Copyright © 2026 by Mackenzie Hamelin

Book Cover by Mackenzie Hamelin

1st edition 2026

# Playlist

- Creep -Radiohead
- You Found Me- The Fray
- Take on the World- You Me At Six
- Rescue -Lauren Daigle
- Wildflower- Billie Eilish
- Wherever You Will Go- The Calling
- A Lot More Free- Max McKnown
- You Could Start A Cult- Niall Horan, Lizzy McAlpine
- Blindside- James Arthur
- Dusk Till Dawn- ZAYN, Sia
- Look After You- The Fray
- Halley's Comet-Billie Eilish
- Burning Down- Alex Warren
- I know it won't work-Gracie Abrams
- Feel Something-Jaymes Young
- Softcore-The Neighbourhood
- Someone To Stay-Vancouver Sleep Clinic
- Chloe or Sam or Sophia or Marcus- Taylor Swift
- Surrender- Natalie Taylor
- DNA Guarantee- Kodi Rhianne
- Innocence and Sadness- Dermot Kennedy
- Elastic Heart- Sia
- Cinnamon Girl- Lana Del Ray
- Superheroes- The Script

To those whose love is not determined by DNA, but by the power of connection.

And to family. The family we're born into, and the one we build for ourselves.

<u>CONTENT WARNING</u>

This book is heavily based around the foster system and childhood trauma. It includes themes of drug abuse, childhood neglect and abuse, and food insecurity.

Chapter 1

<u>Maisy</u>

I find it deeply ironic that the walls of Wanda's office are littered in serene images and quotes about hope.   If you're sitting on this side of her desk, the last two things you *ever* feel are hope and serenity.

It's more like dread and despair.

Every meeting I've had with our well-kept case counselor thus far has been leading up to this moment. I've known for years that this day was coming, and especially for the last few months. It was only a matter of time, and the situation with Mom last week only further confirmed the obvious.

We're being taken away. My brother, sister, and I. I don't know when, or where we'll go, but the second I saw Wanda's name flashing across the screen of my beat-up flip phone, I knew. I played the words I knew she'd say over and over again in my mind for the entire five-block walk to Wanda's office.

And when I sit in the familiar white chair across from her desk, I know by the solemn look on her face that I'm right. When the word 'rehoming' leaves her lips, I'm not even the slightest bit surprised.

"You know I tried," Wanda says, trying to douse the fire she'd set. It's hopeless, though. There's no amending this situation.

I try to keep my face neutral, to act passive, but some emotion must have slipped through my mask, because Wanda lets out a deep, sorrowful sigh. She takes off her spectacles and pinches the bridge of her nose. "This is the best possible case scenario. You and the kids all staying together? It's the best we could have hoped for, Maisy."

I know that I should be more grateful. I know that the alternative sucks way more than the deal being offered to me. My siblings and I getting to stay together is huge, because finding a foster home for one kid is hard enough, but three? It's practically unheard of. Especially when one's a fragile sixteen-year-old, one's a high strong eight-year-old, and the other isn't even out of diapers yet.

Inhaling a deep breath to steady myself, I clench my eyes shut for a moment, trying to block out the world. "The best possible scenario would be staying with my mother," I whisper, hearing the emotion in my voice clear as day.

Wanda lets out another dejected sigh, digging in her computer bag for something. "Maisy, I tried to help your mother. You know I did. But you can't save someone who doesn't want to be saved, sweetheart."

I rest my hands in my lap and subconsciously twirl my fingers like I always do when I'm anxious. "You'll have to switch school districts," Wanda adds, pulling a manilla folder out of her bag. "But the family you're with—the Marshalls—I think you'll get along splendidly."

I watch intently as Wanda flips through the pages stacked in the folder, wondering how the hell the kids and I are going to survive this. It isn't my first rodeo in foster care; Mom surrendered me for a year when I was six. But CJ and Nat, my little brother and sister, haven't known anything other than my mother. They're still young enough to see things through rose-colored glasses.

I know in my heart that we deserve better. That the things that happen in my house aren't *normal*. But nobody's family is perfect, and I've spent my life trying to keep my family together. Trying to keep us grounded. And sometimes that meant telling little white lies to the counselors, or fabricating stories to teachers at school.

But after last week, I don't know how much longer I can play the game. I know that Wanda has been looking for a home for the kids and I for a while now, but the foster system is a slow one. I genuinely think the timing between The Incident and our placement is entirely coincidental.

"They live in Elksborrough," Wanda continues, pushing a piece of paper towards me. "The father, Tim, he's a doctor. And the mother, Amanda, is a lawyer."

"So, they're rich?" I blurt out, then clench my mouth shut, embarrassed by the comment that should've stayed in my head.

Wanda chuckles, adjusting the sleeve of her white pantsuit. "You could say that." Her features sober, the lighthearted version of her melting back into the stoic, professional version that I'm all too familiar with. "They also have a son, Christopher. He's your age."

"Oh. Is he… I mean, does he want…"

"The Marshalls have said that they're very excited to meet you all. *All* of the Marshalls. Christopher included."
There's another question burning the tip of my tongue. I want to ask it more than anything, but I don't think I want the answer. I don't think my heart can take another massive hit today.

"Go ahead," Wanda urges. "I see that twinkle in your eyes, Maisy. I know you have a question."

I can feel the heat creeping over my cheeks as I tuck a stray strand of hair behind my ear with shaky hands. "Yeah, um, what'll happen to Mom?"

Wanda's expression floods with sympathy. She reaches across the desk to place her cold, bony hands over mine, squeezing encouragingly. "Oh, Maisy. You'll still be able to see her. Once a month."

I don't know how the kids and I can be expected to go from seeing our mother every day for most of our lives to once a month. To treat our mother like a car payment, or a lunar phase, or…some other monthly occurrence that I'm too distraught to think of, is absurd.

I get that she's not winning any World's Best Mom awards. I *know* that. But the year I spent away from her was practically torture, and now with the two younger kids added into the equation, I can't even begin to think of the disaster that will ensue when my siblings and I are uprooted from our lives.

"The timing really couldn't be better," Wanda continues, oblivious to my internal dilemma. "With the start of the school year in two weeks, you and CJ will be in the same boats as all of the other kids."

No, we won't. All of the other kids weren't ripped from their homes. All of the other kids aren't starting over at a new school. With a new family.

"This is effective immediately. I'm going to come in the morning to help you and the kids get all packed up, and I'll drive you to Elksborrough myself, okay?" She looks at me with her soulful blue eyes, her expression sympathetic and forcefully optimistic.

I wish she'd just be honest. I wish she'd say to hell with the professional terminology, to hell with bedside manner, and just give me news straight. I understand the fact that she has to sugar coat things for my sake, considering I'm a minor and all. But the least she could do is treat me like an adult. Lord knows I've had to be one my entire life.

After debriefing the entire foster care situation to me earlier, Wanda pulled my siblings into the office for a similar chat. In Nat's case, it was a pointless endeavor, seeing that she's only two and didn't understand a word of what was said.

And, in CJ's case, it was simply a mistake. He went through the five stages of grief in rapid succession, from denial to full on outrage in less than two minutes.

And then the crying started.

Though Nat didn't realize what was happening, she knew that CJ was crying, and that was all it took for her to start bawling her eyes out, too.

I hate it when they cry. I always feel so helpless, so desperate to fix the unfixable. They always look younger when they cry, and it's sobering to see them act their age when every element of our lives has forced us to mature quickly. Quicker than any kids should. The reminder that they really are just kids is always a hard pill to swallow.

I'm still reeling later that night when we return home from Wanda's office.

"What do you want for dinner, CJ?" I ask, pushing the front door open with one hip and re-steadying Nat on my other. "Whatever you want, bud. Tell me and I'll make it."

"Can you *make* them let us stay?" he huffs, putting his hands on his hips defiantly. "'Cause that's all I really want, Maisy. I just want to stay."

Trust me, I've tried.

Throwing Nat's diaper bag on the couch, I lead CJ into the kitchen, trying to think of a way to lighten the situation. I have to harness my internal optimist, because telling CJ that we have no say in the matter doesn't seem like the best idea at the moment.

"I know, CJ," I say tentatively, setting Nat down in her high chair. "But we'll make new friends." *You will, at least.* "And we'll have brand-new teachers."

His green eyes sparkle with interest. "No more snotty Mrs. Snyder?" he asks hopefully, referring to his loathed teacher from last year.

"No more Mrs. Snyder," I confirm, making my way to the fridge to prepare the last dinner I'll make in this house. Probably ever, but at least for a long time.

"And we'll have a whole new bedroom. We might not even have to share a bed anymore." That's the only tantalizing thing about this whole ordeal. I may actually get a bed to myself.

"How does pasta sound?" I ask, pulling a half-full can of tomato sauce out of our almost-empty refrigerator and setting it on the counter. CJ nods absentmindedly. "Hey, can you watch Nat for me, please? I'm going to go see if Mom wants dinner."

Wordlessly, CJ pulls out the chair next to Nat's high chair and plops down. I figure I have two minutes before he loses interest and abandons his post, so I hightail it out of the kitchen and up the narrow staircase that leads from our tiny main floor to our even tinier second story.

We live in a two-bedroom, one bathroom Terrace house in the poorer part of town.

Poorer is a nice way of putting it. Parksfield is the crime hotspot of the area. There's a burglary almost every night, a drug bust every fortnight, and some sort of public brawl or gang face off at least once a month. After a while, the sirens became like white noise. I could sleep through a hurricane thanks to the countless squad cars and ambulances that have raced down the street right outside of my bedroom window.

When I reach the landing, I stop outside of my mother's bedroom door and knock lightly.

I let myself in, knowing better than to wait for her to answer. I shut the door behind me so the kids can't hear what I'm about to say, and turn to face my mother. She's in her bed, staring aimlessly at the ceiling. No surprises there.

"Mom, did you know we're being moved tomorrow?"

No response.

"Mom," I try again, my tone firmer. "The kids and I are being put in foster care. As of tomorrow morning, we won't be here anymore."

Silence.

"Great, glad we cleared that up." Shaking my head, I wrap my hand around the doorknob, ready to leave this room as quickly as possible. "I'll leave dinner outside of your door."

As I'm slipping out of her room, I hear her weak voice.

"Bring my pills up, would you, Maisy?"

Rolling my eyes, I force out an annoyed *"sure"*, and latch the door shut behind me.

I'm not apathetic. I'm not heartless for not caring about my mother. She's not sick—not in the physical sense, at least. But she's entirely dependent on her medication and has a tendency to hole herself up in her room at the slightest inconvenience. She's been up there for two days now, which means that, for two days, I've played mommy to my younger siblings. *Again.*

I'm not heartless. My empathy just has a breaking point, and I have long past reached it. Mom could have gotten help. Wanda gave her every resource under the sun, but she refuses.

Hence the foster care.

When I make it back down the staircase, I halt in the doorway, listening to the voice in the kitchen.

"I know, Nattie," CJ sighs, resting his elbows on the table. He's got all of his attention trained on her, and his back to the doorway I'm currently standing in. "But Maisy says it's all gonna be okay. We might even get our own beds. How cool would that be?"

Nat obviously doesn't respond, but she gives him a gummy smile in return.

"And we're getting a new brother. That's what Wanda said. Do you think he's gonna be okay with it? With us all sleeping at his house?"

Nat makes a cooing noise, slapping her hands down on the tray of her high chair. "Yeah, you're right. Who doesn't like a big sleepover?" CJ chuckles, straightening his back in the chair. He reaches out and pats Nat's slobbery hand. "Good talk, Nat. We're gonna be okay. Maisy said so."

My heart cracks at the interaction, then cracks again with how much blind trust my brother has in me. For all of our sakes, I hope I'm right. I hope we'll be okay.

Later that night, after the kids are fed and bathed and clad in their choice pajamas for the night, I lie awake, just staring at the ceiling and thinking.

I wonder what our new foster brother is like. I wonder what my new school will be like. I wonder how long this family will keep us before deciding we're too much and turning us back over to Wanda. I wonder who will take care of Mom when I'm gone.

CJ's soft voice breaks my mental spiral. "Are you awake?" he asks, poking my ribcage with his elbow.

"Yeah."

Turning onto his side to face me, he looks me right in the eyes and says, "I'm nervous, Maisy. Like, super-duper nervous."

My heart cracks wide-open in my chest. "There's no reason to be nervous, bud. It's all going to be okay."

"But what if they don't like me?"

"Who? The new kids at school, or the foster family?"

"Both," he sighs wearily. "The foster parents."

"Of course they'll like you." This time, I'm not lying. He really is the sweetest kid ever. He may be a bit high-strong at times, but he's still a great kid. "You're the best."

"Are you sure, Maisy?"

"I'm super sure, CJ." I ruffle his hair before turning on my side, facing away from his anxious eyes and towards the window instead. "Now, get some sleep. We have a long day tomorrow."

That's the understatement of the century.

Chapter 2

<u>Colton</u>

"No way. I'm not doing it."

My asshole of a best friend tails after me, following me into the gym locker room like a lost puppy dog. "Come on, Colt. You never do anything fun anymore. It's all *hockey* this and *Princeton* that. We're almost seventeen. Live a little bit."

I toss my water bottle in my gym bag on the bench, then continue walking towards the showers in the back, ripping off my shorts in the process.

"Chris, you know we can't be drinking during pre-season. Actually, we can't be drinking at all," I amend, stepping into a shower stall. He steps forward, like he's going to follow me in. I cock a brow at him. I mean, I know we're close, but we're not *that* close. He steps back, holding his hands up sheepishly.

I strip down and toss my remaining clothes over the stall door, cranking the water as hot as it'll go.

"It's just a party," Chris continues. "You don't even have to drink. Better yet, you can be our DD. Just get out and do *something*. It's not even until next week."

"Don't care," I murmur. "I'm still not going."

"Come *on* Colton," my best friend whines, sounding scarily similar to a toddler. "You're obsessed with hockey. Like, more than usual. It's an addiction."

"An addiction?" I can't hide my snort. To be completely honest, I don't even try. "Says the one who's trying to get me to blow off training to go out *drinking*."

"It *is* an addiction," Chris says matter-of-factly. "A destructive one. Consider this my official intervention."

"I don't need an intervention. I'm fine where I'm at, thank you very much."

And that's the truth. Maybe I *am* dull for my age, and maybe I *am* hyper-focused on my performance, but I didn't get to this point by slacking off.

I was the top pick for our age division in the country this year. The sheer number of boarding schools that tried to recruit me on full rides is insane. The number of scouts visits I have lined up for this season is even more insane. I didn't get here by blowing off training for a house party, or wasting calories on shitty beer.

I have a regimen that's proven to work, and I have no desire to break it.

"You have time to think about it," Chris adds, a promising hint in his voice.

"I don't need time," I bite out. "My answer is no."

"Sleep on it."

Groaning, I finish my shower while simultaneously questioning my life choices.

How *I*, the most type-A, organized, driven person alive, became acquainted with *him*, the most life of the party, spontaneous, wild child is beyond me.

How we became best friends is even more of a mystery.

I've known Chris since I was five years old, and up until the last two years, I've matched his spontaneity limb for limb. But that was when we were kids. That was before we had scouts breathing down our necks and college to think about.

We all have to settle down sometime.

Though I'm not sure that time will ever come for Christopher Marshall.

I'm more boring than the average sixteen-year-old. I'll admit that much. I don't party often, if ever, I don't drink, and I don't screw my way through girls like most of my teammates do. My sole focus is on hockey and maintaining my grades, with the end goal of playing for Princeton when I graduate in two years, and the NHL after that. I've worked my ass off to make it to the U18 league, but there's no contract binding me to the team. If I slack off, if I mess up… I'm gone. There are dozens of other kids waiting to take my spot. I can't afford to slip up.

Junior year is the most important year for standardized tests and grades, and I'm captain of our school's hockey team, too. There's a lot of pressure on me this year, and I can't afford to mess it up before the school year even starts.

"Anyway, what time are we hitting up the gym tomorrow? I need to prepare myself to die again." Chris makes a big deal of massaging his biceps as he follows me back to the lockers to get changed.

"I don't know? Early in the morning again?" I offer, throwing off my towel and reaching for the pair of sweatpants I left in my bag.

"I have to be home by ten."

I turn to face him, cocking my brow curiously. "What the hell do you have at ten?" He never works on Sundays, he doesn't have a girlfriend, he doesn't have schoolwork, and I know for a fact that we don't have practice tomorrow. The school season hasn't even started yet.

"Oh right, shit, I forgot to tell you."

"Tell me what?"

"Mom and Dad got a call a few weeks ago. They were approved to foster again," he explains, his tone taking on a slightly somber note.

My eyes widen in surprise. "Really? How old is the kid?"

I don't know how the Marshalls do it, other than the very real fact that they're saints. Mr. and Mrs. Marshall have somehow found the perfect balance between their extremely successful careers, spending adequate time with their son, and still having the healthiest marriage I've ever seen. Seriously, they're the best people I know, and I genuinely consider them to be my second set of parents.

"Well, actually, there are three," he says, reaching his hand up to cup the back of his neck. "A sixteen-year-old girl, an eight-year-old boy, and a two-year-old-girl."

"Damn." I breathe, rustling through my bag for the T-shirt I threw in there earlier. "And your parents are taking in three kids why?"

Chris shrugs, like this is an everyday conversation that people normally have while standing half-naked in a YMCA locker room. "They're siblings. Nobody else would take them, and they'd have to be split up. Mom and Dad have always wanted a bunch of kids, anyway."

"Don't go getting any ideas with the girl," I warn, zipping my bag shut and throwing it over my shoulder.

"Relax, Colt. My parents have already given me the whole spiel," he huffs, rolling his eyes. "No tapping the foster sister. Got it."

"You are so tactless, Christopher."

He grins devilishly at me, pushing the locker room door open with his ass. "Yeah, but you love me, anyway." His expression falters a bit, his smile sobering. He does this a lot. Puts on a happy, joking façade to cover up when something's wrong.

"You're nervous again, aren't you?" I ask, eyeing him sympathetically.

If I were anyone else, Chris would deny it. He'd give his whole "it's okay, I'm okay" mumbo jumbo and be done with it. But he knows I can read him like a book, and we both know it'd be pointless to lie to each other.

"Yeah." He nods solemnly. "I always say I won't get attached, cause it's so much harder when they leave." He shrugs, helplessly. "But I always do, anyway. And then I'm all depressed when they leave."

Don't I know it. I spend a lot of time at the Marshall house, and I've been known to bond with the kids they foster, too. The difference is, I know in my realistic mind that it's a temporary situation. I have a balance between forming a relationship and wearing my heart on my sleeve. Chris does not. He's your definition of a golden retriever, and the guy attaches himself to people way too easily.

Every round of foster kids his parents get starts the same; with Chris saying things will be different this time around. And every round of foster kids ends the same, too; with Chris crying and blaming his tears on allergies while also sulking around for weeks on edge.

"Do you want me to come over tomorrow?" I offer, mentally shuffling through the things on my to-do list. Gym, game tapes, summer assignments. That was my plan.

I hate going against my schedule, but I know how stressful the first day is for him, and after twelve years of friendship, I owe it to him to be there. I love the big dope like a brother and I'd never make him go through something like this alone.

"Nah, it's okay. I know you're busy," Chris says, shrugging nonchalantly.

But I saw it. The brief look of relief in his eyes. Which is why I say, "I'll head home with you after the gym, yeah?"

As stressed as I am about going against my pre-set plan, I know I should be there for Chris. Also, I haven't stopped in to see Chris' parents in a while. I owe them a visit after everything they've done for me through the years.

"Hey, Colt?" he calls out, walking towards his black Mercedes parked on the opposite side of the lot from my car. "Thank you."

"Yeah, of course. Any time."

And I mean it. He's my ride or die.

Chapter 3

<u>Maisy</u>

After a grand total of two hours, and an uncountable number of tears, our few belongings are packed and the kids are situated in the back of Wanda's Honda Odyssey.

It didn't take us very long to get our things packed. All I own is a Ziploc bag of toiletries, a backpack for school, half a trash bag full of clothing, my phone, a pair of headphones, and a beat-up Walkman. And a pillow and blanket. That's it.

CJ has some action figures and Lego sets he's accumulated over the last few years, and of course his clothes and bedding, and Nat has the most stuff, considering she's still in diapers and needs sippy cups and all of that. But between the three of us, our possessions fit in the trunk of Wanda's car, with plenty of room to spare.

It took us the longest to say goodbye to Mom. It should've taken a few minutes, tops. But she wouldn't get out of bed, and Wanda refused to take us without a proper goodbye from her. I told her to save her breath. Mom was in a funk and would be for the next God knows how long. She wouldn't get out of that bed if the house was on fire.

When Wanda finally admitted defeat, I brought my siblings upstairs to say goodbye, promising them that we'd see her again soon. CJ cried inconsolably, Nat burrowed into my side like a scared animal, and Wanda stood in the doorway, shaking her head.

The Marshall's house in Elksborrough is a half an hour away from the Terrace, and I spend the entire drive silently reeling, fidgeting in my lap and staring out the window at the passing scenery.

"Did you kids eat breakfast?" Wanda asks conversationally as we drive through the consumer-y part of town. "We can stop and get something if you'd like."

"No thanks," CJ says politely, tugging at his seatbelt. "Maisy woke up extra early to make me pancakes. And a tiny one for Nat, too." He sighs contently, flashing his missing front teeth. "Maisy's the *best* cook."

Yeah, he'd think so, because I'm the only one who has *ever* cooked for him. I don't say that, though. Instead, I keep my mouth shut and my eyes glued on the window.

Wanda glances at me through the rearview mirror, smiling sadly. I hate it when she looks at me sympathetically like that. When *anybody* looks at me like that. Like I'm a charity case who's liable to crumble at any given moment. Like I'm just a fragile, lost little girl.

I mean, maybe a part of me *is* fragile, and maybe I *am* a charity case, but I'd like to believe that people see me as more than that.

The rest of the drive is spent in silence as the ETA on the center console slowly counts down the minutes separating my siblings and I from our new life.

With a minute left in the drive, Wanda turns into a neighborhood full of the biggest houses I've ever seen in real life. As in actual *mansions*.

She pulls the van into the fourth house on the right. Instantly, I take in the gray stone house, which could easily fit five of my houses inside of it. My gaze wanders to the driveway, with three cars parked in it.

Not just any cars. An Audi, a Mercedes, and a Bugatti.

So, they're rich *rich*.

My eyes wander over the clean-cut, lush green grass surrounding the gray loop in front of the house. The beds of flowers, the perfectly clean siding, the ivy stretching up the side of the house. It's gorgeous, and that fact fills me with hesitation and doubt.

They clearly aren't fostering for the money. Why do people who live like *this* want to take in three scraggly kids from the Terrace?

"Oh my gosh, Maisy!" CJ squeals, tugging on the sleeve of my oversized hoodie. "It's a castle!"

Still not trusting any part of this situation, I paint on a smile for my baby brother. "Yeah, it is pretty big."

The front door swings open, and two of the biggest men I have ever seen file through the doorway, followed by a woman not much taller than me.

The first man is probably around fifty, with a strong jawline and salt-and-pepper black hair. He must be at least six-foot-two, probably taller. *Tim Marshall*, I recall. *The doctor.*

The woman nestled beneath his arm looks no older than thirty, but I know from what Wanda has told me that she's just as old as Tim. She has her blonde hair tied back in an impressive ponytail, and an expensive-looking white pantsuit. *Amanda Marshall.*

The next isn't exactly a man, but he's far too big to be a boy. He's slightly taller than his father, with the same jawline and blue eyes, but his mother's high cheekbones and her dimples and blonde hair. He waves at the car. *Christopher Marshall.*

I know it sounds strange, but the first adjective I can think of to describe this family is *warm*. They're all smiles and glowy skin. They just look *lovely*, and I feel guilty for tainting their perfect American family with the trauma and baggage that's associated with my siblings and I.

They seem like people who vacation in the Hamptons and have family dinners every night that *don't* result in tears and slammed doors. They seem like the kind of people who have scented candles for every season, who have family game nights and give their spare change to homeless people.

They couldn't be more different than us.

Our Terrace and bus passes have nothing on their mansion and fancy cars. Our tattered clothes and skinny frames have nothing on their designer outfits and athletic builds. Our teary-eyed, has-seen-a-ghost expression pales in comparison to their smiley, welcoming nature.

We really are two different types of people.

Wanda is the first to push her door open, stepping onto the asphalt driveway with a loud clap of her hands. "Okay, kids," she says peppily, rounding the car and tugging open the passenger side door. She unbuckles Nat from her car seat, then extends a hand to CJ, who takes the offer with a tentative expression painted on his face.

I give him a reassuring nod, opening my own door and stepping that much further into the unknown.

Wanda joins me in facing the Marshalls, with Nat on her hip and CJ tucked beneath her arm. We look like a pack of skittish foals, eying our new foster family with wariness and curiosity.

"Do you guys have a cow?" CJ comes right out and asks.

My cheeks burn in embarrassment. Honestly, I expected him to say something like this. There's no telling what'll come out of his mouth. He's got no filter and no shame.

"A cow?" Christopher chuckles, furrowing his brow in confusion. "Uh, no. Not that I know of."

"Oh," CJ muses, his disappointment evident. "Maisy says that milk makes you grow big and strong, and you're *very* big." He points to Mr. Marshall, who is doing all he can not to laugh. "And you're even bigger," he adds, pointing at Christopher. "I just thought you guys must go through a *lot* of milk."

Christopher barks out a laugh, tucking his hands in his sweatpants pockets. "Are you fat shaming me, little dude?" He eyes CJ curiously, like he's not quite sure what to make of him.

"No, no, no," I cut in, a ferocious blush spreading down my neck as my embarrassment threatens to swallow me whole. "He, uh, he just… he means *athletic*. And, uh, tall," I choke out, cringing at my awkwardness. I should've just kept my mouth shut. I *always* bomb in social situations, but I couldn't sit back while my brother burned bridges in our first five minutes with our foster family. By fat shaming them, nonetheless.

"Relax, I'm just messing with him. I'm Chris, by the way," he says, closing the space between us to shake my hand.

"Nuh-uh," CJ challenges, shaking his head. "Wanda says your name is Chris*topher*. Not just Chris."

"It's a nickname," I explain, turning to my brother.

"Like how your real name is Christian John, but you go by CJ."

Realization floods his curious green eyes. He nods, looking up at me. "Like how Mommy called that one handyman *daddy*? Wasn't that funny, Maisy? How she called him daddy? He wasn't her father!"

Chris legitimately snorts, which earns him an elbow to the ribs from Mrs. Marshall.

"Okay, moving on," Wanda says, desperately trying to redirect the conversation. "This is Natalia." She points to my sister, who has her head buried in Wanda's neck.

She's an overall terrified child. Spooks at the slightest little noise. And she's young enough that she still subscribes to the whole "*if I can't see you, you can't see me*" ideology.

"Mama," she cries, her voice breaking. "Mama, mama, mama."

The smile on Chris's face drops, replaced with that same look of pity I'm so used to seeing. Mr. and Mrs. Marshall look at each other, their expressions sad and slightly guilty.

"She means Maisy," CJ fills in, pointing at me. "She calls her '*Mama*'."

Nat continues her crying, reaching out towards me. Wanda sighs, handing my baby sister over to me with a dejected look on her face.

Nat nuzzles her tear-soaked cheek against my neck, her muscles untightening the second my arms wrap around her.

"It's not because I, uh… I mean, she knows we have a mother," I amend, tucking a piece of hair behind my ear. "It's just because my name starts with *MA*."

None of the Marshalls look like they believe me, and I can't say I blame them, because I don't believe me, either. I changed a hefty percentage of her diapers—I still do. I'm the one who stayed up late and woke up early while Mom was either unresponsive in bed or doing God knows what with her boyfriend of the week. I'm the one who fed her, the one who bathed her, the one who did everything in my power to keep her safe.

So yeah, maybe she can't say Maisy, but it also isn't unfathomable that she thinks I'm her mother.

"Well then," Mr. Marshall says, smiling warmly at my siblings and I. "Why don't we get started on bringing everything in, shall we?"

Wanda pops the trunk of her minivan, and exposes the high chair, cot, two garbage bags of clothes, and the bedding.

Wordlessly, I readjust Nat on my hip and take as much as I can carry in my free hand.

"Here," Chris says, rushing forward to take the bag out of my hands. "I'll take that for you."

"Thanks."

We each have something to carry in, and I know before he even opens his mouth what Chris is going to say. I pray I'm wrong—I'm genuinely not sure that I can survive any more embarrassment—but I've become a master at reading people.

He's staring at our stuff curiously, his head cocked to the side. "Do you have a U-Haul or something coming?" he asks, his tone perfectly genuine. I know he isn't trying to be rude, but the comment makes my heart sink in my chest.

"Christopher!" Mrs. Marshall barks, eyeing him dangerously.

Panicked about already starting trouble, I quickly intervene. "It's okay, Mrs. Marshall. I, uh… this is all we've got."

Chris's face floods with sympathy again, and I understand it this time. I haven't been inside his house yet, or seen his room, but I have a fantastic imagination. I'm sure he's got closets full of clothes, all of the newest gaming equipment. Probably a nice laptop and a fancy new phone, too.

"I'm sorry, that was a crappy thing to say," Chris says awkwardly, scratching the back of his neck. "C'mon. I'll show you the way. Follow me."

I do just that, handing my sister over to Wanda and blindly following the giant boy whose house I'll be invading until further notice.

Everyone else stays behind in the driveway, which means that only Chris witnesses the way my jaw hits the floor the second we enter the foyer.

I'm hit with tall ceilings, crisp, white walls, marble white flooring, and more statues and vases than I'd know what to do with.

"Oh, Jesus," I murmur, doing a quick spin and glancing at the grand staircase and adjoining sitting room.

"I know," Chris chuckles, peeking at me over his shoulder. "It's kind of a lot to take in, huh?"

"Well, yeah, but I was thinking more along the lines of the damage my brother could cause here," I admit, flinching at the image of the immaculate statues and vases on the floor.

"CJ is kind of a walking hurricane."

"Mom's used to it," Chris laughs, gesturing for me to follow him up the stairs. "When the guys come over, she hides all of the good China."

"The guys?"

"My teammates," Chris clarifies, flicking on the light in the upstairs hallway. "Hockey players are walking tornadoes, too."

All I can say is "Oh," because I'm so enamored by the hallway full of doors in front of me. At least six, from what I can count.

"So, here's your room," Chris says, leading me to the door directly across the landing. He pushes it open with his hip, and I have to try extremely hard to stop the gasp from escaping my mouth.

There's a gorgeous white wooden desk against one wall, a queen size bed pressed against the back wall, and a vanity in the corner. And... Two doors?

Noticing the curious expression on my face, Chris tosses the bags on the floor and brushes his hands together. "That's your bathroom," he says, pointing to the door on the left. "And that's the walk-in."

Stunned speechless, I take in the white faux fur rug, the white bedspread, and the gold accents of the room. It's bigger than the entire kitchen in the Terrace, and that isn't an exaggeration.

"Walk-in?" I ask, puzzled by his description of the other door.

Chris cocks his head, like he doesn't understand my question. Then realization sparkles in his blue eyes and he clarifies. "Closet. Walk-in closet."

A walk-in closet? A bathroom? An actual place to do homework other than my bed or the floor?

I genuinely think I might faint.

"I, uh, I hope it's okay," Chris says, gesturing to the room. "The bathroom is a full, but there's no tub. Just a shower." He shrugs again. "If you want to take a bath, you can use my bathroom. I don't mind."

Does he seriously think I'll be upset about the lack of a bathtub? This one room has more space than I had in the entire top floor of the Terrace house. It's clean-kept and gorgeous, and I genuinely can't think of a single complaint. Sharing a queen bed with CJ will be so much better than the tiny full that we shared at the Terrace.

"No, we'll be okay in here. Thank you, Chris," I say, still a bit breathless. I'm so in awe with the sheer size of the room that I barely notice the puzzled look on his face.

"We? Are you French," he quips, plopping himself down in the white fuzzy swivel chair by the desk and staring at me curiously.

My cheeks burn with embarrassment and I shift under the weight of his stare. "The kids and I," I explain, my voice mousy. *Don't shut down. He's not the enemy.* "There's plenty of room for CJ and I. And for Nat's crib."

His confused look intensifies, and I don't know how else to explain it. I don't get what he's not getting, and I feel myself growing more flustered by the second.

"Maisy, this is your room," Chris says slowly, his brow furrowed.

"I know that."

"Just yours."

Now *I'm* the confused one. "But the kids…"

"Have their own rooms. Christ, you should see what Dad and I built for CJ," Chris chuckles, blowing out a breath. "Giant bunk beds built into the walls," he adds proudly. "He's gonna lose his shit when he sees it. Prepare for the screams. And Mom had a *blast* with the nursery."

We have our own rooms? As in, these people dedicated three rooms of their house to my siblings and I?

Why?

"We have our own rooms?" I ask, sounding like an idiot reiterating what Chris literally *just* said.

He nods, folding his hands behind his head and leaning back in the office chair. "You didn't before?"

I feel like I can tell him the truth. I'm a pretty good judge of character, and I can tell that there's nothing harmful about Chris Marshall. Or his parents. They seem too…soft, to be dangerous.

Friend or foe? I glance at his curious expression, at the lax way he's sprawled himself out at the desk, and it's all the mental confirmation I need.

Friend. *Definitely friend.*

"No. I've always shared a bed with CJ. I haven't had my own bed since he was a toddler, let alone my own room." He looks horrified, but all I can do is shrug awkwardly. "It's always been the three of us together."

"In the same room?" he gapes, looking at me like I just told him we had been rooming in a dumpster.

"Yeah. It wasn't so bad." And it wasn't. People have it way worse than I did. At least I had a bed. And a house. I'm not complaining.

"Well, not here." Chris shakes his head, still looking mildly disturbed. "This is your space, Maisy. Just for you."

Chapter 4

<u>Colton</u>

There are a thousand things I *should* be doing. I should be training. I should be finishing my summer reading for my English class. I should be at the shop helping my dad. I should be so many places, but instead I'm pulling up outside of the Marshall's house to comfort my best friend.

He's done worse for me, though. The least I can do is support him during the huge fucking shift happening in his life right now.

I can't imagine how hard it must be, opening your house up to a bunch of strangers. Befriending those strangers, knowing that they're going to leave soon. I'm scared to meet these kids, if I'm being perfectly honest, so I can't even begin to comprehend how hard it must be for Chris.

I knock on the front door, even though I have my own set of keys. I've never been a fan of barging in, no matter how comfortable I am somewhere.

"Colt!" Amanda, Chris's mom, exclaims when she swings open the front door. "I didn't realize you were stopping by."

Amanda Marshall is the definition of a saint. The woman cooks like nobody else I know, is a partner at a law firm and the top-rated lawyer in our area. She's cutthroat and terrifying at times, but really, she's just a giant softy. A softy who dedicates all of her free time to fostering kids.

If you split the woman's kindness into thousandths and distributed it, she'd still be the nicest person I know, hands down.

"Hi, Amanda. Chris asked me to come over… I think he's, uh…" I glance around the foyer, looking for little ears. When my search proves empty, I shrug. "Move-in day is always hard for him. Figured I'd come over and make it a little bit better."

"Well, that was very sweet of you," she smiles, patting my forearm. "The kids are all in their rooms, but you know where to find Chris."

I nod, making my way towards the staircase. I all but fly up the stairs and towards my best friend's bedroom door. Knocking twice, I push open the door to find Chris lying on his bed, staring at the ceiling with a puzzled frown.

Shit, this is bad.

Chris is the golden retriever of our little group. He's always lighthearted and joking around, so the fact that he's looking all serious and deep in thought is alarming.

Chris doesn't think—ever. So, when he does, you know something is seriously wrong.

"Hey, Chris," I say nonchalantly, throwing myself down on the cushy gaming chair by his desk. "What's up?"

He just shakes his head, no sign of his normal playful self. "This is so bad, Colt. So, *so* bad."

"What is?"

"These kids, man." He blows out a breath, combing his fingers through his mop of blonde hair.

"Okay," I say cautiously. "Start from the beginning."

He nods, sitting up and resting his elbows on his thighs. "Well, Mom and Dad won't tell me why they're here. Just that there was neglect, which, *obviously* there was if these kids got uprooted from their house," he scoffs. "But something feels different about these kids, C. I don't know what, but they just seem... broken.

"Like, all the kids my parents have fostered were quiet. I guess it's a given. But these kids seemed almost *scared* to talk. Like they were waiting for us to lash out. They just watched us, all wide-eyed and cautious. And they're *so* skinny, man. Like, skin and bones skinny. I just want to give them my whole candy stash so they don't look like a breeze could blow them over.

"All they came with was two trash bags and the stuff for the baby... they literally had nothing else. And they all had to share a room before. They had to share a bed, Colt. A *bed*. You should've seen Maisy's face when she found out she had her own room."

"Maisy?" I ask, struggling to keep up with his downward spiral.

"The girl our age. Oh, and speaking of her, she seems like she's on the verge of a breakdown. I don't know. I just feel like I *need* to protect her, which is weird as hell because I don't *know* her."

He's quiet for a long moment, just cradling his head in his hands. Something about seeing him stress like this hits me hard. Probably because I know how hard he is to rattle.

"You know how there's a baby?" he asks, peeking up at me from his behind hands. I nod. "She calls Maisy *mama*. Maisy played it off as the first two letters of her name are *ma*, but I think it's more than that," Chris says sadly, shaking his head.

"Meaning?"

He looks broken when he says, "I think she sees Maisy as her mother."

I exhale a long breath. "Shit."

"Yeah. Shit."

I don't know what to say to all of that, so I don't say anything. I know that spewing a bunch of verbal bullshit won't do anything to help Chris right now, so instead, I opt for something that I know will. The only way to calm him down is to help him take his mind off of things.

"You want to play Call of Duty?" I ask, grabbing two controllers and waving them in front of his face.

He sighs but nods, dropping to the floor by his bed and facing his television. I flip on the PlayStation and mirror him, wishing there was more I could do for him.

"These kids are going to destroy me, C. I can feel it," Chris says after our first game. He's got a sad look in his eyes, and I know he's not bullshitting me. My best friend feels way too much, and I know that he's right. I know there's a high chance that he goes and gets attached to these kids and his heart gets a little bit broken in the process.

"They might, Chris. But you'll survive it. Do the best you can while they're here. Be who they need now. That's all you can do."

He pauses the screen, turning to face me with a sad smile. "Oh, and fair warning, we are thoroughly fucked when school starts."

"Oh yeah? Why's that."

"I anticipate a problem with Maisy."

"A problem?"

"The guys on the team. The guys in general. Mark my words, dude. They'll be feral."

"Shit. She's pretty?" I ask, already knowing the answer before the question even leaves my mouth. He nods, smiling faintly. "Don't go getting notions about your foster sister, asshole. I'm not saving you if your mother catches you and castrates you. Consider yourself warned."

Chris raises both of his hands defensively. "Hey, I'm not talking about me here. I'm thinking of the others. I'm actually worried here, Colt. I'm gonna need your help."

Great. That's all I need during the biggest year in high school. More fights on my record. More bridges to burn with the idiots at my school.

I'll do it, though. *Of course* I'll help him protect her. I wouldn't question it if she was his sister, and in a way she is. The guys on the team are good dudes, for the most part. But there's a select few who are problematic, and I can't blame Chris for worrying.

I wouldn't trust them with my sister. Or sister-adjacent. And he's my best friend, so his fights are my fights.

An hour or so later, Chris is still sulking. He's finally calmed down about the three kids who just dropped a bombshell on his life. This new tantrum is about how many times I kicked his ass in COD.

"Kids!" Amanda's sugary-sweet voice calls from the hallway. "Dinner's ready!"

I notice the apprehension return to Chris's expression, so I hold out a hand, gesturing for him to let me pull him up from the floor.

The thing about our friendship is that it can do a complete three-sixty at any given moment. And it does; all of the time. I don't know anyone that can go from busting each other's balls to going to war for each other quite as quickly as we can. But I've forever got his back, and he forever has mine. No matter how much we joke around, we both know it.

"They're just kids," I murmur as we make our way down the giant spiral staircase and towards the kitchen. "Just be you, man."

In true Chris fashion, he brushes off his very obvious anxiety with attempted humor. "Watch out for the little one," he warns, voice low as we stroll towards the dining room. "He's ruthless."

The moment the Marshall's eight-person dining room table comes into view, I know Chris was on-point about two things.

The first: there's something about these kids that screams *broken*. The identical look of fear in their eyes as they take me in is all the proof I need. *Something happened to these kids. Something really, really fucked up. Something beyond neglect.*

They look like timid animals, wearing the same look opponents do when you're ahead in a fight on the ice. A look that says, *"I know what's coming next, and I know there's no chance of stopping it."*

Chris's micro-panic up in his room suddenly makes a hell of a lot more sense. There's something haunting about these kids. Something heartbreaking.

And the second thing he was right about?

We're in for a world of trouble with the girl. Because holy shit, I've never seen anything like her before in my life.

I've seen my fair share of girls. Christ, hockey players are *inundated* with them. Pretty ones. Ones with legs for days and double Ds. But I have never seen someone so…symmetrical? That's probably a horrible adjective, but I'm kind of drawing a blank on how to put *that* into words.   She's got these full pink lips that stand out against her olive brown skin. Long brown hair that's flowing well past the middle of her back in loose, undefined waves. A light dusting of freckles, and, fuck me, the oddest colored eyes I've ever seen.

They're the color of whiskey, with the slightest bit of green. Like hazel, but not really hazel.

I just stand there in the doorway for God knows how long, reeling. Trying to figure out why this girl has my jaw on the floor and my full, undivided attention without even saying a word. Without even making *eye contact*.

It's those eyes, I think. It's the haunted look in them, a look that says she's seen things that I won't even encounter in my worst nightmares.

I'm used to puck bunnies. I hate that term—it seems so wrong to refer to people as bunnies—but goddamnit, that's what they are. Girls who chase jerseys and want the thrill of being with a hockey player without actually *being* with a hockey player.

It's not as much of an issue with the school team as it is with the under-eighteen team. The Ravens—New York's U18 team—travels all over the country. Literally, my teammates and I were in Colorado last weekend for a tournament. And when we stay in hotel rooms…

Let's just say, we've had to call security more than once. Batshit crazy girls looking for a "good time", whose presence is sure to ruin whatever good time my teammates and I had been having.

I'm used to that; to girls who love the chase. The type that's so in-your-face sexual that you're either into it or you're repulsed by it.

I have always been, and will always be, the latter.

But there is not an iota of an ounce of that energy coming from the haunted looking girl at the Marshall's dining room table.

And maybe that's it. The reason I can't seem to make myself function like a normal person. The reason that I don't immediately take my seat next to Chris at the table. The reason I'm lost for words.

"Maisy, CJ, Nat, this is Colton. He's my friend," Chris says cautiously, moving slowly towards the table like the kids will spook with any sudden movement. "He's been my best friend since we were younger than you, CJ."

The little boy looks at me, a mix of trepidation and curiosity swimming in his bright green eyes. "So, you trust him, Chris?" he asks warily.

Chris nods, not even having to think about the question. "Absolutely. With my life."

Both the girl—Maisy, apparently—and the boy, CJ, seem to relax a little bit at that, their shoulders dropping as their muscles relax.

"Does *he* have a cow?" CJ blurts out, nodding his head of brown curls at me. "Cause he's even bigger than you, Chris, and you're *huge*."

"CJ," Maisy sighs dejectedly, shaking her head. "We've been over this. You can't comment on people's size. It's offensive."

"He's okay," I cut in, watching Maisy cautiously, expecting some kind of retaliation. When none comes, I just shrug. "I'm not a small guy. I know that."

She nods shyly, blushing the cutest shade of pink and tucking a stray lock of her hair behind her ear.

Somehow, I feel like her shyness is worth noting. I want to start a mental diary to sort through my thoughts right now. Maybe then I can figure out what the hell this girl is doing to me.

"So, Colton," Chris's dad, Tim, interjects. "How was Colorado, son? I'm sorry I couldn't be there."

Tim has been my biggest fan since Chris and I started mini minors in the second grade. He's always been in the stands at my games, cheering the loudest, wearing the team-colored face paint.

He's not a stranger to foam fingers, either. It used to mortify Chris and I, having his father in the stands screaming our names and looking like a fandom threw up. But now that I'm older, I appreciate the hell out of the man that served as my second father. He was always at my games— even the away ones, even when my own parents weren't.

Mom and Dad work a *lot*. They run our family garage, so getting a day off for them is a lot harder than it is for Tim, who manages his own schedule at his private-practice dermatology office.

He couldn't come to the Colorado game, though he hadn't told me why at the time. He'd told me it was *something confidential*, and that he'd explain later. Well, it's later, and I have a feeling that I'm staring at the three confidential reasons why my bonus dad had to stay back in New York.

"No worries, Tim," I say, claiming the seat next to Chris at the table. And I mean it. There really aren't any hard feelings. "We won. We were undefeated," I add, grabbing the bowl of mashed potatoes Amanda hands me and plopping a giant scoop on my plate.

"Of course you were," Tim chuckles, taking a sip of his water. "So, are you ready for the school year?"

I'm not sure if he's addressing his question to me, or Chris, or Maisy or CJ, but when nobody makes a move to speak, I fill the awkward silence following Tim's question. "I'm a little stressed, but that's kind of a given, right?" Tim nods in understanding.

"I got stuck in math lab again, Pops," Chris groans, raking his hand through his wavy blonde hair. "I'm sorry. I really did try, I just couldn't *learn* the way they were *teaching*. It just never clicked." He shrugs, and I can see the shift in his usually happy-go-lucky mood.

I'm prepared to come to his defense. To tell his parents that he'd spent nearly every sports study hall in his Algebra teacher's classroom, that he'd done every homework assignment and retake humanely possible. He even put his ego aside and asked me to tutor him—which I did—but he still couldn't quite make the benchmark. But I should've known Mr. and Mrs. Marshall wouldn't berate him.

"As long as you try, Chris, you know your father and I don't care about your grades. We know you work your tail off, and you know what we say." Amanda smiles warmly, reaching over to pat her son's shoulder.

"You can do anything but not everything," Chris recites like a trained puppy dog.

"Exactly." Amanda nods.

"How about you, Maisy?" Tim asks, shifting his attention to the still very frightened looking girl across the table. Her eyes go comically wide at the sound of her name and she snaps her head up, looking around like she's in trouble.

"Me?" she croaks, looking at Tim anxiously.

"You," he confirms with a calm nod, staring back at her with patient eyes. "Are you excited to start at your new school?"

She looks torn for a moment, but she ultimately nods and drops her gaze to the untouched food on her plate. She pushes a piece of broccoli around, staring at it like it's a foreign entity. "Uh, I guess so."

"You're starting at St. Mark's, right?" I ask stupidly, referring to mine and Chris's co-ed private school. I know damn well she is. It's part of the reason Chris had spiraled earlier, worrying about the douchebags at our school giving her trouble. I know the answer, but for some inexplicable reason, I want to keep her talking.

"Yeah."

Give me more than that. "You're a junior, right?"

Chris eyes me warily, probably wondering why I'm asking questions we both know he'd answered earlier. I shoot him a glance that says *trust me*, before he can open his mouth and scare the girl back into her shell.

"Yeah. Same as Chris."

I try to rack my brain for something to say to her, a follow-up question to ask, but before I can, CJ chirps up from across the table. "I'm going into the third grade, Collin," he says proudly, puffing his chest out like he's the hot shit. "I've grown *so* much over the summer. Chris said the girls will be all over me."

Amanda shoots Chris a dirty look, and he shrugs sheepishly.

"Wow, the third grade? You're basically an old man already," I quip. "And my name's Colton, bud."

"Oh," he says, scrunching his nose up. "That's a weirder name than Collin."

We go back and forth like that, for the rest of dinner. Getting roasted by the kid gets old after a while, but the slight blush creeping up his sister's cheeks with every offhand comment definitely doesn't.

Chapter 5

Maisy

Hours after family dinner ends, I'm lying face-up in my new bed, staring at the ceiling aimlessly and letting my thoughts run wild.

The entire night had been so weird. There was a table full of food, for starters. Food I didn't cook. Made with ingredients that weren't chosen because they were defective and therefore were being sold for cheaper prices. Dinner with people who asked questions and laughed with each other.

I didn't know what to make of it. I still don't.

And the boy?

I have even less of an idea what to make of him.

He's taller than Chris, which I previously would have thought was impossible. He's also bigger than Chris. Not fatter, despite CJ's claims. Just… stockier. You can tell he spends as much time in the gym as I do in the kitchen and counseling office. Everything about him seems firm, his jawline, his muscles, his personality.

But when he talks, he mellows out a little bit. He's intense, but not in a scary way. In an intriguing way.

According to Mr. Marshall, Colton is some sort of local hockey prodigy. He plays with kids two years older than him in a national league and travels, like, every weekend to play in different states. Apparently, he's on the fast track to D1 hockey, and maybe even the NHL.

It felt strange, to be sitting at that table. Not just because I don't know them, or because my siblings and I were obviously intruding on some sort of routine. But because everyone at that table was *something*.

Colton is on his way to a serious career in professional sports. Chris is one of the top players for the elite private school team. Mr. Marshall has a doctorate degree and his own private practice business. And Mrs. Marshall is a kickass lawyer who is simultaneously feared and respected.

But me? I barely made it out of sophomore year, I come from deadbeat parents and a rundown Terrace in the worst part of town, and I can't hold a proper conversation to save my life.

I'm not even exaggerating.

The Terrace was like fire. Threatening to burn everything—and everyone—to the ground. Threatening to consume me until I was nothing but ash.

But the Marshall house? It's like ice. Infinitely peaceful. Kind of beautiful, too, if you take a step back and just marvel at it.

I'm not quite sure how my siblings and I are going to fit into their dynamic, if I'm being honest. And I definitely don't know how I'm going to fit into an elite private school for the uber-wealthy. I have enough trouble with peers as it is. I don't need to be broadcasted as an out of place new student on top of that.

Somewhere in the middle of my mental spiral, there's a soft knock on my door. "Hey, Maisy? It's Amanda. May I come in?"

Of course you can. It's your house.

"Yeah," I say instead, still keeping my eyes locked on the white stucco ceiling.

The door inches open, and I see a flash of Mrs. Marshall's blonde hair as she hurries into my room and shuts the door.

She glances around the room with a sour look on her face, shaking her head slowly.

Oh, God. What did I do? I left my bag of clothes on the floor, mostly because there hadn't been enough time before dinner. I spent the few hours in between our arrival and dinner time calming CJ down and helping him unpack. I really did plan on cleaning up my space, too.

God, you let-down. She's pissed. You haven't even been here twenty-four hours and you've already messed up.

I open my mouth to apologize, but no words come out. So, I close it, then open it again, like some sort of desperate, oxygen-deprived fish.

"I'm sorry about this," Mrs. Marshall sighs, gesturing to the room. "It's so… bland."

I blink at her disbelievingly. "Huh?"

"There's no color. No posters or fun pillows or… character. It's like a skeleton of the room I had imagined for you."

"Respectfully, Mrs. Marshall, the only thing this room doesn't have that my old room did is cockroaches." Mrs. Marshall squirms and I groan at my pathetic attempt at humor.

"I haven't had my own bed in forever, let alone my own room. This is more than enough. It's… It's more than I ever could have asked you for. So, thank you."

She eyes me sympathetically; her brown eyes filled with a strange mix of emotions. "I'm glad you like it, sweetheart, but I want to take you out. We can get whatever you want—whatever you think you'll need to make this room yours. And clothes, too. Whatever you need."

I shake my head, mortified. "Oh no, Mrs. Marshall. I'm alright, really. I've got clothes," I point to the floor, at my trash bag of clothes. Granted, most of the garments are the wrong size or are hanging on by a thread, but they still count. "You've done plenty for me already."

"Maisy, we gave you a bed and mashed potatoes," Mrs. Marshall deadpans. "That's hardly extraordinary."

"It is to me." Placing my hands in my lap to fidget, I drop my head to avoid her sad eyes. "I don't need fancy things. I just need to get through this. To get my siblings through this. I'd rather the kids get nice stuff."

She studies me for a moment, her head cocked to the side. "There's plenty for all of you. Both CJ and Natalia will have everything they need and want, too, but you don't have to sacrifice for them. Not anymore, okay? Why don't we go out on a little shopping spree?"

I know that Mrs. Marshall is a stubborn woman. I've gathered that in my few hours here, and she sort of has to be, given the nature of her job. I know that I'm probably going to have to cave eventually, but the thought of going out and spending this nice woman's hard-earned money on materialistic items is repulsive.

I feel guilty enough for the bare essentials she's providing me.

Calling on my old friend deflection, I make a big show of checking the alarm clock on my nightstand. "Oh, eight o'clock already? I should go get Nat ready for bed," I say, standing from the cushy mattress, ready to make a run for it.

"Already done." Mrs. Marshall stands to her feet, clearly taking the hint and heading for the doorway. Before she exits the room fully, she turns around to face me again, a small smile dusting her lips. "Nice try at deflection, though. I'm a very persuasive person, so consider this conversation far from over."

"I really don't want to spend your money, Mrs. Marshall, and I don't have any of my own. I promise this is more than enough for me," I say quietly. "And, uh, thanks for taking care of the baby."

"That's what I'm here for, sweetie. I know it'll be an adjustment for you, not being responsible for your siblings, but you need to be a kid. I mean, don't be as stupid as my son," she quips, nodding towards the shared wall between mine and Chris's rooms. "But live your life. Let Tim and I worry about the kids, okay?"

I nod, discomfort and unfamiliarity swirling in the pit of my stomach. It's been so long I don't know that I *can* take a backseat in my siblings' lives. But it's nice to know that I have the option, at least.

"Oh, and Maisy?" Mrs. Marshall says, turning around in the hallway. "Call me Amanda. Mrs. Marshall makes me feel old."

And then she's gone.

Chapter 6

<u>Maisy</u>

Four days after we moved in, I have my first real conversation with Chris.

I learned quickly that he isn't home much. Between the gym, his part-time job at the car garage, and spending time with his friends, he's usually only at the house for dinner. I've only talked to him in passing or while discussing our days.

That is, until Wednesday.

I'm lying on my bed with one of the books I took from the library downstairs. I'm not exaggerating when I say library, either. A whole wall of the family room downstairs is a floor to-ceiling bookshelf, filled to the brim with books from various different authors and genres.

Tim reads mostly historical fiction, classics, and the occasional memoir, while Amanda goes for romances and murder mysteries. Combined, I have the world's most eclectic selection of books at my disposal.

It felt weird, taking something from the Marshalls, but after Amanda caught me staring longingly at the bookshelf, she told me to take one. When I initially declined, she pulled the strangest, most boring titles from Tim's collection and said she would pile them all up in my room if I didn't pick one that I actually wanted.

Her tactic worked, because the fear of having to read The History of Cattle Farming drove me to my current selection.

The Book Thief. I'm completely enthralled by it, and I've barely made it a quarter of the way through.

I'm mid-page when I hear the soft knock on my bedroom door, followed by the deep timbre of Chris's voice. "Maisy Mae, can I come in?"

He insists on calling me by my first *and* middle names, claiming that it sounds better than plain old Maisy. I called bullshit, because nobody else seems to have a problem with my first name.

But he's as relentless as his mother.

I'm still getting used to the prospect of knocking. I'm used to my brother just barging in whenever he feels like it, and lord knows my mother was never out of bed for long enough to consult me about anything.

"Yeah, sure," I call back, placing my bookmark on the page and setting the book on my nightstand.

My door swings open then, and seconds later Chris is plopped down on the foot of my bed, lying on his stomach with his feet in the air.

"So, how're you?" he asks, resting his head in his hands. "What's new in the life of Maisy?"

"Absolutely nothing." Leaning against my headboard, I can't bite back my smile looking at my foster brother. He's a giant goofball, and I honestly doubt he's ever gone a full day without smiling or ripping one offhand joke or another. It's hard to be sad when Chris is around. His energy is contagious. I have nothing against Tim and Amanda, but I think Chris is my favorite Marshall.

I have a crippling fear of authority—understandable, given my parental predicament— but Chris is different. I can relax in his presence, which isn't something I can say about very many people.

"Boring," he drawls, grinning wider so I know he's joking.

I shrug. "Well, it's not like I have very many friends to hang out with."

Mischief twinkles in his blue eyes. "Yeah, about your lack of friends…" My face falls a bit at his bluntness. "Shit, that was kind of harsh. Sorry. But there's this pool party on Friday. I think you should come."

"A party?" I haven't been invited to one of those since I was five. And that was when it was custom to invite your entire class to a birthday party, so you didn't leave anyone out. "For who?"

Now it's Chris's turn to shrug. "High school parties usually don't have a recipient. But it's at a girl from school's house. Mia.

She's pretty cool, and her parties are always a ton of fun. Especially her pool parties."

"I don't get it. How would she have invited me to her party? I don't even go to your school yet."

"*She* didn't invite you," Chris says slowly. "I did."

"Chris, I can't just show up to a random girls' party. That feels…wrong."

Chris adjusts his big body on my bed, so he's sitting criss-crossed on my duvet, his expression showing no indication of debauchery. He's looking at me like he seriously expected me to say yes to going to a random girls' party. Like it's crazy of me to turn the offer down.

"Maisy, half of the people who'll be there weren't invited. I was only invited because Mia wants a piece of this." He grins mischievously, gesturing up and down his body. "I mean, can we really blame her?"

That makes me chuckle. "Yes, we can. Ego much?"

"I'm so serious here, Maisy," Chris says, still grinning. "I want you to come. Do some networking before the start of the school year. Break out of that little tortoise shell of yours."

"Even if I had a desire to go—which I don't—I don't even have a swimsuit, Chris. And I don't know anybody. And I should stay back here, just in case the kids need something—"

"Maisy, Maisy, Maisy," Chris says, holding a hand up. "One crisis at a time. First, I'll take you under my wing. You're welcome. We'll go shopping, okay? Second, you know Colt and I, and I won't let you out of my sight if that makes you feel any better. And third, that's what my parents are for. Come have some teenage fun for once. It'll be good for you."

I think Amanda would be very proud of him right now. He certainly got his persuasion skills from his mother in addition to his stubbornness.

It could be good for me to get out, right? I mean, I'm going to have to face a bunch of new kids on the first day of school, anyway, so what's the harm in speeding up the process? Amanda said she wants me to have normal teenage experiences, and it doesn't get much more normal than a house party, right?

I let out a sigh, nodding my head hesitantly. "Okay. I'm in."

Chris claps his hands together happily, jumping off of my bed. "Perfect. We'll go shopping after my work out tomorrow morning, okay?"

What have I signed myself up for? I wonder as I watch my hyper-energetic foster brother skip happily out of my bedroom.

This will either be a ton of fun or a total disaster. I guess only time will tell.

Chapter 7

<u>Colton</u>

"Lorenzo!" Coach Caldwell bellows from the bench as the rest of my teammates skate of off the ice. "My office."

I follow my teammates off of the ice, dread stemming in my gut. It's never good when Caldwell wants to see you. It isn't going to be for a pat on the back or a gentle thumbs up, that's for sure.

More like a spit-filled berating disguised as "tough love".

Racking my brain for what I could've possibly done to piss him off, I wave goodbye to my teammates and take a left towards his office.

Is it about Colorado? I played beautifully and scored at least one goal per game. I had no penalties. Was it something from this practice?

Think, Lorenzo. Fucking think.

I need the upper hand here. If I know what I did wrong, I can calculate how I'll react to his criticism. I can plot a way to make up for it…

I'm still clueless by the time he joins me in his office a few minutes later.

Feigning calm, I stare back at his towering frame from across his thick oak desk. "What's up, Coach?"

"First of all, great practice today." *Ok, good start…* "But I wanted to talk to you about Colorado."

Shit. "What about it, sir?"

He runs his hand across his scraggly beard, looking off into the distance thoughtfully. Everything about this feels *wrong*. He should be yelling at me. Telling me about how much of a fuckup I am. It's almost more unsettling seeing the man calm than it is to watch him raging.

"Your performance was insane, kid. Far beyond this division. I know you've been working your ass off all summer, and it shows."

"Thank you, sir," I say wearily, waiting for the *but*. He has to be pulling my leg here. There's no way in hell Caldwell is actually complimenting me. He doesn't do compliments. *Ever*.

"As you know, we lost Reinhardt this year," he drawls, referring to our old team captain, Leo Reinhardt. He was a hell of a player, but he aged out this year and left the U18 team captainless.

It's been up in the air about who will take his place, and everyone assumed the position would go to Alex Turner, our goalie, since he's one of the older guys on the team. It'd make sense—he's been here for three years, and he's more than responsible enough to take on the role.

It never once crossed my mind that I could be considered. I'm the baby of the team by well over a year.

"Your performance was unmatched, Lorenzo. The guys all know it. They all look up to you. I want you to take the captaincy."

I search my coach's face for a sign of sarcasm, but I find nothing. *No fucking way.* "You're serious?" I ask, quite frankly a bit dumbfounded by the entire ordeal. "You want me to be captain?"

"Are you deaf, kid? Yeah, I want you to be captain." Caldwell rolls his eyes, his friendly façade slipping. "Don't make me regret this," he warns, shooting me a stern glance.

"I won't, Coach," I promise.

He shoos me out of his office, and I swear to Christ, I could levitate out of there.

At sixteen, I'm captaining the New York State U18 team. The *state* team.

Holy *shit*.

I know that logistically I should be freaking out for entirely different reasons. I have a loaded schedule this year, between school, work, and now captaining two teams, but I can't bring myself to care.

I pull my phone out of my bag to call Chris, but I guess we're even more freakily in sync than I thought, because my phone starts vibrating in my hand as I type in my passcode.

"Hello?" I push open the locker room door, checking to make sure I'm alone before putting the call on speaker. I set my phone on the bench so I can work on untying my skates.

"Colt, my man. Are you ready for the party tomorrow?"

"No," I growl into the phone. Damn Chris and his persistence. "Because I explicitly said I'm not coming."

God, first Maisy, now you?" Chris tuts over the line. "Doesn't anybody trust my party judgment anymore?"

That catches my attention. Trying to push the curiosity and excitement out of my voice, I aim for nonchalant and say, "Wait, Maisy's going?"

The same Maisy who's been stuck in my head for five days straight? I know it sounds creepy, but I can't stop thinking about her eyes. How haunted they looked. There's something about her that makes me uneasy. Her skittishness, maybe?

I have no right to worry about her—I don't know the first thing about the girl—but that doesn't stop me. Tortured whiskey eyes are on the forefront of my mind whenever her name is brought up in conversation. I'm trying really fucking hard to contain my curiosity and *not* come off as a creep, but it's no easy feat when every instinct in my body is screaming at me to learn her story.

"Yep. I talked her into being my plus-one. Figured it'd be in her best interest to get to know some people before school starts, you know?"

"Good move." Chris's good ideas are few and far between, but sometimes he really strikes a good one. "I mean, I guess I can go. But I'm not getting drunk."

I'm not like my teammates. I can't get absolutely hammered and then function like a normal human being the next day. Hangover-Colton skates like a one-legged foal and has skull-splitting headaches for two full days.

It's just not worth it.

"Fine by me. Hey, what're you doing today?" Chris asks.

I pull my jersey over my head and toss it into my gear bag, digging to find the T-shirt I threw in here earlier. "I'm still at the rink. I had U18 practice today."

"Duh," he drawls, and I know he rolled his eyes, too. "But what are you doing *after*?"

"Nothing," I say skeptically, not trusting whatever it is he has planned. "Why?"

"Well, I promised Maisy I'd take her to get a swimsuit for tomorrow. I was wondering if you wanted to tag along. Get to know her a little better."

I really should say no. I should go home and study for the upcoming SATs. I should finish my summer assignment for English. I should go help my dad at the garage.

But the idea of getting to spend the day with Chris and Maisy trumps my other plans. Mostly the Maisy part.

I finish getting changed, zip my gear bag up, and kick it under the bench. Double checking that I didn't leave anything behind, I pick my phone up off of the bench and set it between my shoulder and my ear. "Yeah, I'm in."

"Great. Meet me at my place."

So that's exactly what I do.

"Ah, my favorite asshole," Chris muses, hopping into the front seat of my truck. "Look who finally had room for me in his schedule."

I roll my eyes at his antics, watching the backseat through the rearview mirror. Maisy flung the door open, but she's looking at the car like it's her archnemesis.

It occurs to me then that the girl isn't much more than five foot, and my lifted truck may be a bit of a challenge to get into. She may have to run and jump into the backseat. No joke.

Chris follows my gaze, his eyes shining with humor as he takes in Maisy's current predicament. "Oh, you poor, poor, dwarf girl," he tuts, sliding out of the passenger door. "I'd recommend a step stool, but I don't think we have one of those. Here—" He gets on his hands and knees, and I have so many questions, I don't even know where to start.

I've been friends with him for long enough to know that asking questions is a dangerous game. Most of the time, you're better off not knowing what's going through his head.

But this is one of the times I'll let my curiosity get the better of me. "Why the hell are you doggy style, Christopher?" Maisy's cheeks flush bright pink as she stares from Chris to the truck, and finally up to me.

"I'm being her step stool, dumbass," Chris deadpans, like kneeling on his driveway is a totally normal thing to do. "Hop on, Maisy Mae."

"*Chris*," she whisper-hisses, her cheeks flushing darker. "I'm not stepping on your back. I'll hurt you."

Chris rolls his eyes. "Okay, first of all, you're, like, eighty pounds. I bench almost triple what you weigh. And second, I spend my free time getting slammed into boards, so I don't think a little weight on my back will break me. Hop on."

Maisy sighs and seems to weigh her options for a moment before caving and stepping on Chris's back.

Even on his back, she has to lunge into the truck.

Jesus, she's tiny.

A part of me wonders if her size—or lack thereof—has something to do with malnutrition, but I feel like I'm better off not knowing. I have a feeling that the answer will upset me, and I honestly don't have the mental capacity to deal with knowledge like that.

Chris reclaims his spot in the front, sinking into the seat casually, like he wasn't just on all fours like a goddamn animal. All I can do is shake my head, because honestly, what does one say to that?

Mackenzie Hamelin

I peer at Maisy through the rearview mirror, stealing a fleeting glance at her side profile as she buckles her seatbelt.

You're staring. Snap out of it before she notices you, creeper.

Breaking my gaze, I snap my eyes to the windshield. "So, Maisy," I drawl. "What do you listen to?"

She looks up, startled. "Huh?"

"What kind of music do you like?" I rephrase, opening my phone and clicking on the Spotify icon.

"Oh, uh, I don't care." She stares out the window, a clear attempt at shutting down the conversation. Shrugging, I hit random shuffle, and back out of the Marshall's driveway.

The car is quiet—something that never happens when my best friend is involved—but I can say with a hundred percent certainty that he's afraid to scare the girl in the back seat.

I know that because I am, too.

She's fidgeting, cracking her knuckles and bouncing her leg restlessly. Her apprehension is palpable, and it suddenly feels like I've kidnapped her or something. She's clearly uncomfortable, and knowing she feels that way because of me does something funny to my gut.

When we roll up to a stoplight, I turn to face Chris, nodding my head to the back seat. "*Do something*," I mouth, trusting him to say the right thing. He knows her better than I do, and I don't trust myself enough to not accidentally screw things up.

"So, Maisy Mae," Chris drawls, drumming his fingers against the window. "What are you thinking of getting?"

"I don't know," she sighs, stilling her hands. "I don't know what people wear to these things." She pauses for a moment, as if she's debating saying something. "I don't go out much."

"Don't worry, Maisy," Chris says reassuringly. "Colt and I have *plenty* of experience with women's clothing. Particularly with taking it off, but it still counts."

Maisy blushes and retreats back into that shell of hers. I groan, wanting to knock my best friend over the top of the head. Hard. Maybe then I can knock whatever's loose back into place.

"Shit. I went too far again, didn't I?" Chris shrugs sheepishly. "I'm sorry, Maisy."

"What about me?!" I exclaim, pinching my eyebrows together. "I'm the one you just outed, asshole! I feel violated."

Maisy chuckles at my outburst, and I feel my rage dissolve. Fuck, she's got a great laugh. Surprise flashes on Chris's face, and I know without him saying a word that he hadn't heard that from her before, either.

Progress.

I try to keep my attention on the road, to get us to the mall in one piece, but it's a hard feat to achieve when all I can focus on is all of the ways I can make her laugh again.

Chapter 8

Maisy

Sitting in the backseat of Colton's truck, my mind seems to be stuck on one thought.

These two are idiots.

Colton less so than Chris, but as I watch them start scream-singing a horribly off-key rendition of *Call Me Maybe*, I'm thoroughly convinced that these boys are actually ten-year-olds impersonating high school juniors.

When we make it to the mall, I start to panic a little bit. I hate the idea of using the credit card Amanda placed in Chris's hand on our way out the door. I hate the thought of taking any more from this family than I already am, but Amanda told me that if I come back from the store without something cute to wear, she'll be very upset.

I'm pretty sure she was only joking, but I'm not certain. I really don't want to make her upset, but I also feel incredibly awkward spending the Marshall's hard-earned money on a skimpy bikini that I'll probably only wear once.

And the fact that I'm shopping for said skimpy bikini with two giant hockey players only amplifies my mortification.

Why, why, why *did I say yes to this?*

"Okay," Chris says happily, clearly oblivious to my internal turmoil. "I say we start at Darcy's, and then try Bloom Boutique, and then we can stop and get pretzels, because I'm hungry as fuck." He turns to me with a megawatt grin. "How does that sound, Maisy Mae?"

I nod, struggling to stay in step with the boys. Their legs are so much longer than mine. Every step they take is equivalent to six of mine. "Yeah. That sounds good."

"Chris, slow down. The girl's jogging to keep up with us," Colton says through a chuckle, grabbing the back of Chris's T-shirt and yanking him back. "There." Colton nods, slowing their strides to a more manageable speed. He looks down at me and smiles. "How're you doing down there, Shorty?"

I want to be embarrassed—it's practically my second nature—but Colton's goofy grin and teasing tone make it hard to take his words to heart.

Instead, I instruct myself to stay cool and match his humor. Or try to, at least.

"Pretty good. How's the weather up there, BFG?" Both boys cock their heads at me, clearly not getting the reference I'd made. This time I *am* embarrassed, and I feel the heat rise up my cheeks as both boys scrunch their eyebrows in confusion.

"Huh?" Colton and Chris say in unison.

"Big Friendly Giant," I mumble, hanging my head to hide my flushed cheeks. "It's, uh, it's from a Roald Dahl book."

"Aw, you think I'm friendly?" Colton goads, nudging me with his elbow playfully.

"You haven't seen him when it's his time of the month," Chris grumbles. "He's more hormonal than any chick I've ever met."

Colton narrows his eyes at his best friend. "I'm so friendly, I'm going to ignore that *very* untrue statement."

We stop in front of a small boutique, with mannequins all dolled up in expensive-looking jeans and cute tube tops.

I've never been clothes shopping outside of the thrift store, and even then, I only went once in a blue moon. A hefty amount of the checks my mother brought home went towards an endless mountain of bills, a significant chunk of it went towards fulfilling my mother's addictions, and the rest of it was used for groceries and whatever CJ or Nat needed.

I've always been the one in charge of finances at home, and while most teenagers given passwords to their parent's bank account might go on a shopping spree, I couldn't. Even the small amount of left over money we did have was set aside, in case of emergencies.

Most of my clothes were hand-me-downs from my mother, and those that didn't were taken from Goodwill or the thrift store down the road from the Terrace.

The jump from that lifestyle to this one is threatening to give me whiplash. I never would have dreamed about splurging on something like this, but as we walk into the shop, neither Colton nor Chris seems the slightest bit fazed by the price tags and flashy items filling the store.

I don't know whether to be amazed at the stark contrast between our lifestyles, or jealous of them.

"Oooh this one!" Chris squeals, running off towards the back of the store. I try to peer around him to catch a glimpse of whatever it is he saw, but nothing stands out to me. He holds up a white scrap of a bikini triumphantly. I look at Colton, whose face is distorted in the same horrified expression as mine.

"Chris, there's no bikini in that bikini," Colton says, eyes wide. "She might as well show up naked."

Chris rolls his eyes, waving his free hand around flippantly. "It's not for her, dumbass. It's for me. I should go try it on, shouldn't I?"

I want to laugh, but I'm honestly not sure if he's joking or not. You can never really tell with Chris.

"If you put that on, I'm going back to the parking lot and driving away without you." Judging by the disapproving scowl on his face, I don't think Colton's joking. He probably *would* drive off without Chris.

Chris mumbles something unintelligible, but he turns around and re-racks the bikini.

The next few he grabs are more modest, but not by much. There's a baby blue one, a yellow one, and a purple one, and I know for a fact that I'm not going to find anything more concealing. Not in this store, at least.

Still very much regretting coming out on this particular excursion, I take the bathing suits from Chris and head to the fitting rooms.

The blue swimsuit is way too big, and the purple one is way too small, but the yellow one fits semi-decently.

I stare at the floor-to-ceiling mirror in the dressing room, not recognizing myself without my usual getup of unintentionally oversized jeans and an old ratty T-shirt. I feel…different. *Pretty,* even. I think the fact that it takes an item of clothing for me to feel this way is a bit alarming, and can probably be identified as a self-confidence issue, but oh well. For once in my life, I feel confident, and I'm taking that fact and running with it.

"How's it going, Maisy Mae?" Chris asks from the other side of the fitting room door. "Did you like any of them?"

"Yeah," I call back. "I like the yellow one."

"Perfect. Put real clothes back on and we'll move onto phase two of Project Maisy."

"Which is?" Colton asks skeptically.

"Uh, *duh.* She can't just show up to the party in a swimsuit, Colton. She needs something to go over it. *Obviously.*"

I can hear the eyeroll in his voice, as strange as it sounds. I feel a bit panicky at the thought of costing the Marshall's even more money, but I picture Amanda's hopeful face when she found out Chris and I were going shopping, and I sigh, knowing that my desire to please her outweighs my natural instinct of saving money at all costs.

As I'm pulling my jeans back on, I decide that I'll go for the cheapest thing I can find, and call it a day. I'll do minimum damage on their bank account, and Amanda will be happy. It's a win-win.

I hang the two discarded swimsuits on the return rack and walk over to meet Chris and Colton at their perch across from the fitting room door.

Chris gets a head start, running off to look at the dresses, but Colton hangs behind with me.

"I'm really sorry about this," he says, blowing out a breath. "This Project Maisy shit. Just know he doesn't mean any harm by it."

"Harm?" I parrot, slightly confused. "How would it be harmful?"

"Because he's trying to change you, Maisy, and I kind of hate that. You should be able to just be you, how you are, without needing a new wardrobe or a new attitude or whatever to fit in." He looks down at me with soulful brown eyes, and I somehow just *know* that he means every word. "For the record, I think you're great the way you are." He shrugs, tucking his hands in his pockets. "If the kids at school don't like you, then fuck them. It says more about them than you, anyway."

I'm a bit lost for words, still reeling in Colton's compliment turned advice session. It's a long time before I can think clearly enough to come up with a coherent response.

"I appreciate it, honestly," I admit, tucking my hair behind my ears anxiously. "I don't have the clothes I have because that's my style. They're just all I *could* have."

I don't think I've ever said those words out loud, and I honestly can't tell you why I chose *Colton* of all people to admit that to. Besides the fact that I feel eerily comfortable around him.

"What do you mean?" he asks, puzzlement flashing across his expression.

"There were more important things to spend money on." I shrug, unsure of how else to explain it. "I made my mom's old stuff work. I know it's kind of…different than what normal teenagers wear, but there's a lot about my life that's different than normal teenagers."

"Like?"

I'm *this* close to telling him, to testing to see if he'll run away when he hears my story, like so many people have in the past. There's nothing appealing about being a sixteen-year-old head of the household, and the mother figure to two kids I had no part in creating.

It scares people away. As it should.

A masochistic part of me wonders if Colton would follow that pattern. He seems more level headed than most of the other kids our age, but I wouldn't blame him for taking one look at my baggage and deciding he wants no part of it. Even if he's only hanging out with me to pacify Chris.

Before I can answer him, Chris rejoins us, holding a white tube top and a cute jean skirt in front of me like a fisherman holds his prized catch.

"Okay, try these," he says, holding the clothing out to me. "And also, these." He sets a shoebox in my hands, with the words *Dr. Martens* stamped on the top.

"Jesus, Chris, you're treating her like she's a Bratz doll." Colton shoots me a sympathetic glance, which I return with a what-can-you-do shrug. We both know Chris won't drop it until I cave, so I take the items from him and turn back towards the dressing room.

I actually don't hate the outfit. The shoes are adorable, and make me look several inches taller than I actually am. The skirt is cute, too, and makes me look way curvier than I thought I was.

Chris should be a personal stylist, because the boy has taste. I wouldn't have guessed it, given that I've never seen him in anything but sweatpants and T-shirts, but I'm more than a little impressed with his creative eye.

"Come on, let us see!"

It's a bit awkward, going all fashion runway for Colton and Chris, but it's hard to feel uncomfortable with Chris's drunk-on-life grin. If it were anyone else, I probably would have refused to come out of the dressing room, but there's something about the two massive boys staring back at me that makes me feel grounded.

"Give us a spin!" Chris nods in approval as I do a stationary three-sixty. "God, I'm so talented," he sighs wistfully, clapping Colton on the shoulder.

"Don't be so cocky, Chris," Colton murmurs, rolling his eyes at his best friend. He waves a hand in my general direction, motioning up and down my body. "That has *nothing* to do with your clothes and *everything* to do with the girl in them."

I don't think Colton meant to say that last part out loud, because his cheeks flush a little bit. Not as hard as mine do, though.

I run from my discomfort, as per usual, using the changing room as my safe haven from whatever the hell *that* was.

Unfortunately, it's only a temporary, because as soon as I get changed into my street clothes, I'm forced back into the proximity of the boys.

"I'm sorry," Colton says quietly as we wait for Chris outside of the store. I had a slight freak out about how much everything would cost, and Chris banished me from the line. Being the gentleman I've seen him be, Colton offered to wait with me.

I'm honestly more embarrassed by my instinct to run at the first sign of discomfort than I am by Colton's suggestive comment. I'm sure he meant nothing by it. I mean, look at *him*, and look at *me*.

Colton finding me attractive is about as likely as Channing Tatum finding Tinkerbell attractive.

Maybe even less than that. I have no idea what Channing's into.

"I didn't mean to make you uncomfortable," Colton continues, turning his head to face me. "I just wanted to shut him up."

I drop my gaze to my tattered sneakers, not nearly strong enough to meet his eyes. "I know."

He cocks his head, his dark brown eyes boring into my face. "Then why'd you run?"

He sounds genuinely curious, and as ashamed as I am about my less-than-stellar approach at confrontation, I feel like I owe him some semblance of an explanation.

"I always do." I shrug. "I guess running is hardwired into my brain."

"Well, you don't have to do it from me," he says, smiling down at me. "I don't bite." He pauses, pointing in the store window at Chris, who's still waiting in line. "Him, on the other hand? Bites like a rabid rottweiler."

I can't help but smile, and Colton jumps on it like a fish that's been offered a line. "How come you don't do that more often?"

"What?" I ask quizzically. "Smile?" Colton nods. "I guess it's just kind of hard to be happy, after everything."

Yet another thing I haven't admitted out loud. Christ, does he have some sort of truth-spilling pheromone or something?

His eyebrows furrow as he studies me. "Everything?"

I'm trapped in a corner now, where I can admit to him the reason I'm here, or I can shut down and run off. When Chris plants himself between us, holding up the shopping bag victoriously, I've never been happier to see his stupid, dopey face.

"I'm perished," he groans, patting his stomach for emphasis. "And I was promised pretzels."

"You promised yourself pretzels, dumbass," Colton points out, seemingly annoyed by the distraction.

"Regardless. I want food." He slings an arm around my shoulders, tugging me away from Colton, who frowns. "Now, Maisy, let me introduce you to the glory that is Mama Tina's Pretzels."

He's covered in cinnamon.

His face, his hands, his jeans… Not even my baby siblings are as messy as Chris.

"You're delusional if you think I'm letting you get in my truck like that," Colton says, setting his soda on the table and sinking into the seat next to Chris. "Seriously, man, you got more cinnamon on your face than in your mouth."

I can hear Colton and Chris bickering back and forth like an old married couple, but my attention is locked on the table over Chris's shoulders.

It's a table of girls, about my age, whose attention is locked on *me*.

"Um, Chris, don't look, but…" I lean over the food court table, whispering so that the people around us can't hear the paranoia in my voice. "I think they're watching us," I say, pointing to the group of girls shooting me death glares.

Seriously, I don't think I've ever seen as much sheer hatred in a pair of eyes as I do with these girls. Not even when my mother looked at me. And that's saying something.

Chris swivels his head around, blatantly glaring at the table of girls. "Dude. She said don't look." Colton rolls his eyes, but then he also turns around to check out what I was talking about.

When the boys face me again, their expressions have been covered by a storm cloud, their scowls blatant. "For fuck's sake. School hasn't even started yet and we're already on the receiving end of their bullshit?"

"Whose bullshit?" I ask, thoroughly confused. "Who are those girls?"

"The Fatal Four." Is Chris's tortured response.

Noticing my still-puzzled expression, Colton begins to clarify. "They're girls we go to school with. They're the worst of the jersey chasers." I'm still lost. Colton continues, his voice mellow despite the annoyance shining in his brown eyes. "The girls obsessed with sleeping with every athlete in the goddamn school."

"When pertaining to hockey, they're called puck bunnies," Chris adds, nodding his head grimly. "And those four? They're by far the worst in the school."

I nod, my neck flaming with embarrassment. That explains why they're looking at me like they want to gut me like a fish. They think I'm a threat.

Hardly. These boys are only here with me out of pity and probably a bit of bribery on Amanda's part. They'd never tell me that upfront—they're both too kind for that—but two uber-popular hockey players must have *something* better to do during the last week of summer break than going shopping with the town orphan.

"Oh." I look down at my lap, forcing myself not to crumble under the intensity of the girls' stares.

Chris leans over the table, tipping my chin up with aching tenderness. "Chin up, Maisy Mae." He forces my eyes up to his, smiling softly. "Remember, you're here with us because we want you here. You were invited. *They* were not," he says, tilting his head back towards the table of furious females.

His words are somehow just what I needed to hear. Like he can read my mind. Honestly, knowing the little bit that I know about Chris, it wouldn't surprise me if he *could* read minds.

Chapter 9

<u>Colton</u>

I have never been more nervous for a party.   I'm not nervous for me. I'm sure I'll get swarmed by unwanted and unreciprocated female attention, but that isn't why I'm dreading the party.

I'm *terrified* that the Fatal Four are going to terrorize Maisy. After seeing their mean girl scowls at the mall yesterday, it doesn't take a genius to know that they're jealous as hell.

And jealousy? It paints all sorts of ugly pictures.

The worst of the group, Sierra, has been after me since freshman year. Since we were baby fourteen-year-olds. There's nothing baby about this girl, though. She was sleeping around before we even hit high school.

Normally, I wouldn't ever recite a piece of information like that. I'm not keen on feeding the rumor mill, but the fact that she hooked up with Jason Murphy—our school's quarterback—isn't a secret. No, the sex tape she uploaded right afterward is all the proof the school needed. Of course, her loaded lawyer daddy had it removed, said she was hacked or some lame shit like that, and it was taken down. But nobody at school ever forgot.

Sierra's friends aren't much better. Trish, Brianna, and Fiona are no angels themselves. But in a way, they're worse than Sierra will *ever* be, because they're so spineless that they're at Sierra's beck and call every second of every day.

At least Sierra has the balls to be a leader.

One of my teammates on the school team, Tommy Zalinsky, refers to them as Sierra's "posse of poisonous pussy" and honestly, I can't think of a better way to describe them.

They follow her in everything, especially in her pursuit to screw every member of the ice hockey team.

Myself included.

Some of the guys on my team are lust-clouded horndogs, who were unfortunate enough to fall into their trap.

But the girls are relentless in their pursuit of one thing.

The captain. Sacred number twenty-two. *Me*.

I'm terrified that seeing me with Maisy is going to be the equivalent of strapping a giant *KICK ME!* sign on her back, but I'm not scared enough to drop her entirely. She needs someone right now. Not only is she starting over in a different school junior year, when the rest of us have been together for three years, but she's starting over in a new family, too.

Plus, there's something… fragile, about her. Like she could be blown over by the wind and just *shatter*. I have a feeling that the girl is barely hanging on by a thread, so Chris and I have made it our mission to make sure she acclimates okay.

It won't hurt that we're the two biggest hotshots on campus. That's not a brag, it's a fact. Being the captain of a championship hockey team and the beloved class clown have their perks, including a seemingly unlimited supply of friends.

Our plan is to spend the off-season getting her into her own little circle, so that by the time school hockey is in full swing, she'll have her own group.

I'll be too busy by then to so much as look at the girl, but until that point, I've promised Chris to help him help her out. The truth is, I'm busy enough as it is, what with SAT prep and summer assignments and the new U18 captaincy, but when Chris needs help, you bet your ass I'll be the first one by his side.

And, honestly, I don't think I can take a back seat with this whole Maisy thing. Something inside of me is all but demanding that I look after her, and whether that urge is justified or not, it isn't something I can ignore.

I stroll into my kitchen at quarter to five, with the hopes that I can sneak in and out.

My folks won't care that I'm going out tonight—they don't give a shit what I do, as long as I keep up my grades and stay on top of hockey—but if my mom catches me in her firing line of questions, I'll be late to pick up Maisy and Chris.

To my dismay, Mom is at the kitchen island on her computer, typing furiously. There's still a chance of maintaining invisibility, so I avoid the floorboards I know will squeak if I put weight on them and creep towards the garage door to snatch my key ring.

It's only when she hears the garage door creak open that she perks her head up.

"Were you really going to sneak out without saying hello to me first?" She bats her long lashes at me, frowning. Well, frowning as much as the Botox allows.

There's nothing explicitly *wrong* with my parents. I just don't agree with their way of life. It feels so… fake, I guess. Mom's all about weekly trips to the salon, dyed black hair because *God forbid* she has a couple of grays. And Dad's all about buying cars and tangible shit that's way outside of our budget. It's all fine, but they put on this happy, look-at-me front, when deep down, I know that they're miserable. They work non-stop and spend the little time off that they have pretending to live fairy tale lives. It's exhausting.

"Sorry, Ma," I concede, stepping back into the kitchen. I know that my most promising option right now is playing Devil's advocate, so that's precisely what I'll do.

"Where're you off to tonight?" Something occurs to her and hurt dances across her dark brown eyes. "Christopher's again?"

Ah, fuck. Here we go again.

"Well, yeah," I say cautiously. "But only to pick him up. We're going to a little get together. A back-to-school thing."

It isn't a total lie. It is a back-to-school thing. *Little* just isn't the proper adjective to describe it. I'm willing to put money down on the fact that people will be bombed before we even get there, and I give it until ten before the cops are called. "Oh. I figured you'd be going to see the Marshalls." I don't miss the hint of disappointment in her voice.

For whatever reason, my mother can't wrap her head around the fact that I respect the hell out of Tim and Amanda Marshall. She's under the impression that I cannot possibly have room in my life for adult role models outside of her and my father.

She turns into this raging jealous lunatic wherever Amanda's concerned, which I find strange as hell.

"Nope. I'm just dropping by to grab Chris. Hey, I've gotta run, but I'll talk to you later, okay?" I say dryly, turning back towards the door before she brings out the crocodile tears and I go from *fashionably late* to *asshole late*.

It crossed my mind that I didn't tell her about the U18 captaincy. She'll just lecture me about my use of time again, and I honestly don't think I can take any more of her disappointment tonight. I just have to hope she doesn't find out that I told Chris before her.

I have my second *oh fuck* moment of the day twenty minutes later, when I pull up outside of the Marshall's house to pick up Chris and Maisy.

I'm pretty sure I'm staring at them like a gape-mouthed idiot. Chris shoots me a look that says "*I know*" as he trails after his foster sister.

We are so, so, *so* screwed.

Even in the Doc Martens, she's a good foot shorter than Chris, but Christ, they make her legs look long. It's the same outfit she showed us yesterday at the mall, but sometime between then and now, my brain forgot how much of a smoke show she is.

She's got on this tiny jean skirt that hugs her small waist and a tiny tube top that hugs her *not* small *everything*.

Before she even gets in the car, I've come to the conclusion that I'm going to get in a fight tonight.

Damnit.

Chris boosts Maisy into the truck, and being the masochist I am, I force my eyes forward, careful not to study the way her skirt rides up when she dives into the back seat of my truck.

When she's settled in the back, and Chris is strapped into the front, I pull out of their driveway. "You look very pretty, Maisy," I say nonchalantly, even though there's about a million other adjectives I could be using.

She blushes fiercely. "Oh, um, thank you," she stutters, tucking her hair behind her ear. I've noticed she does that a lot when she's nervous. "You, do, too. Look pretty, I mean." I glance at her through the rearview mirror and cock a brow. Maybe it's wrong of me to be enjoying this interaction so much. She blushes harder, though I previously thought that that was impossible. "I mean not *pretty*. But, well…" she sighs, slouching her shoulders in defeat. "Never mind."

I catch her gaze in one fleeting moment and smile warmly before returning my attention to the road. "It's okay, Maisy. I know what you meant."

Chris clears his throat from beside me. "Um, can I just point out that nobody's calling *me* pretty?" he grumbles, feigning hurt.

Maisy leans forward and pats his shoulder consolingly. "Don't worry, Chris. You're very pretty, too."

The big doofus smiles. "God, you're such a baby."

He turns to look at me, grinning widely. "Yeah, but I'm a *pretty* baby."

Chapter 10

<u>Maisy</u>

Mia's house is huge.

Like, it is seriously *ginormous*.

I feel like I stand out like a sore thumb here, even though I know my little getup helps me blend right in. It looks like I belong here, externally. But I feel like I can't possibly be farther away from these kids.

Everyone here has fancy new iPhones and name brand clothing. They all have a certain look about them. A certain *glow* to them. They walk and talk and *breathe* like they have always belonged, like this is where they're meant to be.

With every one of my five senses I can tell that all of these kids have lived an insanely different life than I have. I can smell their Dior and Chanel perfumes, can taste the fancy sparkling water from the wine-looking bottle. I hear it in the way they talk, see it in the way they walk, and feel it in the lighthearted nature of their conversations.

Nothing about these kids fits my life. It doesn't fit sharing a bed with your siblings, or catching rats in makeshift traps because the traps they sell at the hardware store are too expensive. It doesn't match the empty pantries and the breath of relief when a month goes by without unaccounted for expenses.

Nothing about this situation feels like I belong. Chris and Colton? Absolutely. They're the biggest attraction at this party, swarmed by boys and girls alike, laughing and talking seamlessly with more people than I can count.

But me? I do my best to hide behind one or both of the boys for as long as I can.

At least, until Colton picks up on my evasion tactics and forces me in front of him, so that I *have* to socialize. "C'mon,

Maisy. There's somebody I want you to meet." He puts his big hands on my shoulders and leads me towards the back door.

"Colton, I don't like this," I say quietly, wishing more than anything that I could be back at the Marshall's house, watching TV with my siblings or reading in the quiet sanctuary of my room.

"If you really don't want to do this, that's okay. I won't make you. But this girl is super sweet, so I think you should give her a chance." Colton peers down at me, his expression genuine and full of promise. "I won't leave your side. And, after you meet her, if you still want to go, we can ditch Chris and I'll take you back to the house. How does that sound?"

I nod, blowing out a steady breath. One conversation. One *hey, nice to meet ya*, and I can be back in a place I'm semi-comfortable.

Colton smiles, then wrenches the sliding glass door open and all but drags me out with him. "Yo, Lainey!" he calls out.

A pretty redhead turns around at the sound of his voice, breaking into a devilish grin. "Colton!" she squeals, running towards him and hugging him tightly. She makes a big show of it, which draws in a ton of stares, but she either doesn't realize or she just flat-out doesn't care.

I have a feeling it's the latter.

"Oh my God, how are you?" She studies him carefully, fixing her green eyes on his chiseled face. "I haven't seen you all summer!"

I'm about to ask how they know each other, but Colton beats me to it. "Maisy, this is my baby cousin, Lainey. Lainey, this is Maisy."

"Baby cousin?" she scoffs, punching his bicep. "Hardly. He's two months older, and he's terrorized me about being the baby of the family my entire life." She rolls her eyes at Colton before reaching a perfectly manicured hand out to me. "It's so nice to meet you, Maisy!"

I shake her hand, and when I'm met with a powerful grip, I wonder if she's on caffeine or drugs. God, this girl's got more energy than CJ. And that's saying something.

"Hi, Lainey," I mumble, feeling my cheeks grow redder than her hair.

She releases the death grip she has on my hand, her smile never once faltering. "So, did Colty finally find himself a girlfriend?" she goads, looking between Colton and I.

My face flushes harder.

"No," Colton says, a bit too quickly. "She lives with Chris."

Realization flashes over Lainey's features, and I wait for the sympathetic light to shine in her eyes. I wait for the high-pitched voice, for the fragile treatment I'm so used to getting.

But it doesn't come.

"Ooooh, a new Marshall? Are you starting at St. Mark's this year?" she asks, cocking her head in a way that makes her curls bounce.

I nod. "Yeah. I'm a junior."

Someone calls Colton's name, and he wanders off in search of the voice. *Turncoat.* I stay there on the deck with Lainey, wanting to make a run for it, but not wanting to abandon the only person who hasn't looked at me like I'm some sort of foreign specimen.

"So, what's it like living with Chris Marshall?" Lainey asks, her tone genuinely curious and not at all pitchy like all of the other girls I've met so far. I come to the conclusion that this girl isn't like the others. She doesn't seem like she has a fake bone in her body.

While everyone else is in tube tops and miniskirts and booty shorts, Lainey's in a pair of acid wash jeans and an oversized Carrie Underwood T-shirt. While everyone else has on full faces of makeup, Lainey is very clearly going all natural. She doesn't seem to care about everyone else.

It's kind of relieving, honestly.

I study her kind eyes for a moment before deciding that she's definitely a friend and not a foe. "He's actually been really good to me. To us." She looks confused for a moment, so I clarify. "My siblings and I. There are three of us."

Her eyebrows shoot up to her hairline. "Three? Damn, girl. I can barely handle one sibling, how do you handle two?"

I shrug. "It's all I've known, really."

I don't mention that I've taken care of them their entire lives, and that we have a different dynamic than most siblings. I'm no social expert, but that doesn't seem like a tidbit of information you share during your first interaction.

"Well, I'm hot as hell. Wanna go in the pool?"

I *want* to go back to the house, like I was promised, but Colton's nowhere to be found. Also, I kind of hate the idea of taking him and Chris away from their fun and ruining their night. Besides, Lainey seems harmless. Another hour or so of partying won't kill me. So, I nod, and follow Lainey back into the house to grab our swimsuits.

Three hours later, and I'm still in the pool with Lainey.

The sun is starting to set, but the party is still going strong.

It's kind of shocking how easy it is to be around Lainey. When I don't know what to say, or how to be social—because, let's face it, I clam up more than I don't—she just keeps talking. She doesn't look at me like a charity case, or grill me with questions about the two boys I showed up here with. Being with her is like a breath of fresh air. It's even easier than being with my classmates at my other school, which is weird, because I've known those kids my entire life.

Maybe it's because Lainey only knows what I want her to know. She hasn't seen the really bad parts of my life yet, and it's nice to know that there's someone out there that hasn't been tainted by the exposure of my past yet.

I was right about my previous assessment—the girl couldn't care less about what anyone thinks. Peer pressure is afraid of *her*.

When this one boy—Mitch, I think? —came over and started being gross, I blushed like a tomato. But Lainey? She looked him dead in the eyes and said to take his *"inability to take no for an answer elsewhere"* because his *"small dick energy is putting a damper on our good time.*" He walked away grumbling, but he obliged.

Then, there was the group of football players that came over and tried to get Lainey and I to have a drink with them. I said no. I've never tried alcohol, and I don't plan on starting, but the boys were not very receptive of that.

They brought two drinks over, despite our nos. Lainey snapped, and it was the first time all night I saw her fully lose her cool. "We said no, assholes. Do we need to say it in another language? How about sign?" And then she flipped the main boy off.

"Chill out, Lane. I'm not talking to you. I'm talking to her." The boy had pointed to me and smiled one of those creepy, slimy smiles that brought back memories of *him* and made my toes curl and my stomach flip uneasily.

"Yeah, well, she said no, too, asshole," Lainey huffed. And then she did the last thing I expected. She took the drink from his hand and dumped it over his head.

Suffice to say, I don't have to worry much when she's around. She's strong enough for the both of us, and for the first time since I arrived at the party, I felt the promise of the impending school year.

But then Lainey went home. She punched her number into my crappy flip phone and told me to text her my school schedule, and hopped in the cab of someone's truck.

I decided it was in my best interest to get out of my still-soaked bikini, and trudged up the grand staircase towards the upstairs bathroom, where I'd left my clothes.

Except when I get there, they're gone. In their place are two girls, one blonde and one brunette. They're much bigger than me, with mean scowls and malice in their mascara-coated eyes.

They look familiar. They're the girls from the food court, I realize.

And that's when the dread hits me in the chest with the force of a semi-truck. What was it the boys called them? The Fatal Four?

"I don't think we've been properly introduced," the blonde girl says icily, folding her arms across her chest. "I'm surprised your *boyfriend* didn't introduce us," she sneers. "I'm Sierra."

My danger scale is off the charts, telling me to abort mission, but as I turn towards the door, the brunette dives for it, blocking my only way out.

Sierra laughs maliciously. "No way, bitch. We've been waiting here way too long for you to leave already. We need to talk about your little game, okay?"

My little game? I just wanted to grab my clothes and *leave*. How on Earth is that a game?

"Does that confuse you?" she mock-pouts, batting her obscenely long lashes at me. "Wow, what a trifecta. Slutty, stupid, and an orphan. What a catch you are, huh?"

I feel the familiar prick of tears behind my eyes, but I will them away with every ounce of strength I have left in me. Crying in front of these girls would be detrimental.

"I know what's going on here. You're living in the same house as Chris, probably riding him, can't blame you there." She smirks, her blue eyes glimmering dangerously. "Fuck Chris all you want. But stay away from Colton."

I want to ask why, because I know for a fact that Colton hates her. But I'm not suicidal, so I keep my mouth shut.

"Don't cross the line here, you little slut. Got it? Colton is *mine*. If I have to tell you again, I won't be so nice." She tosses her blonde hair over one shoulder and marches for the door.

I catch a glimpse of her tote bag as she strides away, and in it, I see my clothes, my dignity, and any shred of fun I'd had tonight.

Chapter 11

<u>Colton</u>

It's been four hours since I left Maisy with my cousin, and I haven't seen her once in that time.

I'd be worried, except for the fact that I'd willingly put my life in Lainey's hands. Aside from Chris, she's the person I trust the most. Sure, she marches to the beat of her own drum, and sure, her filter is practically non-existent, but the girl has a hell of a head on her shoulders and she'd die before she gave into peer pressure.

But when Chris comes to ask me if I've seen Maisy, and I tell him she's with Lainey, and he informs me that Lainey left an hour ago, I kind of panic. Just a little bit.

"It's fine. It's not like she's a small child that needs supervision. We should probably just… find her." Chris is trying to sound nonchalant, but I can see the tiny crack in his cool façade.

We split up and wander around the party, covering double the area in half the time. I feel like a dick, because I promised her that I'd stay by her side, and then I ditched her. Granted, it was with good intentions. I was only trying to help her make friends besides Chris and I, but now she's sort of missing, and I feel like I'm to blame.

"Zalinsky?" I say, coming up behind my buddy and clapping him on the shoulder. "Hey, man. Have you seen the girl we came here with? Maisy?"

Z tosses back the rest of his drink before meeting my eyes. "Yeah, she left half an hour ago."

"I'm sorry, she *what*?"

We're a twenty-minute drive from the Marshall house, in an area entirely unfamiliar to her. Plus, it's dark outside. It's not like she walked back to the house, and she sure as hell didn't take my truck.

I guess she could've caught a ride with someone, but given what I know about her social anxiety, I don't see her asking any strangers for rides.

"Okay. Thanks, man." I'm panicking more than is normal. I mean, really, it's not like she's my sister or girlfriend or anything. There's no reason for me to feel worried.

But I do.

I yank my phone out of my back pocket, typing in Chris's number by memory and holding it up to my ear as I push through the crowd of people and towards the front door.

He picks up on the second ring. "Um, Houston, we have a problem."

"God, don't tell me that," Chris groans.

"Z said she left thirty minutes ago."

"Where the hell would she have gone?"

I run an exasperated hand through my hair, blowing out a sigh. "Fuck if I know, man."

This is the kind of tie-up I try to avoid. The kind of drama I don't need in my life. But does that knowledge stop my heart from racing or my mind from spinning with worst-case-scenarios?

No. No it does not.

"Okay, so here's the plan," Chris says, scarily calmly. Between the two of us, he's always the calm one in a crisis. Go figure. "You look around the neighborhood. I'll double check the house. You catch any sign of anything, call me. And I'll do the same. If we can't find her in twenty minutes, we call my mom. Got it?"

"Got it."

And then the line goes dead.

A few of my hockey buddies live in this neighborhood, so I'm kind of familiar with the surrounding area. But not familiar enough to efficiently manhunt.

She's not on the front lawn, or in my truck, and I'm about to concede and text Chris, when a thought occurs to me.

It's a long shot, but there's one last place I can check.

I part through the backyard, not giving a shit who I knock into or maul. I make it to the end of the property, to the line that crosses the clean-cut, lush green grass with the acre or so of woods behind it. I follow the narrow trail back for about five minutes, until I hit the creek.

And, wouldn't you know it, there's a person there.

Please be her. Please, please, please be her.

A branch crunches beneath my feet, and the figure turns around, searching for the source of the noise.

And, lo and behold, a pair of tortured whiskey eyes meets mine.

Thank God.

"Jesus Christ, Maisy," I mutter, stopping at the bank of the creek where she's sitting. "You gave Chris and I a heart attack."

"I'm s-sorry," she sniffles, wiping her eyes with the back of her hand. I take out my phone flashlight and shine it down on her face. And the sight there makes my heart clench in my chest.

Her eyes are red and swollen, wet streaks spread down both of her cheeks. She's been sitting out in the woods alone, crying.

And then I look again, and notice that she's only in her swimsuit. Her wet swimsuit. And she's shivering.

Fuck.

I pull my hoodie over my head and sit down next to her. "Arms up," I tell her, my tone leaving no room for debate. I slide my hoodie over her head. "I'm going to call Chris and tell him you're safe, and then we're going to talk. Okay?"

All I get is a nod in return.

I call Chris, who tells me that he's on his way to the creek, and then I pocket my phone and turn all of my attention back to the girl on my right. The girl that's *still* silently sobbing.

"Maisy, where are your clothes?" I ask gently.

"I l-lost them," she chokes out.

"You lost them?"

She nods, her long brown hair fanning over her face with the movement. I reach forward, tucking the loose strands behind her ears before cupping her chin, forcing her to look up at me.

"I need you to tell me what happened, okay?"

"It's nothing. Really, I just have allergies."

Allergies my ass. "Maisy, I'm no fool. Something happened. And if you don't tell me, I'll hear it from someone else."

She looks hesitant. Weary. She looks like the scared girl from the dinner table that first night, not like the sweet, funny girl Chris and I had coaxed out to the mall with us. She seems… retreated, almost. Broken.

"It was her," she whispers. Her voice is so quiet, I would've missed it if all of my attention wasn't focused solely on her.

"Sierra?" I ask, feeling my heartbreak and concern slowly morph into blind rage. I don't even have to wait for Maisy's response. I just *know*. "Who the fuck am I kidding?" I scoff. "Of course it was her."

"Colton, please don't do anything," she sniffles, her sad eyes now wide with panic. "Seriously, please just leave it alone."

"What did she say?" When my request is met with silence, I make my tone firmer. "Maisy, what did she say to you?"

She's dwarfed by my hoodie, but she attempts to cross her arms, anyway. She folds them protectively across her stomach, like that will hide her from me. "I don't want to talk about it."

"What about Chris?" I ask, trying to soften my tone despite the rage filling me. "Do you want to talk to him about it instead?"

That just makes her sob harder.

Christ, I'm bad with emotions. I'm only immune to two of them; stress and anger, and I solve both of them with hockey. I don't have a clue what to do with these many tears.

"Do you want a hug?" I ask helplessly, seriously pulling at straws here. To my absolute shock, she nods, and it's all the permission I need. I tug her into my chest, cradling her in my arms. I want to squeeze the shit out of her, but I'm all too aware of our size difference, and I'm a little bit afraid of crushing her.

We stay like that, with her wrapped up in my arms, until Chris reaches us five minutes later.

"Christ, Maisy Mae," he pants, out of breath. He probably ran the entire way here. "Don't you ever scare me like that again.

Maisy's tear-soaked face is still tucked into my chest, so I take the opportunity to glance up at my best friend. I widen my eyes and give my head the slightest shake, as if to say, "*It's worse than we thought.*" And, because we're scarily in sync, he nods, somehow knowing exactly what I'm getting at without either one of us saying a word.

"C-can I have a minute with j-just Chris?" Maisy asks, her voice muffled against my chest. Chris's eyes widen, but I ignore him and release Maisy from my hold.

"Of course. I'll be right up the trail if you need me, okay?"

I step just out of earshot, but close enough that I can run right back if she needs me.

How the *fuck* did I get here? Soaked in the tears of a girl I met less than a week ago, yet I couldn't care less. In fact, I want to sprint in there and tug her back into my arms. At least then I know she's safe.

I don't know why I feel like that about her. I hardly know her. I just know that she needs somebody.

It's because you promised Chris you'd help look out for her.

Bullshit.

Yeah, I signed myself up for this for Chris, but it's something more. I don't know. The chivalrous part of me sees that there's something fragile about her, and it aims to protect. I can't explain it, because I don't understand it.

I'm mid internal meltdown when I hear two sets of footsteps crunching through the leaves behind me. "Okay, here's the plan," Chris says when they reach me. "We're gonna crank the heat in the truck, set Maisy in the front seat so she doesn't go freezing into a block of ice on us, and then Colt and I will go say goodbye to everyone. Then we'll go back to the house and you can borrow some sweats and we can watch whatever movie you want. How does that sound?"

All she can manage is a nod.

Chris's voice sounds gentle, but I know him. I can tell by the slight tinge in his voice that he's seething. I see the fire in his eyes. Either Maisy is too new to his antics or too distraught to notice.

The second we make it back to the truck, we plop Maisy down and crank the heat as high as it'll go. Chris even gives her his beloved shotgun seat so she has access to the seat heaters. "We'll be right back, Maisy Mae. Don't freeze on us, okay?"

"I'll t-try not to."

The second we're out of earshot of the truck, all hell breaks loose. The fire fully engulfs Chris's expression, and I can't recall a time I've ever seen him so visibly angry.

"That motherfucker. Call Lainey," he seethes, not an ounce of sarcasm in his voice.

"Uh, why? What did she tell you?"

He's storming towards the house so fast that I have to reach out to steady him.

"That fucking bitch." I don't need to ask to know that he means Sierra. "She called her an orphan. And a slut. And told her that everyone knows she's 'riding me'." He runs an exasperated through his hair, gripping the ends so hard I don't know how he's not wincing in pain. "She told her that stealing her clothes is her fair warning not to fuck you."

Oh *hell* no.

Now I'm seething right alongside him. "What does Lainey have to do with this?"

"Because I can't sucker punch a chick, C. But Lainey can," he says grimly. "And she would." Yeah, he's right about that much. "I swear to God, where does she get off calling Maisy a slut? Ms. Sex-tape-at-thirteen, of all fucking people!"

"Okay, nobody's sucker punching anyone," I say, even though I wish more than anything that someone would knock some sense into Sierra. "We'll go and talk to her."

Chris looks thoroughly disappointed with that idea. "I do not want to *talk*. I want to *argue*. With my fists."

"And that will solve *nothing*." I shoot him a serious glance. Chris would never hit a woman—I wouldn't either—but the dangerous gleam in his eyes tells me he's liable to pummel the first thing that gets in his way. He's harmless ninety percent of the time, but that other ten percent…

I catch a glimpse of Zalinsky playing cornhole on the front lawn, and the first step towards justice unfolds itself. I cup my hands over my mouth to serve as a megaphone. "Zalinsky!" His big body turns to face me. "Watch my truck, would you?"

He nods like the loyal bastard he is, even though he has no idea what he's watching for. I know it's solely out of curiosity when he asks, "For what exactly, Bossman?"

I scowl at the nickname. According to my teammates, I'm a bossy prick on the ice, but that's a captain's job, is it not? I decide to lecture him about the shitty nickname another day, when I have less pressing problems on my hands.

"Blonde-haired spawns of Satan," I grumble, grabbing Chris's T-shirt and dragging him up the driveway with me. "Maisy's in the truck. Make sure nobody fucks with her."

I don't even check to see if he nods, or responds at all. I know Z's got my back, even though he doesn't know what's going on at the moment. Tommy Zalinsky's good like that.

Once Chris and I make it into the house, it takes us all of five seconds to find the succubus herself.

Dry-humping on the couch, of course. It absolutely blows my mind that someone as overly sexual as Sierra has the nerve to slut shame anyone, let alone someone as mousy and shy as Maisy.

I'm seeing red, and the only guaranteed way to feel better is by ramming my fist into something. Or someone. But I won't do that, because there's a frightened girl in my car as it is. I don't need to make things worse by adding assault charges and bloody knuckles to the mix.

She's already afraid of everything. I don't want her to be afraid of me, too.

I don't take the time to wonder why I'm so worked up over a few hurtful words. If it were anyone else in Sierra's firing line, I probably wouldn't bat an eye.

But it's because it's *her*.

"Sierra!" I shout, my voice barely audible over the heavy bass reverberating from the speaker in the corner of the living room. She pauses her attempt at sucking the face off of her current victim, snapping her head towards me.

"Colt," she acknowledges with a nod.

The amicable move only pisses me off more. "Don't fucking '*Colt*' me," I growl, clenching my fists at my side. "What the hell is wrong with you?!"

She bats her fake lashes at me, feigning innocence. "I have no clue what you mean, but it hurts my feelings that you're insulting me right now."

The nerve. The fucking *nerve*. I throw a hand out to intercept Chris, who has taken several steps forward, towards the couch seating Sierra and her man candy.

I know what he's thinking. Because the same thought crossed my mind, too.

Hit the guy. We can't hit her, but what better way to send a message than pummeling the face of her tonsil hockey partner?

I remind myself that I'm monitored by the state team, and neither one of us needs the hassle involved with throwing the first punch. Plus, Amanda would kill the both of us if we knocked someone's face in. She's a damn good lawyer, but I know she isn't keen on the idea of having to defend our asses if we get charged with assault.

I clench my fists tighter at my sides and force a breath through my nose, willing my blood to stop boiling.

It doesn't work.

"That's rich, Sierra," I hiss, my voice lethally cold. "You know what actually hurts feelings? What's actually insulting?" She stares at me blankly. Of course she doesn't get it. Heartless bitch. "Try meeting your new classmates for the first time and having some bitch steal your clothes, call you an orphan, and slut-shame you for doing literally *nothing* wrong."

"It's her fault!" Sierra exclaims accusingly. "She should know bet—"

I'm trying to be diplomatic. I really am. My best friend on the other hand… he couldn't care less if he's diplomatic or not.

"Ughhhh" Chris groans loudly, running an exasperated hand down his face. "It's still talking?"

Sierra scoffs at him. "Oh, go fuck yourself, Chris." Her words make his face break out in a wry grin.

Don't say it. Whatever it is you're thinking, don't fucking say it, man.

He blinks innocently at her, and I know right then that all hope is lost. "I do. Every other day. But unlike this," he sneers, holding up his right hand and wiggling his fingers. "You'll never have the absolute *pleasure* of touching me. And that fact makes you all sorts of bitter, doesn't it, Serena?"

"My name is Sierra and you know it," she hisses.

"Is that not what I said?" Chris asks, fluttering his lashes at her, his tone high in mock-innocence.

I pinch the bridge of my nose, fed up with their little game of back and forth. I turn to Sierra, my expression serious. "Just stay away from Maisy, and we'll be fine."

Her glossy lips curl up in a malicious smirk, indicating that this conversation is far from over. "She deserved what she got. She was playing in the wrong girl's toybox."

And just like that, the humor evaporates from Chris's expression as his mood does a one-eighty. He has a limit, and Sierra just plowed right over it.

"You're a fucking psycho!" Chris shouts, his face nearly purple with anger. "Colton doesn't want you. He *never* wanted you. Grow the fuck up and stop tormenting innocent girls because you're a jealous bitch!"

Sierra doesn't even flinch. "Wow. Looks like someone's pussy whipped," she deadpans, eyeing Chris with disgust. "I thought you had more taste than that, Marshall. She's just so…"

"Finish that sentence," Chris sneers manically, shaking with rage. "I fucking *dare* you, Sierra. Try me."

"Stay away from her. Got it?" I spot her tote bag in the corner of the living room, and, sure enough, Maisy's clothes are poking out of the top of it. I stomp over and grab her things before returning to Chris's side, not trusting him to stay put if he's provoked.

"Just a little PSA," I announce, grabbing Chris by the shirt and dragging him out of the living room before he can cause any serious damage. He's gone and lost his temper entirely, and I'm not far behind him. We need to get the hell out of here before I fall over the precipice and follow Chris's lead. "You fuck with the new girl, you fuck with us. Understand?"

The various people who had watched the altercation nod, but Sierra just stares at us blankly. "Make sure that's a well-known fact. And you," I say, pointing at the evil bitch in front of me. "Don't test me. Leave. Her. Alone."

Sierra crosses her arms over her chest. "Or what?"

"Or I will make your life a living hell."

She narrows her smokey eyes at me. "Is that a threat, Colton?"

"Nope," I toss over my shoulder, exiting the room. "It's a promise."

Chapter 12

<u>Maisy</u>

I don't pray often, but last night I prayed for a spontaneous case of the measles. Or whooping cough. Or scurvy. I really didn't specify a serious illness. I just need one.

Since my disastrous attempt at socialization on Friday, I've been a nervous wreck about the first day of school. Which happens to be today.

I want to feign an illness, to stay in my bed with the covers drawn over my head and the outside world entirely blocked off.

Unfortunately for me, Amanda called my bluff and is making me go to school. It's the first time I've seen her put her foot down with me, and while I don't appreciate the unceremonious end to my torment-avoiding tactics, I get where she's coming from.

Amanda and Tim paid good money for me to attend St. Mark's with Chris. I should be thrilled to get a quality education at one of the best private schools in the state. I should be bowing down to them, thanking them immensely for everything they're doing for me.

Instead, I'm hiding in my bed like an absolute wimp because of a mean girl.

I don't care that she called me an orphan. I pretty much am one. I don't care that she called me stupid. What I do care about is the slut allegations. All I need is for people to think I'm hooking up with Chris. All I need is for that particular wretched label to follow me from the Terrace.

Things were bad enough at my old school. The last thing I need is for the slut-shaming to repeat itself at St. Mark's.

My general inability to speak to anybody—especially the male population—ensures that I have absolutely no experience in the romance department. Zip. Zero. None.

But all it takes is one little rumor…

"Maisy?" CJ's muffled voice calls from outside my door. "May I come in?"

Secretly grateful for a reprieve from my depressing thoughts, I yell for him to come in, while simultaneously sliding out of my bed and making my way to my desk.

"Looking sharp, bud," I say, nodding towards his blazer and trouser pants. He's too young to be at St. Mark's, but he's going to some prep school for kids from kindergarten to fifth grade. Like me, he also has to wear a uniform.

That's actually the one part of school I *am* excited about. Nobody can comment on my wardrobe—or lack thereof—if I'm in the exact same uniform as everyone else.   "Thanks," CJ murmurs absently, tucking his hands in his pants pockets and staring down at his feet. "Maisy, I'm really nervous."

I knew he would be. CJ may come off as overly social and charismatic, but deep down, he's a fragile kid. He wears his heart on his sleeve and has more anxiety than any eight-year-old should. But that's kind of expected, given our past and all.

I force a smile, even though I feel like crumbling inside. My life is in shambles at the moment, and I feel like I'm barely hanging on, but he can't know that. I have to be strong for him, even if it's fake strength.

I zip up my backpack and turn to face my brother. "Don't be scared, CJ. You're going to kick school's butt. Everyone is going to love you."

He looks up at me, his big green eyes swimming with hope. "You really think so?"

God, I hope so. "Absolutely," I confirm, pushing every shred of uncertainty out of my voice. "You should probably get going. Tim's driving you soon. But I expect to hear all about your day tonight, okay?"

He nods, the anxiety fading from his expression. I feel awful for lying to him, for potentially giving him false hope when, in reality, I have no idea how today will go. But what was I supposed to do? Tell him that the other kids will probably bully him for having foster parents? That the bullies might call him a fraud for being at a private school when he comes from the most rundown terrace in the area?

CJ wraps his arms around my waist and hugs me tightly. "I love you, Maisy."

"I love you more."

He runs out of my room, flying down the staircase and yelling something to Tim.

I know that I have to start getting ready soon. Chris is taking me to school and he said that we're leaving in an hour, on the dot, but the deflective part of my brain hopes that I can draw out the time leading up to that. The more I procrastinate getting ready, the longer it'll be before the reality of the situation seeps in.

I creep out into the hallway and towards the nursery. Amanda really did go all out in here, and my chest clenches with guilt at the thought of how much time and money she must've poured into this room.

The walls are a pale pink, and there are flowers *everywhere*. A mural on the wall. Hanging from the mobile above the crib. In photo frames.

Tim and Amanda are paying for some obscene daycare program. Top-of-the-line childcare at some ritzy chain establishment that's housed tons of celebrities' kids.

I know Nat will be safe, and way better off than she was at the daycare attached to Mom's office. But that doesn't stop me from worrying about her.

I came in here to avoid getting ready, yes, but she also needs her diaper bag packed for the day, and she needs to be changed before Amanda drops her off, and…

It's all done. Her bag is propped in the corner, filled to the brim. And Nat is in her crib, fully changed and dressed in a frilly pink strawberry dress.

It's all done.

A strange mix of gratitude and sadness swirl together in the pit of my stomach as I take in the gesture.

It's still weird, not being accountable for my siblings. I'm used to them needing me. To things only getting done when I do them.

Having Tim and Amanda take the brunt of responsibility with my siblings will probably always be uncomfortable for me. Because up until this point, everything relied on *me*. They always needed *me*.

And now that they don't, I don't quite know what to do with myself. I don't know how to be Maisy the teenager, and not Maisy the mother figure. I don't know what I'm worth if I'm not needed.

What if it's too late for me to learn?

"Maisy, Chris!" Amanda yells up the staircase. "It's six-thirty!"

I'd appreciate the time check in the event that I overslept. But you need to fall asleep to oversleep, and I couldn't do that last night. Not with the anxious pit in my gut and the endless worries swirling through my skull.

"Thanks, Ma!" Chris calls back, his voice husky. He probably just woke up from a nice, long slumber free of worries. Because why would he worry? He's Mr. Popularity.

Stop it, I chastise myself. *Chris isn't the enemy here.*

I give Nat a kiss on the top of the head and make my way back to my bedroom. There's no more delaying the inevitable.

Wrong. This feels… wrong.

I'm staring at the full-length mirror in my bathroom at my uniform-clad reflection.

A blue sweater with St. Mark's school crest lies over my white undershirt. I'm wearing tights under my blue, gray, and green plaid skirt. I don't think I've ever worn tights before. Or a sweater this nice. I feel like a walking price tag, and the fact that I don't feel like I belong in the uniform tells me that I probably don't belong at the school.

No. Scratch that. I *definitely* don't belong at the school.

Everything is way too big on me. I don't fill out the uniform the way it's meant to be filled out, and I'm all too aware of the sharp protruding of my hips and shoulders.

There's a knock on my door, followed by Chris's soft voice. It's not his typical, goofy voice, or his lighthearted banter voice. It's almost like he knows that I'm struggling right now without having seen me yet today.

I may have only been here a week, but Chris is freaky attuned to me. He just… *knows*, without me having to utter a word.

It's equal parts scary and intriguing.

"You almost ready?" he asks, his voice infinitely patient.

"I'm having a crisis," I groan, stomping out of my bathroom and flopping onto the bed. Maybe I'm being a tad bit overdramatic, but who can blame me?

"Can I come in and help with said crisis?" He pauses for the briefest moment. "Wait, it's not about your, um, lady issues, is it? Cause I don't care how much I like you, Maisy Mae, I *will* pass out. Or puke. Or both."

"No," I choke out a laugh. Leave it to Chris to make me chuckle when I'm mid-meltdown. "You can come in."

My bedroom door creaks open, and his big, blonde head pokes in, like he's double-checking that the coast is clear.

"I hate this," I whisper, feeling the familiar burning of tears behind my eyes. "Everyone's gonna know, Chris." I swat at my eyes with the back of my hand, willing my cheeks to stay dry. "That I don't belong. That I'm such a screw-up, my own parents don't even want me. I belong at the Terrace." I shake my head, giving up on holding back the waterworks. Warm tears trickle down my cheeks as I slump my shoulders forward in defeat.

"Hey," Chris says, his voice achingly gentle. He makes his way over to my bed and sits down beside me, rubbing soothing circles on my back. "You *do* belong here, Maisy. Okay? I promise you, nobody's going to say anything."

"Yeah, right. They already did. They know I'm a fraud, Chris." I shake my head, my cheek brushing against his shoulder as he tugs me closer to him. "I don't think I can do this."

"Well, tough shit. Cause I happen to know that you absolutely, one hundred percent *can* do this. So dry those pretty eyes, give me a hug, and then go kick today's ass."

I sniffle, blinking the tears away. "You have an awful lot of faith in me."

He shrugs. "What can I say? I'm intuitive."

"Or stupid," I murmur.

"Yeah," he chuckles, slinging an arm over my shoulder. "I'm that, too. But not about this. Not about you. You're gonna be just fine, okay?"

I nod, only half believing him, but hoping with my whole heart that he knows what he's talking about.

Chapter 13

<u>Colton</u>

Different year, same bullshit.

I know I have it good at St. Mark's. The hockey team is the top in the division, for starters. We've got a hell of a training facility on campus, with top-of-the-line equipment and a damn good coaching staff. We also have insanely good teachers and a curriculum that is tailored to all different types of students.

I've got myself in three AP classes and two college courses this semester. I chose more rigorous coursework, partially because I get bored easily and need a challenge, but also because if I want a fighting chance of playing for Princeton, I need to load up my schedule to the best of my ability.

But it was a *choice*. There are also tech classes and arts and languages and normal level classes. Electives galore, in pretty much every subject you could ever dream of.   Plus, the campus is gorgeous. It looks like a castle, with lush green grass and flower beds around every corner.

But the students? They leave room for desire.

There's a fair number of pompous assholes. While there is a chunk of decent kids, there is also a percentage of my peers that survive on Daddy's money and unnecessarily inflated egos.

It isn't cheap to attend St. Mark's, especially not for the kids who choose to board and live in the dorms on campus. I'm here on a full hockey scholarship, but I'm one of few. Most of the people here come from money, and it shows.

My first two periods of the day are relatively light. I had English first period and History second, but by the time lunch rolls around, I've heard enough stories about European vacations and private yachts to last me a lifetime.

If I have to hear one more goddamn kid talk about their goddamn sailing experiences, I am going to flip a desk.

I'm not even joking.

Luckily, I have lunch in between second and third period, so I have a brief reprieve from the goading.

I walk into the giant cafeteria and head for our normal table. I try to avoid sitting with all of my teammates. Most of them spend the entire lunch period with a chick in their lap and not one but *two* tongues in their mouths. And, let's be honest, it's hard to eat when you're watching your buddies make it to second base right next to you.

We usually sit at a table in the back of the cafeteria. And by we, I mean Chris and I, as well as Lainey and some of my more tolerable teammates, Zalinsky, Vinny, and Davie.

But by the time I grab my food from the lunch line and make it to our designated table, I notice an extra person. One who's caught the eye of each one of my friends.

Long, brown hair, small frame, glued to Chris's side. It doesn't take a genius to figure out who it is.

"How are you doing down there, Shorty?" I ask, plopping down onto the bench beside her, and praying that she remembers our banter from the day at the mall.

I don't want her to think I'm teasing her. I probably should've thought of that before I opened my mouth, but there's no turning back now.

"Pretty good," she says shyly, tucking a piece of hair behind her ear. "How's the weather up there, BFG?"

Oh, thank God. My friends—minus Chris—look at me quizzically, but their confused expressions can wait. Because for the second time ever, Maisy's smiling at me.

And, fuck, it's so much better than watching her cry. I haven't been able to shake the image of her tortured whiskey eyes from my mind since Friday night. Haven't been able to stop thinking about the rage that ignited in me when Sierra pulled her shit, either. I still don't get it. Why I cared as much as I did. Why she's a permanent fixture in my brain now.

"Nice and sunny," I reply with a wink. She blushes. "How's your first day treating you?"

She shuffles away from Chris, just slightly, but I count it as a win. She gravitates towards him, and I know she feels safe with him. Comfortable. So the fact that she's letting her guard down, even just a little bit, must mean that she trusts me not to hurt her.

Baby steps.

"It's, uh, it's going okay," she says. She sounds genuine. Looks pretty close to happy, if not a little bit stressed out. "I've gotten lost twice, though," she admits.

Vinny laughs. "Babydoll, I've been going here for three years and I *still* get lost."

"Babydoll?" I echo, raising a brow at my overly flirtatious defenseman. Vinny's a good guy, but he's the definition of a womanizer. The only reason he's not ostracized with the rest of the manwhores on the team is because he's got the decency to be anti-PDA.

"Look at the size of the girl. And her face. She looks like a doll," Vinny says defensively, no doubt noticing the murder glistening in my eyes.

There's a slight blush tainting Maisy's olive cheeks, and as much as her shy nature intrigues me, I hate knowing that she's even the slightest bit uncomfortable. Especially at the hands of my friends and teammates.

I can't explain what I feel for this girl. Between the rage I felt at the party, and the surge of protectiveness I feel watching her squirm, I'm a total wreck of emotions wherever she's concerned.

My brain tells me that I don't know the first thing about her. Not really, anyway. I know she has two siblings, and that she's the Marshall's foster child, but that's surface level shit. I don't know her favorite movie, or her pet peeves, or what she does in her free time. My brain knows that the feelings Maisy elicits from me are insane.

But my heart doesn't care.

"Goddamn it, Wessie!" I curse as the two-hundred-pound winger slams me into the sideboards. "Motherfucker."

"Sorry, Bossman," Brian Wesley grins sheepishly, not hesitating to snatch the puck and skate away. I'm all for practicing how you play, but body checking me into the sideboards during a scrimmage seems excessive. Even for overachievers like Wessie and I.

"You shouldn't risk injuring your own teammates before a game, *Brian*," I grit out, putting extra emphasis on his first name.

Wessie has been Wessie since the day he was born. The guy despises his first name, which makes it all the more fun to use when he really pisses me off. It's a surefire way to rile him up.

"Next time skate away faster, *Colton*," he snickers, returning the first-naming favor.

His roughness aside, Wessie is my favorite teammate on the U18's. He's seventeen, turning eighteen next month, and the guy's an old soul. He's the one you go to when you're in a jam, or when you need solid advice free of judgement.

Besides Chris and Zalinsky, he's probably the most trustworthy guy I know.

He's helped me out of too much shit over the years to hold a grudge about the whole body slamming thing, but I make a mental note to target him the next time we're faced against each other during a scrimmage. I can't let him completely off the hook. I'm not *that* nice.

Coach Caldwell blows his whistle three times, signaling the end of practice. "Home game tomorrow at seven. Be here by five-thirty."

The guys all grumble their responses, skating towards the tunnel that leads off of the ice and towards the locker rooms.

It isn't until I'm stripped down in the shower that I notice the implications of the hit I took from Wessie.

"Damn, dude," Wessie groans from the stall beside me, frowning sympathetically. Each stall has a saloon style door, so everything from your midsection above is fair game for the rest of the guys to see. And, in my case, the entire left side of my body is already starting to bruise. "I'm sorry."

I shrug, because I've had worse. Bruises will fade. "Eh, I'll survive." I turn off the faucet and grab my towel from the hook right outside of my stall door. "You ready for tomorrow?"

We've got our first game of the season, and—lucky us—we're going up against Massachusetts. Our rivals. They play nasty, and we spend more collective time in the penalty box during Mass games than literally any other game of the season. They love instigating fights, and we're a team of short-tempered hotheads. It isn't a good mix.

"I was born ready, baby." Wessie smirks, dragging his own towel over his hair. "Wait, you started school today, right?" I nod. "How'd it go?"

"School itself? Boring as shit," I chuckle, swinging open my stall door and sauntering off towards the lockers. Wessie follows me, rustling through his bag as I toss my towel on the bench and tug on a pair of sweatpants. "But it was intriguing in other ways."

"Yeah?" Wessie cocks a brow, clearly interested in what I have to say. "How so?"

I would never in a million years dream of talking about Maisy to ninety percent of my teammates. Not that they're bad dudes. I love most of them like brothers. But I don't trust that they wouldn't go seeking her out on their own. And, knowing what I know about her, it'd embarrass the shit out of her.   But I know I can trust Wessie, and quite frankly, if I don't talk about my strange emotions soon, my head might explode. Chris is out of the equation, because he's too close to the situation. Plus, there's some physical attraction laced in with the emotional bullshit, and he sees Maisy like a sister. Going up to him and admitting that I'm attracted to her is basically asking for a knee to the nuts.

"You know my friend Chris?" Wessie nods. "Well, his parents foster kids, and there are these three kids living with them now. One of them is a girl our age."

Realization sparkles in Wessie's eyes. "You like her." It doesn't sound like a question. It sounds like he knows the answer already. Which is crazy, because I'm not even sure *I* know the answer to that question.

"It's…complicated." I drop my gaze from his, and spend an excessive amount of time neatly folding my practice jersey and repacking my gear bag.

"How so?" Wessie asks, crossing his arms over his chest and leaning his hip against the lockers.

"Well, for starters, she's my best friend's foster sister," I deadpan. A fleeting glance in Wessie's direction tells me that my answer does not impress him. "She makes me feel all sorts of disoriented. I was worried as hell about her at school, and this whole thing happened with some nasty bitches from school and I absolutely lost my shit." I shake my head incredulously, still not understanding my own feelings. "But there's something… off, about her. She's really quiet. Skittish."

Wessie furrows his eyebrows. "Well *duh*. She's in foster care. Obviously, some really messed up shit happened." He stands up straight again, leveling me with an expectant look. "But you think she's hot?"

Does that cut it? Probably not. Plenty of people are *hot*. Adrianna Lima. Megan Fox. Betty Bop. But I feel like something's different about Maisy.

I nod, albeit reluctantly.

"Okay," he says, with absolute finality in his tone. "Ask her out."

"Really?" I balk, blinking at my teammate. "That's your advice? I don't know anything about her!"

"Then get to know her, dipshit." Wessie rolls his eyes, like his answer is obvious.

"I can't go out with her. She's basically Chris's sister. I can't do that to him."

I can tell by his expression that Wessie isn't buying an ounce of my bullshit. "From the stories I've heard, Chris isn't the kind of guy to care."

True. "I don't have time for a girlfriend, Wes," I admit, voicing my other major concern regarding Maisy. "I feel too much when it comes to her as it is. I'm afraid that if I get to know her, it'll only get worse. And I really, *really* don't have the time."

That's not a lie. I'll be up to my neck in coursework before I know it. I'm the captain of two separate hockey teams, and I need to be one hundred percent on my game. There will be scouts at some of our games, and I need to succeed. I've fought too hard to get to this point to let a lapse in my focus take it all away.

"Christ, you're acting like I told you to marry the girl and father her quadruplets." Wessie rolls his eyes again. "You don't have to date her. But get to know her. Be a friend." He shrugs. "Sounds like she could use a few more of those."

Maybe he's right. I might not be able to go *there* romantically with Maisy, but what the hell is stopping me from getting to know her? From being a real friend, not just an acquaintance as a favor to Chris?

That little spark of realization marks the slow start of Operation Befriend Maisy. Maybe being her friend isn't everything I want, but it's a step.

A small one, but I'm hoping it's enough.

Chapter 14

Maisy

"Oh Maisy!" Chris sing-songs, flopping onto my bed. I turn in my swiveling desk chair, eyeing him cautiously.

I was mid Algebra homework when he asked to come in, and I'd take any distraction at this point. I hate math with a burning, fiery passion, so any excuse to procrastinate this assignment is much appreciated.

But I can tell by his extra-lightheartedness that Chris has an agenda, and I've learned to proceed with caution when it comes to Chris and his ideas.

"Yeah, Chris?"

"How much homework do you have?"

I eye my backpack on the floor. I've got math homework and a chapter to read for English, but none of it has to get done right this second. "Not much. Why?"

His face lights up with a grin. "How would you like to have a night out?"

"Chris, it's *Tuesday*," I remind him. "And we've got school tomorrow."

"No shit, Sherlock." Chris rolls his eyes. "I'm not talking about partying. Colton has a game tonight, and I wanted to see if you want to tag along with me."

I'm honored that he thought to ask me. Truly, I am. I'm not used to being included in activities. You can only cancel on people so many times before they stop trying to invite you places.

But secretly, I always feel like I'm in the way with Chris. He's never given me any reason to feel unwelcome. It's just my own insecurities talking. But hockey is his thing, and he's been so kind and included me in almost everything he's done since the kids and I moved in.

I don't want to take this from him, too.

"Thanks for the invite but I don't know the first thing about hockey." It's not a total lie; I'm fairly clueless about the sport. I'm not opposed to learning about it, but it seems like the easiest way to turn Chris down.

I can't tell him the truth. He's the kind of person who would tell me to come, anyway. Hell, he probably doesn't even see things in the same light. But he needs his time away. He needs some normalcy in his life, or he's going to grow to see me as a burden.

And I like our little spur of a friendship too much to sit back and let that happen.

"That's okay." Chris shrugs, his smile unfaltering. "I'll teach you."

Well, so much for that plan.

I try again. "I'm supposed to help CJ with his homework." Also not a total lie, though the last time I checked. he was almost done with his assignment. But Chris doesn't need to know that.

"Already done. We hammered it out earlier. Any other shitty excuses you want to pull on me, Maisy Mae?" Chris goads, leaning back on his elbows.

I study him, searching his expression for any shred of hesitation or a sign that he's bluffing about wanting me there. I come up empty handed. "If you're sure?" Chris nods, his smile widening. "Okay, then. I'm in."

"You're gonna love it, Maisy," Chris says, pulling himself to his feet. "I promise."

"Oh my God this is *awful*!" I exclaim, hiding my face behind my hands as two gigantic boys smash each other into the sideboards. "It's so… so…"

"Violent?" Chris offers with a chuckle. "Chaotic? Fast-paced?"

I shake my head, cringing as another player from the Massachusetts team bodychecks one of Colton's teammates. "I was thinking homicidal, but yeah, those all work."

Chris laughs again before turning all of his attention back to the ice. He looks absolutely enthralled, watching the game with a twinkle in his eyes that I haven't seen before.

He's tried his best to explain the ins and outs of the game, but it's a hard feat to achieve when our conversation was interrupted by Chris's choice expletives to the ref or the occasional gasp when the game took a turn. You can't look away for a second without missing something major.   "So, he's a center," I echo, pointing at the spot on the ice where number twenty-two is skating. LORENZO is spelt out in big black letters across the back of his light blue jersey, but I could've spotted him even without the name tag.   Colton is much faster than the other players on his team.

Seriously, you can hardly see him in action, because he zips around before you can even blink. He's got an energy to him, a sort of confident vibe that makes his success seem inevitable.

I thought that Tim had been overexaggerating Colton's talent that night at dinner, but sitting here watching him, I can say that this boy is going places. I may not know the first thing about hockey, but the sheer speed and agility he has, coupled with the number of people in charge of blocking him, tell me that he's a serious asset to his team.

Chris leans over to explain whenever something important happens, but for the most part, we spend the rest of the game with our eyes glued to the ice.

Well, Chris does. My eyes are glued on the twenty-two jersey as I take in the addictive sight of Colton skating and shoving other people into walls.

It's the weirdest thing, actually *liking* watching him. I don't know him all that well, but at the same time, I can't tear my eyes off of him to save my life.

When the clock runs out, the scoreboard reads 2-0, with Colton's team in the lead. Chris is beaming with excitement as we shuffle down the packed ramp that leads from the bleachers to the lobby area near the entrance.

"You're awfully happy," I acknowledge, stepping to the side on the ground floor. "Two points doesn't seem like a lot."

He gapes at me, like I spoke in a foreign language or something. "Two points is huge, Maisy. They shut Mass out."

I cock my head. "Huh?"

"It means that they didn't let the other team score at all," Chris explains, grabbing my forearm and tugging me to the side.

The lobby area is absolutely packed, and the amount of people who almost maul me is insane. I know that I'm tiny, but seriously, people? You can't walk through me, no matter how hard you try.

"C'mon," Chris says, ushering me towards a separate hallway like I'm a stray sheep who wandered away from the flock.

I follow him, secretly wondering where we're going, and if we're even allowed back here. I can't imagine we are, because if this was a public space, everyone clogging the main area would be in here. But I don't say anything, because, again, I know nothing about the subject. And I don't think Chris would ever do anything to deliberately get me into trouble.

At the end of the hallway, there's an oak door, which Chris tells me leads to the locker room. We only linger for a moment before the door swings open and the first wave of players floods out.

It's another five minutes before Colton emerges.   He's one of the last players out, and he walks out of the locker room with his head turned, talking animatedly to a tall, black-haired boy who looks a bit older than him.

I take the opportunity to study his features. For longer than I should, no doubt. But he's so interesting to look at that I literally *can't* look away.

His wavy brown hair is wet and poking up in a thousand different directions. The sharp lines in his chiseled face are lax as he smiles at his friend, his brown eyes glowing with happiness.

He's so pretty. I know it's not a great adjective for boys, but I genuinely don't know how else to describe him. He's saying something to his friend, but I don't catch it, because I freak myself out with my own thoughts.

Do I *like* Colton?

I mean, I like Colton, Chris's friend who has a really tall truck and comes to deserted creeks to rescue me when mean girls make me cry. I like watching him play hockey, even though it's stressful. And I like the Colton who answers my brother's crazy questions and calls me Shorty.

But do I *like* him?

I don't have much experience when it comes to boys. I'm too shy to talk to them, too invisible to be noticed by them, and too busy to entertain the idea of engaging with them. Plenty of girls at my old school had boyfriends, but I never felt any sort of *anything* for a guy.

I've always thought that there was something wrong with me. A miswiring in my circuit board.

But my heart does a little flip when he turns his head and catches my eye. His expression floods with surprise, but it's a good kind of surprise. Like what I'd imagine kids look like on Christmas morning. Or for a surprise party.

That little heart flip leaves me wondering if I really *am* capable of feeling normal teenage things for boys.

Or maybe it's just this one boy in particular.

Chapter 15

Colton

Holy fuck.

She's here. She's actually *here*.

My first question is *how*, but that answers itself when I'm finally able to tear my gaze away from her face and glance down the hallway. Chris is leaning against the wall, grinning like the town idiot. My next question is *why*, but that one answers itself when Maisy looks up at me and tucks a stray piece of hair behind her ear.

"I hope it's okay that I came. Chris invited me, and, well, I really don't know anything about hockey, but you did a really good job. I think," she adds, scrunching her nose. "I mean, you didn't fall on your butt or get cut with a skate, so that counts for something, right?"

I chuckle, hiking my gear bag up higher on my shoulder. "It's a start, I guess. But you liked it? The game, I mean."

She nods eagerly. "Well, I was confused for a lot of it, and nervous for the rest of it. You guys really like to be violent, huh?"

I don't miss the fact that this is the most words I've heard her say at once. I blame it on the adrenaline rush that comes with watching a ton of guys pummel each other into walls for an hour straight.

I'm suddenly a lot more grateful for my slapshot in the second period. Knowing that Maisy was here to see the gorgeous goal makes the victory that much sweeter.   She shrugs. "You're not too shabby, BFG," she says with a teasing smile.

A smile. A whole motherfucking *smile*.

God, I'm going to turn into one of Pavlov's dogs. Start doing outlandish shit in the hopes of getting a reaction from Maisy. Because that smile is a *fabulous* reward.

"'*Not too shabby*,'" I parrot, shaking my head. I can't bite back the smile curling my lips. Not that I want to, anyway. "I should put that on a T-shirt."

I'm going to be honest, I may be a shitty friend, because during my little moment with Maisy, I completely forgot about my two friends in the hallway.

Apparently, so did Maisy.

"Oh, hi," she says quietly, turning to face Wessie. "I'm—"

"Maisy," Wessie fills in with a megawatt grin. "It's nice to finally meet you."

Abort! Wes, what the hell are you doing?!

Chris eyes me curiously, probably wondering how the hell my teammate knows about Maisy. And I'm sure Maisy's wondering the same exact thing.

It's not like Wessie goes to our school or would've ever seen her in passing. The only way he'd know her name is if I brought it up. Which I did, but I could really do without Chris and Maisy knowing that tidbit of information.

"Finally?" she asks, narrowing those whiskey eyes in confusion.

"Colt bailed on a boys' night to go to that party on Friday." Wessie shrugs, lying through his teeth. "He mentioned your name."

Yeah, I was supposed to go over to Wessie's house that night, but it's not the reason he knows about Maisy.

I'm momentarily relieved, grateful for his white lie and the catastrophe we just narrowly avoided. But the relief slips away when I watch Maisy's expression fall guiltily.

"You ditched your friends for the party?" she asks, her voice small. "Was it because of me?"

Yes. "No." I'm a dirty liar—dirtier than Wes—but what else can I do? Tell this extremely fragile girl in front of me that I bailed on gaming at Wessie's place to escort her to a party? Because I can't tell her that without explaining how nervous I was that someone would start shit, especially after the stare down in the mall the day before. And there's no way in hell I'm telling her how disoriented she makes me.

"I felt like catching up with some of the kids from school."

Chris eyes me from his spot against the wall, his expression telling me that he sees right through my lies. I pray he has the brain-to-mouth control to not call my bluff right now. He must see the relief in Maisy's eyes at my tiny lie, though, because he doesn't mention it.

I can tell she's re-shelled herself. Wessie's comment succeeded in bringing back the shy version of Maisy, but I can hardly be pissed at him for it. Because now I've had a taste of sarcastic, goading Maisy, and it's like a goddamn high. It's like a drug that I don't think I'll ever be able to get my fix of.

I think back to my conversation with Wessie about being her friend, and I know that I have to follow through with it. There's no way in hell that I can see her smile like *that* and keep her as an acquaintance.

I have to go slow, though. I have a feeling that if I throw myself at her, even platonically, I'll scare her back to a place I may not be able to coax her out of.

I don't mind proceeding with caution, though. I didn't get to where I am by rushing things. I can be patient if I want to be.

And for Maisy, I will be.

Chapter 16

<u>Maisy</u>

It's been three weeks since the start of school, and I've surprised myself with how well I've acclimated.

All of my classes are going smoothly. I'm getting better grades than I ever have, and I have a feeling that has to do with the lack of responsibility I have at the house. I don't have to cook dinner and clean. I don't have to stay up late rocking my teething baby sister to bed. I'm not being woken up in the middle of the night by CJ's bony elbow being jammed into my ribs. I can actually focus in class instead of worrying about everything I have to do later.

I've even made friends. Ish. I've spent a lot of time with Lainey and her group of friends. And although I get constant questions about Chris—most of which are disturbingly sexual—Lainey's quick to shut them down.

We've got a few classes together, which is nice. She makes me laugh a lot, which isn't something I'm used to. I'm getting the hang of it. Being a student, not a parent, and having a group of people who aren't related to me or depending on me.

I'm still struggling with stepping back from my siblings' lives. Amanda and I set up a system to wean me off of the responsibilities I carried. Chris said it reminds him of a rehab program. I punched him in the arm for that one.

I still help get Nat ready for bed. I help CJ with his homework, and occasionally sleep on the top bunk in his room. It was nice, the first few days of having my own room, but it was harder than I thought it would be. Lonelier. The silence allows my brain to wander, to stumble across memories I tried to lock deep in my brain. They all come rushing back when I'm alone.

I help Amanda with the laundry, too, but I only help out when I have time. It's up to me how much I do and when I do it, and it's been a great way to transition between having everything settling on my shoulders to having nothing at all.

I'm finally content with our arrangement, with the temporary life I've built with the Marshalls.

And then D-Day hits. Yes, I'm probably being overdramatic by referring to it as D-Day, but I don't care. It's a day out of hell from the very start.

I wake up late. Not by a lot, but it's enough to rattle me a little bit. I run around like a madwoman to get ready for school on time, though it's a bit easier today. It's the last Friday of the month, which means it's casual day at school. I settle for my signature outfit—an oversized hoodie and baggy jeans. I have to hurriedly shove my books in my bag and rush to tie my shoes, all the while cursing Chris and his lazy smile watching me scramble.

Nothing fazes him. Ever. It's disorienting and annoying as hell sometimes. I'm a constant ball of anxiety, but Chris lets things roll off his back.

When I'm finally ready and Chris and I stop in the kitchen for smoothies before we take off for school, the real tragedy strikes.

Amanda's worried face is the first indicator that something's wrong. The fact that Tim and CJ hung back instead of leaving at 7:00 like they always do is the second indicator.

"I really didn't want to tell you in the morning, because I don't want you all to have a storm cloud over your Friday," Amanda says, her tone laced with sympathy. "But I got a call from Wanda today."

Terror crashes into me like a freight train. Smack in the center of my chest. My first thought is that we're being taken back. That, somehow, Mom won back custody. Or one of our dads stepped forward…

Don't be stupid. That'd never happen. I chastise myself.

CJ looks mildly worried, but I don't think he fully understands the situation we're in. He sees our foster family as a giant slumber party, not a temporary replacement because our parents are incompetent. But Chris *definitely* understands just how bad this news could be. His face pales, his grip tightening on the straps of his backpack, his knuckles turning white.

It's a long time before I can force the words out. "Are we being sent back?" I croak, dread creeping higher up my throat with every passing second.

"No, no, no." Amanda shakes her head, her tone firm and certain. "But you do have a visitation with your mother next month." I don't miss the flicker of anger in her eyes at the mention of Mom. She conceals her emotions quickly, but I caught it.

"Do we have to go?" I ask, filled with dread for a totally different reason. I don't feel like putting up with her bullshit again. I don't feel like sitting there and pretending I miss her, that I want to go home.

The Terrace wasn't home. It was a roof and four walls. Because at home, you're supposed to feel safe and welcome, and those are two things I *never* felt living with my mother.

Not once.

Tim chimes in, nodding his head. "It's in your best interest. But it's only once a month, okay? Try to keep your heads up, kiddos."

CJ frowns, looking up at Tim. He's formed an especially tight bond with our foster father, and I don't doubt that it has something to do with the constant lack of a father figure in his life. He saw some semblance of a male role model and grabbed onto it with both hands.

Their relationship worries me when I think about leaving. Because we *will* leave. It's just a matter of when.

"But I don't want to see her," CJ pouts, his distaste clear in his voice. "She's *way* meaner than Amanda. Why can't we just stay here instead?"

I see the sadness settle in the adults' expressions. I exchange a frown with Chris, who is probably starting to piece things together. I haven't told him anything about our past, but it doesn't take a rocket scientist to combine his previous knowledge with CJ's comments to paint a bigger, uglier picture.

"You can stay here, squirt," Tim says consolingly, ruffling my brother's curly brown hair. "It's just a little meeting. And you don't even have to go back to your old house. You can just go out to eat, or go to the park."

"Like a date?" CJ asks, cocking his head to the side.

"Well, not exactly…"

"A playdate, then," CJ amends, nodding his head. "I can do a playdate with Mom. Only one, right? Then I can come back here to my bunk beds and food?"

"Yeah, only one," Amanda says sadly, glancing at Tim with pure heartbreak in her eyes. "And I'll make a big, yummy dinner that night. How does that sound?"

CJ's eyes twinkle as he nods enthusiastically.

Tim takes my brother to school, and it isn't until Chris and I are alone in his Mercedes that we start to deconstruct the bombshell that was dropped in the kitchen.

"So," he says cautiously, eyeing me when we stop at a red light. "How do you feel about seeing your mom again?"

"You want the honest answer, or the one I give the adults and my siblings?" I ask, stretching my legs out and relaxing in the front seat.

"The honest answer," Chris replies, pure conviction in his tone. "I always want the truth from you, Maisy Mae."

"I'm dreading it. She… it's just…" I shake my head, willing a coherent sentence to form in my head. "She's so *good* at what she does. At making me feel like crap for things I can't control. For blaming anything and everything on me. And I know she's a bad person—she's done nothing but prove that over and over again—but I still want to make her happy. I still went out of my way to make sure she was taken care of when she was too high or out of it to get out of bed. Figure that one out," I scoff, still hating myself for my weakness with my mother.

I'm not an outgoing person. At school and with peers, I take whatever is thrown at me without much argument. I try to stay in the shadows, because being invisible has always been the safest option for me. But with my mother? Being spineless was a huge curse, because she *knew* what power she had over me, and she used that power to hold me to impossible standards. To excuse her horrible behavior.

Chris smiles at me sadly before returning his eyes to the road. "It's not a bad thing to care about people, Maisy. Even if you're the bigger person, even if they don't reciprocate it. It isn't a bad thing to have a bigger heart."

"It is when my own mother chose random men over her kids." I still, wholly aware that I'd just admitted that out loud for the first time. But I don't regret it. I'm angry at her for how she's treated my siblings through the years. I don't care about myself; I'm too far gone. I've been her second priority my whole life. Her highs and lows color my entire childhood. But those two kids? They don't deserve that. They deserve way better. And she has failed them miserably.

I think I hate her for that more than anything else.

"Shit," Chris murmurs.

"Yeah, shit."

"I'm sorry, Maisy." He looks at me again, his blue eyes swimming with sadness.

I shrug, because I honestly can't think of anything else to say or do.

The second hit of the day comes during second period. We're so close to lunch that I'm counting down the seconds.

That's another new thing for me—the food. I've always had a thing about eating, always struggled to eat in front of other people. I've definitely gained some weight over the few weeks I've spent with the Marshalls. My ribs don't protrude as much as they once did. My hips don't jut out quite as alarmingly as before.

It took me a while to eat in the cafeteria, because I felt like everyone was watching me. All I could do was poke around my plate and think self-deprecating thoughts.

Colton caught on, I think. We never discussed it—we never really talk about anything serious like that—but I could tell by the mix of sadness and fury in his eyes that he knew about my whole anti-eating dilemma. He pulled me to the side after lunch one day and asked me, point blank, if I was eating.

I like that about him. How frank he is. Since the social workers appeared in my life at the age of five, everyone has always skated around me. Like I'm some glass artifact that might break if you're too curt. But Colton doesn't beat around the bush or sugar coat things in the way that I'm used to.

I debated telling him the truth, but I still felt like I could trust him, so I did. Well, part of it at least. Not about the food insecurity piece of my past, but about the aversion to eating in public. I told him I felt like everyone was watching me, and I honestly expected him to laugh at me.

He didn't, though. But the next day at lunch, and the day after that, he positioned his body next to me on one side, and Chris mirrored him on my other side.

I'd thought they were crazy, but then I realized what they were doing. Using their giant frames to block out the rest of the cafeteria, so my mind was at ease.

I haven't had a problem since.

The bell rings, signaling the end of second period and the start of lunch. The teacher takes off first, and I'm tempted to laugh at her eagerness to get away from the class. We're kind of a rowdy bunch. I spring out of my seat, eager to make it to Lainey's classroom so we can walk to the cafeteria together. But before I can reach the doorway, a tall frame steps in front of me.

"Where are you rushing off to, Annie?" Sierra snarls, crossing her arms over her chest in typical bully fashion.

She insists on calling me Annie, because I'm little, I'm an "orphan," and she's too lazy and uncreative to come up with a better derogatory nickname.

"Heading back to Goodwill for another round of shopping?" Her jab would hurt less if it wasn't true. My clothes *are* from a donation bin. "It's funny how much of an outcast you are, don't you think?" She tilts her head, looking at me with pure hatred in her eyes. "It's obvious you don't belong here. Crystal clear."

I shove past her, no longer laughing at our teacher's absence. Though I doubt Sierra would've cared. She'd probably torment me in front of the teacher just so she had an audience.

She's cruel like that.

I speed walk down the hallway towards the single stall bathrooms. I can't run and draw more attention to myself, but I also have to hurry. I can feel the familiar sting of tears in my eyes, and I really don't want to break down in the busiest hallway in the school.

I slip in the doorway unnoticed and flip the lock on the bathroom door. I sink down, my back sliding down the door as I stop fighting the tears threatening to escape.

I hate that I'm letting another person affect me like this. I hate giving her power. But it's hard not to when her insults and cruel remarks mirror my insecurities.

Everyone else is in cute tops and jean skirts or leggings for casual day. All designer brands and spotless garments.

Everyone except for me.

I let all of my frustration from this morning, all the impending dread of seeing my mother, and all of the hurt from Sierra's comments out as I sit in the dark bathroom and just cry.

I cry. I cry for the things I've been stuck with my whole life, and I cry for the things I never had. I cry for the unfairness of it all, for my siblings and for myself.

I cry until I run out of tears, and then I cry some more.

Chapter 17

Colton

"The fuck is that look for, Bossman?" Zalinsky asks, eying me skeptically from across the table. "You look like your Spidey senses are tingling."

As ridiculous as he sounds, he's right. Something's wrong. Lainey came to the lunch table asking if we've seen Maisy, even though those two usually travel as a pair. I didn't miss the worry in her eyes, and my cousin is hard to rattle.

But Maisy's absence rattled her. It rattled Chris and I, too.

Nobody else seems to see a problem with it. The guys said she probably got held up in class or went to the bathroom or something. But I don't think so. There's an uneasy feeling in my gut that's too strong to ignore.

When the first ten minutes of lunch go by with no word from Maisy, I've officially lost my shit. My Spidey senses *are* tingling.

"Fuck it, I'm going to look for her." I stand up from the bench, looking at Chris and Lainey expectantly. "Are you coming with me?"

"Uh, duh," Chris says at the same time Lainey says, "Obviously."

At the large oak doors at the entrance of the cafeteria, Lainey heads left towards the girls' locker room and west wing of the school, Chris heads straight, towards the common areas and main lobby, and I head right towards the east wing.

I'm pretty sure her last class was over here, which gives me the highest odds of finding her. Don't ask me why that bit of information fueled my decision. I guess I don't trust Lainey and Chris to text me right when they find her. And the unease I'm feeling right now needs to be put to rest, ASAP.

I check the lifestyle hallway and the science hallway first, poking my head into each of the classrooms and growing a little bit more anxious with every empty room I encounter.

At the end of the language hallway, I hear it. The running sink from the single stall bathrooms. Every student at St. Mark's has lunch this period, which means that every student should hypothetically be in the cafeteria right now.

It's not a teacher in that bathroom. They have their own, much nicer facilities around the corner. It's definitely a student in there, but the question is, is it the student I'm looking for?

I knock softly on the door, but I can't hear much over the sound of the water hitting porcelain. I have a feeling that might be intentional. "Maisy, are you in there?" Silence.

It occurs to me that someone might have left the sink running by mistake, but then I hear a choked sob, and I know that that's not the case.

"Maisy?"

"Nope, sorry. Not Maisy," a voice calls from the other side of the door. Except that the voice is lying, because even through the nasally, tear-choked pitch, I know that voice. It's the same one that's been tormenting me, fucking with my mind since the first time I heard it.

"Bullshit. I know it's you." I hear a sniffle and decide to soften my voice. "Can I please come in?"

"B-but this is a girls' b-bathroom, Colton."

I choose to ignore the way my heart stutters with the knowledge that she knows my voice, too. I never announced who I was. She just knew.

You're pulling at strings here, Lorenzo.

"Fine. It's not Colton. It's Coltona. Can I come in now?"

There's a long pause of silence, and I'm convinced that she's either ignoring me or just straight up didn't hear me. But then I hear the turn of a lock and the creaking of hinges, and I'm no longer staring blankly at the bathroom door.

I'm staring at a puffy-eyed, bloodshot Maisy. And damned if my heart doesn't shatter at the sight.

"Maisy—"

"Just come in," she murmurs, grabbing my hand and tugging me into the bathroom. "I don't want anyone else to see me like this." She shuts the door behind us and crosses her arms across her stomach, looking down at her feet like she's ashamed.

I've got two questions, neither of which I have the strength to ask. The first is who the *hell* did this to her, and the second is, why the *hell* is she ashamed in front of me?

I'm usually a logical guy. I usually think things through, make rational decisions after weighing the pros and cons, but there's nothing rational about the way I step towards her and wrap her in a bear hug.

I'm probably squeezing her too tightly, but seeing her hurting breaks my fucking heart. I can't even explain the devastation I'm feeling right now. She's stiff at first, and I kind of regret forcing myself on her. I don't know the first thing about what she went through before she came to the Marshall's house. I don't know if she's a touchy person. I don't know if she wants this.

I'm about to pull away and start a long string of apologies when she fists my hoodie with both hands, keeping me pressed against her. "Please don't leave me."

I don't think I could ever fully leave her. This girl has made it past every defense I've set up for the alternate sex. I couldn't shake her from my mind if I wanted to. And believe me, I've tried.

"I'm not going anywhere," I promise, squeezing her tighter. And, true to my word, I don't pull back. I'd stay here with her for the rest of the day if she asked me to. I'd keep her in my arms for as long as she asked me to. I'd do anything to stop the silent flow of tears falling from her eyes right now.

After several minutes, she pulls back reluctantly. "I'm sorry," she sniffles, looking up at me with sad eyes. She looks tired. Defeated. "I soaked your shirt."

"I don't care." And I really, truly don't. "Maisy, what happened? You had us all worried."

"I'm sorry," she chokes out, her voice thick with unshed tears. "I just… I couldn't go out there. I-I've only been here for a m-month and crying in front of the whole s-school seems like social suicide."

Yeah, she's not wrong there. But… "Why are you crying, Maisy?" I ask, my voice gentle even though I'm not above forcing an answer out of her and then pummeling whatever name she gives me. It was a person that did this to her. I know it was.

She shakes her head, her expression still looking dejected. "I don't want to talk about it."

"Maisy—"

She looks up at me again, and the sadness in her eyes makes my heart crack all over again. "Please don't make me, Colt."

As much as it breaks me to see her like this, I know that forcing an answer out of her is only going to make things worse. And I don't want to do that to her. I *can't* do that to her. So instead, I wipe my palms on the front of my cargo pants and look down at her. "What can I do?"

"I don't need—"

"Maisy, I'm going to go crazy. Crazier," I amend with a small smile. "Please let me help you."

She thinks for a moment, fidgeting with her hands inside of her oversized sleeves. "I don't want to be here," she says after what feels like an eternity. "Can you text Amanda and see if she can come and get me? My phone's all out of credit."

"How about I take you back to the house instead?" I offer, inexplicably thrilled by the idea of having her alone in my car for the ten-minute ride to the Marshall's house.

Not like *that*. I don't want to try anything. I wouldn't dream of it, especially not right now. But when she's with me, I know she's safe. I know that I have a better chance of figuring out what happened to her. Of getting her to open up to me.

"But you have school," she objects. But I hear the fractured hope in her voice, and that's how I know it's bad. Whatever happened to her, I mean. The one thing I do know about Maisy is that she won't ask for anything, ever. She could be drowning at sea and she wouldn't ask a nearby boat for a buoy. Or she would, and she'd give it to her siblings. The fact that she'd consider taking a ride from me means that she really needs to get away.

But it also means that she trusts me to help her.

"I've got thirty minutes of lunch left. The house is only ten minutes from here." I scoop her discarded bag off of the floor and sling it over my shoulder. When she doesn't object, I reach out and sling an arm over her shoulder. "C'mon, Shorty. Let me take you home."

She barely reaches my armpit. Somehow, I always forget just how small she is until we're right next to each other.

"Okay." She nods obediently, following me out of the bathroom and into the harsh light of the hallway. "Hey, Colton?"

"Yeah, Maisy?"

"You really are friendly for a giant."

Chapter 18

Maisy

The entire car ride home is silent.

I can tell by the tension in his shoulders and the worry in his eyes that Colton would like to change that, but he has the good sense not to push me. I don't think I'm capable of producing words right now. Especially not to him.

I know that I can trust him, but I also know that if I told him what Sierra said, he'd go fight with her again. And sending Colton and Chris to fight my battles isn't going to help the accusations that I'm sleeping with them. Plus, I'm already enough of a burden just being here. They don't need to be getting into trouble to defend my honor when there isn't enough of it to be worth defending.

Superheroes by The Script starts floating through the speakers, distracting me from my inner turmoil. Colton turns up the volume. "I love this song," he says awkwardly, clearly attempting to break the strained silence between us.

I listen intently, not breaking the silence, but absorbing the lyrics.

When Colton pulls into the driveway, I notice Amanda's silver Bugatti, and I feel even worse. I know for a fact that she had work today, but I have a feeling that Chris texted her when Colton told him he found me.

"Do you want me to come in with you?" Colton asks, putting his truck and park and looking at me with kind eyes.

I shake my head. "You've got school," I remind him, swinging open the side door and sliding out unceremoniously. "You've done too much for me already."

Colton frowns. "It was just a ride, Maisy."

"One that was out of your way," I point out, grabbing my bag from the floor.

"It was a ride," he reiterates. "Not a kidney."

"Still." I tuck a piece of my hair behind my ear, blushing under the intensity of his stare. "Thank you, Colt. I… um… it's…" I shake my head, looking down at my feet. "Thank you."

"Anytime. Text me if you need anything, okay?"

I nod, not wanting to mention that I don't have his number, and even if I did, I don't have any credit left anyway. I feel like that would just open up another can of worms that I don't particularly want to deal with right now.

I feel his gaze boring into my back as I walk up the driveway, but I try to ignore it.

Once I'm in the foyer, I feel the familiar sting of tears again, but I blink them away when I see Amanda rush towards me from the kitchen.

But they return the second I hear the worry in her tone. "Maisy, honey," she coos, looking at me with a kind of maternal anxiety that I've never seen before.
"What happened?"

I shake my head, feeling the tears rapidly welling in my eyes. Amanda wastes no time pulling me into a hug, and the moment her strong arms wrap around me, I lose it for the second time today.

Amanda couldn't calm me down. She tried—God bless her heart—but even the tea she made me and the soft music she played from the kitchen speakers couldn't stop my stream of tears.

It gets bad like this every once and a while. I've got a bad habit of pushing everything down deep, internalizing every single thing until one day something happens and it unleashes months' worth of emotions.

Today was that day.

There was only one person I wanted to talk to, and it was Chris. I had to wait for a few hours before school got out, but he came right home to check on me.

"Maisy Mae." He's standing in my doorway with his hands on his hips and a soft expression on his face. "Skipping class? What are we gonna do with you?"

I manage a shrug, pulling my duvet up to my chin to hide the way my body is still convulsing from my latest fit of tears.

I'm such a wimp. People have said way worse to me than what Sierra said today. But it's that, plus the pressure that comes with seeing my mom, plus the unchecked emotions around moving in here and starting at a new school… all of it combined today, and it all just *broke* me.

Chris walks into my room and closes the door behind him. He sets his backpack down at the end of my bed and pulls out a folder. "I got the work from your last two teachers," he says, waving it in the air. "I told them you had a migraine." He sets the folder on my desk before returning to the unoccupied side of my bed.

I sniffle again, wiping my swollen eyes with the backs of my hands. "Thank you."

Chris blows out a breath, shaking his head. "Well, this is bumming me the fuck out. Scooch over."

"What are you—"

I can't even get my sentence out before he launches himself onto my bed. I narrowly escape getting crushed by his WWE move, but I scramble out of his way just in time. He sits up against the headboard, making himself comfortable before glancing down at me. "Hi, Maisy Mae," he says, flashing me his signature goofy grin.

I can't help but chuckle. I think he might be the only person who could've made me laugh given the state I'm in. "Hi, Chris."

"So," he says casually, crossing his hands behind his head. "Care to tell me what happened today?"

I bite down on my bottom lip. I know it isn't healthy to carry it all in, but I'm nervous to tell him. Not because I don't trust him, but because I've seen how overprotective he and Colt are of me.

I don't understand it, but apparently, they almost started a fight a few weeks ago at the party over me, and that fact has been crushing me with guilt.

I don't want a repeat of that.

But the way Chris is looking at me, all comforting and open, I come to the conclusion that if I have to confide in someone, he's going to be the easiest option.

"If I tell you, you can't tell Colton."

Chris's brow furrows in confusion. "Do you not trust him?"

"No, I do," I amend quickly. "But I just… I don't want any more fights, okay? Please, Chris, just don't tell anybody, okay?"

Chris looks hesitant, but he nods, his features sobering as he studies me.

"I… I was leaving class before lunch, you know, to meet up with Lainey, and Sierra stopped me." His expression darkens, his bright blue eyes taking on a homicidal glint. "She, uh, called me *Annie*. She's been doing that a lot," I admit.

"Annie?" Chris looks confused. "Is she fucking stupid? Maisy sounds *nothing* like Annie."

"It's not a sound thing," I murmur, feeling my cheeks burn in embarrassment. "It's because I'm small, and, um, your parents foster me. Little Orphan Annie, you know?" His expression darkens further. He looks like he wants to punch something. But I don't feel scared. I know Chris would never hurt me. "She basically just told me that I don't belong. Made fun of my clothes and told me to go back to Goodwill."

"That *bitch*," Chris snaps, clenching his fists. "*She* needs to go back to Planned Parenthood. Lord knows she has to get her fucking punch card stamped for the week. She's—"

"She's not wrong," I say, dropping my gaze to my lap in shame. "I don't belong there, Chris, and I don't belong here, either."

I feel all of the testosterone-induced energy melt in the air as the tension leaves Chris beside me. "Maisy," he whispers, his voice taking on a sad note. "Don't say that."

I feel the tears start up again. I'd assumed I'd run out after my third consecutive hour of crying, but I must have massive tear ducts. "You know it's true, Chris. I don't dress like them, I don't act like them, guys don't like me like they like them. I have *nothing* in common with any of the other girls. I'm the black sheep. Sierra just had the guts to say it out loud."

"Hey." I feel Chris's hand tip my chin up, forcing me to look into his now-softened blue eyes. "You *do* belong here. Can I tell you a secret?" I nod. "Mom and Dad have fostered a lot of kids, but I think you're my favorite."

"You're just saying that to make me stop crying."

"Nope. You're my favorite. But if you tell your brother I said that, I *will* deny it." Chris shrugs, releasing his hold on my face. "You're the easiest for me to talk to. Sometimes it's easier to tell you things than it is to tell Colt, and I've been best friends with him since I was five."

I search his expression for a clue that he's lying, but I can't find one. "I don't get it."

"I don't either. But I trust you more than I trust most of my friends and teammates. No joke, Maisy Mae, you're one of my favorite humans." Chris smiles softly down at me. "So maybe you're not like some of the girls at school, but that is *not* a bad thing. Trust me. You're *you* and that's way better than being *them*."

"You sound like my therapist," I chuckle, blinking away a few stray tears.

"Thanks. Contrary to popular belief, I'm more of a genius than I look." Chris grins down at me, running a hand through his wavy blonde hair. "Okay, I have a plan. Wanna hear it?"

"Hit me, Mr. Genius."

"You're gonna go out with my mother, and you're going to humor her by getting some new clothes." I try to interject, but Chris holds a hand up between us to stop me. "No objections. I know you don't like spending money, and I get it, but the woman is dying for an excuse to go shopping. If you want to still wear your clothes for casual day, go for it. Don't let Sierra ruin what you love. But if you do want new clothes, or shoes, or whatever the hell it is that girls buy, then get them."

"But I'd be putting your parents out," I whisper, dread filling me at the thought of Amanda paying for my clothes.

"Maisy, it would make my mother's day to take you out. I promise you. You don't have to go crazy, but get a few things. It can't hurt."

I'm no less weary of spending money now than I was when I first moved in here, but I don't think I can relive today once a month. Or more, if I count potential encounters with my classmates on weekends. I don't want to let Sierra win, and I don't want to change myself, but maybe Chris is right. Maybe I could strike a deal with Amanda. Pick up extra chores around the house to compensate for the money I spend or something.

The more I think about it, the more excited I get.

As it turns out, striking a deal with Amanda is the equivalent of striking a deal with the devil.

She literally laughed at my proposal to pay off what I spend. Laughed right in my face.

She wanted to go to some fancy designer store in the mall. I said that I was already uncomfortable and that name brand items would only intensify that discomfort. I recommended Walmart. She counter-offered with Carina's, a trendy store for teenagers that Lainey is constantly raving about. I countered that with Macy's.

We ended up at Carina's.

A word of advice? Don't try to negotiate with a lawyer.

"You know," Amanda muses, flicking through some of the hangers on a nearby rack. "I always wanted a girl. Of course, Chris was a miracle and I love him, but that kid has bought the same rendition of clothing since he was twelve. Shopping for a boy is *boring*. Please, Maisy, save me. I beg you."

I smile at her pleading eyes. Chris was right; if shopping was an Olympic sport, Amanda Marshall would be a gold medalist. She gets this flicker of excitement in her eyes whenever she sees something cute, and a giant smirk whenever I pick something up on my own accord.

I still hate spending the money. I hate feeling like a burden. But the sheer happiness radiating from my foster mother in waves almost makes my discomfort worth it.

I end up leaving the store with several pairs of new jeans, a few cute sweaters, some tighter-fitting tops, and a couple pairs of leggings.

"Okay, I was trying to save this for the end, because you're going to kill me," Amanda warns, readjusting one of the many bag straps on her elbow.

"What a great way to start a sentence."

Amanda grins, stopping outside of a store with a pink and orange poster in the window. My eyes skim the words quickly, and my heart stops momentarily in my chest. "No," I breathe, looking at Amanda in horror.

"Maisy, it's a safety thing. You need to have a phone." I know she's being logical. I know that I should be able to contact her or Tim or Chris in the event of an emergency. But the price tags attached to the shiny new iPhones in the store's window are debilitating.

"It's too much," I croak out, dread climbing up my throat. God, the clothes were already way outside of my comfort zone. A shiny new piece of technology is about as far north of comfort as one can get.

"I'll have my people bill your people," Amanda says with a teasing wink, ushering me inside the store.

"Amanda, you *are* my people," I remind her, giving a greeting nod to the salesman sitting in the corner.

"Exactly," she says with a bright smile. "And I'll be sending that call straight to voicemail."

Chapter 19

<u>Colton</u>

I usually adore Friday nights. It's the one night a week that Chris and I are able to work together at my family's garage. We both get paid to tinker with cars and dick around together for four hours. It's great.

But this particular Friday night, I'm filled with anxiety waiting for Chris to show up at the start of our shift. I no longer want to know how Maisy is doing. I *need* to know. For my own sanity.

It killed me that she didn't want to talk during the ride from school today, but I wasn't about to push her.

No, instead I've spent the last several hours in my own head like the self-loathing masochist I am.

I expected the adrenaline tied to finding her in the bathroom to die down.

It didn't.

It took a different form—paranoia—as I thought of all of the different reasons she was locked in there, alone. I spent the entire hour I had allocated to SAT prep worrying myself sick, and the entire ride to the garage drowning in a pit of what-ifs.

See this? My inner logic sneers. *This distraction is exactly why you don't entertain girls. What if you had practice tonight? How off your game would you be?*

"Shut up," I mutter, tugging on a pair of overalls and grabbing a toolbox from the corner.

"Wow, what a lovely welcome," Chris muses from the doorway. The garage isn't big—just enough for two cars to fit in, plus a tiny office—but it works just fine. The small size makes it easy for Chris to plant himself by my side as he also reaches for a pair of overalls.

"I was talking to myself."

"Yeah, I could tell, you lunatic." Chris's grin widens as I flip my middle finger up at him. "Which car are you taking?"

I glance between the blue SUV and the gray Sedan. The former needs an oil change, and the latter needs a full inspection. I'm not in the headspace to be trusted with serious machinery right now. I can change oil in my sleep, but I don't trust myself not to miss something major running an inspection.

"I'll take the SUV." Chris nods, stepping towards the Sedan and lowering himself to the creeper on the floor. He salutes me before rolling under the car.

When his face is out of view, I can ask the question I've been dying to know. Call me a coward, but I can't handle the guilt that I know I'll feel if he asks me about my intentions with Maisy and I have to lie. Because I *will* have to lie. Despite what Wessie said, Chris would lose his ever-loving shit if I told him that I'm into Maisy. For good reasons. He's incredibly protective of her, and I don't have the greatest track record when it comes to girls and commitment.

"So, how's Maisy doing?" I ask, praying that my voice sounds a hell of a lot less curious than I feel.

"She's rattled. But she'll be okay," Chris replies, his tone even.

"What happened today?" I hate myself for prying, but I also need to know. Chris and I warned people not to mess with her, and whoever did should be dealt with accordingly.

Chris rolls back out from underneath the Sedan, leveling me with a serious expression I'm not used to seeing from him. He props himself up on his elbows, glancing up at me intimidatingly. "That's her business to tell. Not mine."

"Chris, it's *me*," I argue, disappointment and anger swirling inside of me. We never keep shit from each other. Ever.

Hypocrite. You're not exactly being honest about Maisy either, are you?

Damn conscious.

Chris shrugs nonchalantly, wiping his hands on an oil rag nearby. "Yeah, and if it were up to me, I'd tell you."

"What the hell is that supposed to mean?" I snap, cocking a brow at my best friend.

"What Maisy tells me in confidence will stay in confidence. I love you, man. You know I do, but she asked me specifically not to tell you. I'm going to respect her wishes." He shrugs again. "Sorry."

I choose to ignore the pang of hurt that hits me when his words sink in. Maisy asked him not to tell me?

"*Chris*," I say, my voice pleading. "Whoever did that to her needs to pay. You saw her. How can you let them get off scot-free?"

"I'm not." He grits his teeth, staring off at a point in the distance. He looks extremely conflicted, which I guess is expected. He's torn between confiding in his best friend or upholding the wishes of his foster sister. With a resigned sigh, he rolls back under the car, making it clear who he's choosing.

Maisy.

Goddamn loyal bastard.

Chris continues to talk from his perch beneath the Sedan. "Maybe—and here's food for thought—she doesn't want us fighting her battles. Maybe she doesn't want fights, period."

"It was your idea to protect her in the first place," I remind him. It was only a month ago that he broke down in his bedroom thinking about the difficulties Maisy and her siblings would undoubtedly have. He all but begged me to help him look out for her, and now he's upset with me over it?

"Yeah, well, that was before I got to know her. She's strong enough to fight her own battles." There's a long pause of silence before I hear Chris's resigned sigh. "She's a lot stronger than we thought, Colt. She'll be okay on her own."

"But—"

"She doesn't want the attention we bring. Having two of the most popular guys at school play bodyguard is only causing more problems for her. We've gotta back off, man," he says, his tone firmer now.

I want to ask what he means by that—that we're causing more problems for her—but I know he won't give me a real answer, so I don't even bother.

"She doesn't need us to fight for her," Chris reiterates. "So, consider yourself off the hook."

I should let out a sigh of relief at that. Less Maisy related stress means more focus for hockey. More focus for school and test prep.

So why does disappointment hit me square in the chest at the thought of not having her in my life anymore?

Maybe you like the distraction…

"Maybe I don't want to be off the hook," I shock myself by saying.

Chris's voice carries no remorse when he replies with, "Well, tough shit, because you are. We both are."

I weigh my options. Go along with him and cut my Maisy fix cold turkey, or admit that I like her. More than I want to. More than is healthy.

The first option feels all wrong, and the second seems homicidal given the mood Chris is in, so instead I settle for something in the middle.

"She's kind of growing on me," I admit, thanking God that he's halfway under a car so I don't have to stare back at his assessing eyes. "I just… I guess it's refreshing, hanging around someone who isn't trying to get something from me, you know?"

"You can say that again."

It didn't occur to me that his attachment to Maisy might mean something similar to him. He's no stranger to the puck bunnies, or the hordes of attention he gets because of hockey and his parent's money. Maybe the breath of fresh air I can breathe around her is similar for him, too.

"I don't think I want to cut her off, Chris."

"Then don't."

He offers no more advice outside of those two words, but we're in sync enough that I know what he's getting at.

Be her friend. Just because we can't play bodyguard anymore doesn't mean we can't just hangout like normal friends would, right?

I guess this means it's time to up operation befriend Maisy.

Chapter 20

<u>Maisy</u>

"I give it two minutes before it collapses," Lainey muses, nodding her head towards the swing set. "Actually, scratch that. I give it a minute and thirty seconds."

Lainey, Chris, Colton and I took my siblings to the playground down the road from the Marshall's house for the afternoon. Amanda had an important work call, and CJ had way too much energy to burn off.

But our current predicament has nothing to do with my hyperenergetic baby brother. No, our problem has to do with the two two-hundred-pound hockey players competing to see who can swing the highest.

"Chris!" CJ whines, stamping his foot in the mulch. "I want to go on the swing. You said it could be my turn."

"Okay, little man," Colton says, his voice carrying his smile. I can't really explain it, but when Colton *really* smiles, you can actually hear it in his voice.

He hops off of the swing, glaring disapprovingly at his best friend, who is still on his swing. "Chris, give the kid a turn."

Chris is a bit more hesitant to give up his beloved swing, but he obliges with a sigh, barreling towards Lainey and I with a grin.

"Where's my girl?" At the sound of his voice, Nat pokes her head up from the sandbox, smiling up at him.   Over the few weeks we've spent at the Marshall's house, several bonds have been formed. CJ has all but glued himself to Tim's side, and he gravitates towards Colton with a sort of awestruck curiosity. I've built a silent friendship with Chris. Neither one of us talks much about serious things, but we just *know*. When he's around, I can read his mood faster than his parents at times, and it goes both ways.

But the most heartwarming, by far, is the way Chris adores my baby sister. Every day after school, Chris checks in on Nat first, and when he gets back from the gym or work, he checks the nursery to make sure that she fell asleep okay. She smiles whenever she sees him, and he smiles whenever he sees her.

It's the cutest thing I've seen in a long time.

"Kiss." She holds her hands up in the air, clenching and unclenching her fists at him. "Kiss, kiss."

She can't quite say his name, but she's trying, and that's more than she's done previously. A few weeks in the Marshall house has done my siblings and I wonders. Especially the younger ones.

Chris scoops my baby sister up, nuzzling his cheek against hers. "Hey, Nattie." She wraps her tiny arms around his neck, giggling. "Should we go down the slide? Yeah?" He takes off in the direction of the blue twisty slide attached to a larger playhouse.

"I have a feeling he's going to get stuck halfway, but I don't want to say anything," I say to Lainey, chuckling as Chris monkey climbs up the ladder with one hand, holding my sister in the other. "I kind of want to see how this plays out."

"Oh, for fuck's sake," Colton sighs, stopping next to Lainey and I and placing his hands on his hips. "I swear to God, this idiot never learns."

Lainey and I look at him, equal parts intrigued and confused.

"He got stuck going down that slide earlier this summer. We almost had to get butter to loosen him," Colton explains, amusement dancing in his dark brown eyes. "You know what, let him. I'm not pushing his ass when he gets stuck, though."

"Lainey!" CJ interrupts. "Come swing with me!"

If I'm being completely honest, I think CJ might have a little crush on my new friend. I asked him about it the other day and the way he blushed was all the proof I needed.

"Sorry, folks. Duty calls." She salutes us and jogs towards the swing set, disappearing in a flash of red hair and pink sneakers.

"And then there were two," Colton muses, staring down at me with a lazy smile that makes my stomach flip.

I've been trying to keep myself distracted lately, which hasn't been hard. Between reading, coursework, helping CJ with his schoolwork, and maintaining blossoming friendships, my mind hasn't had a lot of time to wander.

But when it does wander, it almost always ends up homing in on a certain dark-haired hockey player.

My little crush on Colton hasn't gone away, even though I've done my very best to ignore it. It's the first real crush I've had on a guy, and I don't know how to act around people in general, let alone people I'm attracted to.

At least, I think that's what it is. I feel more jittery than usual whenever he's around. Butterflies erupt in my stomach whenever he flashes me one of his lax smiles or teasing winks.

I have no experience with this sort of thing, but there's nobody I can really ask. Colton is Chris's best friend, so talking to him out of the question. He's Lainey's cousin, so I feel like that would just be plain weird. And Amanda… as great as she is, I'd rather gouge my eyes out with a plastic spork than go to my foster mom for relationship advice.

I guess I'll have to settle on being clueless.

The new phone Amanda bought me pings in my pocket. I pull it out and glance down at the screen, reading the new message. It's Amanda, saying that her work call ended and we're free to come back whenever. I type back a quick reply, but before I can repocket my phone, Colton pipes up.

"When'd you get that?" he asks curiously, cocking his head at me.

"Oh, Amanda got it for me last week. She said it was a 'safety thing'." I put air quotes to emphasize how pathetic the excuse was. Flip phones and older models are just as safe. I secretly think Amanda wanted me to have the best of the best, to fit in with everyone else.

"I agree." Colton nods. "Wait—I'm offended." He places a large hand on his chest, feigning hurt. "You've had it for a week and you haven't asked for my number?"

The butterflies are back, fluttering around rapidly in the pit of my stomach. "I just… You…" I sigh, shaking my head. "No, I haven't."

"Well, we should fix that, shouldn't we?" He takes the phone from my hands, letting it hover by my face so it unlocks first. I peer over the screen, watching as he types in his name and contact information. "There you go. I texted myself so I have your number now, too."

I nod, not having the slightest idea how to respond to him. I'm oozing discomfort, which is a problem, because I don't want Colton to think he's making me uncomfortable. I mean, he is, but it's not because I feel unsafe or he's been unkind. It's got way more to do with me and my own internal turmoil than it does him.

"So, listen," he says, tucking his hands in his sweatpants pockets and rocking up on his toes. "I wanted to ask you something, but I won't be offended if you say no." He looks more awkward than I have ever seen him before. He's usually the epitome of calm, cool, and collected, but right now, he looks like he wants to melt away. "Well, um, Chris told me you like to read."

Okay, I can talk about this. "Yeah," I say warily. "I do."

"Well, I've been studying for the SATs a lot, and I… I can read," he adds hastily. "It's just… I'm kind of horrible at the interpretation part." He hangs his head, looking ashamed. "Like, how am I supposed to know what Joe frickin' Smith meant by a poem he wrote in the eighteen hundreds?"

"So, you want me to tutor you?" I ask cautiously, fairly certain I'm not understanding him. I've seen his schedule; it's jam packed with AP's. He's one of the top kids in our class. The idea that he's struggling with English, of all subjects, strikes me as odd.

But big tests *do* word questions differently to try to trick you, so I guess it isn't totally unfathomable.

He nods, looking at me with hopeful brown eyes. "I'll pay you. Whatever you want. And we don't have to meet all that often. I know you're busy…"

I wave that idea off. "You're not paying me to help you, Colton. It'll be my way of repaying you for the two separate times you've saved my ass." He smirks, his eyes twinkling with mischief. "What?"

"Nothing. I just haven't heard you swear before. Didn't think you had it in you, Shorty."

I shrug. "There's a lot you don't know about me."

Holy crap. Am I *flirting* with Colton?

He cocks a brow. "Is that so?"

And is he flirting *back*?

A long silence stretches between us, where he's studying me intently, and I'm trying not to melt under his scrutiny.

"So, are you around tomorrow?"

I nod. "Yep. You know where to find me."

I'm actually shocking myself with how naturally I'm talking to him. I haven't stuttered or fidgeted once during this entire interaction.

Colton smiles lazily, and I feel the butterflies take off again. It shouldn't be fair for someone who looks like *that* to have so much undiluted charm. Save some for the rest of us, for Pete's sake.

"I'll bring—"

Our conversation is interrupted by Chris's panicked shout from a few hundred feet away. "Uh, guys?" he calls out, the defeat evident in his tone. "I think I might be stuck."

Colton and I swivel our heads at the same time to find Chris lodged firmly between the two sides of the slide. Colton sighs. I chuckle.

"You really can't bring him anywhere, can you?" I ask as we make our way over to the slide.

Colton sighs again, shaking his head. But I can see the amusement dancing in his dark eyes. "Nope. I'm surprised you didn't pick up on that sooner."

Chapter 21

<u>Colton</u>

I am a deceptive piece of shit.

But you know what? I don't care.

Tutoring my ass. I'm doing great in all of my classes, especially English. That's the one subject I've never struggled in. I'm not one to brag, but I can spew literary bullshit with the best of them.

But Maisy doesn't need to know any of that.

I'm not a big liar. I hate it, to be honest. But I couldn't think of another way to hang out with her without coming on too strong. If I invited her to a game, she'd be suspicious, or try to bring Chris. And as much as I love the guy, that defeats the purpose of trying to get to know her.

I already see her at lunch, but she's usually too busy chatting with Lainey or Chris.

And I can't invite her out to dinner or a movie without it seeming like a date. Which I don't want. I'm not looking for anything romantic. I just want to talk to her. To be her friend.

That's it.

I don't really know when I became so goddamn needy, but it happened, and here I am, dealing with the aftermath.

When Chris made a fleeting comment the other day about Maisy's love of reading, I saw my in.

Do I feel bad for lying to her? Yes. Do I feel like an ass for going behind Chris's back to hang out with his foster sister…
Also, yes.

But does that stop me from pulling up to the Marshall's house the next day? No.

I usually go to the gym on Saturday nights, but I went this morning instead so I could meet up with Maisy. I'm choosing to ignore the fact that I've never altered my schedule for a girl before. Never even thought of it. But that doesn't mean anything, right?

I also chose this particular night because I know Chris will be working at the garage until ten. I'm not opposed to him knowing about our little agreement, but I also know that if he confronts me about my intentions, I'll spill the truth. The *whole* truth.

And I'm not ready for that. Not yet.

With an uncanny excitement bubbling somewhere in my chest, I knock on the Marshall's front door, my test prep book under one arm and a bag of Swedish Fish under the other.

Yes, I did some prying. And yes, I'm also indebted to my cousin for the information I got from her. But I was desperate, and asking Chris for Maisy intel wasn't an option. I did what I had to do, and I have no regrets.

The front door swings open, and I'm met with Amanda's smiling face. "Oh, hello, Colt!" She says peppily.

"Hello, Amanda."

"Chris is at work tonight." She frowns, dropping her gaze to my book. "Unless you're here for someone else?" A knowing smirk curls her lips, and panic settles into my gut. If anyone in this house was going to pick up on my little Maisy infatuation, it'd be her. The woman has a sixth sense when it comes to reading people.

"Yeah, I, uh, I'm here for Maisy, actually," I say, trying to be casual. I don't think it works, though, because her smirk widens further.

She cocks her blonde head at me. "Is that so?"

I swallow, hard enough that she can probably hear it. As much as I love the woman, she scares the shit out of me.

One time, when we were about thirteen, she caught Chris and I with a bottle of Titos we'd swiped from the liquor cabinet downstairs. She didn't scream at us, or kick me out, or even lock up the liquor. *That* was what we had expected.

No, instead she turned the basement—our favorite hangout spot—into her personal yoga studio, robbing us of our lair. We'd stood on the basement stairs, gap mouthed in horror, almost brought to tears when we realized our air hockey table had been replaced by a little waterfall, and our vending machine had been replaced by a table of incense.

She said that if we couldn't respect her rules and her personal things, she wouldn't respect ours.

That was the last time we ever snooped around Tim and Amanda's things.

That's only one of the many times she's punished us in one of the many frightening ways of hers, and I'm not keen on throwing myself in the way of her wrath again.

"Well, I was struggling with some of the English stuff on the SATs," I lie, holding up the prep book in my hand. "And Chris told me Maisy's really good with that kind of thing."

"Yeah, she is." Amanda's face takes on a softer note, pride settling in her brown eyes. "She's a smart girl." I nod, not sure of what else to say. "Well, I won't keep you."

The moment the words leave her lips, I all but sprint towards the staircase, pausing halfway up when I hear my name. "But Colton?" She smirks again. "Door open."

Yeah. She definitely knows.

Maisy's room is the first door on the landing, right next to Chris's. It's a little bit strange, being here but not barging into his room the way I have for the last twelve years.

I value Maisy's privacy more than his, though, so when I make it outside of her door, I knock twice before twisting the knob and letting myself into the room.

"Oh, hi Colton," Maisy says, smiling as I walk into her room. She tucks her bookmark into her book before setting it on her nightstand.

"Hi, Maisy." I let my eyes linger curiously, but only for a second. She's in sweatpants and one of Chris's St. Mark's hockey T-shirts.

I'd be lying if I said that seeing the Spartan logo on her chest didn't do something to me. She looks amazing in our signature blue and gray colors.

Fuck that. She looks amazing, *period.*

Her long brown hair is tied in a loose bun, her whiskey eyes framed by long, dark lashes. She's got a light dusting of freckles across her nose, and the smoothest olive skin I've ever seen in real life.

"I just did some laundry today. I stole Chris's clothes because I had none," she explains, gesturing to her Spartan's Hockey shirt.

I'd correct her, tell her that the jersey wasn't why I was looking, but it's probably better for me if she thinks I'm staring because I'm intrigued by her shirt.

I tear my eyes off of her before my staring grows suspicious. I've never been in her room before, so I take a moment to look around. It's the neatest space belonging to a teenager I've ever personally seen, and that's not an exaggeration.

Everything on her desk is organized in neat piles, every stray item of clothing is in her hamper, and her bed is perfectly made.

"I think this is the cleanest room I've ever seen," I muse, walking away from the door and towards her bed.   She blushes slightly at the compliment. "I've never had my own space before. I like to keep it clean."

I nod. "So, where do you want me?" I ask, mentally sorting through the reasons I feel this nervous. I've talked to pretty girls before. I've done a lot more than *talk* with girls, for Christ's sake.

So why do I feel this disoriented just being in Maisy's space?

"Oh, um, I only have the one chair at my desk," she says quietly, tucking her hair behind her ear nervously. At least it's not just me feeling this irrational anxiety. "So, either the bed or the floor."

Anything for You

Lying in bed with her will one hundred percent *not* help my case, but I also don't feel like cricking all of my muscles by sitting on the floor.

"The bed works." I sink onto the mattress at the foot of the bed, careful to leave ample distance between us. I have no aversion to being close to her, but I don't know that she feels the same way.

I don't know what demons haunt her past. I don't know why she's here, or what she's been through. And I'm not about to take away the peace in her normally tortured eyes by forcing myself into her space and potentially bringing back unwanted memories.

I don't want to assume that something like that happened to her, but I've also seen how quiet she is. Her slight flinch when one of the guys is too loud, or sounds angry. I've seen the way her shoulders stiffen when Vinny miscalculates the available space and brushes her shoulder.

Her reactions are almost invisible, but I'm so accustomed to picking up on her every little detail that I usually notice them. And they paint an ugly picture, one that tells a story that I'm desperate to know but also terrified to hear.

My lack of knowledge is why I'm here. I can't sate my thirst for knowledge by going to Chris or Lainey, because they both refuse to tell me anything serious about Maisy.

"If you want to hear her story, be somebody worth telling." Those were my cousin's exact words, and they'd hit me like a spear in the chest.

"Wait, are those Swedish Fish?" Maisy asks, snapping me out of my trance.

I smile at the obvious excitement in her voice. "Yeah. For you." I toss them towards her, grinning when she tries to catch the bag and fails miserably.

She eyes me with a mix of curiosity and appreciation. "How did you know that they're my favorite?"

I shrug, too much of a coward to admit that I begged my cousin for intel. I don't want to seem like a creep. "A true magician never reveals his secrets."

She frowns. "What does this have to do with magic?"

"The candy? Nothing." I smile lazily, relishing in her confusion. "But your smile is pretty magical."

I didn't mean to get all flirty with her, but the line was *right there*. I couldn't *not* say it. I expected her to blush; that was part of the point, because it's freaking adorable when she blushes. I expected her to freak out and start stammering for words.

I do not expect her to laugh at me.

But that's what she does. She laughs so hard she starts crying. And it'd be a huge milestone for me—for us—if it wasn't such a knock to the ego.

"Oh my God, that was the worst thing I have ever heard," she says, wiping away the tears of mirth pooling in her eyes. "I thought you were supposed to be good at the whole seduction thing."

"I am," I grumble.

"No, you're really not." She fake pouts, shooting me a sorrowful look. Like I'm a little kid in need of emotional reassurance after a hard truth was delivered.

There's no sign of the silent, scared girl I'm used to, and it's throwing me.

"What happened to shy Maisy?"

"She's not here right now."

I cock a brow at her, fighting a smile at the sudden sincerity in her tone. "Why not?"

She shrugs, looking right into my eyes. "I don't have a reason to be afraid right now." She breaks our eye contact, focusing her attention on the bag of candy I'd brought for her.

"And why's that?"

"Because it's only you," she says matter-of-factly. "You're too nice to be afraid of." She shrugs again, and a slight blush works its way up her cheeks. "Plus, you brought me food. I have to let my guard down after that, don't I?"

She says it so surely, like the prospect of being afraid of me is insane. Which it is.

"What changed?" I ask, genuinely curious. Just last week she couldn't make herself speak in front of me. We spent the whole ride from school to the house in silence, and I didn't miss the way she fidgeted anxiously the entire time.

But today, she's like a different girl. A girl with sarcasm, a girl who's seemingly immune to my charm.

"What can I say? You're growing on me," she says casually, tearing open the bag of candy and offering the bag to me.

"In a good way?" I ask hopefully, accepting her offer and stealing some of her candy. "Like trashy reality TV?"

"In a neutral way." She smiles maliciously, her eyes twinkling with trouble. "Like mold. Or barnacles."

I feign hurt, trying to bite back a smile. "You're really terrible for a guy's ego, did you know that?" Her grin widens.

I thought I liked seeing her shy smile. I thought I liked seeing her hushed conversations with Lainey at lunch. But the feelings those experiences brought about are *nothing* compared to the adrenaline rush that I get from bantering with her.

Chapter 22

<u>Maisy</u>

I thought St Mark's was pretty before, but the campus in the waning days of summer is nothing compared to the campus in the fall.

It's only early October, so most of the trees still have their leaves. But they've started to change colors, so the old, ivy-ridden stone buildings are accompanied by bursts of red, yellow, and orange.

It looks like a scene out of a movie, or a picture on a postcard.

Lainey and I have spent almost all of our free time outside, because we're under an agreement to spend as much time as possible outside before the harsh Northeastern winters hole us up inside for half of the school year.

Like today, for example. We bought coffees and donuts from the school's café, and are sitting in the courtyard beneath a particularly colorful oak tree.

"So, what was that I saw earlier?" Lainey asks, the accusation clear in her voice.

When she caught me talking to the boy in the hallway, I'd promised to tell her *later*, but I had done it mostly in a desperate attempt to get away as quickly as possible. My new friend has a tendency to react first and ask questions later, and in the moment, I wanted to get away as quickly as possible.

"With Mitchell?" I ask stupidly. Of *course* she was asking about the hot hockey player who'd stopped me after class. In a busy hallway.

I wanted to die.

"Obviously," Lainey scoffs, rolling her eyes. "What'd he want?"

I shrug. I hadn't let him talk for long enough to be sure, but I get a strange feeling around him. A slight twinge in my gut that warns me of potential danger.

It's nothing like the twinge in my gut I feel when Colton's around. I don't know how the two feelings are different; they just are.

"I think he was asking me out?" It comes out more like a question, because I'm not really sure. I'd been more focused on getting away from him than listening to him.

"He mentioned something about the movies."

"Mitchell Wilcock asked you out?" Lainey exclaims, almost throwing her coffee cup in exasperation.

"Say it a little louder," I hiss, feeling my cheeks flush with embarrassment. "I don't think the entire school heard you."

"Sorry." Lainey flattens a hand down her plaid skirt in an attempt to compose herself. "Did you say yes?"

"No, I didn't say yes!" My mortification doubles. I don't even like being in a room with strangers. The thought of going on a date alone with one makes me want to anxiety vomit. "I barely know him."

"Good," Lainey murmurs, her tone grave. "Keep it that way. He's all sorts of trouble."

I've begun to gather that a lot of the boys at this school are trouble. St. Mark's is a big athletic school, and most of the boys here belong to one team or another. Couple that with immense wealth, and you build some pretty strong egos. And a thirst for girls, apparently.

I've heard stories about all of the boys here, mostly unwillingly. I don't try to eavesdrop, but it's hard not to overhear the conversations in the tiny locker room before gym, or in the bathrooms.

The general trend is that these guys get around. Even Chris, though I quickly excused myself from that conversation, because I see him as a brother and hearing about his sex life was deeply disturbing.

I also tried extra-hard to tune out of the conversations about Colton, but for entirely different reasons. Hearing girls talk about him like some sort of prize or sex symbol was upsetting, especially when I know he has a lot more going for him than they seem to see.

I've gotten to know him a lot better these last few weeks. It's hard not to, given that we've spent two nights a week studying together. *Alone.* I haven't mentioned our meetings to Lainey or Chris, but Colton hasn't, either. I think he might be embarrassed about needing extra help, and I don't want to humiliate him in front of his cousin and his best friend.

My complicated feelings for him haven't changed much. I feel comfortable around him—enough to joke around—which isn't something that comes easy for me. I'm trying hard not to read into it, though. I'm trying to remind myself that I'm the last girl he'd go for at a school full of near models, so getting all tangled up in a silly little crush is a horrible idea.

Of course, with my luck, the one guy that I have even a remote attraction to happens to be the most popular kid at our school. I'm like a walking cliché, and I kind of hate myself for that.

I trust that the feelings will pass eventually. I can't stay enthralled by him forever, right?

"So, I messed up," Colton announces later that night as he waltzes into my bedroom. He tosses me a bag of Swedish Fish that I catch easily, having anticipated them this time. He's brought one to every one of our meetings, as a form of payment, I guess.

He's got on a pair of sweatpants and a tight-fitting gym shirt. His hair is wet and disheveled, like he's fresh out of the shower. I try not to ogle the way he stretches out the thin material of his shirt, because the last thing I need is for him to catch me staring at him.

Even though it is really, *really* tempting.

"I came right from the gym, and I kind of forgot to bring my SAT book with me." He scratches the back of his neck sheepishly, smiling in that boyish way of his that makes my stomach twist. "My bad."

"Oh." I tuck a piece of hair behind my ear, swallowing the irrational disappointment that comes with that news. I've started to enjoy the time we spend working together.

Working with Colton gives me a sense of usefulness I lost when my siblings and I moved into the Marshall's house. I'm no longer needed to handle the day-to-day problems. CJ talks to Tim and Chris about the social and academic problems he used to come to me about. I know in my mind that him having a network of support is good. Having more people to turn to, more people to bond with, is helpful for him. I know that.

But it doesn't take away the pang of sadness that comes whenever he turns to someone other than me. I'm so used to being a parent figure that a demotion to a regular sibling relationship was a sort of whiplash I wasn't ready to handle.

I went from having all of the responsibilities to none of them, and that left a hole in me. But helping Colton makes me feel useful, even if it's only small things we're working on. It's nice to feel needed again, even if it's only for a few hours a week.

I push past my little pity-party. "That's fine. We can always do extra next time."

Colton sinks onto my desk chair, spinning around in circles and flashing me a grin every time our eyes lock. He constantly does one-eighties like this. He's so unserious sometimes—like now—and so serious other times. Whenever he mentions his hockey training or academics, he turns into some sort of hyper-focused machine.

I like this side of him a lot better, though. The playful side.

"Or I could stay here and annoy you." He spins again. "I mean, why waste the gas? I'm already here."

"Are you serious?" I ask, studying his expression for a sign that he's kidding. I mean, what could he possibly want to do with me if he's not studying? Colton nods, his expression one of pure sincerity. "Why?"

"Why do I want to stay? Gee, I don't know. Maybe because I like hanging out with you?" He looks at me like the answer is obvious, even though it's the last thing I would've guessed he'd say. "Friends don't usually interrogate each other for reasoning, just an FYI."

"But are we?" I blurt out. "I mean, are we friends?"

I wait with my heart in my throat for his response. I genuinely thought he just wanted to be tutored. I mean, I guess he has looked out for me a lot, too, but I kind of chalked that up to him being Chris's friend. I assumed he was roped into caring.

Maybe I'm just a pessimist.

He blinks at me. Blinks again. "Of course we're friends, Maisy." He sounds incredulous. Like I had asked him what color the sky was, or how many letters are in the alphabet.

"Oh." I try to mask the surprise in my voice, but judging by the way his brow furrows, I don't do a very good job of it.

"What did you think we were?" he asks cautiously, his brown eyes narrowed.

"I just thought you wanted to be tutored." I drop my gaze to my lap, trying to hide the blush creeping up my cheeks.

"And what about the day I drove you home from school?"

"I figured Chris put you up to it."

He rakes a hand through his wavy brown hair, and his little growl of disapproval tells me that he isn't very fond of my answer. "Jesus. No, Maisy, Chris didn't put me up to it, and I asked you to tutor me because I already considered us friends."

"Oh. Okay." I twirl my fingers together in my lap, melting a little bit under his scrutiny. "Um, can I ask why?"

"Why what?"

"Why do you want to be friends? I mean, don't you have enough? In case you've missed the memo, everyone at school worships the ground you walk on."

His eyes glaze over slightly, anger simmering in his dark irises. I feel bad antagonizing him like this, but I'm also genuinely curious. He doesn't know anything about me, so either his desire to be my friend comes from intrigue or pity.

I really hope it isn't pity.

"Can I tell you something without sounding like a creep?" I nod. "I'm used to being flocked with attention. It's been that way for a while now, and I'm not used to having to work to win people over. It usually just happens." He shrugs, his expression cooling into one of fascination. "But you were…different. I didn't know a thing about you, not really, and that bothered me. You're the first person I've met in a while who doesn't give a shit about who I am or where I'm going, and that's refreshing."

"So, it isn't because you feel bad for me?"

"Maisy, I don't know anything about you. How could I seek you out out of pity?"

Fair point.

"So, we're friends now?" I ask, sounding like a complete moron. He gives me a half smile and a nod. "Just like that?"

"Yeah, Maisy," he says with a lopsided smile. "Just like that."

Chapter 23

<u>Colton</u>

I'm an asshole.

These last two weeks, I've been rearranging my schedule, spending my days waiting to come over and hang out with Maisy. And this whole time, she thought I was only here for tutoring.

And everything before that she thought was a favor to Chris.

Which, I mean, it did start that way. But it stopped being about Chris a while ago, and started being about the fierce protectiveness I have over this girl that I barely know.

I thought my intentions were clear. I've wanted to be her friend for weeks now—since that first conversation with Wessie—and I thought the conversations we've had were reflective of that. But apparently, I was wrong.

She seems genuinely shocked that I want to associate with her, which is both heartbreaking and confusing. I saw the old Maisy today, the reserved, anxious one. I didn't realize how much I'd miss our banter until it all but disappeared.

Now that we're on the same page, though, the anxious version of Maisy has faded back into the more playful one.

"No way," I object, shaking my head.

Maisy bats her lashes at me pleadingly. It's adorable, and I almost give in, but my willpower is *just* strong enough to combat her offensive strike. "Please, Colton?"

"Well, when you say it like that," I smirk at the hopeful look in her eyes. "*Fuck* no."

She huffs, sinking deeper into her side of the bed. We've been stationed here for an hour, just talking. Mostly about school and how she's adjusting, though she tries to deflect the conversation back to me whenever she gets the chance. I've noticed she doesn't love talking about herself.

We'll work on it.

It's growing dark outside, and since we have a good three hours before my curfew and Chris's arrival home, I brought up the idea of watching a movie.

I was a gentleman and left the choice up to her, but I didn't expect the petite, fragile girl beside me to choose the most gruesome horror movie on offering.

"I didn't realize you were such a wimp," she goads.

"I'm not a wimp," I say defensively. "I just prefer not to spend eighty minutes watching people get murdered. That's not the sign of a coward; that's the sign of someone who's mentally sound."

"Boring," she drawls, clicking on the trailer despite my protests. "Look, it's about hockey! Right up your alley!"

I appreciate her persuasion skills, and usually I'd be all over a movie about hockey, but… "It's about an entire team that gets murdered by a frickin' rink demon. Not the same."

"What if we make a deal? You watch the movie, and I'll…" Her voice fades off as she stares off into the distance, clearly trying to think of a fair trade. "Owe you a favor."

"A favor?" I cock a reluctant brow. "What kind of favor?"

Maisy shrugs. "Whatever you want."

I smirk, and she sighs. "You're a pig, Colton Lorenzo. Not *that* kind of favor." I chuckle, which earns me a throw pillow to the side of the head. "I'm turning the movie on."

It isn't a horrible movie, if you ignore the predictable plotline. Seriously, who goes into the storage closet to check on the skate blades *alone* when all of the lights are out?

I call that Darwinism, thank you very much.

I don't utter a single complaint about the movie, though, because just being here with Maisy is nice. It always is. I don't have to perform for her, because I know she doesn't see me as some sort of status symbol, or another check mark for the list of athletes she's bagged. She asks me things about me—not just hockey related—like she's genuinely curious about the answer.

She pauses the movie every once and a while to ask random questions as they occur to her, and I honestly think I owe her a thank you for the reprieve. I secretly think she's timing her pauses out, and halting the movie after the particularly gruesome scenes to give me a break.

She'd never admit that, though, and I'd never ask.

"Why did you start playing hockey, anyway?" she asks, after the team captain gets mercilessly speared by a hockey skate.

"Chris dragged me into it, actually," I sigh wistfully, crossing my arms behind my head. "His parents desperately needed to find an outlet for all of his extra energy, so they signed him up for a hockey camp. Little wuss didn't want to go alone, so he dragged me along with him." I smile at the memory. "I think we were six, maybe? I was obsessed. I loved every single thing about it. Still do." Maisy nods, looking like she's pocketing that information for later. "What about you? Did you play sports when you were little?"

A look of nostalgia passes over her expression, her eyes glittering with a mix of sadness and the familiar shine of fond memories. "I was a dancer."

"Really?" I ask. "Wait. You said was. What happened?"

I figure she had a bad injury. One bad ankle twist or leg wound that limits mobility could rob you of the whole sport.

She falls into a long lapse of silence, and I can see the resigned look in her eyes. I can see her retreating back into herself, distancing herself from the conversation.

"Maisy?" I probe, desperate to keep her from withdrawing again. It felt good to finally have her open up to me. To chat like a normal pair of friends. I'm not ready to lose that yet. "Where'd you go just then?"

"Sorry. I, um, I stopped when I was eight," she says quietly, suddenly very interested with her fingernails.

"Why?"

She shrugs. "I didn't have the time."

"Why not?"

I know I'm being annoying, prying her for details like this. It's clear that she doesn't want to talk about it, but I'm persuasive when I want to be, and I can't watch her shut down on me. Not again.

She doesn't answer me, so I try again. "Maisy, why didn't you have time?"

She looks up at me, that familiar hint of torture in her whiskey eyes. "I became a parent."

Her voice is so quiet, I have to strain to hear it. Her words shoot right into my chest, halting the beat of my heart for a moment. I'm convinced I heard her wrong. "Wait, you have a kid?"

It doesn't seem possible, but then again, what the hell do I know?

"Oh God no." Crimson rises up her cheeks at the misconception. "I mean, not biologically, anyways. But I raised both of my siblings. When my mom brought CJ home… I had to choose between dance or CJ being fed and changed and looked after." She shrugs helplessly, a self-deprecating smile curling her full lips. "It was never really a question."

A wave of empathy and frustration washes over me. I can't imagine what it must've been like, being responsible for a whole other person at such a young age. I don't want to imagine, to be honest. My initial assessment of her was spot on; she's seen and experienced things I've never even imagined.

And frustrated because… "Where were your parents?"

"Mom has her… she has her issues," Maisy explains quietly. I can tell she's being vague for a reason, and I'm careful not to push her. She's already shared more with me tonight than she has in the month and a half that I've known her, and I don't want to jeopardize that.

"What about your dad?"

Maisy doesn't seem put off by my question. Thank God, because I was foolish for thinking that learning pieces of her story would be enough. Now I need the whole thing.

What can I say? I'm a greedy son of a bitch.

"CJ's dad was never in the picture."

"CJ's dad?" I cock my head curiously, not following the conversation. "Wait, you don't have the same parents?"

"We have the same mother, but Nat, CJ, and I all have different fathers."

Huh. Her mother's genes must be iron-strong, because all three Williams kids look like altered versions of the others. They all look like full siblings.

"Well, your mother was a busy woman, huh?" I grimace at my words, instantly realizing that it was probably a comment that should've stayed in my head. "Sorry, I shouldn't have said that."

I'd have to be blind to miss the way her expression darkens. "No, you're right."

I have a feeling that there's more to the story, but again, I don't want to push or pry. If she wanted to tell me, she would, and I don't want to take this moment for granted.

I have a piece of her narrative now. A piece of the reason she's here to begin with.

I want to ask why it took eight years for them to be put into care.

I want to ask what happened with their fathers.

I want to ask how she survived it.

But instead, I take her silence as a hint, unpause our movie, and settle beside her with the knowledge that this girl has more unexpected layers than I ever could have imagined.

Chapter 24

<u>Maisy</u>

One day. One goddamn day and then I have to face *her* again.

I've been in a downward spiral all week, with the only solace coming from my late-night tutoring sessions with Colton. It's easy to talk to him. It's fun to hang out with him. But, more than anything, it's a time that I don't have to worry or anticipate. For a few hours, everything just *stops*.

It's probably ridiculous of me, to take so much meaning from a few silly tutoring sessions, but that's just the way it is.

With the pressure of impending doom growing in my chest, it's getting harder and harder to pretend that I'm not nervous about tomorrow. I'm afraid that seeing my mother again will undo all of the progress I've made the past month and a half. The kids, too.

The truth is, my mother has the capability to hurt me worse than any bully at school. Even Sierra. I give her a power over me that's cowardly and absurd, but I don't know how to stop it. She has a direct line to my mind, to my emotions, that nobody else has ever tapped into. It doesn't matter how many times she betrayed me, how much she hurt me. I always forgave her.

And what if tomorrow isn't any different? I know she can't get custody back that easily, but I've purged her toxicity from my system. I've cleansed myself of the complications she brings into my life.

And now I'm welcoming it all back with open arms.

I've spent the better part of my night panicking. Chris is at work, so I can't talk his ear off, and I still feel strange going to Tim and Amanda.

Once again, I only have myself.

I have to put a mask on my emotion, though, when I hear the soft knock on my door at a quarter to six.

"Maisy?" CJ's soft voice sounds tentative, like he isn't sure if he should come in or not. I know Tim and Amanda had a talk with him about boundaries and respecting my personal space, and he's been extra cautious about it since. "May I come in, please?"

My heart cracks at his voice. I know that tone. He's hurting.

If my mother has a line to my emotions, then I have one to CJ's. The kid wears his heart on his sleeve to begin with, but I've always been able to read him, even when he tries to hide it.

"Of course, bud." The door swings open, and CJ shuffles into my room. I pat the spot on my bed beside me, gesturing for him to join me.

He doesn't ask questions. He jumps onto my bed, curls into my side, and starts bawling.

Sobs tear from his tiny body in gut-wrenching waves, his breath quivering with exertion.

I can tell he's on the brink of a full-blown panic attack, and I feel absolutely helpless as I stroke his hair consolingly, counting out breaths with him like that, of all things, will take his pain away. "Shhh, it's okay. In and out, buddy. Good job," I praise as he takes a choke-free breath. "You're so strong, bud."

After what feels like an eternity, but in reality, is only a few minutes, his breathing evens, and his tears slowly stop falling.

"What happened, CJ?" I ask gently, rubbing circles on his back. "Did somebody say something at school?"   His lower lip quivers, threatening another onslaught of tears. "N-no. I'm j-just being a big b-baby."

"That's not true. You're allowed to have feelings without being a baby, CJ."

"Yeah," he says, but his voice is distant, like he's not sure he believes me. "I'm really scared, Maisy. I don't want to see Mom again."

My heart breaks clean in two for the second time since he showed up at my door.

He's such a strong kid. Unbreakable, for the most part. Seeing him this distraught is sobering. Sobering and heartbreaking.

"What are you afraid of?"

That she'll be drunk. Or high. That she'll bring him *up. That she'll make me feel like shit for reporting it.*

Shut up. I command my inner voice. *This is about CJ. Not you. Take the backseat.*

"I'm afraid she'll have The Dark Eyes," he croaks, his voice raw from crying.

The Dark Eyes is his way of describing when our mother is high off her mind. Her pupils get huge, engulfing her entire eye in a black void. All of the light, all of the sparkle, leaves her eyes and she just looks…empty.

When Mom is high, we fight. That's when her most hurtful words are spewed, when her worst threats are given out like cars at an Oprah show.

I never had the heart to explain to him what The Dark Eyes actually mean. I think he's too young to find out. "Wanda won't let her near us if she's got The Dark Eyes," I say, my voice sounding way more confident than I feel. I hope I'm right. I really, truly do.

"What if she tries to take us back?" he asks, his voice full of fresh worry.

"Amanda and Tim would never let that happen. All we have to do is sit with her for one lunch, and then we can come back here. Okay?" CJ nods. "I'll be there with you the whole entire time."

"Can we make a code word?" he asks hopefully, some of his usual peppiness seeping through the cracks of his earlier despair.

"Sure. If you say it, we'll go to the bathroom and take a breather. How does that sound?"

His face breaks out in a grin. "Can our code word be butt crack?"

I chuckle. "We should think of something a little more discreet, bud. How about 'apple'?"

CJ rolls his eyes at my boring suggestion. "Ugh. Fine."

"How about you go shower, and then I'll come tuck you into bed? Does that sound good?" I offer.

"I don't need you to tuck me in, Maisy. I'm almost nine, you know." He puffs his chest out, acting like he's the most macho man on Earth. "But, if you happen to come in, I won't stop you."

He leaves my room, sauntering off towards the bathroom between his room and Nat's.

I feel no relief watching his renewed personality, because I know he's only calm because of my lies. I promised him things I don't know are the truth. But I'm worried about the same things he is. How can I console him when I'm an anxious wreck, too?

I know what I have to do, but it doesn't make it any easier.

Up until this point, I would have rather died than depend on someone. Rather slit my own wrists than ask for help. Adults have failed me my entire life, especially the ones that were supposed to love me the most. How can I depend on them? *Why* would I depend on them?

But this isn't about me. This is about my siblings and their wellbeing, and they will always take precedence over my pride.

Which is why I find myself outside of the familiar barn style sliding door half an hour later, torn between knocking or running back up to my room with my tail between my legs.

Ask.

Don't ask.

Screw it.

I bring my fist up to the white wooden door, knocking three times.

There's no turning back now.

"Come in!" Tim shouts from inside his home office.

I inhale a sharp breath, willing the oxygen to work quicker and make my head stop spinning.

"Maisy," Tim regards as I step into his office, his voice oozing pleasant surprise. He caps his highlighter and sets it on his desk, peering at me over the rim of his reading glasses. "How're you doing, sweetie?"

"I'm fine," I lie. I've acclimated a lot these past few weeks, but I haven't fully gotten used to Amanda and Tim's kindness. I always feel like there's a punchline waiting, like I'm one misstep away from being ostracized.

Wrong house. That's the Terrace.

"I have a question. Actually, it's more like a favor," I amend. "A question-favor."

He folds his hands, setting them on his desk and looking at me with undivided attention. "I'm all ears."

"Right. Well, I had a talk with CJ tonight…" It feels so wrong, relaying our conversation to Tim. But I know he'll help CJ more than I ever can. "And he kind of broke down." Tim's face falls, worry penetrating every inch of his expression. "He's okay now, though. I talked him down. But he worried about meeting Mom tomorrow. Like, panic attack level worried," I confess, shocking myself with the weight that leaves my chest with the admission.

"I see." Tim takes off his glasses, running a hand through his hair the same way Chris does. "He hasn't had another one since coming here though, right? A panic attack," Tim clarifies.

I shake my head. My baby brother used to suffer from them at least once a week, but they've ceased completely since we came to live with the Marshalls.

"But he really idolizes you, so I was wondering if you could go talk to him. Don't tell him we talked, but just… check in on him. If you have time."

Tim's features soften, his blue eyes swimming with a mixture of admiration and sadness. "Of course, Maisy. I always have time where you kids are concerned. I'll check on your brother."

I thank him and turn to leave. I already feel guilty enough about interrupting him and adding another thing onto his already full to-do list.

"Maisy," Tim says, stopping me before I can reach the door. "How're you doing?"

"Me?" I croak.

"Yes, you. Do you want to talk about seeing your mother tomorrow?"

I know he's being sincere, and I know that if I did want to talk, he would listen. But I don't want to project my personal demons onto him. Not when he has enough to worry about with my siblings.

"There's nothing to talk about. I'm okay."

I think he can see through my lies, but he doesn't say anything. And, at the moment, I appreciate that more than words can express.

As it turns out, I am very much *not* okay, but I wait to break down until family dinner is over and I'm locked away in my room.

Alone.

I've had sad music playing for the past hour, each gut-wrenching lyric a bit more healing than the last. That's been my favorite part of my new phone so far—the music streaming subscription.

I have access to almost every song ever written, and it's healing, for lack of a better word. There's a song for every emotion I could possibly feel. It cures some of the loneliness I've grown accustomed to feeling. Some of the isolation.

I've had Billie Eilish playing on loop for the past half an hour, serving as the background music to my moping. I'm in the pure darkness, just staring at the ceiling, like the answers to all of my problems will be etched across the plaster if I stare hard enough, for long enough.

By the time I'm halfway through *Halley's Comet*, there's a soft knock on my door.

I curl deeper into my mattress, trying to ignore the knocking on my door so I can stay in my little bubble of sadness for a while longer.

"I was good at feeling nothing, now I'm hopeless. What a drag to love you like I do."

God, it hits too close to home.

"Maisy Mae?"

I don't answer. I don't think I can.

"Maisy?" There's a long silence, and I think for a moment that the voice is gone for good. But then, "Fuck it. I'm coming in."

Light pours in from the hallway, and my blissfully dark cave is flooded with brightness.

"Shit," Chris mumbles, staring at my huddled frame from the doorway. "I knew it was bad when I heard the Billie.... But it's *really* bad, huh?"

There's sympathy in his voice. Sadness.

"You're home early," I manage, breaking my trancelike stare to glance at his shadowy figure. He shuts the door behind him, so the only light illuminating the room comes from the window behind my bed. It casts dark shadows across the room, making it so I can only see Chris's faint outline.

"Not really. It's nine." He eyes me skeptically, worry written all over his expression. "Maisy, what happened?"

I can't give him a simple answer. There are so many things wrong, so many thoughts on my mind, that I can't choose. So instead, I go with the easiest answer. The one I'm so used to giving. "Nothing."

"Yeah, that's bullshit." He kicks off his sneakers, setting them neatly by my desk. He sits at the foot of the bed. Close to me, but still so far. "Maisy—"

I shake my head, feeling the familiar sting of tears behind my eyes again. I *just* stopped crying. But seeing the worry in his eyes, hearing the hurt in his voice…

"I don't want to talk about it, Chris. Please don't make me," I beg, looking up at him with pleading eyes.

"Okay." Chris nods, but he sounds hesitant. "Okay, I won't make you." He pauses for a moment, turning his head towards the door before finding my eyes again. "Do you want me to go?"

A lot of things are in limbo right now. But not this. Not him. "Please don't leave me, Chris."

He smiles down at me sadly. "Glad you feel that way, cause that was a rhetorical question. I'm not going anywhere, Maisy Mae."

We sit in a heavy silence for hours. Or maybe minutes. I'm not really sure. Time has stilled completely, and the only things distracting me from my mental prison are the music from my phone and the soothing circles Chris is drawing on my back.

It's a role reversal from earlier. I've taken CJ's place, and Chris has taken mine as I sit in the dark and cry inconsolably.

I don't think he knows that he's drawing the circles. But I'm afraid to bring it up, because it's so soothing, and it's one of the only things grounding me to reality right now. I'm afraid that if I mention it, he'll stop.

I'm prepared to sit in silence all night, or at least until Chris leaves. I don't have the heart to break the quiet, and I don't think Chris does, either.

So, it shocks me when he speaks first. But not as much as the weight of his words do.

"I used to be really jealous of Colton," he admits, shame and sadness dripping from his usually peppy voice.

"What?" My mind is cloudy. I'm sure I heard him wrong.

"I was always jealous of Colton growing up," Chris repeats. "He was just… he seemed like the son my parents were meant to have, you know? Perfect grades. Perfect character. A promising future in hockey. It only made sense that the perfect kid would be given to the perfect set of parents."

"You're good at hockey too, though," I point out, my heart cracking once again at the insecurity in his voice.
Chris shakes his head. "Not like him. I was always the inattentive problem child. I had to work my ass off, and I'd only get half of the success I watched Colt get. I stopped comparing myself years ago, but it always sucked, feeling like I was a shadow in my own house. Even if it was only in my mind."

God, don't I know it.

I'm really glad that the room is dark. It means that Chris can't see the resigned look in my eyes, the fresh tears trickling down my cheeks, or the way my face caves at the thought of my mother.

A shadow in my own house.
The darkness allows me to make my confession.

Everything is easier to admit in the dark.

"My mother hates me," I whisper, my voice deathly quiet.

I feel Chris freeze beside me. "What?"

I've never admitted that out loud before. Not to my slew of therapists through the years. Not to Colton. Certainly not to Wanda or Amanda. But something about my foster brother screams *ventable*. I feel like I can tell him anything, and honestly, I probably can. I haven't known him for long, but I know that I can trust him.

His own admission opened the floor for my truths. I have a feeling he did that intentionally. Told me something personal to bring me out of my shell.

"My mother hates me." The words feel like bile rising up my throat. I've lived with the truth my whole life, but I've never told another living soul. "She told me so herself."

Chris's voice takes on a somber note. "Maisy, sometimes people say things they don't mean in the heat of the moment."

I shake my head. I wish that were the case. It would be an easier pill to swallow. "I know from her words *and* her actions. She… she's not a good person, Chris."

"Yeah," he says sadly, rubbing his thumb over the ridges of my spine. "I kind of gathered that."

"She does a lot of drugs. Abuses prescriptions. And she drinks a lot. Like, *a lot*, a lot." The more I talk, the easier the words flow. "I had a talk with CJ tonight, and you know what he said?" I chuckle humorlessly. "He's afraid of seeing her with The Dark Eyes tomorrow. That's what he calls it when the drugs suck every ounce of life from her.

"When she gets high… she says some really messed up stuff. Tells me she hates me. Says she wishes she'd gotten the abortion. Blames me for—" I cut myself off, pain and sadness gripping my heart with bloodied claws.

"What does she blame you for, Maisy?"

"She blames me for my dad leaving." Yet another story I haven't regaled anybody with. But Chris's kind eyes and his encouraging expression make the confession so much easier. I've held the truth in for a lifetime. I've saved it for someone I thought genuinely cared, someone I trusted enough to tell.

Chris is that person.

"My parents fell in love when my mom was seventeen. My father was twenty-five."

"Yeah, that sounds legal," Chris scoffs, disgust written across his features. "Sorry. Continue."

A small smile ghosts my lips at his commentary. "She was a waitress at the restaurant he managed. It was a whole thing, and it ended with me being conceived. Mom was thrilled. She loved my father. He was her first true love, all that crap. But when she told him, he was… less thrilled.

"Turns out, Pops had an entire second family. A wife and two kids. He wanted no part of a bastard child—me—and he left my mother. Never turned back. She blamed me for robbing her of his love. Said that if I wasn't conceived, she could still have him. She's always resented me for it."   "How is that your fault?" Chris asks, his tone gentle despite the underlying anger I can hear shine through the mask he'd placed over his emotions. "You didn't ask to be here. He should've wrapped his shit. First of all, what creeper sleeps with a seventeen-year-old? And second of all, it takes a real coward to walk away from his girl and his baby like that. That alone says a lot about him." Acid coats his tone as he continues to rub his thumb back and forth. "And your mother? How can she blame you?"

"It gets worse."

"Oh God," Chris croaks out.

"I don't have to tell you, if you don't want." I swallow hard, glancing down at my lap. "It's a lot to take in."

Chris's voice is determined when he says, "No. You need to get it out, Maisy. Tell me."

"Well, after my dad, she slept around. A lot. There was a new guy every month, pretty much. There'd be a honeymoon phase, then they'd see her on her meds or drunk off her mind, and they'd flee."

"Smart bastards."

"But I think…" I feel awful for saying it—for even thinking it—but it's my perception, right? I can't be held accountable for having my own opinion. "I think she tried to trap our fathers. Nat, CJ, and I."

Chris stills beside me.

I continue.

"My father, I know she loved. CJ's dad, Ryan, he had a lot of money. When he and Mom were together, we stayed at his house in the outskirts of town and it was…" I sigh wistfully. "It was a mansion. I liked him a lot. Mostly because when we were with him, I got three meals a day. I had heat. I had a stable place to live. I think Mom saw that, and assumed a baby with him would cement that life for… well not for *us*. She didn't care about me. But it would cement that life for *her*."

Chris sighs beside me, his expression laced with pity. "That's all kinds of fucked up."

I nod in agreement. "And Nat's father was similar. A really nice guy, with a ton of money. They started fighting a bit, and all of the sudden, a surprise pregnancy. Once is understandable. But three unexpected pregnancies with three different guys she happened to be fond of, who were threatening to leave her?" I shake my head. "That's not a coincidence. That's a pattern."

We fall into a heavy silence, and I relish the space in my chest. It feels like I can breathe easier without the weight of my truths weighing me down.

"Can I ask you something?" Chris whispers, his tone tentative.

"Ask away. We've blown boundaries out of the water tonight, Chris."

And we have. There aren't massive secrets looming between us anymore—at least not on my side—and I know, deep down, that this is a huge milestone in our relationship. I've never opened up to someone the way I opened up to him tonight, and that can't go without acknowledging.

"When you said CJ's dad—Ryan, was it? You said he gave you three meals a day." His voice is deathly quiet, like he's as afraid of asking the question as I am of answering it. "Did you not have that before?"

I've already told him so much tonight, it's go big or go home at this point. "I usually had meals. But if Mom went on a big spending spree—for booze or pills—food wasn't guaranteed." Chris turns rigid again. "And after the kids… it wasn't a guarantee, either. I always let them have the first food. Sometimes the only food. Your house is the only place I've been a hundred percent guaranteed meals since Ryan's house when I was seven."

His voice is raw, filled with emotion and pity. "Maisy…"

"Don't feel bad for me, Chris. Please. I made the choice to stay in that house. I could've gone forward… but I knew we'd be put into care. So, I stayed quiet. All of the years I struggled were because I lied to everyone that could've helped me. Everyone that *tried* to help me. So don't feel bad for me."

"You were just a kid. You shouldn't have had to make that call," Chris protests. "That's not fair."

"Yeah, well, life's not always fair."

We fall into another bout of silence. I thought he'd fallen asleep, but then he stirs. "Maisy? If you stayed quiet, how'd you get here? How'd you end up in the system?"

That day replays before my eyes. The screaming. The threats. Rob's meaty hand on my wrist. CJ's sobs.

The sound of sirens.

"I called the police," I confess. "I called them, and I told them everything, knowing that we'd get taken. Knowing that we'd probably be split up. Because if we stayed in that house, we would've died."

Chris blanches. "Died?"

"My mom's last boyfriend… he was a lunatic. Tried things with me behind my mom's back. I obviously said no, and he never pushed it farther than that. Until he did." I swallow the bile threatening to escape as the horrible images from that day replay before my mind. "Mom walked in before he got anywhere," I say, hoping it'll ease Chris's horrified expression. It doesn't. "But instead of yelling at him for trying to rape her teenage daughter, she yelled at me for trying to steal her boyfriend."

"You're fucking kidding me," Chris seethes, clenching his jaw.

"He threatened to kill us all if we told. But he'd kill us all anyway, even if we stayed silent. I just knew it. So, I called it in." I heave out a breath. "And here we are."

Chris stares at me, gape-mouthed, for what feels like an eternity. "I can't believe she's allowed to see you after all of that. She should be locked away for good. God, Maisy, I don't even know what to say. I'm sorry." His voice breaks as he looks at me with pure sincerity etched on his face and unshed tears in his bright blue eyes. "I'm so sorry."

"I am, too. But I mean, I guess I don't seem so pathetic for crying like a baby earlier."

"I never once thought you were pathetic," he says steely, tucking a piece of hair behind my ear. "You're a goddamn warrior is what you are."

"All I did was survive, Chris. I'm hardly a hero."

He shakes his head, his expression infinitely confident. "I disagree."

I don't have the energy to fight with him, so instead, I let us settle into a taut silence. I can tell he has more questions—I would too if I were him—but I don't have it in me to answer them. Not tonight, at least.

"Hey, Chris?" I say a while later. "Can you stay with me? Just for the night."

"Of course, Maisy Mae," he says, his voice still sad and his eyes still swimming with sympathy. "Anything for you."

Chapter 25

Colton

The sun hasn't even risen yet, and I've burned a thousand calories. I've done my laps around the YMCA's track, I've done my squats and my bench presses. Every muscle in my body is screaming from exertion, but I *love* the feeling.

The ache means I was successful. It means I'm pushing myself to get somewhere. I'm bettering myself.

My best friend, on the other hand? He passed out on the bench press an hour ago. I would have woken him up, but he looks so peaceful when he's sleeping that I felt bad disturbing him.

I let him snooze while I finished my workout, but now I'm done and ready to go.

I hover over the bench, poking his forehead with a sweaty finger. "Oh Sleeping Beauty, it's time to wake up," I sing-song. He groans in response. I jab him again, this time with less patience. "You're drooling on the bench, dumbass. Get up."

He mumbles something unintelligible, before attempting to roll over onto his side. He looks like he's trying to snuggle the air. But the problem is the bench is only so wide, and Chris isn't a small dude. He thinks he's burrowing deeper into his nice, comfy mattress, but instead, he runs out of room and rolls right off of the bench and he hits the floor with a loud *thud*.

I can't help it. I know I'm a horrible friend, but I laugh my ass off. I can't even ask if he's okay, because I can't catch my breath for long enough to get the words out.

His eyes snap open as he lays there on the gym floor, his limbs spread out to each side, like he's trying to make a snow angel or something. "Motherfucker," he grumbles, rubbing his eyes. "What the hell happened?"

"You fell asleep," I say, wiping tears of mirth from my eyes. My expression sobers when I notice the confusion in his expression. He must've really been out of it. "Are you feeling okay? You're never this tired."

Chris is a ball of energy ninety-nine percent of the time. Even our early morning sessions don't usually affect him. "Yeah," he yawns, sitting up and resting his weight on his forearms. "I'm fine."

I offer him a hand and tug him up to his feet. "Did you have a late-night last night?" I ask, smirking. He's been talking to this one girl for a while, and, well, it isn't inconceivable that he took her home. His reputation with girls is a hell of a lot worse than mine.

"You could say that." Chris starts walking towards the locker rooms, not entertaining my question at all.

"That's it? You're not going to tell me about her?" Every time he hooks up with someone, I get the full debrief the next day, whether I like it or not.

Whoever said girls are the biggest gossips have clearly never had guy friends. We talk *constantly*, even when we probably shouldn't.

My comment seems to get his attention. He snaps his head to face me, alarm coloring his tired features. "Her? What're you talking about?"

I cock a brow at him curiously. "I figured you hooked up with someone." His expression floods with relief as he pushes open the locker room door. "What are *you* talking about?"

Chris looks hesitant for a moment before he lets out a reluctant sigh. "I fucking hate doing this. I'm such a *dick*." His voice is bitter, dripping with self-loathing. I'm thoroughly confused. "She trusted me and I'm standing here about to tell you."

"Tell me what?" I ask, still lost. "Who's she?"

He looks at me with the vulnerability of a wounded animal. "Maisy."

My heart sinks in my chest. I was just with her the other day. What could have happened between then and now? And why hadn't she told *me* about it?

We've been texting back and forth a little bit. Funny memes we find, crazy things that are going on. That kind of thing. But if something massive happened—something big enough to pull this reaction out of Chris—she'd tell me, right?

I clear my throat, trying to push past the gravel in my voice. "What happened?"

"I'm not telling you the details," he says, with a finality in his tone that I don't dare argue with. "That's her place. But I… we…" He runs a hand through his hair, tugging harder than necessary. "*Fuck.*" He punches the metal locker, and the sound of the impact echoes through the empty room.

I hold my hands up, stepping back. He looks like he does before a fight. Black eyes, rigid expression. I don't know what I did, but I sure as hell don't want to take the brunt of his tantrum. "Woah, Chris. Jesus."

He takes a deep breath, and then another. I watch the steady rise and fall of his chest curiously. I haven't seen him this worked up in a while. Not since that night at the party with Sierra.

Which also happened to be about Maisy. The pattern doesn't escape my attention.

"We stayed up late last night. Talking. About everything. What her and those kids went through…" He shakes his head, his expression darkening again. "And they have to go meet their mother today. I slept on her goddamn floor because she was hyperventilating so much, I was afraid she'd forget how to breathe." He tightens his fists into balls, clenching his jaw so hard a muscle starts ticking. "I just watched her sleep like a fucking *stalker* because I was afraid to look away. I thought… I thought if I looked away everything that bastard woman put her through would fucking *drown* her."

Shit. I'd known something was off with Maisy's mother. She always flinches when the subject comes up, and she tries extra hard to redirect conversations away from her parents. But whatever happened must be way worse than I'd imagined.

"And after all of that, she's allowed to see them again." He shakes his head in disbelief, pacing around the locker room like an expectant father. "She doesn't deserve to call them her children. It's so fucking unfair!"

I don't know what he's rambling about, but I also don't ask, because I know for a fact that he won't tell me. I won't know her past until I hear it right from Maisy, and I've grown to be at peace with that. It isn't my place to know, and it isn't Chris's story to tell.

"Chris, this rage isn't going to help the situation," I say carefully, taking a step towards him.

"You don't think I know that?" he snaps, glaring at me with an intensity hot enough to melt the remaining ice caps in the arctic. "There's nothing I can do. I just have to sit there and listen to her pain and I can't do a fucking thing about it!"

I understand that helplessness. I feel it with Maisy, too. Though probably to a lesser extent than her frazzled foster brother.

The idea hits me like a ton of bricks. It won't cure her pain, and it won't eliminate the demons from her past, but it *will* put a smile on her face. And sometimes that's all you can do.

"Chris, you said Maisy's gotten really into music, right?" He nods, his expression sullen. "I have an idea."

"You can say it now." I put the truck in park and grin at Chris's expression. "'*Colton, you're a genius*'. Go ahead. Say it."

"Usually, I'd tell you to shove your ego up your ass, but this actually is kind of genius." He rubs a hand down his face, staring in awe at my choice store.

Joanie's Records has been in this strip mall since before we were born, but they've done a great job keeping things up to date. You can buy record players and vinyls ranging from old classical music to eighties rock, to modern hits. They've got everything.

Chris was difficult to persuade. Especially when I told him to leave his car at the YMCA—I didn't trust him behind the wheel of a motorized vehicle—and take a trip with me downtown. But he looks pleased now that my genius idea has revealed itself, so at least there's that.

My plan is to get a record player for Maisy and some vinyls we think she'll like. I know that you can't buy people's happiness, and no purchase will erase everything she's been through.

Tangible objects won't heal invisible scars. I *know* that. But music makes her happy, and sometimes music can help heal scars.

At the very worst, she'll hate it, and we can put it in Chris's room, or my parent's garage. I'm willing to take that risk if it means we have even the smallest chance of seeing her smile.

Chapter 26

<u>Maisy</u>

She's sober.

At least, I think she is. She's responsive and her eyes are clear, so I guess that's a start.

Somehow that makes it harder, knowing that she's sober. When she's intoxicated, I can blame every hurtful comment on the toxins flowing through her veins. She doesn't really mean it; it's the drugs talking.

But I can't use that excuse when she's as sober as a judge.

I take in her small frame. Like me, she's all skin and bones, all hollow features and sullen eyes. But her appearance has more to do with drug-induced weight loss than malnutrition.

Seeing her ghostly appearance used to make me feel sorry for her. Like she was just as much of a fragile victim as the rest of us.

But seeing her now, all I feel is disgust. Shame that I've spent so many years of my life making excuses for her.

"Hi, kids," my mother sniffles, dabbing at her eyes with a tissue. *Crocodile tears.* I'd recognize them anywhere. "I've missed you all so much."

Translation: I've missed having a live-in chef and maid to care for me when I can't take care of myself.

Both kids shy away from our mother, choosing to burrow into my side instead. My mother frowns at their reactions.

I don't think she understands why the kids gravitate towards me. I genuinely think that she can't wrap her head around the damage she's caused us. She honestly thinks she's the mother of the year.

Nat and CJ don't have the same psychological draw to Mom as I do. They've always had me to rely on; I had nobody *but* my mother.

I thank God for their connection to me every day, though. Relying on my mother is draining, as is the mental prison she's kept me locked inside for the majority of my life. I'm glad that they don't have to experience it the way that I do.

"I'll be right over there," Wanda announces, pointing to a small table in the corner of the shop. We came to a small café in downtown Elksborough, mostly so that the kids and I didn't have to return to the Terrace and be inundated with bad memories.

Given Mom's history with substance abuse and the danger she put us in by inviting Rob into our lives, she was granted visitation only if it was supervised. At least there's that. She can't do too much damage with Wanda sitting twenty feet away, can she?

We take our own table, settling in with our hot cocoas and playing a mental game of chicken over who'll initiate a conversation.

My mother caves first. "So, how are your new schools?"

"Fine," CJ and I answer in unison.

My mother gulps. I think this is the moment she realizes her three children aren't going to be jumping with joy to see her again. None of us are pleased about seeing her, even the baby. And we make no move to cover our disapproval, either.

Her green eyes sadden, though I'm fairly sure it's an act. "And your new family?"

I know she words the question purposefully. It's intended to make us feel guilty for leaving our actual family. Aka, her. But my real family is wherever my siblings are. My mother plays no role in it for me.

I'm well aware that I'm hyper analyzing her behavior, down to the drum of her fingers against the table. I seem paranoid and pessimistic, but after sixteen years of dancing this dance with my mother, I know the score. She can hide her intentions from plenty of people, but I'm not one of them. I can read her like a poorly written book,

"They're lovely, actually. Very welcoming. The food is delicious. And, you know, *present*." There's an unusual bitterness to my voice, a hatred in my tone that isn't usually there.

But after my talk with Chris last night, it's hard to look at her. After admitting everything that this woman has done to me—and how little she's done *for* me—it's hard to act all lovey-dovey and pretend like I've spent the last month and a half missing her.

"Maisy," Mom says breathlessly, looking aghast. "You know I tried my hardest for you kids." Lies. "And I'm so sorry for the way we left things." More lies. "I've been fighting for you guys, though."

My heart stills for a moment. "What?"

"I've been going to meetings," Mom explains, her green eyes sparkling. "I've been sober the whole time you've been gone. I'm working on getting a better job and turning my life around. There's still a chance that we could be a family again…"

"Maisy!" CJ interjects, cutting off my mother's hopeful rant. "I really need to use the bathroom," he says, way too loudly. "I think I have toilet paper stuck in my *butt crack*." He places extra emphasis on the last two syllables, signaling at our code word.

So much for *apple*.

Several patrons turn their heads to stare at my brother with varying expressions. Some of humor. Some of distaste. All of curiosity.

What can I say? He's nothing if not discreet.

"Okay, bud. Let's take a quick bathroom break." My mother scowls, no doubt upset that her limited time with us is being interfered with. "We'll be right back, Mom."

She purses her lips, but has the good graces to keep her mouth closed. She's aware of Wanda's eyes burrowing into us right now, no doubt.

I collect my siblings and make a break for the family restroom in the back of the café, sending a crystal-clear message. I don't trust her with either one of them, but especially not with Nat.

I lock us in the small bathroom, trying to ignore the smell assaulting my nose. "CJ, it reeks in here, and we don't have much time," I say, propping Nat higher up on my hip. "Why'd you call a timeout, bud?"

His green eyes are welling with tears, a look of vulnerability shadowing his features. "Is she really gonna take us back? I don't wanna be family with her again." His lower lip wobbles, and it makes me want to cry, too. But someone here has to stay strong, and I know that someone logistically should be me. "I don't want to leave the Marshall's house."

"I know, CJ," I sigh, wishing there was something else I could say. I don't dare promise him anything, because the truth is, I don't know what the future holds. Mom *could* take us back. She won back custody of me when I was six, and she could do it again. It'd expose a major fault in the system, but it's a possibility. "All we can do is take it day by day, okay? We have to trust that the grown-ups will fight for us." I think of the fire in Wanda's eyes, the tightness in her jaw when she saw my mother. She tried to keep a professional front, but again, I can read people with freakish ease. My survival used to depend on it. "Wanda isn't going to go down without a fight."

"You're right," he sniffles, swatting away the tears in his eyes. "At least she doesn't have The Dark Eyes Today. That's a good sign, right?"

No. It means that she's listening to her lawyers for once and actually attempting to get us back. Her sobriety is alarming. "Yes. It's really good," I say instead, choosing not to squash my brother's fragile hope. "Now, let's go back out there and finish our hot cocoa so we can get the heck out of here."

Chapter 27

Colton

"You're still the worst," Chris tells me, hours later. We've set up the record player in Maisy's room, and made a whole array of the records we picked out. We went halfsies on it, but I know that if she doesn't like it, he's going to throw me under the bus. "I can't believe you wouldn't let me get the disc."

He's been pouting like a little baby for the past two hours because I vetoed his Weird Al Yankovic vinyl. I had a feeling he wanted it for his own selfish reasons, and I'd rather use our resources to get her music she'll actually *like*. Call me crazy.

"You can listen to *Eat It* on your own time, fat ass," I quip, standing back to admire our arrangement. All twelve of the vinyls we picked out are scattered on the bed, in rainbow order, obviously. We got everything from Abba to One Direction. It's eclectic as hell, but how else are you going to discover what you like and don't like?

It feels weird being in here without her, like an invasion of her privacy. But Chris left his only pair of clean-ish socks on her floor when he slept in here last night, and he had to retrieve them, anyway. We were already in here.

I just hope she won't be mad at us. I know her privacy is super important to her, especially because before moving in here she had none. Hopefully the sentiment outweighs the betrayal.

We hear the front door open, followed by CJ's shrill voice announcing his presence. "Honey, I'm home!" His initial announcement is followed by mumbled chatter and Maisy saying she's going to put the baby down for a nap.

As in, she's coming upstairs, while Chris and I are still in her bedroom.

"Shit," Chris mumbles, staring at the doorway with a conflicted look on his face. The sound of Maisy's footsteps echoes through the hallway, proving that we have no way out.

The nursery door looks right at Maisy's bedroom door. There's no way we can escape without her noticing us. "Well, it's not like she's not gonna know we were in here," I point out, nodding towards the array on her bed. "I mean, that didn't just magically appear."

"Yeah, but we're still loitering around in here. That seems weird."

It does, but there's quite literally nothing we can do about it. Maisy is understanding enough; hopefully she won't be *too* mad at our invasion. I've never seen her mad. I can't even imagine it, honestly.

"What if we hide in the closet?" Chris offers, looking at the closet door like it's a watering hole in the middle of a desert.

"No way in hell," I protest. "Cause then when we come out, some asshole will frame it as '*Chris and Colt came out of the closet together*', and think about how *that* sounds."

"Like you'd be so lucky," Chris scoffs, genuine defensiveness in his voice. "Being gay with me would be an *honor*, thank you very much."

"Yeah, I'm not having this conversation with you." I walk towards Maisy's desk, resting my ass against it and glaring at my best friend. "Seriously, I'm not addressing your level of crazy."

"Gay does not equal crazy, Colton," Chris huffs.

"No," I agree. "*You* equal crazy."

He pats my head, like I'm some troubled little child. "I'd still love you if you came out, you know."

"Thanks, I'd still love you too, but I'm not, you're not, and I'm still not entertaining this discussion."

Before our conversation can get any further, the doorknob shifts, telling us that someone's coming in. Thank God. I'd take Maisy's prospective wrath over this conversation any day.

When she spots us hovering near her desk, she freezes. I try to make out her expression, try to decipher the odd glint in her eyes, but I don't spot a trace of anger. She just looks confused. Rightfully so.

She glances between Chris and I, her gaze conveniently missing the display we'd set up on her bed.

"Hi, Maisy Mae." Chris gives her his signature awe shucks little boy grin. The one that *always* works in his favor. "How's it going?"

"Can someone explain this to me in simple terms, please? My brain is fried." She glances at Chris, curiosity flooding her features.

Chris and I glance at each other, silently deciding who's the sucker who has to explain this to her. Chris cocks a brow at me, a wordless reminder that this was my idea. I sigh. "Well, um, I know you had kind of a hard morning."

Her eyes flood with panic as she turns to look at Chris. "You *told* him?" There's hurt and betrayal etched in the high squeak of her voice. And the pain in her expression makes my best friend panic just as much as me.

Chris holds his hands up defensively. "I didn't give him any specifics. Just that I was worried about you."

"Yeah," I chime in, relishing in the way her shoulders drop and her features sober. She's back to looking relatively calm. Or at least as calm as one can be walking in on two unexpected guests. "I'm clueless."

Chris rolls his eyes. "Yeah, I've been saying that for years."

I shoot him a dirty look. "We knew you were going to have a hard morning, so we wanted to surprise you." I gesture towards the bed. "I'm really sorry we came into your room without permission, but I—"

I can't finish my sentence, because she flings herself at me. As in, she literally launches herself into my arms and clings to me like a koala.

It feels so damn right, having her in my arms. Like nothing can hurt either one of us. She presses her face into my chest—thank you, height difference—and squeezes me tightly.

It's pure bliss, and I honestly wouldn't mind just staying here like this for the rest of forever. Intertwined like we're the missing piece of the other.

Unfortunately, my best friend is a jealous prick who robs me of the moment. "Hey, I helped too!" he protests, storming towards us in long strides. "Group hug!"

And then he throws himself at Maisy's back, sandwiching her between us with his hands around my shoulders. I'm momentarily worried that we're going to suffocate the poor girl, but she makes no attempt to move.

She just squeezes me tighter.

I'm so lost in the moment, in the sensations, that I don't feel the wet spots on my shirt. It isn't until I hear her muffled sniffle that my brain acknowledges the tears soaking my chest.

"Aw shit." I pull back to look into Maisy's leaky eyes. "I didn't mean to make you cry."

I hate seeing her cry. It makes something crack in my chest.

"No, no, no," she says quickly, shaking her head. "I'm… it's just…" She turns to look between Chris and I, lost for words. "This is the nicest thing anyone has ever done for me," she sniffles. "Thank you."

She ducks beneath Chris's arm, heading over to her bed to check out our display. Her fingers brush each title delicately, a faint smile curling her lips.

She's always been gorgeous. Even that first day, when she was terrified out of her mind. She just kind of…glows, I guess. But when she smiles? Forget it.

She doesn't do it nearly enough, but I really hope she makes a habit of it. I mean, obviously I want her to be happy, but it's also kind of a selfish wish.

"Chris, if you could hear my phone through the vents, what are you gonna do now?" she jokes, grinning at her foster brother.

He shrugs. "Jam out to Taylor Swift with you? There are worse fates, Maisy Mae."

Amanda yells up the stairs then, interrupting our little triad of smiles. "Chris! It's eleven!"

He groans, throwing his head back. "That woman is like a freaking alarm clock." He straightens himself, offering us each a smile as he saunters towards Maisy's bedroom door. "Well, boys and girls, I'm going to work. I'll be home by ten. And Maisy," he adds, grinning at us from the doorway. "I expect a karaoke night when I get home, yeah?"

She giggles and nods, waving goodbye. When Chris disappears from the doorway, she turns to face me. And, my God, I love having her attention all to myself.

"So, I have a question for you, Shorty," I say casually, ignoring the little jump in my chest when she glances up at me. "I have a home game tonight. How badly do you want to come?"

"I'd love to." Then her face falls, and my sudden burst of happiness falls right with it. "But I've got no way of getting there. Chris is working tonight."

"You could always walk," I tease. But her frown deepens, and I don't think she gets the joke. "I'm kidding. I'll drive you. You'll have to get there a bit early, but you can watch warm-ups. And get really good seats."

I give her a moment to think about it, but she still looks hesitant. "Please? It can be the favor you still owe me," I say, referring to the deal we struck a little while ago, during one of our earlier tutoring sessions.

"Are you sure?" she asks, uncertainty ringing clear in her voice. "I don't want to intrude or anything."

"Maisy, I'm inviting you. You're not intruding on anything, I promise."

I see a flash of excitement in her whiskey eyes, and her frown of uncertainty flips into a warm smile. "Okay, then. I'd love to go. I like watching you play."

Sweetest words I've ever heard.

Chapter 28

<u>Colton</u>

Our side of the ice is buzzing with energy. It's palpable, the anticipation, the nerves… everything.

It's going to be a good game. The Jersey team is one of our closest matches skill-wise, and it's always a battle.

I prefer it this way, though. It's more fun to be fighting tooth and nail than it is to cruise through a game. It makes the victory that much sweeter.

The rink is packed. It's never usually this crowded for regular games. Playoffs, sure, but we never see this kind of turnout on a regular old Saturday night.

"Why is it so crowded?" I ask Mac, one of the left wings.

"Fuck if I know." We both make our shots, then skate to the back of the line, having completed the drill. "It's like they're handing out free Playboys or something."

"I bet you it's because of Prescott," Wessie chimes in, skating beside us. He's referring to Isaac Prescott, Jersey's newest recruit. He's got speed on his side. A hell of a shot. The last game they played, he was a goal short of a hat trick. His debut game in the league. Everybody is fascinated with the sixteen-year-old boy wonder from the middle of nowhere, which means one thing.

He's a threat.

"I think you're right," Mac says darkly, glancing at the kid skating laps around his teammates.

Rookie move. Save your energy. His screw-up makes me feel better, though, because it means he's got more to learn. It means I still have a leg up.

For now.

Warm-ups end, and as the guys and I all skate towards our bench, we're all a bit rattled. The threat Prescott poses wasn't something any of us considered, but after watching his performance during warmups, we're all a bit shook.

"You look like you've seen a ghost," Caldwell scolds, facing the row of us. "You better man up, boys, because if you're going to let one semi-decent opponent rattle you, I've got a sparkly pink pair of Bauer's in my trunk. You can go join the girls' team."

Jesus.

"Yeah, they've got Wonder Boy, but we've got Wesley's slapshot, Lorenzo's speed, and McDowell's temper. Instead of being pansies and freaking out about what they have, focus on the asset you bring to the team, and max it out. Go get 'em, boys."

It's about as inspirational as Caldwell gets.

The first six of us skate out to the ice, taking our positions and stamping down the earlier nerves. Caldwell's right. One player doesn't make a team, and while Jersey has the benefit of mystery, we've proven our abilities as a team time and time again. We play like a well-oiled machine, and we've got three of the top ten best players in the country on our side.

I win the faceoff easily and pass the puck to Wessie, who takes off like a bullet towards Jersey's goal. Unfortunately, the fucking Flash catches up to him no problem and leads a breakaway, switching things up before we even get a fighting chance.

I'm able to get possession of the puck back, but the Jersey defense is stuck on me like glue. There's a hole in their line, though, so I take the chance and send the puck flying towards Mac. It hits his stick seconds before someone slams me into the boards.

With my face pressed against the glass I have the briefest moment to look out at the crowd, and I notice her. Maisy. Sitting in the third row, gnawing on her fingernails anxiously.

Those whiskey eyes find mine, and I can't help but smirk at her as the defensemen releases me and I skate away.

The game goes back and forth for a while, with Prescott's speed keeping them in the running, and my speed keeping us in the game.

The first period ends, with the score still 0-0.

In the second period, they get a bit more inventive. Start playing a little bit dirtier. Every hit they make is legal, up until I get the puck back from Prescott for the billionth time today.

I skate up the ice, the cold air nipping at my face as I avoid the two defensemen who make half-assed attempts to stop me. I'm hugging the side a bit tight after having to swerve to avoid a guy in the center of the ice, but I'm in the perfect position to sink a goal.

And then I get hit with a triple-whammy. A guy from God-knows-where comes up from behind me and slams me into the boards with a firm shoulder to the side of my head.

I'm not opposed to checking—I'm guilty of it myself— but it was way harder than necessary. Not to mention it was a hit from behind, which is a firm no. With the hit to my head, it's a trifecta of problems.

I'm not surprised when I taste copper in my mouth. And I'm not surprised when the ref's whistle blows moments later as I'm scrambling to get back onto my feet before I get mauled.

However, I'm surprised as hell when the ref calls it a legal hit and instructs us to continue the game.

No way in hell that hit was legal. Coach Caldwell must agree, because he starts screaming profanities at the ref, who refuses to budge on his previous call.

I honestly think it's an ego thing. Like the ref is stuck to his initial call and too desperate to be right to pay attention to the point-blank facts of the situation.

The ref rants something about unintentional contact and my head not being the primary target, and there's no penalty.

I try to wipe away the blood trailing down my face, but I guess it doesn't really matter. It's pooled all over the ice beneath me, anyway.

"Fucking hell," I grumble, feeling the ache in my nose. It's probably broken again, but I couldn't give a shit less about that. I've broken my nose more times than I can count.

It's the blood filling my mouth that I worry about. If the Jersey fucker knocked out one of my teeth my parents are gonna gut me like a fish.

"Lorenzo!" Caldwell bellows. "Get your ass in here and get stitched up!"

I hang my head, making the skate of shame from my bloody mess on the ice to our team bench.

I've only made it a few feet when I hear his voice.

"Sorry about that, *Bossman*," Mitch sneers, placing emphasis on my hated nickname. But he doesn't say it jokingly like my friends do. He says it like an insult. Like a jibe.

Mitchell Wilcock has been the bane of my existence since we started at St. Mark's three years ago. He's a rich, entitled prick from Jersey shore that lives off of Daddy's money and a horribly inflated ego.

He doesn't play for the school team anymore, thank God, but the years he did play were torture.

He goes to St. Mark's, but he boards from out of state. Since he's from Jersey, and his parents live there, he plays for their U18 team.

Think of the dumbest person you know. And I'm not talking just academically—I'm talking full circle, survival skills, conversational skills, intellectual abilities. Take the dumbest person you know, cut their IQ in half, and they'd still be smarter than Mitch. No joke.

It doesn't shock me in the slightest that he's the asshole who was dumb enough to charge me from behind.

"You're not sorry and you know it, Mitch the Bitch." Maybe it isn't the most creative nickname ever, but Chris and I weren't the most creative freshmen.

I can practically see the smoke seeping from his ears, cartoon style. "Watch your back, Lorenzo."

"Yeah, I have to. Seems like my back is the only place you can get a good hit, huh?"

And with that, I skate off towards the bench, leaving a gushing crimson trail behind me.

Chapter 29

Maisy

The entire stadium is dead silent the entire time Colton is on the ground. It isn't very long—maybe a minute, tops—but stress and high-pressure situations like these have a way of making a few seconds seem like a few hours.

I wish Chris was here with me to explain what the hell just happened. Everyone around me boos and makes vulgar comments about the ref after the call. The hit Colton took was nastier than the other ones delivered tonight. More aggressive. Deliberate.

I have no idea what happened, but I don't need to understand it to be filled with an uneasy hum of worry. He's bleeding a lot. From his face, by the looks of it.

I watch in strained silence as he stands to his feet and wipes a stream of blood from his lower lip. Like that'll make a difference.

He gets stopped on his way to the bench by Jersey's number nine. *Wilcock.* The last name sounds familiar, but I can't think of where I'd know him from.

Colton rips off his helmet, revealing his slightly crooked, gushing nose, and blood-stained teeth. He says something to number nine, and his expression darkens as he turns to skate away, dripping blood everywhere.

The game resumes immediately, but my attention isn't on the ice anymore. It's on the brooding player on the team's bench, who looks about ready to kill whoever comes near him.

Even gushing blood, he really is good looking. His mop of brown hair is disheveled, stuck up in certain areas with sweat and ruffled from his helmet. His legs are spread apart, with one elbow resting on each of his thighs. He looks like he's teeming with anger, like he can't wait to get back on the ice.

These guys are wild. They get all beat up, smashed into boards and bruised and bloody, and yet they *still* can't wait to get back out. It's insane to me.

I watch the way his jaw clenches and unclenches as he listens to what the first aid person is telling him. His brown eyes are simmering with anger as he murmurs something back.

I think there might be something seriously wrong with my cardiovascular system. The way my heart jumps watching Colton be so angry isn't okay. Neither are the butterflies that take residence in my stomach when I think about what he did for me earlier today.

Chris helped, too, but my heart is set on the fact that the record player was Colton's idea. Because he knows nothing about my relationship with my mother, nothing about my past, and yet he still knew that I'd be struggling and wanted to make it better.

And that… it ignites something within me.

I know my crush on him is stupid, but seriously, who can blame me? He brings me candy and flashes me the sweetest half smiles while simultaneously looking like a Greek God. And then he goes out trying to make my day and bringing me to his games?

Whose heart *wouldn't* get a bit lost in translation?

As though he senses that I'm thinking about him, Colton glances up from the bench, his eyes scouring the stands. Like he's looking for something. Or someone.

He smirks when he looks towards my section, though I'm not nearly naive enough to assume he's looking at me. He's the best player here. I'm sure there are plenty of fans he's acknowledging.

But then he does the single hottest thing I think I have ever witnessed in my life. Still smirking, he brings his right hand up to wipe a fresh stream of blood from his lower lip. Then he looks right at my seat, right at *me*, and winks.

I feel myself blushing, but the good news is, nobody around me will really notice because it's so damn cold in here, everyone's cheeks are a little flushed. I offer Colton a shy wave in return, which makes his grin widen.

What the heck was that? I wonder, watching as he stands to his feet and heads back out to the ice.

I spend the rest of the game with my eyes locked exclusively on number twenty-two, trying to ignore the confusion clouding my brain and the butterflies taking residence in my stomach.

One hour ago, I thought Colton was good-looking from afar.

But the image of him on the bench has *nothing* on him up close.

He finds me almost instantly, like he knew where I'd be without even discussing it with me. He's got his gray sweatpants hung low, a tight white workout shirt outlining every fine ridge, every bulge of muscle.

Are teenagers even allowed to be this built?

He hikes his gear bag higher up on his shoulder and claps his friend on the back. I recognize the guy from before. Wessie, I think his name was. He says something that makes Colton chuckle before heading straight for the exit.

Moments later, the smell of Colton's cologne assaults my senses as he stands right in front of me, towering over me.

He smiles, completely ignoring the people staring at him curiously and trying to congratulate him. "Hi, Maisy."

"Hi, Colton." I point up at his face, at the black and blue running up his nose and the dried blood on his lip. "How's the face?"

He grins devilishly. "Still as devastatingly handsome as ever."

He's not wrong.

"I'm glad the incident didn't damage your humor at all. Or your ego." I roll my eyes, giving into the smile that had been threatening to take over my expression.

"Thank God for that, right?" Colton blows out a relieved breath, still grinning.

"I don't know the first thing about hockey, but that hit didn't look right. The old guy next to me cupped his hands over his mouth and screamed '*Ref! Ref, does your wife know you're screwing us?!*'. His wife wasn't very happy with that one, but it got a lot of chuckles." I shake my head, smiling at the memory of the unhappy gentleman.

Colton barks out a laugh. "That's one way of putting it," he says, holding the door open for me before stepping through himself.

I start walking towards Colton's familiar white truck in the distance. "I didn't realize people got that into it."

"It's the state team," Colton explains, reaching into his pocket to withdraw his keys. "Most of the guys will go on to play D1 or pro, so they see it as kind of a cheap behind the scenes league."

"I guess that makes sense."

I stand at the passenger side of Colton's truck awkwardly, acutely aware of the fact that I can't make it up on my own. Colton, though, is oblivious to that fact. He tosses his gear bag into the bed of the truck before sliding into the driver's side. Only then does he realize that I'm not already nestled in the passenger seat.

He shakes his head, and I worry for a moment that he's annoyed with me. But then I catch a glimpse of his smile. "I forgot I've associated myself with one of Snow White's dwarves," Colton quips, walking around the back of the car.

And then he clamps a hand on each side of my hips, the heat of his fingertips burning my skin through the denim of my jeans.

He lifts me into the truck wordlessly, setting me on the seat like I weigh five pounds.

I'm grateful for the dark cab of the truck. It means Colton can't see just how red his simple gesture made me.

"So," he drawls, flicking on his lights and pulling out of the rink's parking lot. "You're really not upset about Chris and I sneaking into your room earlier?"

I shake my head, keeping my eyes trained on my hands in my lap. "No. It was really sweet of you guys. I really don't mind."

"Chris had me scared you'd hate us for it," Colton admits, offering me a quick glance before turning his attention back to the road.

"I don't hate anyone. Especially not you or Chris." I think about my words for a moment, feeling the icy dread that fills my chest whenever I think about *her*. "Well, actually, that's not entirely true."

"You hate us?" The slight note of panic is clear in his voice as he whips his head towards me again.

"No, of course not," I chuckle, watching Colton's shoulders relax and his expression soften. "I mean, I think I only hate one person."

He nods knowingly, his brown eyes sparkling with recognition. "Your mom?"

I nod. "It's complicated." I really don't want to offer him anymore. I know I can trust him, and I know that he's curious, but I don't want to scare him away. With Chris it was different—we live under the same roof. He's stuck with me.

But Colton isn't, and I know there's a risk of him running when he finds out about all of the baggage I carry.

"I bet it is." He switches on his directional, turning onto the stretch of road that will take us back to the house. He does it all so casually, like it's a normal, everyday occurrence for people to admit that they hate their parents. Like I'm not something he should pity.

I appreciate that more than I can put into words.

"So, I have a question for you. You can say no, if you want," Colton says, rolling to a stop at a stoplight. He turns to glance at me. "Zalinsky is having a Halloween party at his place next weekend. I wanted to know if you'd be my plus one."

I search his expression for a sign that he's joking, but all I can see is shining sincerity and a bit of excitement. Still, there's a logical part of me that's holding up red flags to warn me.

I mean, why would Colton, the most popular guy at school—and the best looking—want to take me to a party? He could bring literally any other girl at school.

"Why me?" I ask, hating the insecurity in my voice. "I'm sure there are plenty of other girls that would want to go with you."

"The other girls aren't you," he says simply. My heart stutters, and I watch the panic take over his expression. "I just mean that... I mean, you're my friend, and I enjoy hanging out with you." I'd have to be blind to miss the slight blush on the apples of his cheeks.

It's not like him to be so nervous. That's usually my job.

I tuck my hair behind my ears nervously, trying to find a way to let him down gently. "I don't really party much."

"You went to the back-to-school thing," Colton points out, turning back towards the windshield as the light turns green.

"Yeah, and that's the only party I've ever been to."

Colton furrows his brow in confusion. "Why? Weren't there parties at your old school?"

At my old school, I was never invited to the get-togethers. I'd turned down too many invites through the years to take care of the kids that people eventually stopped asking. I had wished I had more friends, but I was secretly okay missing out on all of that partying.

But the real reason cuts a bit deeper than that. I haven't even admitted it to Chris yet.

Can I trust Colton like that? Or will he run?

"Yeah, it's just..." I glance over at him and make a split-second decision to trust him. "I'm not a big fan of the alcohol scene."

Maybe he won't ask follow-up questions.

"Why not?"

Well, so much for that.

I take a deep breath, deciding on admitting a part of the truth while staring out of the window. Baring my scars to him will be way easier if I don't have to watch the pity overtake his expression.

"My mom has a problem with addiction," I admit, feeling slightly lighter with the confession. "Mostly with pills, but she's always had a drinking problem."

He nods like he understands. "And seeing people drunk brings back bad memories?" There's a sympathy in his voice that I simultaneously hate and find comforting. I don't want to be a subject of his pity, but there's something in the lull of his voice that soothes the sudden ache in my chest.

"Not really. It's just… I'm afraid of being like her. I'm afraid that it's genetic, and if I party, I'll drink, and I'll turn into *her*."

I was never afraid of conventional things as a child. I wasn't afraid of monsters under my bed, because the biggest one slept across the hall from me. I was never afraid of the dark, because darkness came before sleep, which was the one time a day I could sit back and just *breathe*.

I was, however, petrified of looking in the mirror one day and seeing my mother look back at me. I was afraid of drawing any parallels between our lives.

"Maisy," Colton sighs, pulling into the Marshall's driveway and putting the car in park. He turns to look at me, his eyes flooding with sadness and another heavier emotion. "I don't know much about your mom, but I promise you, you aren't her."

"But what if I become her?" I ask quietly, locking my gaze with his.

"I have an idea," Colton announces, unbuckling his seatbelt and turning his giant body to face me completely. "I'm not saying you have to go to the party. I'd never ask you to do something you're uncomfortable with. And if you do go, you don't have to drink. *But*," he says, smiling at me softly. "What if I watch over you? Make sure that if you want to drink, you can without getting too out of control?"

There's hope in his brown eyes that warms a part of me. He seems genuinely willing to give up his fun at the party to babysit me, but while I appreciate the gesture, I kind of hate the idea.

"But then you can't enjoy yourself. I don't want to take away from your fun, Colton."

"I don't drink during the season," he interjects, like he saw my point coming and had prepared for it. "I can't function the next day, so I just don't do it. I only go because Chris drags me and I don't mind hanging out with our other friends."

"Are you sure?" I ask, searching his expression for a sign that he isn't.

"Anything for you, Maisy." He grins, his brown eyes flashing with sincerity. "Come party with me. I'll look after you."

This seems like a normal teenage thing to do. Trust, sure, but also partying and going out for Halloween instead of taking my little siblings trick-or-treating. I tell myself that that's the reason I accept his offer—for the experience—and definitely not for a night as Colton's first choice companion.

Chapter 30

<u>Maisy</u>

I'm blushing. It's nothing new, but the cause of it is.

"Lainey, there's no way we can wear any of this," I balk, staring at the rack of less than conservative costumes. "They look like lingerie."

"Exactly," Lainey says with a malicious sparkle in her eyes. "They're perfect."

The Halloween party I'm going to with Colton is in three days, and Lainey convinced me to come out shopping with her at the costume store in the Elksborough Mall.

I've only been here once before—the time Colton and Chris took me out—so I've been following Lainey's lead. But only in the direction sense. I refuse to follow her lead when it comes to our costumes for this weekend.

First, she wanted to be sexy cops. Then it was sexy nurses, and now it's sexy construction workers. Pretty much just pick a profession and add the word *sexy* and it's an idea that has crossed her mind.

The more time I spend with Lainey, the more I wonder how we make our friendship work. She's everything I'm not; daring, snarky, strong-willed. And while I stick to leggings and hoodies when I'm not in my St. Mark's uniform, Lainey falls back on more…revealing clothing.

Our differences rarely cause disagreements, but sometimes, like right now, they do.

"Why don't we just get onesies?" I offer, even though I know her answer is going to be no.

"Maisy," Lainey sighs, turning to face me with empathetic green eyes. "Haven't you ever watched *Mean Girls*? We'll draw more attention to ourselves if we dress in onesies than if we wear one of these," she says, gesturing towards the wall of various colored corsets.

"So? You love attention," I point out.

"True, but I love these more."

In the end, we compromise. Lainey gets her corsets, and I get my semi-innocent concept of a costume. I mean, sexy Disney princesses are more innocent than sexy cowgirls, right?

"We're gonna look so hot," Lainey says excitedly, slinging her bag over her shoulder as we exit the Halloween store. "God, I can practically see it now."

"See what now?"

"My cousin's face," Lainey says in a *duh* tone of voice. Like it's common knowledge.

"Colton?" I ask like an absolute idiot. Of course she means Colton. He's the only cousin of hers that I know.

"Of course." Noticing my confusion, Lainey furrows her brow at me. "Oh, c'mon. That boy is so obsessed with you, it isn't even funny."

"No, he's not." I shake my head, feeling heat creep up my cheeks for the second time in twenty minutes. "We're just friends."

"Yeah," Lainey sighs, looking at me like I'm a naïve child. "That's what they all say. But the way he looks at you?" She shakes her head. "I've known since the day he found you in that bathroom, he's got it bad."

"He said we're friends. We're only going this weekend as friends." I don't know why I'm so desperate for her to believe me. Maybe because I know deep down that this information will give my stupid, confused heart false hope. Hope that I don't need, because there's no way that Colton could ever like me the way that I like him.

"Right," Lainey says, making a popping sound on the *t*. It sounds like she doesn't believe me. "Because he doesn't have enough *friends* to take. He likes you, Maisy." She waggles her brows at me, mischief dancing in her green eyes. "And I know you like him, too."

"I do not," I lie.

"You're blushing," Lainey points out, holding out a manicured fingernail to my red-stained cheeks.

I bat her hand away, stifling a giggle. "I always blush."

"Yeah, especially when Colton's brought up," Lainey goads. "'Cause you *like* him."

I'd deny it again, but really, what's the point? I'm sure it is painfully obvious that I have a tiny crush on Colton, but half of the school does. It's not like I'm a minority when it comes to being attracted to him.

Plus, Lainey's my best girl friend. We've told each other a bunch of embarrassing stuff—including her childhood crush on Bob the Builder—so really, how is this any different?

"Yeah," I sigh, sinking into a table at the food court. "Maybe I do."

It feels good to tell someone else after keeping it inside for so long. But the moment of relief shatters when Lainey's jaw drops and she stares at me, shocked. "Wait, really? Ew, babe, that's my *cousin*."

"What?" I chuckle, pinning her with a glare of my own. "I knew him before I knew you. Plus, you brought it up."

"Yeah, because I thought it wasn't true!" she blanches, shuddering slightly. "Yuck. You know he used to pick his nose as a kid?" She looks at me, willing me to see how "gross" her cousin is. It isn't working. "Ugh, speak of the devil," she groans, pointing over her shoulder.

I turn, glancing in the direction she's pointing. Standing probably twenty feet away in the Smoothie Man line is none other than Colton.

I stare at him for longer than I probably should, at the way his jeans hug his lower body, at the way his shirt clings tightly to the taut muscles in his chest, even though it's supposed to be loose-fitting.

His hair is perfectly disheveled, like he rolled out of bed and merely scraped his hand through it a few times.

"Did we manifest its presence?" Lainey whisper-yells, eyeballing where her cousin is standing a few feet away. "We did, didn't we?"

"Don't be ridiculous," I chuckle. But the chuckle dies on my lips when he shuffles, and we get a glimpse of who he appears to be talking to.

Because it isn't anybody I know. No, of course Colton's talking to the prettiest girl I'd ever seen.

He's smiling at her, laughing at whatever it is she's saying. I think that would be bad enough to witness, watching the way he bends down to wrap her in a tight, intimate hug is even worse.

"Fuck it. I'm texting Aunt Jenny to give up hope of ever getting grandbabies," Lainey hisses, pulling out her phone. "I'm going to castrate her golden child of a son."

Something prickly crawls up my chest. It feels a lot like jealousy, but that's impossible. We're just friends. And friends don't care that other friends talk to pretty girls in mall food courts.

Of course, Colton and his mystery guest take the table behind us, so we can hear every word they're saying. He's got his back to our table, so he can't see us, but we can see him perfectly. I can hear him pretty clearly, too.

And, like the masochist I am, I listen to every single word. Hoping that I'm wrong.

I don't seem to be, though.

"It's good to see you again. I'm really excited for you to come over," the girl says, smiling all happy-go-lucky at Colton.

"I'm excited, too. It's been way too long," Colton replies, smiling a genuine-looking smile right back at her.

"Since you've been to my house, or since you've seen me?"

"Both."

"Oh my God, I cannot watch this," Lainey gags, standing up from our table and marching away. I follow her, also more than content to leave that conversation behind, and the strangely jealous feelings it evoked inside of me.

"What am I going to do about Saturday?" I ask, dreading faking my way through a party when the guy I'm supposed to go with would obviously rather take some other girl.

"You're going to get dressed up. You're going to look hot as fuck, and then you're going to ignore my shitty, slimy cousin. Show him where he is on your list of priorities, babe."

I know she has a point, but I don't know how I can even *talk* to Colton with this strange ache of betrayal residing in my chest, let alone show up to that party on his arm.

Chapter 31

Colton

I am getting really sick and tired of having to play detective to figure out what the fuck is going on in my life. Everyone's acting weird around me—Chris, Lainey, Maisy. Even Amanda seemed off when I went over for my weekly tutoring session. During which Maisy barely talked to me.

Like I said, weird. And I don't know what the hell I did.

Usually, Chris wouldn't miss an opportunity to point out my faults. He'd tease me ruthlessly, sure, but I wouldn't be walking on eggshells, racking my brain for where I went wrong. Same goes for Lainey. She loves rubbing it in my face and reminding me I'm a fuckup whenever possible. So their silence means I must've done something really, really bad.

"Hey, Chris?" I ask tentatively, glancing over my shoulder. Ready for him to snap. *Again.* "Can you please tell me why everyone's treating me like I've got the plague?"

His body goes rigid under his *Lorenzo's Auto Repair* jumper. He rolls his shoulders back—a sure sign that he's livid—and turns to glare at me with pure disgust in his blue eyes.

I've never seen that there before. That hatred. Chris and I have had a lot of ups and downs through the years, but we always find our way back to each other. We always make up. It's been two days of this, of him looking like he wants to punch me in the face. Two days, and he *still* won't talk to me.

"Maybe because you fucked up," Chris replies dryly, returning to his perch beneath the hood of the Volvo in the garage.

Our Friday night shifts together are usually my favorite part of the week, but tonight the garage is liable to implode from the pressure between us.

"Yeah, I've gathered that," I snap, crossing my arms over my chest. "But I don't understand what I did."

"Then that just makes this even sadder." He shakes his head. "Think long and hard, man." I have. I've racked my brain for days and I still can't come up with anything. "Why would Lainey and I both be mad at you?"

That's the thing. My cousin and my best friend have very different moral compasses. They rarely agree with each other on anything. Except for… "Does it have something to do with Maisy?"

"Ding, ding, ding, asshole," Chris mumbles.

Unease courses through me, clenching tightly in my chest. How the hell did I upset Maisy? I haven't really talked to her since the night of my game. Since she agreed to go to the party with me. And the last few days she wouldn't even look in my direction, let alone talk to me. She retreated back into her little shell, cowering away from everyone except for Lainey and Chris.

How could I have done something so bad if I haven't even talked to her?

"What did I do to Maisy?" I ask, still thoroughly confused.

"You fucked with her, that's what you did." Chris straightens again, abandoning his work under the hood and stalking towards me. "I've been so on edge making sure she's fitting in at school, making sure the fucking Fatal Four doesn't mess with her, but it was *you* who hurt her. Not Sierra. Not the assholes on the team. It was *you*."

I clench my fists at my sides to ease some of the tension, to erase some of my anger, but it doesn't work. I hate being accused of things. I hate the loathing bite in his voice.

"I didn't do shit to her! All I did was invite her to the party!" I grit out defensively.

"Mhm. There's the start of it. Now, Colton. Think about what asking a girl to a party sounds like. Read between the lines here, pal," he says condescendingly.

"Well… I mean, it sounds like a date." I feel my face flush a bit. Yeah, it sounds romantic, but that isn't how I meant it. I just want to spend time with her. "But that isn't how I meant it. She just… she never gets out, and I wanted her to have some fun for a change."

I don't know why I'm explaining myself to him. But I can't help but wonder… is that why Lainey and Chris are so pissed at me? Because I went *there* with their best friend and foster sister? Is it a line I crossed over or something?

But then why would Maisy be ignoring me?

God, my brain hurts.

Chris folds his arms, his eyes still burning with disdain. "And if a girl thinks she's going on a date with a guy, she'd be pretty hurt to find him all buddy-buddy with another girl, wouldn't she?"

Wait, did Maisy see this as a date? I mean, I don't hate the idea. I know how I feel about her—whether I'm going to act on those feelings or not is a separate debate. But if she's pissed about seeing me with some other girl, does that mean my feelings aren't totally unreciprocated?

I mean, she blushes a lot when I'm around. But she always blushes. Her gaze lingers on me a little bit longer than it does on everyone else, but I guess I just assumed she was hyper-focused.

Holy shit, does Maisy like me?

"Colton?" Chris urges impatiently. "She'd be pretty hurt, wouldn't she?"

"Well, yeah," I admit, shrugging my shoulders. "But I wasn't '*buddy-buddy*' with any other girl."

The only girl I've entertained lately is Maisy, and that's mostly accidentally. Lewd thoughts that come when they shouldn't, slip-ups when I'm talking to her, uncontrollable smiles when I'm with her. I'm not intentionally seeking these feelings out. They're just *there*.

Come to think of it, Maisy has been the only girl in my orbit in a long time.

"Really?" Chris quirks his head, arching a brow disbelievingly. "That's not what the girls saw. Or heard."

"I'm not… I didn't…"

I don't have words to say to Chris right now. Not really. It hurts that my best friend doesn't believe me, but it hurts even worse knowing that I've upset Maisy in some way. And it drives me crazy that I can't figure out how I've hurt her, because that means I can't fix it.

I can't apologize if I don't know where I went wrong.

I can't grovel if I don't know why she's angry.

Chris shakes his head, looking a bit like a disappointed parent. "Figure it out, man. But you hurt her. Bad enough that I went home and frickin' Lizzy McAlpine was playing. Her sad music went to you. Let that one sink in."

It doesn't need to. The second the words leave his mouth, I feel like total shit.

I don't want her to be sad ever, let alone over me. Nobody is worthy of her tears. Especially not me.

"I'm really upset with you. I care about her a lot, and you hurt her. So, I'm going to go back over there and finish working so I can leave before I punch you in your big, stupid face. 'Kay?"

I nod, and decide that I'm going to figure out exactly who Maisy could have seen me with before our party "date" tomorrow night.

It's six o'clock on Saturday—aka when I'm supposed to pick Maisy up for the party—and I still can't figure out who I was seen with.

I know that that's going to be a major problem; the tension in the air between us. It'll be pretty damn hard to have a good time when I can't get her to look at me, but I'll find a way.

But my problems double when Maisy and Lainey come out of the Marshall's house. Chris is close behind them, saying something that has both girls smirking. But it doesn't even matter. The other two don't even matter.

All I can see is Maisy.

Maisy, in a turquoise corset and a matching mini skirt.

Bedazzled gold bands run across the hems of her skirt and top.

She looks like Princess Jasmine, if she fumbled the whole royalty thing and became a Playboy model.

And, judging by my cousin's Princess Ariel costume, that's exactly what the girls were going for.

My eyes rake over Maisy's body, catching on her smooth, tan skin and the gold thingy she has dangling around her perfectly curvy hips. She doesn't look real.

Holy shit, I'm in so much trouble.

Because suddenly, I want this to be a date. I want to have a reason to knock out the guys who look at her, because this is a sight that I don't want to share.

The back seat of my truck opens, and Chris helps both girls into my truck before sliding into the passenger's seat.

Silently, because he still won't talk to me, either.

The ride to Zalinsky's house is uncomfortably quiet, filled with brimming tension and a communal hatred of my guts.

The worst part is, I have training in the morning, and I'm driving, so I can't even drink to take the edge off. I have to sit and watch my friends get shit faced while I just stew in my discomfort and self-loathing.

Fun times.

When I pull into Zalinsky's driveway, Chris and Lainey dive out of the truck, like they can't escape my presence fast enough. Maisy tries to join them, but she's just a second too late.

"Maisy, wait up," I say, reaching into the backseat to curl a hand around her wrist. There's a palpable electricity that passes over my skin at the contact. And, judging by the look on her face, she feels it too.

I drop her hand like it scorched me, clearing my throat. "I know you aren't happy with me. But I'm sorry. For whatever it is I did."

"It's fine." She waves her hand dismissively, making a break for the door. "Thanks for the ride. And, uh, have fun tonight."

"Hey, Maisy?" I call out, catching her right before she slams the door. "I'm still up to keep my end of our deal. To watch over you tonight."

She shifts uncomfortably, looking at Zalinsky's front door longingly. "Uh, yeah. You do that."

And then she slams the truck door and practically bolts away from me, and I'm left even more confused than before.

Chapter 32

<u>Maisy</u>

I'm breaking all of my pre-set rules tonight. And I couldn't care less about it.

I've tried my whole life to be the perfect daughter. To be the perfect sister, role model, the perfect *parent* to the two kids I had no part in making, but every part in raising.

I've always crossed my t's and dotted my i's, but you know what? Trying to be perfect is exhausting.

Tonight, I've got no responsibilities. I'm at a party with kids my own age, in an outfit that would give a conservative adult a heart attack, sipping on a drink that I'm too young to drink but too at-ease to care too much about.

I'm doing everything I've never done before and I *love* it.

I'm not drunk, but I'm not sober, either. I'm that steady, in between buzz. Where I'm sober enough to make pretty educated decisions, but tipsy enough to have checked my social anxiety at the door. Buzzed enough to have normal teenage fun without feeling guilty about it.

Lainey and I station ourselves in the living room, sitting pressed against each other on one of the sofas. So far, we've been able to avoid Colton, which is fabulous, because I really hate the idea of having to see him right now.

I know I'm being petty. I know that neither of us are tethered to the other, and we should be able to talk to whomever we want, about whatever we want. My head knows that.

But my heart? It feels betrayed by the fact that he's out chatting with Vogue-level girls days after he asks me out. Even if it isn't a romantic outing, common courtesy would tell you not to go out and flirt with other girls.

So, yeah, I'm taking the easy way out and avoiding him. At least until I get a better grasp on my emotions. Until I push this pesky little crush out of the way for good.

"Hey there, Maisy," a familiar voice drawls, plopping down on the seat beside me.

I turn to look at the tall frame beside me. Jet-black hair, strong jaw. Overly toothy grin. An overpowering stench of Axe body spray.

"Oh. Hi, Mitchell." I smile politely, even though I don't really like the guy.

"Ugh my grandmother calls me Mitchell," he sighs, angling his body towards mine and making us feel that much closer. "Call me Mitch."

"Okay. Can I help you, Mitch?"

His grin widens, revealing two deep dimples in his cheeks. "You can, actually. Some of the guys want to play spin the bottle."

"Spin the bottle?" Lainey scoffs. "What are we, ten?" She's a little drunker than I am, with rosy-pink cheeks and a slight glaze over her green eyes. But she's taking it like a champ. I still wouldn't mess with her.

"Hey, entertainment is entertainment." Mitch shrugs.

I want to say no. This is something old Maisy definitely wouldn't do. I haven't even had my first kiss yet, so wasting it on a tipsy game of spin the bottle seems a bit insane. But then my eyes wander over Mitch's shoulder, towards the hallway. Towards Colton's deep scowl and fiery brown eyes. He looks pissed to see me talking to Mitch, and isn't that ironic? It's almost like he didn't do the exact same thing three days ago.

"You know what? Sure. Count us in." I clap a hand down on Lainey's fishnet clad leg, hitting Mitch with a sure smile. Even though I don't feel so sure about the whole thing, seeing the pure anger on Colton's stupid hypocritical face is *so* worth it.

There are five boys and five girls sitting cross-legged on Tommy Zalinsky's living room floor.

Lainey and I are joined by a girl named Sam from my biology class, as well as two other girls I recognize from school but whose names I'm blanking on.

Across from the girls are the guys; Tommy, Mitch, Vinny, Davie, and another guy who I don't recognize. I think his name is Brad? Or Brody?

Lainey goes first, and although she didn't love the idea of this game before, she seems pretty content when the empty beer bottle lands on a nervous looking Tommy.

"Pucker up, Zalinsky." She grins devilishly, crossing the circle of people and kneeling right in front of him.

"She's been tormenting the poor guy since elementary school," Vinny whispers, filling me in on why Tommy looks like he's about to cry. "He doesn't have the same feelings, though." Tommy leans in and kisses Lainey, but instead of breaking apart immediately like everyone expected, Tommy laces his hands in Lainey's curly red hair, deepening their kiss. "Or at least I thought he didn't." Vinny stares at his friend in awe.

Chuckling, I pick up the bottle for my turn. Leave it to Lainey to land a kiss with her childhood crush during a game of spin the bottle she didn't even want to play.

Before I can take my turn, I hear heavy footsteps behind me. A low voice clearing their throat.

I don't even have to turn around to see who's behind me, because Davie outs him for me. "Oh, hey, Bossman. Are you gonna join the game?" he asks.

"No, thanks," Colton replies breezily. "I need to talk to Maisy." This time I do swivel around to look at him. "Can you come outside with me really quickly?"

He asks politely, but I can hear the anger in his voice. I can see the impatience swimming in his irises. Normally, I'd play along and go with him. But apparently alcohol makes me defiant.

"I'm okay. Thanks."

Colton sighs, tucking his hands in his sweatpants pockets. "Please, Maisy?"

I'm weaker than I thought, because after hearing his pleading tone, I find myself standing to my feet. Mostly so we don't make a scene. But also because even though I'm furious with him, that note of desperation in his voice does something to me.

I stand slowly, to avoid a wardrobe malfunction. But I don't miss the way Colton's face sags in relief.

I'm following him, but it doesn't make me any less upset with him.

"What's up?" I ask coldly the second we're alone on the porch.

Tommy's back deck is screened in, and the cold October air is seeping into the small space, sending goosebumps erupting over my bare skin. I fight the urge to shudder, though. I need the upper hand here, and shivering like a wimp won't give me that.

"What's up?" Colton mocks, his voice taking on an angry note. Anger and disbelief. "You were about to kiss one of our friends, that's what's up."

"And?"

"And that's not like you, Maisy," he says, gentler this time. "I made a promise to keep you in line, remember?"

I can't help but scoff. "Yeah, thanks, but I'm not drunk. I can handle myself." He cocks an eyebrow at me, as if he's saying, *can you*? "What? Maybe I wanted to kiss someone tonight."

"And is that person Davie, Vinny, Brody, or Zalinsky?" he asks accusingly. "Because you've never given any of them a second glance. And I know you sure as shit don't want to kiss Mitch the Bitch. He makes you uncomfortable."

He's not wrong. That first party, when he tried to talk to Lainey and I and that day at school… I'm not Mitch's biggest fan, but what do I know about him? I obviously can't trust my instincts about people. I've been wrong about a person's character before.

Exhibit A; Colton.

But I never told Colton any of that. I didn't even tell Chris any of that. So how the hell does Colton know about the prickly feeling I get whenever Mitch is around?

"You're pretty easy to read, Maisy. I see the way you clam up when he's around. And it's not the same way you clam up when I'm around." Oh God. He's noticed? "No, it's a totally different type of nerves, isn't it?"

"I don't know what you're talking about." I cross my arms over my chest, partially to stay warm, and partially to feed into my confused act.

"Yeah, I think you do. And it isn't Mitch you want to kiss, is it?" He takes a step closer to me, and even though butterflies erupt in my stomach, I don't move an inch. "It isn't the others, is it?" He tucks a stray piece of hair behind my ear, smirking to himself like the cocky jerk he is. "It's me you want to kiss, isn't it?"

Somehow, I push past the lump of nerves in my throat and manage a coherent sentence. "Why did you really pull me out here?"

Colton chuckles darkly, humor lighting up his eyes, visible even in the dimly lit patio. "I said I'd look after you, and I think you'll seriously regret kissing any one of those guys. You're welcome." He steps closer, filling the little space between us so we're all but pressed together. "But also? The thought of watching you kiss one of my friends makes me really fucking angry. And the thought of watching you kiss Mitch?" He shakes his head. "That just makes me homicidal."

I can't think clearly with him this close to me. I can't even breathe correctly. I think there's a lack of oxygen in this tiny bubble we seem to exist in.

But I have enough strength left in me to feel a tiny bit hurt by his actions the other day. A tiny bit of pettiness left, too.

"I didn't realize you had room in your schedule to worry about two girls."

Colton takes a step back, raking a hand through his wavy brown hair with a sigh. I should be grateful for the extra space between us. Maybe I can think clearer now.

Instead, I find myself missing the feeling of him that close to me. Missing his extra body heat.

"Yeah, can you explain that one to me? Everyone's telling me that I was all suspicious with another girl, but I don't... I haven't..."

He looks genuinely confused, and that makes *me* confused. Can he really not remember three days ago? Does he flirt with so many girls that he can't keep up?

I'm tired of playing cat and mouse with him. I'm tired of having my feelings hurt over a guy who very clearly can't see the error of his ways.

If he needs it spelled out for him, so be it.

"The mall food court? Really pretty blonde girl? Agreement that it's been '*way too long*'?" I don't miss the bitterness in my tone. I also don't miss the hurt that prickles in my chest.

Colton's brown eyes remain clouded with confusion for a moment, his face scrunched as he deciphers my words. And then, "Wait. This entire thing was about *Morgan*?!"

I sag my shoulders, officially giving up on my grudge. "If Morgan was the girl you were flirting with, then yeah. I know I don't have a right to feel jealous. I know that, okay? But... you asked me to this party, then you talked to her like that... I was just confused. And hurt."

I have to admit, it feels good to be honest. My chest feels a little bit lighter.

But then Colton starts laughing. Like, actually chuckling. "For fuck's sake, Maisy. I'm not interested in Morgan, and she's not interested in me."

"That isn't what it seemed like."

"Yeah?" He quirks his head before planting one of his hands on either of my shoulders and turning me towards the window that peeks into the living room. "She look familiar?" The blonde girl from the mall—Morgan, I guess—is sitting on the couch, mid-make out with an equally gorgeous brunette girl. "Yeah. That's her girlfriend, Tammy. Trust me, I'm the last person she'd be flirting with." He spins me back to face him, his eyes searching my face. "She's Zalinsky's sister. She said it's been too long since she's seen me because I used to come over here all the time. Before training took off. And, well, the party's at her house, so..."

Yeah, it's official. I'm an idiot.

A jealous, assumption-making idiot.

"Colton… I'm sorry." I let out a long exhale, wishing I could melt into the floorboards. "I was kind of a jealous bitch, and I had no right to be."

"It's okay. I was a jealous bitch tonight, too. Stopping you from kissing those guys in there and all." Colton shrugs, not looking particularly sorry about his actions. "For the record, I'd be pissed if the roles were reversed. If I asked you out and you were flirting with a different guy. But in the future, just ask me, yeah? I'd never play you like that, Maisy."

I nod, not trusting myself to say the right thing.

"I'm sure I'll fuck up again," Colton continues. "I kind of do it a lot. But I'd never hurt you on purpose, okay? So just ask me. Before we waste two days being angry at each other." He blows out a sigh, a ghost of a smile dancing across his lips. "I mean, think of all of the horror movies we could've watched in two days."

I nod again. It seems to be the only thing I'm capable of doing right now.

It makes so much sense, and now I feel super guilty for holding a grudge against him. For dragging Chris and Lainey into it, too.

Colton's been nothing but sweet since the day I moved into the Marshall house, and how do I thank him? By stirring up a bunch of drama that makes everyone's lives awkward as hell for days on end.

Typical.

"Are we good?" he asks, eyeing me skeptically. "You and me?"

I'm definitely "good" with him; it's me I'm having a hard time with right now. But he doesn't need to know that, and I've already done a lovely job of putting him through hell, so I just nod and say, "Yeah. We're good."

Chapter 33

<u>Colton</u>

How does sainthood work? Are you nominated, or can anyone apply?

I think I deserve a spot next to the greats. I had the girl I've been fantasizing about for months pressed up against me on Zalinsky's dim-lit patio, and I didn't make a move. Not even a kiss. Even though I wanted to.

And, holy hell, I *really* wanted to.

I didn't make a move on Maisy for a few reasons. My hesitation was mostly because she's been drinking. It was also partially because I don't want to lead her on.

I threw that bit about her being flustered in there as bait. Sure, I have my speculations, especially after my chat with Chris last night, but Maisy's kind of an awkward person. I considered the fact that she might not like me, and she's all quiet and fidgety around me because I make her uncomfortable.

But when I brought it up tonight, she didn't deny it. She didn't correct me when I said she had feelings for me.

I tell myself it's because she's drunk. Or maybe she didn't hear that part of my spiel.

Unlikely.

I don't know how I feel about it, to be honest. It was easy to ignore my feelings for her when I thought they weren't reciprocated. It was creepy to stare at her, wrong to text her, weird to spend extra time with her. Because she didn't feel the same way.

Except that now she does. *Might.* But I don't know where that leaves us, exactly.

I still don't have time for a girlfriend. She's still in a pretty vulnerable position. She's still basically Chris's sister.

I can't just brush that all away anymore, though. Not when it's her heart on the line, too.

It's a conversation for another day, though. Tonight, Maisy's too tipsy to have any really meaningful discussions.

The alcohol makes her feisty, and in a way, I'm thankful for it. I like seeing all of the different sides of her. And the side that wants to rip my head off? Might just be my favorite.

Maybe I'm a masochist.

Probably.

"You ready to go home?" I ask her. She's been staring at the patio door for the last few minutes, lost in her own little world. "We can go grab the others and make a break for it, if you'd like."

Her whiskey eyes dance across my face, like she's trying to read my expression. "You're not having fun?"

"Not really," I say honestly. "I stopped having fun when Mitch the Bitch tried to trick you into kissing him."

Slimy bastard. I hated him before, but now I fucking *loathe* the guy. Yeah, he's a dirty player on the ice, and he's privileged and has a massive ego, but now he tries to coerce half-drunk girls to kiss him?

I know the guy. I know that's what he was getting at with his whole spin the bottle idea. He's had his eye on Maisy for weeks, and now that he knows I'm interested, he's upping his game.

It's an asshole move to come onto someone's date. But it's a whole other thing, knowing someone's uncomfortable around you but forcing yourself on them, anyway. Waiting until she's drunk to make a move.

I want to kill him. Unfortunately, the U18 league frowns upon premeditated manslaughter, and they also don't condone fights, so I'll have to wait until we're on the ice. But I'll be strategic. I'll fuck him up and take no punishment for it.

I just have to wait.

I notice Maisy shiver, which I'm surprised she was able to suppress until now. She doesn't have much on—a fact I'm trying really hard to ignore—and it's pretty cold out here.

Wordlessly, I shrug off my hoodie. I've always run warm, anyway.

She eyes me curiously. "How are you hot right now?"

"I'm not hot," I say, closing some of the distance I had put between us. "You're cold."

"No, I'm fine," she lies, literally shivering as she says it. I hate the word *fine*, especially coming from girls.

Pro tip? When they say, "*I'm fine*", ninety percent of the time they are, in fact, not fine.

I hold my hoodie out to her, but she shakes her head. I can see the goosebumps on her arms, the slight chatter of her teeth. I'm not an idiot.

But I know her, and she's never going to accept my hoodie when she knows it means that I'll be a little cold.
Selfless girl she is and all.

With a sigh, I place the hoodie over her head. "Arms up," I instruct, tugging the fabric down. She puts her arms in the sleeves and the rest of the hoodie falls down, the hem resting at her mid-thighs.

Jesus, she's tiny.

She looks fabulous in my clothes, though.

"Thank you," she mumbles, looking at me with wide eyes. "Wait. Is that your costume?" Her eyes trail over my upper body and over the Raven's jersey I'm wearing. I give her a spin, mimicking a model so she can see my name and number on the back. "It's just your jersey. That's boring."

"No. It's part of a bigger costume."

She cocks a disbelieving brow at me. "And what's the bigger costume?"

I can't help but smirk. "I'm a sexy hockey player."

Never mind that I did nothing but throw on a practice jersey and sweatpants. It's unoriginal as hell, but my answer makes Maisy laugh one of her rare laughs.

God, I love that noise.

"How humble of you," she says between chuckles.

"I like to think that I'm self-aware."

Her grin widens. "Of course you do."

My eyes wander down her toned thighs, following the hem of my hoodie. It's dangerous territory to be, so I rake my gaze back up, praying that she hadn't caught on to the way I was not-so-discreetly checking her out.

"So, Maisy." I pause to clear my suddenly gravelly voice. "You ready to grab the others and go?"

She nods, and I thank God for the excuse that gets me out of the moonlit porch with the only girl who has the power to screw with my head like this.

Two days later, Maisy and I are alone for another "tutoring session."

I feel like I'm going to have to fess up eventually, but I'm also afraid of her reaction when she finds out I've been feigning stupid for the last month to get her to talk to me.

If you open a dictionary, flip to the p's, and look for *pathetic*, you'll find my picture right next to the definition.

I still have another two months before I take the SATs, but I've upped my sessions with Maisy to three times a week. Because, God help me, I'm so horrible at English.

"So, basically, you need to think about emphasis," she explains, her eyes alight with excitement. She gets this way when we talk about reading. It's adorable. "Like, if you were saying the sentence out loud, where would you have to put the most stress to get your point across?"

Yeah, I get it. I pretend to think about it for a minute, but really, I'm just watching the way her whiskey eyes stare back at me encouragingly. I could probably tell her I forgot how to spell and she'd still look at me like this. Like I have all the potential in the world.

"I think I get it," I drawl, stretching my legs out in front of me on her perfectly made bed. "Like, if you were to say, 'Colton is *hot*'," I add extra emphasis to the hot, popping my t. "Instead of 'Colton is hot', it'd show that you think I'm really attractive, not just mediocre hot."

She rolls her eyes at my wolfish grin. I love how easy it is to get a rise out of her. "God. I mean, technically your answer is right for that example, but I would *never* say that."

"Why not?" I let my face fall, pretending to be hurt. "You don't think I'm hot?"

She blushes an endearing shade of strawberry red, but keeps her verbal game strong. "You and I both know the answer to that, Colt," she sighs.

"That wasn't a no."

"It wasn't a yes, either."

"So, you *do* think I'm hot," I tease, expertly applying her little lesson on emphasis.

She cocks a brow at me in challenge. "I think *you* think you're hot."

Maisy's right: she'd never admit she's attracted to me outright. That's why it's so fun to flirt with her. I get to see her cheeks flush pink, get to see the witty side of her I love so much.

I know it's probably a dick move to mess with her like this, but I can't help myself. I want her to admit it to me sober. I want to hear her say that she wants me as much as I want her.

I'm still hesitant to do anything with Maisy, but I know that if I hear her say it out loud—if I hear her admit that she wants me—my last resolve will dissolve like salt in water.

Honestly, the more time I spend with her, the less my reasons for staying away from her make sense.

My time commitments? I'm already here three days a week.

Her vulnerability? I've never seen her laugh the way she does when it's just the two of us.

Not knowing her? I've heard more stories these last few weeks than I know what to do with. I'm suspiciously lacking in knowledge about the specifics of why she's in foster care, but I've learned pretty much everything else about her.

And as far as Chris goes… that's a battle I can handle.

Sure, he might be pissed off, but he'll get over it eventually.

The only thing standing between us now is her.

Chapter 34

<u>Maisy</u>

How does that one children's book go? 'Twas the night before Christmas and all through the house… blah blah blah.

'Twas the night before Thanksgiving, and all through the house, not a creature is stirring, except for Chris and I. We are very much stirring.

We've done this every night before bed. We each find a song that reminds us of each other and we take turns playing them from our respective bedrooms.

The walls separating our rooms are extremely thin, so we could probably play without the use of our adjoining vent. But it's more fun this way. Plus, we don't have to worry about waking up my siblings or Tim and Amanda downstairs.

Chris goes first, and the notes of Sia's *Elastic Heart* flood into my room. And honestly, props to him for finding such a match. Though I find the whole *"you won't see me vulnerable"* part ironic, because if anybody in my life was going to see me vulnerable, it'd be Chris.

He's the first—and only—person I've ever fully trusted. I can't even really explain it, other than that Chris is the brother that I never got to have. From the moment CJ was born, I was the mother figure. The caretaker. And I love him. I truly do. I'd take a bullet for him, no questions asked. But the responsibility I had in raising him damaged the typical sibling bond we could have had. And I mourned that loss, the loss of innocence.

But I've gotten it back. With Chris.

He's my brother by every definition of the word.

Yeah, he's an unserious idiot half of the time, but that's what I need. A distraction from the dark pit in my mind. A laugh when everything is crumbling down around me. And for the first time in my life, I know that I'm not alone. That it wouldn't matter what time it was, or how far apart we were, if I needed him, he'd be there.

I think this is what family feels like.

When his song dies down and it's my turn, I sit cross-legged over the vent with my phone volume turned up and pressed to the grates of the vent.

And then I sit in silence for two minutes and thirty-two seconds while Jake Banfield's *Thank You for Being You* blasts from my phone's speaker.

I felt like it did a pretty good job of summing up how I feel about him. Of acknowledging how much he's done for me. I don't think the transition from the Terrace to the Marshall's house would have been half as easy if he wasn't here.

It blows my mind that I was worried about how he'd handle our presence in the beginning. Now, I can't imagine this house without him.

There's silence after the song ends, but that's not abnormal. We usually go right to sleep after our little song exchange.

What *is* abnormal is the way my door swings open ten seconds later.

I stand abruptly and turn towards the doorway, equal parts confused and curious. Whoever it is didn't knock. People *always* knock.

Before I can even address him, Chris is rapidly closing the space between us in long strides. He launches himself at me, tucking me into a bear hug. He wraps his arms tightly around me, with one hand pressing my head to his chest, his head resting against mine.

I hug him back just as tightly.

Every time I think he's about to let go, he squeezes me tighter. And I don't oppose. I didn't realize how badly I needed this. How much I needed a hug.

And then he sniffles. Clears his throat. And steps away.

"God, why'd you have to make me cry, Maisy Mae?" he asks, wiping at his leaky eyes. "Not cool."

"I'm sorry," I chuckle, choking back tears of my own. "I didn't mean to. I just… You do a lot for me. Look out for me a lot, and I don't think I say thank you enough."

"You don't have to. That's what siblings do." He's still crying a little bit, his voice all garbled from his tears. "At least I think it is. I've never had siblings before. But you know what, Maisy?"

"What?"

His blue eyes shine with his unshed tears. "You're more of a sister than I've ever had. And I think you're a pretty good one."

I can't hide my smile. Honestly, I don't even try to. "You're a pretty good brother, Chris." Now *I'm* crying, and it's ugly, but I don't have to worry about him running away. Not now, or ever. "And I'm really lucky to have you."

He pulls me into another hug and we just stand there, teary-eyed and laughing at ourselves for crying. There have been so many ups and downs these past three months, but we've held it together. For the most part. But now we're both broken down crying because we love each other like blood.

I'll take it, though. Because the big blonde ape crying into my silk PJ top just so happens to be one of my favorite people.

Chris and I stay up most of the night talking. He gives me fair warnings about all of his relatives that will be coming over for Thanksgiving dinner. I'm a little nervous, to be honest.

I've never had a real Thanksgiving before.

And the Marshall's extended family… What if they don't like me? Or—oh God—what if CJ says something obscene?

"Ok, let's recap," Chris says, rubbing his hands together.

Chris—bless his soul—put pictures of each relative who will be in attendance tonight on my desk. He's told me the must-know facts about each and every one of them.

He points to each picture, and I recall everything he's told me about them.

There's Grandma Jolene, the crazy cat lady who somehow loses her teeth at every single Thanksgiving. Then there's Grandpa

Phil, who cracks a dirty joke at every possible opportunity. They're Amanda's parents.

Then, there's Tim's mother, Sandy, who is materialistic as hell. Apparently, she has so much money that she "could use Benjamins as toilet paper." Chris's words, not mine. The final attendants are Tim's sister, Megan, and her new baby.

The Marshalls are really excited about the baby part. He's only seven weeks old, and nobody's gotten to meet him yet. So, it's his Marshall family debut.

Just like my siblings and I.

"Chin up, Maisy Mae. It's Ryder's first family Thanksgiving, too," Chris goads, poking me in the ribs.

"Yeah, because that's the same thing." I roll my eyes. "They're obligated to like the baby. He's a *baby*." Babies are cute. Stuttering, socially awkward teenage girls?

Not cute.

"And you're you. CJ is CJ, and Nat is Nat." Chris shrugs his shoulders, like the point is moot. "You're all great in your own ways. Everyone is going to love you."

"Do you promise?" I ask, my voice dripping with insecurity.

"Yeah, Maisy Mae. I promise."

Megan is the first to arrive, with baby Ryder in tow. Honestly, props to her. I remember how hard it was getting out of the house with a baby. And not only did she get out of the house on time, she got here way earlier than the others.

Even if I hadn't known she was Tim's younger sister, I could've guessed just by looking at her. She's got the same face shape, the same blue eyes, the same smile. She looks a bit flustered, but considering she's only a few weeks into single motherhood, I can't say I blame her.

"Auntie Meg!" Chris exclaims, barreling down the staircase. I'm close behind him, but I'm taking the steps a bit more tentatively. I can feel the nerves threatening to eat away at my insides.

I've never been good with new people—or people in general—but I've been trying really hard to come out of my shell. It's a lot easier when you're not facing constant backlash or a fear of wrath. I haven't teetered on the edge of overbearing anxiety in weeks. But right now, thinking about meeting a whole group of new "family" members, I'm more than a little nervous.

CJ, though, has no such nerves. "Hello." He smiles his full, toothless smile, waving politely at Meg as she shrugs off her coat. "I'm CJ."

"Well, hello there, CJ." Megan smiles down at my brother, her blue eyes shining. "I'm Megan."

"Meggy!" Tim exclaims, walking into the foyer with his arms out. "How's my favorite sister?" He wraps her in a tight hug before stepping away and glancing down at the carrier holding his first—and only—nephew.

"I'm your only sister, Timothy," Meg chuckles, grinning up at her brother with nothing but pure love in her expression.

After a few tight embraces, the adults take turns holding the tiny baby. But even from my perch on the other side of the foyer, I can see the tension in Meg's shoulders. The tiredness in her eyes.

"Chris," I whisper-hiss, nudging his ribcage with my elbows. He stares down at me, his eyebrows furrowed together. "She's burnt out."

He looks at me, his blue eyes shining with confusion. "She's smiling, though," he whispers back, studying his aunt.

Yeah, she is. But I've been there, too. Taking care of a baby isn't lightwork. It's draining as hell, especially doing it all alone. "Her smile doesn't meet her eyes," I explain sadly. "Look at the tension in her shoulders. The bags under her eyes."

She looks just like I did after the roughest nights.

"Hey, Auntie Meg?" Chris saunters towards the adults, who are standing in the sitting room adjacent to the foyer. "Can I take the baby?"

Relief flashes in her eyes, and I can tell by Chris's tightened smile that he notices it. "Oh, Chris, I can't ask you to do that. I'm sure you have plenty to do without having to babysit…"

"Nonsense." He waggles his eyebrows, holding his arms out and lowering his voice. "Give me the child."

Meg chuckles, shaking her head at her nephew's antics. Chris scoops the baby into his arms, cradling him close to his chest. He's so big, Ryder kind of disappears in his arms. But he's so gentle with the baby, he stares at him with so much love, it makes me smile.

He's so adorably good with kids. Probably because he's really just a big kid himself.

"I'm gonna steal your kid now. Yell up if you want him back." Chris comes back to join me in the foyer, and gestures with his head for me to follow him up the stairs.

When we're halfway upstairs, we hear the adults' muffled voices from the living room.

"I haven't let him out of my sight since he was born," Megan admits, her voice low. But not low enough—I have to grip the railing to stop myself from crashing into Chris's back when he stops short. "I'm kind of scared."

"It's alright, Meggy," Tim says, his voice infinitely comforting. "Chris may be helpless, but Maisy's a great girl. Raised those two kids herself and did a better job parenting them than some of the adults I know. She'll keep your idiot nephew in line."

I feel my heart swell in my chest. I've never had someone outwardly applaud me like that before. I let Tim's words settle into my chest, relishing the way his support and approval makes me feel.

"Rude," Chris scoffs, stomping the rest of the way up the staircase and into my room. "I am *not* helpless."

"Pick your battles, Chris," I chuckle, clicking my door shut behind us.

"Do you want to hold him?" Chris asks, rocking Ryder in his big arms. "I want to go check on Nattie. I feel like I'm cheating on her right now."

I laugh at him. This baby may be his cousin, but Nat is *his* baby. He loves that little girl with his whole heart.

She's napping before everyone gets here, because we didn't want to risk her being cranky for everyone.

I nod and take the baby from Chris, cradling him in my arms as I make my way towards my bed. I sit with my back against the headboard, smiling at the loving gleam in Chris's eyes as he stares back at us from the doorway.

When he wanders off towards the nursery, I glance down at the sleeping baby in my arms. It brings back a lot of memories, sitting here like this.

Except this time, I'm not a scared eight-year-old little girl. I'm not begging him to stop crying, choking the words out through my own tears. I'm not overwhelmed by the tasks at hand, or worried about how I'm going to be able to feed him.

I can just sit here and cuddle a cute baby. It's actually kind of nice.

Chris saunters back into the room a little while later and settles on the bed beside me, staring down at the little bundle in my arms.

"I can't believe it's real." He shakes his head in disbelief. "Like, I've known Aunt Meg my whole life and then all of the sudden she just spawns him? Like, now he's just *here*?"

He stares at Ryder in wonder for a few moments longer, before his expression contorts into what I call his "idea face." "Wait…" Chris's eyes sparkle with mischief. "Set the baby in my lap, and then go hide in the corner."

I open my mouth to ask him what the hell he's planning, but then I think better of it. Sometimes it's better to stay curious when it comes to Chris and his ideas.

I set baby Ryder in his lap and sit at my desk chair, staring inquisitively at my foster brother.

He pulls out his phone, tapping the screen before holding it up to his face. The phone starts ringing, and I start to ask who he's calling, but he holds his pointer finger up to his mouth as if to shush me.

"Yo," a familiar voice says. "What's up?"

"Holy shit, Colton," Chris says, his voice sounding legitimately panicked. "This is bad. It's so fucking bad, man."

"What is?" Colt asks, his voice taking on a serious note. He sounds panicked when he says, "Chris, what the hell is happening?"

"Remember that girl I was with last year? Around Christmas?" Colton responds with a confused *yes.* "Well, uh, her birth control must've failed." He scratches the back of his neck awkwardly. God, he's a really good actor. He's got discomfort written clear across his face.

He aims the camera down towards his lap, giving Colton a perfect view of baby Ryder. "Congratulations, you're the godfather."

I press my fist to my mouth to smother my chuckle. A beat of silence passes. And then—

"WHAT THE FUCK!" Colton exclaims. "You have a whole fucking kid and didn't know the whole goddamn pregnancy!?"

Chris's expression sombers, his head dropping in feign shame. "I swear to God, dude, I just got the call. Girl dropped her off at my door and was just like… surprise!" He rakes a hand through his hair in distress.

"Who the *FUCK* would trust you with a baby?"

"My parents weren't home," Chris replies instantly. It's kind of impressive how much of this he's able to make up on the spot. "I had to take her, C. My parents don't even know yet. I don't know what to do, man."

Chris shuffles, leaning so his face is out of the view of the camera to grin and wink at me. I shake my head, amused by his idiocy.

"You're sure it's yours?" Colt asks skeptically. Chris nods. "Okay, okay, let's think about this logistically. Other guys our age have kids. It isn't ideal, but I mean…" his voice trails off. Leave it to Colton to try to think about this with a level head.

"You know," Chris muses, staring down at the baby with a conflicted look on his face. "Her name is kind of pretty. It's April."

"Yeah, that is a nice name," Colton agrees wistfully.

"Her middle name is Fools." His face breaks out in a shit-eating grin. "APRIL FOOLS, YOU GULLIBLE DUMBASS!"

His exclamation wakes baby Ryder, who starts crying. I swoop in from the desk, chuckling as I pick up the baby and cradle him against my chest. I step into view of the camera, smiling at a very puzzled looking Colton. "Hi, Colton."

His forehead wrinkles in confusion as he stares back at me, dumbfounded. "I'm really fucking confused right now, but, uh, hey, Maisy." I step out of the shot of the camera and he goes right back to interrogating Chris. "So, you aren't a daddy?"

"I'm your daddy," Chris shoots back instantly.

"Please, shut up," Colton sighs, not engaging in his best friend's antics. "Whose baby is that? And why the hell are you and Maisy conspiring against me?"

"He's my cousin, Ryder. Auntie Meg's baby. And to answer your second question, it's because she likes me more than you."

Yeah, I like Chris a lot. But in a very, *very* different way than I like Colton. I don't bring that up, though. It doesn't seem like a good time.

"You're a jackass, Christopher. An absolute jackass," Colton sighs disapprovingly. "But I'm really glad you aren't a jackass with a baby."

Chapter 35

<u>Maisy</u>

I now understand why Tim and Amanda are, well, Tim and Amanda.

I never met my own grandparents. After Mom fell pregnant with me, her parents pushed her away. Last I knew they were living somewhere in Florida. My father didn't want me, and I honestly don't even know if his family knows I exist.

But Jolene and Phil… they're what I always imagined grandparents would be like. Jolene is a tiny woman—even tinier than her daughter—with curly silver hair and kind brown eyes. Phil's a bit taller, but still far shorter than Tim and Chris, with thick glasses and a flashy smile.

Phil has regaled us all with his stories from Vietnam, while Jolene has discussed the latest adventures of her four cats with anyone who would listen. It's nice to just talk with them. To listen to their stories and hear the way everyone laughs together.

But the best part? Neither one of them even blinked an eye at the kids or I. Jolene hugged her grandson, with a big smack of a kiss on the cheek, and then she moved right down the line to do the exact same to me. And then to CJ. And then she did the whole grandma-cheek-pinch thing to Nat.

It was like we had known her forever. Like we were *hers*.

But the party *really* starts when Sandy Marshall walks through the giant entrance to the Marshall house.
She's wearing a pretty purple sweater and a *lot* of jewelry. Big gold hoops and a drooping gold necklace. Both wrists stacked with bracelets, most of her fingers decked out in rings, her wispy blonde hair fanning her face.

Chris says she would never admit it, but the woman has *totally* seen a few Botox injections. She looks five years older than her children, if that.

The second she makes it through the elegant foyer, her excited shriek pierces all of our ears. "Where are my new grandbabies!?" she exclaims.

"Brace yourself," Chris warns me, his voice a low whisper. He turns back to a normal volume as he turns to face his grandmother. "Grandma Sandy!" He meets the eager old woman with a gentle hug. "How are you?"

"Chrissy, let me see them!" She bats her grandson away, pushing through the foyer towards the sitting room where CJ and I are lingering. Nat's playing with some blocks on the floor, but when Grandma Sandy comes through the doorway, she sits up, staring curiously at the new face.

"Oh my goodness!" She cups two bony hands over her mouth, her blue eyes welling with tears. "Aren't you all just *precious*?"

"Oh Jesus," Tim mumbles, his eyes widening when he sees his mother bolt for my baby sister. "Mom, remember what we said. *Boundaries*."

Completely ignoring her son's reminder, Grandma Sandy scoops up a confused looking Nat, holding her up like she's Simba from The Lion King. "Look at that smile! Oh, aren't you just the cutest thing *ever*!"

Nat giggles. Actually *giggles*. A few months ago, she would've screamed her head off until her throat started bleeding if a stranger tried to touch her. But now? She claps her slobbery hands and smiles at the strange old lady hoisting her into the air.

Grandma Sandy sets Nat down and moves for my brother next. "Oh my! Aren't you just a handsome little guy!" she exclaims, ruffling CJ's curls. "Come give Granny a hug!"

He looks up at me with wide green eyes, his face painted in a *WTF* expression. I just shrug. No amount of warning from Chris could've prepared me for the amount of energy this woman possesses. She seems like a lot of fun, but it's also kind of a lot to take in all at once.

CJ gives in and steps tentatively towards the old woman, giving her a hesitant hug.

And then it's my turn.

"Goodness, aren't you gorgeous!" She cocks her head, studying me carefully. "Timmy! Timmy, I should call in a favor with Mark. Remember Mark? From Teen Vogue? Goodness, this face belongs on the front of a magazine!"

And then she bear hugs me. Seriously, I think she might have cracked a rib or two. Whoever said that all old people are frail and weak clearly never got the life squeezed out of them by Sandy Marshall. This woman has an iron grip.

"It's really great to meet you," I say, my voice coming out strained. It's kind of hard to breathe, what with the death grip cutting off my air supply and all.

"Gran, careful," Chris chuckles, coming up behind her and setting a hand on one of her thin shoulders. "You're gonna suffocate the girl."

Grandma Sandy loosens her grip—albeit reluctantly— and takes a step back. She brushes her hands down her fancy white pants before strutting back towards her purse.

"Okay, who wants presents?" I turn to look at Chris curiously. We hadn't prepared for *this*.

I was nervous enough about remembering names and not oversharing when they inevitably asked me questions. I was nervous enough about having to insert myself into their already tight-knit family circle. There's no way in hell I can add accepting a present from this woman into the equation.

Chris comes to stand near me, his signature care-free smile curling his lips. He drops his voice to a low whisper, so that only the two of us can hear what he's saying. "I probably should have warned you. This woman will find any excuse to spoil her grandkids rotten."

I try to swallow past the ball of nerves in my throat. "But I'm not her grandkid."

"Yeah, you and I both know that isn't true. You're family, Maisy Mae. So smile, feed into her craziness, and don't stress. Trust me, stressing won't change this woman's mind."

"Okay, so for you, Chrissy." She digs in her gigantic purse for a moment before pulling out something flat and rectangular.

Chris beams like a kid on Christmas as he takes the PlayStation game from his grandmother. "Sweet! Thank you, Grandma."

"And for you, CJ and Natalia." She holds out an expensive looking Lego set and a fluffy stuffed dog to each of my respective siblings.

CJ squeals—literally *squeals*—with excitement. "Oh my goodness! Thank you so much Misses… I mean, uh…" He looks up at Chris, wide-eyed with panic. Out of the corner of my eye, I see Chris mouth the word *Grandma*. My brother looks uncertain, but still says, "Um, Grandma. Thank you."

"Oh of course, sweetie." She turns to face me, an earnest smile curling her lipstick-clad lips. "And Maisy, yours is my personal favorite." She pulls a small jewelry box from her bag and sets it in my hand.

I tentatively crack the box open, and my breath promptly leaves my lungs. It's a gorgeous golden teardrop necklace that looks like it costs more than my entire wardrobe combined.

Discomfort swirls in my stomach at the gesture. I don't feel comfortable accepting the gift, but I know what Chris said about arguing with Grandma Sandy. Namely that it's useless.

"Thank you very much, Grandma Sandy," I say politely, smiling past my uneasiness. "It's gorgeous."
"Oh, it's so nice to have a girl to buy for. I always wanted a granddaughter," she muses, sighing wistfully.

"What, was I not enough for you?" Chris quips, feigning hurt. "That stings, Gran."

"Oh, nonsense," Grandma Sandy says with a flippant wave of her hand. "You know you're my little bug. But I can't exactly take you makeup shopping, now, can I?"

"Maybe I'd like to look pretty." Chris shrugs, smirking devilishly.

Amanda calls us into the dining room then, interrupting the insane conversation occurring in the sitting room.

The elegant oak wood table is scattered with various plates and bowls. It's more food than I've ever seen in one place, and I'm not sure where to start.

Thanksgiving always consisted of packaged deli meat that was discounted because it was too close to the expiration date and powdered mashed potatoes. Now, I've got my pick of different pies, a gorgeous looking turkey, various vegetables, cheesy potatoes, bowls upon bowls of mashed potatoes and gravy, and a tray of stuffing that makes my mouth water.

I'm paralyzed by indecision. I don't know what to do. Where to start. How much is too much to take.

Chris must sense how overwhelming this culinary freedom is to me, because he sets his own plate down at his table setting and smiles softly down at me. He takes my plate from my hands and drags me towards the start of the food "line", where everyone is gathered around the table.

He doesn't laugh at me or ridicule me. He just gestures towards the spread of food. "Just tell me yes or no, okay, Maisy Mae?" I nod. "Don't worry. I've got you."

He then proceeds to ask me about each individual dish—all twenty of them—without so much as an impatient huff. He isn't worried about his food getting cold, or the odd looks we're getting from some of the relatives that don't know me as well. He just wants to help me.

That pretty much sums up who Chris is as a person.

When we've finished putting my plate together, we plop back into our seats. Once we're settled in, Tim starts reciting things he's grateful for from his perch at the head of the table.

Chris warned me about this, and I'm grateful for that. It gave me extra time to think about what I wanted to say, because we both knew that I'd freeze up if I had to make a quick, on-the-spot speech.

Let's be honest; I'll probably freeze up anyway.

When the chain of gratitude reaches Chris, he clears his throat dramatically. "I'm grateful for my family, and hockey, and Playboy…" Amanda shoots him a warning glance, and he holds his hands up in self-defense. "Kidding, kidding. I'm thankful for my parents and their stupidly huge hearts, because without them, I would never have met these three kids. You guys are like the siblings I never got to have, so, um, thanks for living with us."

That makes the adults smile, and it makes something warm settle in my chest. I never had a reason to believe that Chris didn't like our presence in his home, but it's still nice to hear it out loud.

Eight heads turn to look at me, and I realize that I'm next in our little circle of gratitude.

I'd usually freeze. Go on a little internal spiral and freak myself out about the odds of me screwing up or saying the wrong thing. But these people have done so much for me that I have to at least *try*.

"Um, I… I, uh…" Chris's fingers interlace with mine, and he gives my hand a tight, reassuring squeeze. I inhale deeply and exhale a calming breath. "I'm really bad at this kind of thing," I admit, feeling my nerves eat away at my stomach. "But, um, I'm grateful for the Marshalls. All of them. I've never… I mean, I've always had to be the adult. I've never had even a fraction of the support I have here.

"This is the only place I've ever felt really, truly welcome. And I guess I could list off all of the tangible things you've given me, but, really, the best thing you've given my siblings and I is yourselves. The ability to be normal, carefree kids. You've been the parents we were never fortunate enough to have. And Chris, you've been the best friend that I've ever had. So, thank you," I say, looking at each person sitting at the table. "All of you."

When I glance at Tim and Amanda, it looks like they're seconds away from a full-blown breakdown. Tears well in their eyes, and the weight in my chest disintegrates. If they're this moved, I couldn't have done too bad, right?

Everyone digs into their plates full of food after my impromptu speech, laughing over Grandpa Phil's jokes and reminiscing over old family memories.

In between their mingling, all of the Marshall relatives ask CJ and I a slew of questions. Earnest ones. Like what we want to be when we're older, our favorite movies and books, that kind of thing. It's like they genuinely want to get to know us. Like they actually care.

The whole thing is… weird. Three months ago, it was just the three of us against the world. I never would have imagined that we'd be here, at a table full of people who take genuine interest in our lives. Surrounded by people who give us warm hugs and delicious food.

We went from having nobody to having a table full of grandparents, an aunt-adjacent, a set of loving sort-of-parents, and the best "brother" I could ever ask for.

I've never seen so much love in one place.

And no matter how hard I try, I can't believe I'm on the receiving end of it.

Chapter 36

<u>Colton</u>

It's late Saturday night. Maisy and I are sitting on her bed—in the dark—and my stupid, traitorous brain is getting all of the wrong ideas.

It's just a movie. I got "bored" studying, and suggested that we spend the next two hours of our little tutoring session watching a movie of her choice. Because I'm a gentleman, obviously.

But what I didn't account for is the sheer intimacy of the moment. She's so close I can feel every degree of her body heat somewhere deep in my core. And that's a very dangerous thing when I'm already struggling to keep my thoughts PG.

If she were any other girl, I'd lean down and kiss her. Drag my lips up the slender column of her throat. Drag her onto my lap.

But she's not any other girl, and I can't do any of those things. Not without scaring her. And not without potentially breaking this fragile friendship we've built.

I've ordered my brain to stay platonically blank, and my southern region to cooperate. And it was going okay, up until the jump scare.

It still shocks me that she's into horror movies. She's so quiet and fragile looking. But hand the girl a remote and she'll have you watching *The Exorcist* or something equally traumatizing in seconds.

As the killer clown jumps out of a hidden closet, Maisy also jumps. Vertically. Almost a full foot in the air.

When gravity pulls her back down to the bed, she curls into my side, clutching my bicep like her life depends on it.

Her nails dig into my muscles and I have to swallow a groan.

She doesn't mean for it to be as erotic as it is. I know that. But that knowledge doesn't stop a goddamn thing.

Lust and self-loathing hit me in waves of equal magnitude. Lust because the girl I've been fantasizing about for months on end is curled against me, and self-loathing because she's freaking *petrified*. She's scared shitless, and I'm over here thinking about how badly I want her.

When the scene ends, her fingers stop digging into my arm, but she doesn't let go. She stays pressed against me, her cheek brushing my arm, her small arm curled around my much larger one.

And it's nice. Like, *I want to freeze time* nice. If I could stay here in the dark with Maisy cuddled up beside me forever, I would. I think that notion should scare me more than it does.

I shift around ever so slightly, careful not to ruin the moment. I don't want her freaking out and moving. And, more importantly, I don't want to alert her to the little dilemma she's caused me.

But Maisy does pick up on my slight shift in position, and her eyes widen in horror. I don't think she's picked up on the real issue yet—her eyes haven't wandered far enough south—but she pushes off of me so quickly that I'm surprised her spine doesn't snap in two.

"I'm sorry," she says quickly, her cheeks flushing an adorable shade of pink. "I didn't realize…"

She looks like she's about to die from mortification, and I find it kind of endearing.

I can't fight a smile. "Maisy, it's okay." If she knew half of the things I thought about doing to her—*with her*—she wouldn't be so worked up about clinging onto me.
"It's no big deal."

"It *is* a big deal," she counters, the blush spreading down her neck and across her chest. "I was totally invading your personal space!"

"Maybe I like having you in my personal space," I blurt out. Her lips part, her eyes widening in surprise.

I've rendered her speechless, and the sight of her rendered speechless has rendered *me* speechless.

All I can do is stare down at her, watch the way her chest rises and falls with her shallow breaths. Admire the way her whiskey eyes sparkle, the way her gorgeous features stare back at me in the dim moonlight flooding her room.

Mother*fucker* I can't remember a time I wanted a girl as much as I want Maisy. I don't know that I ever have, to be honest.

There's been a convenient lack of discussion between us lately. Especially about what happened on Halloween. I know she's into me, and I hope she knows I'm into her. I've been waiting to hear her say it, but she's gone on pretending that nothing happened that night. Pretending she doesn't feel the draw we have towards each other.

The tension between us is so thick it's threatening to smother us. Usually, I pride myself on my restraint. On my ability to turn away from temptation. Drugs, alcohol, mindless hookups, I can ignore. I can push past them.

But Maisy? I can't ignore this desire. Not anymore.

She blinks a few times, snapping out of whatever little moment she'd been trapped in. She opens her mouth to speak. Closes it. Then opens it again, and says, "I don't understand."

"I like having you next to me, Maisy." My voice comes out gravelly, thick with the same tension that's stretching between us. "I don't mind you being in my personal space."

She looks up at me, her eyes crackling with heat. The same as mine, I'm sure. She's still flustered—no doubt about it—but she's also aroused.

I always say every new version of Maisy I discover is my favorite, but this one?

This one wins, hands-down.

"But you don't…" she starts, swallowing so hard her throat bobs.

"I don't what, Maisy?"

We're impossibly close. A few inches apart. But it's a few inches too many.

"You don't like me. Not like that," she answers quietly, tucking her hair behind her ears in a move of self-doubt.

God, she's so far off track she's not even in the race anymore. I've liked her *like that* since the moment I saw her. Sure, it took me a while to sort through my feelings, to admit that I liked her and face the mental obstacles I'd erected to keep her away. But I've always liked her. I've always wanted her.

The only difference is that now I'm finally ready to let myself take her.

I'm desperate to touch her again. To feel the heat of her smooth olive skin against me. Underneath me. Around me. I run my thumb over her bottom lip, smirking to myself at the way her breath hitches slightly. "And who told you that?"

"I just figured… I mean, you could have any girl in the school."

"Yeah, I could," I agree with a curt nod. "But I don't want any girl in the school. I want you."

It sounds possessive as hell, sure. But I don't just want her in a sexual sense. I want all of her. All of her versions. All of her demons and her battles. I want her smiles and her laughs and her tears and her hard days. I just want *her*.

"Colt," she murmurs breathlessly, her whiskey eyes locked intently on mine.

I fucking love the sound of my name on her lips. "Maisy," I murmur back, staring right back at her.

"We shouldn't do this," she whispers. But there's no conviction in her voice. It sounds like this is her last-ditch effort. The last thing stopping her from giving into the pull between us.

"No," I agree, keeping my gaze locked on her lips. "We probably shouldn't."

I flick my eyes up to hers, albeit reluctantly. They are swimming with heat, shining with a desire that matches my own.

This could ruin everything. It really could. But I've spent too damn long tortured by the idea of her, by the permanent spot she's taken up in my brain, to put this off any longer.

At this point I'm goddamn *aching* for her. I don't want to be gentle. I don't want to go slow. I'm starving for something I've never even tasted before, and it makes me want to say fuck it all and kiss her long and hard until she forgets her own name.

But I can't do that. Because this isn't another mindless hookup. This is *Maisy*. Even if I'm hungry for her, drowning in desire, it doesn't matter. I know I need to be gentle, at least right now. And that's okay. That's what she needs, and I'd do anything she needs.

I'd do anything for her.

I cup her face gingerly, pressing our foreheads together. It's more intimate than I'm used to, but then again, no girl I've ever been with has felt this important.

I'm giving her plenty of time to pull back. Plenty of time to change her mind and turn me away. Because I'd rather her pull away now and leave me temporarily devastated than her kiss me when she doesn't really want it and regret it later.   I swipe my thumb across her cheeks, my eyes searching hers for any sign that this isn't okay.

I come up empty handed.

"Colton?" Maisy murmurs, her breath tickling my lips.

"Hmm?"

"Can you stop petting me and kiss me already?"

She doesn't have to ask me twice. I thread my fingers through her silky brown hair before dipping my head and planting my lips on hers.

And holy shit, I've never felt anything like this before. Something warm crackles in my chest, forcing every square inch of my body into a warm, tingling state of bliss.

It's slow at first. Sensual. I don't dare change the tempo out of fear of scaring her.

But the kiss deepens itself when she throws one leg over mine, straddling my lap and lacing her fingers in the hair at the nape of my neck.

Maisy has been on my mind since the first day I saw her. I'll admit, I've been preoccupied by her. By the thoughts of her safety. By the worries about her wellbeing. About my own selfish, needy desires.

But now that I've had her hovering over me, now that I've had her hands on me and her lips on mine? I don't think *preoccupied* is the right word to describe the things I feel for this girl.

I think it's more like an obsession.

Chapter 37

<u>Maisy</u>

I've never kissed a boy before, but I can finally say that I understand the hype.

It's kind of like a bomb went off. Like the last few months of tension between us were seconds on the countdown timer, each building up to this moment, when all of our denial and careful restraint imploded.

I don't know what I'm doing, but I know that I don't want it to stop. There's something warm blossoming in the pit of my stomach, a burning need to get him *closer*. To keep him here, beneath me.

He kisses me until both of our lips are swollen and bruised, and then he kisses me some more, dragging his lips up my neck, hungry. Desperate.

"Christ, Maisy," Colton groans, sounding pained and tortured and a thousand other things in between. His hands are locked on my hips, his thumbs dragging back and forth in a tantalizing pattern. "You don't know how long I've wanted to do that."

His dark eyes are almost entirely black, burning with the same desire that's coursing through me. "Actually, I do." I don't know where my sudden burst of confidence comes from. I don't know when I worked up the nerve to tease him—or, better yet, to straddle him like he's a freaking horse—but I guess it has something to do with how comfortable I am around him. Watching him go slightly delirious, knowing that I was the cause of it… it makes it hard to be embarrassed about my own suffocating want. "You've wanted this since the Halloween party."

"Nope," he says, flipping me over playfully and bracketing me under his big body. "Guess again."

I legitimately have no other guesses. I assumed that he'd been jealous at the party, and that's what spurred on the emotions he's had the last few weeks.

When I don't answer him again, he kisses the tip of my nose before pulling back, letting his eyes trail over my face.

"I've wanted you since that very first day. At the dinner table."

"Then why didn't you take me sooner?" I ask, a bit breathless.

Was he being honest? Had he really wanted me all of this time? Longer than *I've* wanted *him*?

He sighs earnestly. "Because sometimes we're our own worst enemies, Maisy. Sometimes we deny ourselves the inevitable because we think it's for the best."

"Then why now?"

"Because if I waited another minute, I think I might have died," he deadpans.

"Okay, drama king." I roll my eyes at his small smile. For holding his type of reputation, you'd think he'd be better at flirting. Better at delivering cheesy one-liners.

"I'm not being dramatic," he huffs, rolling off of his spot on top of me. "If I had to go one more day with the thought of you eating up my every conscious thought, if I had to watch you sit here and blush one more goddamn second, I was going to lose it."

I find it hard to believe that I had distracted Colton *that* much. I mean, he can't be serious.

Can he?

I don't know, and I don't want to offend him by asking, so instead I say the next best thing.

Nothing at all.

It's been two whole days, and I still can't stop thinking about the kiss. I haven't told a soul yet. I wasn't about to tell Chris—not yet at least—and there's no way I was going to tell Lainey over the phone that I made out with her cousin.

But I honestly don't think I can keep it in another second.

Lainey and I are walking into the library so we can spend our free period lounging on the couches and talking. I should probably do some homework, but there's way too much to unpack here.

We spent our first period in math class rolling our eyes at Mitch and his disgustingly forward remarks, so she wastes no time voicing her complaints about him.

She scrunches her nose in disgust. "He gives off the same vibes as a pervy old man. Does that make sense?"

"Yeah. He's just…slimy. I don't know. He makes my stomach lurch," I admit, setting my backpack on the floor and flopping onto the couch.

I found Mitch's games disturbing before. Something about him just has *creeper* written all over it. I think it's his smile. But especially after the party…

Sure, I'd agreed to play spin the bottle, but only because I was sick of being hung up on Colt. He'd talked me into it, knowing I wasn't sober, knowing that he had no chance of getting with me otherwise. And that's shady as hell.

He still hasn't stopped his pursuit of me. I mean, I applaud his dedication, I guess. He's got a longer attention span than most of the boys at my old school ever had with girls, but I hate that I'm the recipient of said attention.

"Nah, the one who makes your stomach lurch is my cousin, remember?" Lainey teases, waggling her eyebrows.

Well, what a perfect segue.

"Um yeah, about that…" I tuck my hair behind my ears nervously. I don't *think* Lainey will have a problem with Colt and I, but who knows? What if she hates me for it?

It's too late, I remind myself. *It's already done.*

"We, um… Well, he came over to my house the other day, and we—"

"Holy *shit*!" Lainey exclaims, slapping her hands down on the couch. Her little outburst earns us a hostile *shush* from two nearby studiers and a librarian. "Holy shit," Lainey repeats, this time much quieter. "Did you hook up with Colt?"

"No. Oh God, no." I shake my head, feeling my cheeks heat up. I hadn't even kissed anybody before Saturday, let alone had sex. "But, um, we kind of kissed."

Her eyebrows shoot up to her hairline. "Define kissed," she says cautiously. "Was it like a grandma peck on the cheek, or like, a porno make out session?"

I think back to the way I'd straddled his lap, to the way his hands had locked on my hips while mine roamed his broad back and the taut muscles in his chest.

If anybody does *that* with their grandmother, then they need some serious clinical help.

"Porno," I say, feeling myself blush harder. "Definitely porno."

Lainey just stares at me for a moment, clearly shocked by my admission. Honestly, I'm still shocked by it, too. We both knew that I liked Colt, but that means nothing. Half of the girls in our school are in love with him. Neither one of us expected it to go anywhere. Lainey would never admit that— she wouldn't want to hurt my barely-there ego—but it's the truth.

I've been at St. Mark's long enough to know that Colton has a certain reputation when it comes to girls. A certain type that he chases.

And that type is usually blonde, athletic looking girls with big boobs and even bigger libidos.

Me? I'm a barely five-foot brunette who hasn't played sports in years. I'm barely rocking a B-cup, and, like I said, I had never even kissed a guy before.

I'm as opposite to his usual type as they come. I had accepted the fact that my little crush on Colt wouldn't go anywhere. Even after our little moment on Zalinsky's back porch. I kept telling myself it was just misunderstanding after misunderstanding, that the blatant signs were all false ones.

And then he kissed me, and now I have no idea what to do. Or feel. Or say to him.

"Oh my God, I can't believe you made out with my cousin," Lainey gapes, her green eyes swimming with disbelief. "I'd ask you for more details, but I might puke if you tell me about my cousin's *tongue* being in your mouth. Sorry girlie." I smirk at her shudder of discomfort. "Oh, Chris is going to *kill* him."

That makes my stomach flip uneasily. It had occurred to me that Chris wouldn't be happy with me making out with his best friend. But of course, it occurred to me after we'd already given in to temptation. There isn't much we can do now.

I really don't want to cause trouble for Colton. Even though it probably didn't mean as much to him as it did to me, I still don't want him to regret it. I don't want him to regret *me*.

"No, he won't. Because Chris isn't going to know." I glance around the mostly empty library, making sure that nobody's listening in. "Because he's not going to find out. At least not yet."

I feel awful lying to him, even if it's only by omission. We've been honest with each other since day one. Keeping something like this from him is going to kill me, but if I tell him, there's a chance that he's going to kill *Colt*.

"Girl, he's gonna find out," Lainey says grimly. "He'll find out when you two cupid-stricken idiots start walking around holding hands and whispering sweet nothings at lunch."

I blanch at the thought of being that public about anything, but especially my feelings for Colton. "That's not going to happen," I assure her. "I don't think anything's going to come from it."

Lainey cocks a skeptical brow, her expression telling me just how much she disagrees with me. "He wouldn't kiss you if he didn't like you, Maize."

I scoff. Loudly. "Lainey, this is *Colton* we're talking about. He's made out with a ton of people. But has he had a legitimate girlfriend?" My point strikes her silent, just like I intended it to. "No, he hasn't."

"But you're different. He wouldn't play games with you. Partially because you're Chris's sister, but also the way he looks at you…" She lets her voice trail off, seemingly losing herself in thought. "He looks at you like he's obsessed with you. Like he'd do anything for you, like he'd give anything to you. I don't think I'd fully count him out yet."

I have caught him staring. On more than one occasion. But I'm not naïve enough to believe that I'm the only one who's captured his eye that way, and I'm not masochistic enough to believe that one little kiss is going to tether him to me. I don't know what any of this means, but the truth is, I'm terrified to assume.

Chapter 38

Colton

I have always been a habitual person. I eat the same meals on the same days of every week. I always wake up at six-thirty, on the dot. I have a set workout schedule that I follow to a t.

So, it isn't much of a surprise when my impromptu visits to Maisy's house become a ritual, too.

A week after our first kiss in her bedroom, I'm back, star fishing on her mattress and watching her intently as she studies her textbook. This has become our thing; I sneak over, and she does homework while I study. And then, once we're both satisfied with our work, we make out until we run out of air in our lungs and adrenaline in our veins.

I have to admit, it's nice. Nice to have this piece of her, to have these moments where nothing matters but the feeling of our bodies pressed together.

I'm completely and utterly weak for her. Before Maisy, I would never have said I was quick on the trigger. But the sheer number of times I've almost come sans-simulation is both depressing and impressive.

Depressing for me, because really, what the hell have I been diminished to? I know that it has been a dry couple of months— what with Maisy setting up a permanent camp in my mind and all—but I didn't think I could grow my virginity back.

And it's impressive for Maisy, because she has to be one hell of a kisser if she's able to draw this kind of reaction from me with just her mouth on mine.

Neither one of us has explored further. Her hands roam my back, and mine roam hers, but we haven't gotten farther.

I don't plan to, either. Even though I really, *really* want to. Obviously, I want to. But even though she's grown a lot during her few months at the Marshall's house, she's still a bit timid. One wrong move and I could scare her back into her shell. I could fuck up irrevocably.

I'm waiting for her to try something first. For her to bring it up in conversation. Because I refuse to ruin this thing between us with my eagerness to learn this girl. I refuse to take more than she's willing to give. To move faster than she wants to go.

I've never fooled around with a girl I really, truly cared about before. I know that sounds horrible, but it's true. It goes both ways, though. The girls I've been with don't want *me*. They want my dick and my title. And I've always been scarily okay with that.

But with Maisy, it's different. With her, *everything* is different.

"Colt?" she asks, resting her head on her hands and looking over at me curiously. "Have you talked to Chris?"

Five little words and my spine is completely stiff. "No," I groan, self-loathing filling my chest. "I haven't. Does that make me a shitty friend?"

She shrugs, closing her textbook and setting it on her end table. "If it does, then I'm an even shittier sister. I haven't said anything, either."

It's only been a week. It's not like we're planning our wedding or anything. We're not even really dating, per se. But Chris is my best friend, and I'd be lying if I said that purposefully not telling him about Maisy and I doesn't make me feel a little bit guilty.

On the one hand, I think he'd be cool with it. He's super protective of Maisy, but he knows I am, too. We've known each other our whole lives. I know he trusts me. Besides, he's not the type to hold a grudge over stuff like this.

But on the other hand… she's basically his sister. I don't know very many dudes who are perfectly fine with their best friends hooking up with their sisters.

"We have to tell him. Eventually." I toss my SAT prep book onto the floor, inching closer to her. "But not right now."

The time will come. I know it will. But until then, we just have to ride it out.

"I like what you did with your hair today," I say, gesturing to her loose bun. Yeah, it looks great on her. Everything does. But I'm also desperate for a subject change, before my guilt threatens to swallow me whole.

"Aw, don't make me blush, Colt," she deadpans, rolling her eyes and flashing me a lazy grin. I've learned that she's not the best at taking compliments. We can fix that, though.

Lord knows there's an infinite amount I can give her.

I smile devilishly down at her, tugging her into my lap. "Give me time and I can make those pretty cheeks blush for a totally different reason," I murmur, pressing my lips to her neck.

She shudders, her fingers curling against the back of my neck. "Damn, that was smooth."

I chuckle against her warm olive skin, nuzzling her neck, trying to get her closer. I can't explain it, but if I could infuse her into my veins, shoot the feeling I get when I'm around her right into my bloodstream, I would. I would in a heartbeat.

Is this what it's like to be addicted to something? To want something more than you want to breathe? Do other people feel for drugs the way I feel for Maisy?

My entire body is thrumming with electricity when my lips find hers. I pull away briefly to ask her a question before the cloud of lust blurs my thoughts and I forget it entirely. "We have a game tomorrow afternoon," I tell her, my lips brushing against hers. "I can get you seats, if you want? You can bring whoever you want with you."

She sighs sadly, and I know before she even opens her mouth that it's going to be a no. "I'm sorry. You know I'd be there if I could, but…" Her body stiffens, grows colder beneath my palms.

My touch turns from hungry and exploratory to soothing, because I know that the mood has been killed, and I'd slit my own wrists before I'd push myself on her when she's clearly not into it.

"The kids and I have to visit Mom tomorrow." I don't miss the grim note in her voice.

"Yeah?" I bring my hand up her back, rubbing soothing circles between her shoulder blades. "How do you feel about that?"

"It doesn't matter how I feel. It has to happen either way."

I frown. "It *does* matter how you feel. It matters very much, actually."

"To who?"

"To me." I catch the glimpse of surprise in her whiskey eyes and smile softly. "So, tell me about all of these mom induced feelings."

I know a little bit about her past from anecdotes I've gotten over the past few months. I know she bounced from house to house, I know that her mother possibly tried to trap three guys. I know about the roles Maisy had to take on, about the food insecurity and the drugs. But I don't know what, exactly, led her here.

Each connecting piece of the puzzle is a bit more painful. Each layer of her makes me feel a bit more protective.

And a little more homicidal.

"Well, seeing her brings up a lot of old emotions." Maisy shrugs. I imagine that's a huge understatement. "Especially since tomorrow will be fourteen weeks exactly."

I scrunch my brow in confusion. "Fourteen weeks?" I repeat. "Fourteen weeks since what?"

"Since the incident," she replies simply. Her answer doesn't help me at all.

She regards my expression, her eyes widening with realization. "Oh, right. I never told you, did I? The reason we're here." She inhales deeply, a slight tremor working through her body at the exertion. "Well, um, long story short, my mom's last boyfriend was an asshole. He, uh… he tried things with me behind my mom's back."

I feel pricks of fury settle on my skin. I feel the temperature of my blood increase, boil over to dangerous temperatures.

"I obviously said no, and he never pushed it farther than that," Maisy adds, probably sensing the change in my demeanor. "Until he did." My heart drops somewhere between my stomach and my ass. The fact that she says it all so casually, that she looks so at peace with her past is just further proof of how goddamn strong she is. "Mom walked in before he got anywhere. But instead of yelling at him for trying to *sexually assault* her teenage daughter, she got pissed off at me for trying to steal her boyfriend."

Forget anger. Red-hot fury courses through me in tidal waves, threatening to blur my vision. What sort of man—what sort of *person*—could do that to someone? Force themselves on a person like that? Especially someone as young as Maisy. And what kind of mother blames their victimized daughter?

"He threatened to kill us all if we said anything," Maisy continues, her tone dark. Detached. Like she's talking about a movie she watched, or a book she read. Like she hasn't yet come to terms with the fact that this is her life. Her story. "But deep down I knew he'd kill us all anyway, even if we stayed silent. So, I called it in."

I fucking hate the fact that her mother's boyfriend had to sexually harass her for justice to be served. These kids were emotionally abused, starved, and dragged along for their entire lives. But nobody would help them. Not until it was almost too late.

"Maisy," I whisper, my voice suddenly tight with emotion. "I'm so fucking sorry. Sorry for everything you've been through. Sorry for everything those monsters did to you."

"It's okay." She smiles sadly, pressing her face into my chest as I hug her tightly against my body. "It's in the past. I just have to survive the meeting, and I won't have to see her for a whole month."

"Is there anything I can do?" I ask, hating the helplessness squeezing at my heart.

Now I get why Chris was so pissed off that morning at the gym. Jesus, he's had to keep this all in. I'd put money on the fact that he's immune to the brand of helplessness clawing at my chest right now.

Maisy looks up at me, her hopeful whiskey eyes trailing my face. "Can you be here when I get back?"

"Of course." I press a soft kiss to her forehead. "Anything for you."

Chapter 39

<u>Maisy</u>

The universe must hate me. I don't know what I did— who I pissed off—but when I wake up the morning of my visit with Mom, I get the world's biggest *fuck you* thrown at me.

It takes me a moment to realize what's happened. I only knew a little bit from the strained, insanely awkward conversations in health class. Lord knows I didn't have this talk with my mother.

Of course I'd get my first period today, of all days. Yes, I'm sixteen and I've yet to be visited by dear old Aunt Flo. The doctors blamed it on stress. Though they didn't have a clue what went on at home, Mom told them about my difficulties at school. And, yeah, stress can mess with menstrual cycles. But I have a feeling my lack of development had more to do with malnutrition than anything else.

It shows up now, go figure, after three months of consistent meals and a fairly stress-free living environment. I wouldn't count that as a coincidence.

I rack my brain for a course of action. I don't have anything, not even a panty liner, because why would I? I'd love to just run out to the store, but I don't think I can make it out of my little en-suite bathroom without butchering my perfectly white carpet.

The options are all equally humiliating, but I don't see much of a choice. "Hey, Chris?" I call out, leaning my head against the bathroom wall. His bed is right on the other side of this wall, and thanks to the thin walls, I know he'll hear me.

"Yes, Maisy Mae?" he grumbles, his voice muffled. He must've just woken up.

"I need a favor. Can you come to my room?" Several seconds later, I hear the sound of his heavy footsteps outside of the bathroom door. "Um, you probably don't want to come in," I warn, recalling what he said several weeks ago about throwing up if he had to help me with my *lady issues.*

"Why the hell—oh my god *ew*." I can practically see his scrunched nose and his slight frown through the door. "Christ, this is why God didn't originally give me a sister."

I can't help but giggle at him. But the chuckle turns into a groan as pain ricochets through my side. "Can you go get your mom, please?"

"Oh thank God. Yes."

I hear my bedroom door shut, and I pull my legs up to my chest, resting my head on my knees. I'm all too aware of the massacre in my linen pajama shorts right now, but I don't even care. Honestly, the first person I want to talk to—the first person I want to *help* me—is Amanda.

I think that's strange. I don't want to talk to my *actual* mother. The woman who birthed me. I doubt I'll even mention it at our meeting later. But the thought of confiding in Amanda? The thought of getting one of her warm hugs, of having her make me tea and tell me everything will be okay?

That calms me more than I can say.

Amanda knocks gently on my bathroom door. "Maisy, sweetie? Are you in there?"

"Yeah. I, um… You can come in." The door opens then, and Amanda's frame stands in the doorway. I take a good look at her slick white pantsuit and snort. I actually *snort.*

Her soft eyes flick between me on the floor, the blood on my legs, and the blood-stained sheets that I set by the toilet. "Not the best getup for me to be wearing, huh?" she chuckles.

I shake my head, shocked out how… not embarrassed I feel right now. I don't want to run and hide. For once, I'm fine staying right here. Maybe it's because I feel comfortable with Amanda. Or maybe it's because I know that she'll take care of me.

She eyes me sympathetically. "Is this your first one?" she asks, her voice swimming with infinite understanding and warmth. I nod. "I figured, since you haven't needed to buy anything. But I wasn't certain." She shrugs, a small smile tugging her lips. "Well, welcome to womanhood."

I rest my head against the wall, trying to ignore the dull ache in my core. "I hate it. It sucks."

Amanda chuckles, crossing the bathroom and sitting down right beside me, mimicking my position. Even though her outfit probably costs more than my old house. Even though I'm a gross, bloody mess.

She pulls me against her and murmurs softly against my hair. "I'm sorry, sweetheart."

"I'm sorry I made such a mess." I nod my head towards my stripped bed sheets, then down at my butchered pants. "I had no idea it was coming. I didn't think to, um, cover up, or anything."

"Don't worry about it, sweetie. These things come out of nowhere." Amanda stands to her feet, reaching out for my hand to help me do the same. "Okay, here's the plan. You're going to get washed up, and I'll start a load of laundry. I can get the stains out, no problem. Then we'll run to the grocery store and get you everything you need, okay?"

I nod my head, smiling softly at her kindness. I'm not surprised; I knew Amanda Marshall would be her usual, warm self. I knew she'd help me out. It's why she's the first person I turned to.

But I think the sheer heart of this woman will always baffle me. Just a little bit.

On the contrary, the sheer *lack* of heart in my mother will also always baffle me. I seem to forget how messed up she is when we're apart. And then I see her again and I'm reminded of what kind of a person she is.

For this month's visit, we met at the park for a walk. My mother and I are on either side of the cobblestone pathway, with CJ in between us, clutching my hand like a vise, and Nat on my hip, burrowed into my side.

CJ sure as hell hasn't forgotten that day. Neither have I.

And Nat… she's too young to fully grasp what had happened, but I think she understands the fear. She won't even *look* at my mother. She froze up the second she approached.

Elksborough was dusted with a thin layer of snow last night, a sheen, crystally white coat that clings to the trees and the grass. It looks like the inside of a snow globe. Mystic. Serene.

It's perfect, except for the terror gripping my chest and the heavy, weighted presence of my mother beside me.

"I see you kids have gotten some new clothes," she says with a rueful sigh. She nods to Nat's coat, then to my boots. "Gucci and Ugg." Her voice is swirled with a mix of sadness and disgust. "Is that why you want to stay with them? Because they're rich?" Her crocodile tears begin to fall, streaking down her cheeks. "Because they can buy you things I never could? You know I tried the best I could."

Is she serious? I fight back a snort. "Mom, if you think we prefer the Marshall house over the Terrace because of name brand clothing, it only further proves my point."

My mother cocks an eyebrow at me. "Your point? What point?"

"That you don't know me," I say simply. "You don't know *us*. If you really, truly believe that we're staying with the Marshalls for clothes, then you're crazier than I thought."

My mother blinks at me. Blinks again. "Why else would you possibly want to stay there?"

This time I do snort. Loudly. Where do I even start? Perhaps with the fact that, earlier today, the first person I wanted to turn to in my heightened female panic was my foster mother. Never once did I yearn for my biological mother's comfort.

Maybe I could tell her about the day that I broke down at school, and all I wanted to do was go back to the Marshall house. Maybe the fact that the first person I turned to for help with CJ was my foster father. Maybe the fact that this Thanksgiving was the first time I ever felt even remotely welcome. The fact that I was loved by a whole group of people who had no obligation to care about me but did, anyway. Or maybe that the strongest non-familial bond I've ever had is with my foster brother.

I don't bother explaining any of that to my mother, though. She wouldn't understand. Like Wanda said all of those months ago, you can't help people who don't want to be helped. You can't make close-minded people understand things that they don't want to understand.

I shrug, putting my thoughts into the simplest form I can. "Because they feel more like family."

I don't say it vindictively or to hurt my mother, I say it because it's true. I've always had my mother, and I've had my siblings for years. But I've never felt the love and support of a traditional, normal family until recently. I haven't felt even remotely cared for until I moved in with the Marshalls.

Mom shakes her head disbelievingly. "Family is blood, Maisy. *I'm* your family."

"See, that's where you're wrong. Family is the people who care about you, Mom. The people who want you to succeed. The people who love you, even when they don't have to."

She looks at me, hurt etched in her expression. "*I* love you. I love you very much. All of you."

"That's the part that I don't believe," I say casually, feeling bolder than I have my entire life. "If you loved us, you'd let us go. You'd let us be where we thrive. You love the idea of us, Mom. There's a difference."

I stun us both to silence with the weight of my words. I've never been one to talk back. I've never been one to talk at all. But I'm so tired of letting her have the upper hand. Of being her personal doormat.

Everyone has their limits, and I've met mine.

We don't talk for the rest of the park loop. I spend the time studying her profile, reading every thought and emotion from the light in her eyes and the different variations of frowns curling her lips.

She looks more fatigued today. Dark black circles line her green eyes, making her look tired and several years older than she actually is.

But her eyes are still crystal clear. *Damnit.* A part of me almost wishes she'd show up high off her ass and spewing her choice of hurtful words. I wish she'd show the case workers her true colors. I wish she'd show them *her*. Because then there'd be no way she could win us back.

Mom has never been sober for this long before. She's tried a few times, but she always, *always* turns back to the drugs that have a hold on her after a week or two.

It's admirable, in a sense, that she's fighting for us. But sometimes it's too little, too late.

I truly believe, in my heart of hearts, that if we had been housed separately, or with anyone other than the Marshalls, I would've found hope in my mother's sobriety. In her attempt to win us back. Hopeful, naïve me would've found sanction in the fact that my mother loved us enough to give up her one true love: drugs.

But, the thing is, we *were* placed with the Marshalls. We've spent the last three months with three meals a day. With heat. With beds and hugs and adults we could run to instead of run from. My siblings and I have spent enough time surrounded by warmth and compassion to realize that what we have in the Marshall house is love.

The sixteen years prior that I spent with my mother? That is *not* love.

I have very little sympathy for my mother. Very few excuses left to explain her behavior. It makes being here with her, listening to her bullshit and watching her phony tears that much harder.

I used to feel sorry for her. But I look at her, look at her withdrawn eyes, and I see desperation. She wants us back to feel like she has the upper hand. So that she gets child support money and whatever mental validation she gets from dragging us along.

The Marshalls took us in out of kindness. They've kept us out of love.

I don't know what it is my mother feels for us. Maybe it's her own twisted form of love. But it isn't as strong—or as pure—as what I feel surrounding me with Amanda and Tim and Chris.

Anything for You

The Marshalls would do anything for us.
My mother would do anything for herself.

Chapter 40

<u>Colton</u>

We win the game in a shutout. 3-0. It was the best game we'd played all year, and it wasn't even close. But I can't find it in me to manage more than half-hearted fist-bumps and back slaps as my teammates and I saunter off of the ice and into the locker room.

I sit through coach's post-game speech drifting in between reality and the worries swirling in my brain.

I should be dripping with pride and excitement. The last goal was a gorgeous slapshot delivered by yours truly, but as my teammates tried to applaud me, my mind wandered to its favorite distraction: Maisy.

It's hard to be happy when I know she's right around the block hurting. When I know that she's being forced to interact with her mother. All I want to do is be with her. That way I know she's safe. Protected.

"You were an absolute bruiser today, Bossman," Wessie says with a proud grin, snapping me out of my trance. "More than usual."

I muster up my best fake smile in response. I know if I continue my sulking, Wessie will catch on. He'll ask what's wrong, and I know that I can't tell him about Maisy's past. I can't explain that it feels like my heart went through the paper shredder in my father's office.

"Thanks." I untie my skates, tossing them in my bag as I work to undress at record speed.

"Trouble in paradise?" Wessie asks, a teasing lilt to his voice.

I pause my attempt to pull my jersey off to stare at him. "Why do you say that?"

Wessie rolls his eyes. "Oh, I don't know. Maybe because you got sent to the sin bin for the first time all season. Maybe because I've never seen you check so many players in a single game. You were a hothead tonight. I'm not complaining, but it isn't like you, man." He eyes me with a look of concern. "Are you okay?"

I let out a sigh. As much as I want to get out of this stuffy locker room, and as much as I want to be on my way to the Marshall's right now, I care too much about Wessie to shut him out right now. He's a good friend for caring.

"I mean, yeah, I'm okay. I guess I was more aggressive today. I just…" *pictured Maisy's past. Saw red whenever I thought about the sacrifices she's had to make. Whenever I thought about the things her mother has done. The things that man did to her.* "I fought with my parents last night. I'm still pissed about it, I guess."

It isn't a total lie. I fight with my parents almost every night, and Wessie knows that. His expression caves sympathetically. "Shit, I'm sorry man."

I feel like an ass for lying to Wessie, but I need to get out of here. I need to get to Maisy. "It's no problem. But I'm uh… I'm gonna get going. So I don't piss them off more."

He doesn't look like he believes me. To be honest, I'm such a shitty liar, he probably sees right through me. But he doesn't say anything. He just nods his head in understanding, giving me one final clap on the back as I make my way to the door.

The locker room lets out into the waiting area, and I weave through the groups of people crowding the hallway, dead-set on getting out of here.

I'm so focused on making it out to my truck that I barely hear the familiar voice calling my name.

"Colton!" Tim exclaims, his voice drawing nearer.   I spin around by the exit door, grinning when I notice my bonus dad trailing behind me.

"Oh, hey Tim." I hold the door open for him, and he follows me out into the parking lot. "I didn't know you'd be here today."

His expression falters slightly, his smile dipping just a little bit. "Yeah. I'm sorry, Colt. I've let you down a lot lately, huh?"

"It's no let down at all, Tim," I say honestly. Nothing is tethering him to me, or to my games. Hell, even my own parents don't show up. "I know you've been busy. With the kids and everything."

He runs a hand through his salt and pepper hair, letting out a deep sigh. "Isn't that the truth. I forgot how tiring boys are." He smiles sheepishly at me. "I've been trying especially hard to make sure CJ accommodates. The girls have attached themselves to Amanda, but CJ…" He shakes his head wistfully, smiling at the thought of his foster son. "Anyway, I'm sorry I haven't been more present. But the kids have gone out with their mother today, so I figured I'd stop by. Like the good ol' days."

I don't miss the tinge in his voice when he mentions the kids' mother. He'd never explicitly say that he dislikes the woman, though. To be honest, I'm not sure Tim Marshall fully dislikes *anyone*.

"How did they handle it this morning? Seeing their mother, I mean?"

Something akin to pride lights his blue eyes. "Those kids are warriors. They weren't happy about it—they never are—but they went without much of a fuss."

"And Maisy?" I ask before I can stop myself. I hope he missed the eagerness in my tone. I sound curious even to my own ears.

"You and Chris are awfully fond of her, huh?" Tim smiles knowingly, and I have a feeling he knows more than he's letting on. I mean, I know he's smart—he's a doctor—but I really thought I was hiding it better than that.

I guess not.

"Um, yeah," I say awkwardly, scratching the back of my neck. The epitome of guilt. "Yeah, she's pretty cool."

Tim's smile widens, but thankfully he doesn't mention my sudden discomfort or the obvious layers of this conversation. He doesn't dig deeper, and I've honestly never been more thankful for his laid-back personality.

"Are you guys studying today?" he asks, placing a strange emphasis on the word *studying*. Like he knows that we're not actually studying—not all the time, at least—but he's okay with that.

He knows me better than to think I'd hurt her. He knows that I'm smart enough to be safe.

"Um, yeah. The test is next month." I shift uncomfortably, hiking my gear bag up higher on my shoulder. I've known this man my entire life. Why I'm uncomfortable around him *now* is beyond me. "Just tying up some loose ends, you know?"

Tim nods, his expression softening. He has this way of looking at you with an intensity that makes you think he knows everything. Honestly, he probably does. It's like he can see right through all of the lies and the bullshit, but not in a malicious way. He's just intuitive.

"For the record," Tim pipes up, pulling his keys out of his back pocket. "I think it's admirable, how much you care about this…test," he says slowly, in a way that makes me think that "test" is a metaphor for something. "I don't think enough people spend enough time with the material. I think people brush it off too easily. I appreciate that you're really taking the time to work through all of the layers of the curriculum. It's very mature of you, Colton."

Yeah, the test is a metaphor, all right. And my bonus dad *definitely* knows something's going on between his foster daughter and I.

And, oddly enough, I'm okay with that.

"But in the future, study with the door open, alright, son?" Tim winks at me, beginning his walk towards his car. "I'll see you at family dinner tonight, yeah?"

I clear my throat, blinking in rapid succession as I try to process that entire interaction. "Um, yeah. I'll see you at the house, Tim."

Mackenzie Hamelin

I guess I'm not as inconspicuous as I thought I was.

I arrive at the Marshall house twenty minutes later, with my decoy SAT prep book tucked beneath my arm. I have no plans of studying. At least not test material, anyway.

Maisy's body? That's a different story.

When I make it past Amanda's narrowed glance and in-depth questioning, I dart up the stairs and towards the first room at the mouth of the staircase.

I knock twice and wait for Maisy's quiet *"come in"* before twisting the knob and letting myself into her room.

She's sitting on her bed, cross-legged and reading her book, her long brown hair acting as a curtain around her.

Every time I see her, I swear she's prettier than she was when I left her. I'm not even joking. It's like when we're apart, I miraculously forget what she does to my circulatory system.

And then I see her again, and my heart stops. Just for a minute. And then it gallops like a racehorse.

At the sight of me in her doorway, Maisy's face breaks out in a wide smile, and my chest constricts. She sets her book on her end table, stretching her arms over her head and cocking her head at me. "How did the game go?"

I shrug. "It was good. We won 3-0."

"That's awesome!" Her face breaks out in a genuine smile, her eyes crinkling just slightly. "I wish I could have been there."

I do too, but I'm not here to talk about my game. I never thought I'd see the day when hockey was second on my list of priorities. But it is. I'd much rather hear about her visit, about how she's doing.

"Enough about hockey," I say, kicking off my Timberland boots and joining her on her bed. "How're you doing?"

Her smile falters slightly, and my heart drops. God, I hope things went okay for her today. She deserves a break. She deserves to just be happy, to have things come at least a little easy for once.

258

"It actually wasn't that bad." I study her expression, trying to see if she's lying. It doesn't seem like she is. Pure sincerity flashes in her whiskey-colored eyes. "Mom was upset because the kids wanted nothing to do with her."

I snort. "Smart kids."

"That's what I'm saying." She smiles self-deprecatingly before dropping her gaze to her hands. "I, uh, I did something kind of out of character today."

"Oh yeah?" I ask, my interest piqued. "And what would that be?"

She looks up at me, her eyes shining with mischief, a wry grin curling her lips. "I snapped at my mother. I told her that family isn't just blood, and that I didn't think she actually loves us. That I think she loves the idea of us more than anything else."

Pride rushes through me. I can't picture the quiet girl from a few months ago saying such a thing. But the girl sitting in front of me now? Yeah, I can see it. She's come so far, so quickly. Tim was right. She's a warrior.

I tug her closer to me, sweeping my lips across her temple mindlessly. "That's my girl."

She blushes slightly, but I don't regret it. I spent so damn long hiding how I felt about this girl. I'm not keen on the idea of going back.

I'm proud of her. So, I'm going to tell her that much.

Maisy clears her throat, her cheeks still burning a deep crimson. "So, do you actually want to study?" She nods her head towards the thick book sitting at the foot of the bed. "Or are you willing to embrace a change of plans?"

I have to swallow a moan at the look of mischief twinkling in her eyes. My mouth curls into a grin as she leans over me, looking like she's going to climb onto my lap. "Oh, I'm more than willing."

She reaches over me towards the end table, giving me a perfect, unobstructed view down her shirt. I know it isn't intentional, but holy hell, I appreciate it nonetheless. I don't know what she's fishing for, but I can't find it in me to care.

I'm too busy thinking about how badly I want to kiss her. Feel her soft, olive skin against mine. How much I want—no—*need* to touch her.

She finds what she was looking for, pulling back to face me. My vision is blurry with desire, my mouth suddenly dry, lust clawing at me from all directions.

Maisy waves her remote control in front of my face, a teasing smirk on her lips. "Does a horror movie sound okay?"

This time I do groan. She knows what she's doing. She one hundred percent knows how much she affects me. How much I want her.

I drop my head to her shoulder, nuzzling against the crook of her neck. "You, Maisy Williams, are a tease."

She chuckles softly, the sound filling the air, smooth like warm honey. I can't even be mad at her, not when she sounds like *that*. Not that I would be, anyway. She's got the reins here, and if she's not in the mood, she's not in the mood.

I've been following this girl blindly since the day she came into my life. I'm not about to stop now.

I flip her over so her back is flat on the mattress, with me lying next to her. "Now, you may continue to torture me with your movie selection." I gesture to her TV. "Your pick."

Her eyes twinkle excitedly. "Really?"

I nod. "Of course. But if I have nightmares tonight, I'm calling you so you have to suffer with me at three in the morning. We're in this together."

She chuckles lightly, burrowing into my side. "Deal." She's quiet for a moment, but I can tell by the look on her face that there's something more on her mind. "Hey, Colt? I'm sorry for teasing you and then pulling away. That wasn't very nice of me."

I furrow my brow at her, my emotions teetering somewhere between awe and distaste. "Maisy, you don't owe me anything, ever. If you don't want to fool around, we don't fool around. Plain and simple. You can change your mind whenever." I smooth my hand over her hair, calming at the way she relaxes further into me. "That being said, you've been teasing me since the day we met. You've had me holding my breath for months now. You just didn't know it then."

Chapter 41

<u>Colton</u>

It's one of those rare days where Chris and I both have off, and my practice schedule is unusually free. We're sitting on his floor playing PlayStation, but deep down I kind of wish I was in the bedroom next door, with a certain pair of hands on me and lips on mine.

I'm a terrible person. A terrible, *horrible* friend and teammate.

I've never been so immersed in my own self-loathing before.

Here I am, with my best friend of twelve years, and he thinks we're hanging out. Bro-time, or whatever. But I'm just sitting here lusting over his sister and thinking about the fact that there are about a dozen places I'd rather have my hands than on his goddamn gaming controller.

I snap out of my little mental vacation when Chris pauses the game, shifting to look at me.

His expression is purely serious. A bit… hurt. Oh God. Serious Chris is *never* good.

"Colt?" he says, his voice sounding a little unsure. Hesitant. "I, uh, I want to talk to you about something."

For a guy who is chronically goofy, the somber note in his voice has my hair standing on end.

Shit. Has he figured Maisy and I out?

"What's up?" I say as casually as I can manage. I hope he misses the high pitch in my voice.

"It's about Maisy." *Oh fuck.* "I'm worried something's going on with her. Or maybe
I did something wrong? I don't know." He shakes his head sadly, staring longingly at the wall that cuts his and Maisy's bedrooms in

half. "She seems like she's been… avoiding me, almost. I don't know. Maybe the kids at school are giving her a hard time, and she doesn't want me to get involved? Or maybe I overstepped somewhere?" He looks at me, his blue eyes shining vulnerably. He looks like a lost little boy, and I feel my heart sink, knowing Maisy's withdrawal is my fault.

Oh my God. I hate myself.

We need to have a talk about telling Chris. Soon, before his puppy dog eyes snap the rest of my resolve.

I've wanted to tell him. I really have. But there's always been something I didn't want to take away from him or distract him from. First, it was the start of the school season. Then it was our first, then second, then third school games. Now that we've caught a break from school practice, it's the impending holiday.

Christmas has always been his favorite holiday. He jokingly says that it's because *Chris* is in the name, but he's secretly a big sap for the whole ordeal, being the big man-child he is and all. And with the holiday coming up, I worry that the news of his Maisy and I will put a damper on his Christmas spirit.

I'm pulling at straws here, I know.

The biggest factor in my silence is that there's no label between Maisy and I. And it isn't for a lack of trying on my part. We've been fooling around for a few weeks now. We haven't gotten farther than hands-up-the-shirt make outs, but I'm more than fine taking it slow. In fact, I don't think I'm ready to move further. Not yet, at least.

It's not like me to take my time, but Maisy's different. I want to learn her first, every square inch of her, and I don't want to rush that exploration.

But even still, I've hinted at the fact that I'd like to be more—my aversion to relationships aside—but she doesn't seem receptive to my casual clues. That, or she doesn't want anything more with me.

I've never folded for a girl like I have for Maisy. I wouldn't care, giving her everything I have. Literally and figuratively. I know she's worth it. Whether she's serious about me or not, I know that she isn't messing around with me for brownie points. She's not using me as a status booster or a tally on a checklist. She's with me because she likes me, whether it's purely physical or not.

Regardless, we're not an official couple, and I don't know how to go about telling Chris I'm getting handsy with his sister without sounding like I'm using her. I feel like he'd be a lot more receptive to the *"hey man, I'm dating your sister"* chat than the *"hey man, your sister and I are hitting first base on the regular"* chat.

We'll figure it out. But I have to talk to him soon.

For now, I need to give him some false hope that his sister doesn't hate him. Because she doesn't. Her distance is solely because she's afraid of slipping up, and all of her free time is spent with me.

"Um, Colton?" Chris probes, looking at me curiously.

"Sorry. No, Chris, I don't think you have to worry. I don't think she hates you. She's probably just settling in now. Finding her sea legs and all of that trivial bullshit."

"Yeah." Chris nods, his expression still forlorn. "I should be happy for her, right? That she doesn't need me anymore." His shoulders slouch, and I can hear the devastation in his tone. "I should be happy that she's found her place. But I just… I don't know, am I a bad brother for missing the time when she relied on me? For missing when she turned to me?"

Am I a bad friend for snowing you over?

Fuck it, why'd I even ask. Of course I am.

"No, you aren't a bad brother," I say cautiously, choosing my words carefully. "She loves you, Chris, and I'm sure there's a reason why she's acting weird. I'm sure it's something small, too. You'll work it out."

His eyes sparkle hopefully. "You think so?"

"Yeah. I know so."

I'll tell him the truth. Eventually. All I can do is hope that when I do, he's in a forgiving mood.

Later that evening, before dinner, Amanda and Tim call Chris and I into the kitchen for a chat.

I'm hit with a wave of déjà vu, remembering the various times throughout our childhood that we've been forced into similar discussions, which usually revolved around what we'd done wrong and how we were being punished.

I can't think of anything in particular that they'd be upset about this time around—minus Maisy and I—but why would they need Chris for that conversation?

I sit at their giant dining room table, casting my best friend a curious glance. But he looks just as lost as I do.

"You're not in trouble, boys, so you can drop your shoulders," Amanda chuckles, sinking into the seat across from us. She clamps her hand in Tim's, looking at him encouragingly.

He clears his throat, glancing between the two of us in a way that has me more than a little panicked.

"Boys, we need a favor. With Christmas coming up so soon, we've been racking our brains as to what to get Maisy," Tim says, his voice strategically quiet.

"Wait," Chris interrupts, feigning a confused expression. "Isn't that Santa's job?" His expression laces with false panic. "Are you telling me Santy Claus isn't real?!"

Tim shakes his head, rolling his eyes. "Moving on," he chuckles, casting a pointed look at his idiot of a son. "We know how important her space is to her. How she hasn't had her own room or any place to call her own previously. We wanted your opinions on potentially renovating her room, as a surprise."

God, they hit the nail on the head. Maisy would *love* that. "We were just worried she'd see a secret renovation as invading her space," Amanda continues, looking between us. "You boys have gotten to know her pretty well. What do you think?"

Chris looks at me excitedly, his eyes sparkling the way they usually do. There's no trace of his confusion or hurt from earlier, just plain joy.

"I think she'd love that."

"I agree," I nod, giving into the smile threatening to curl my lips. "But feasibility wise, how would we surprise her with that?"

"That's where you boys come in. We'd need your help painting and decorating in only a few hours. We can pick whatever day works with your schedule, Colton. We'll have everything ready beforehand."

"I'm free Saturday," I say. That's cutting it fairly close to Christmas, but oh well. "I can recruit Lainey to take her to the mall? She procrastinates everything, so I can have her say she needs to do some last-minute shopping." Both Tim and Amanda nod eagerly. "And let me see if I can get some extra labor, too."

Chapter 42

<u>Maisy</u>

"So, Juliette, how's your Romeo?" Lainey asks teasingly, sipping on her food court smoothie as we wander aimlessly around the mall.

I resist the urge to sock her in the arm. "We aren't dating, Lainey," I remind her. "It's just… It's not serious… we're…"

"You're basically dating," Lainey fills in with a wry smirk. "Colt has never been this focused on a girl before. He's serious."

I have a feeling he is. And that's both comforting and terrifying. I like him, plain and simple. More than I have ever liked anyone else.

He's easy to talk to. Supportive. It's like having my very own cheerleader. He's a great kisser, but that's farther down the list, even though certain parts of me want to put that as number one. There's way more to him than looks and his talented tongue. He's just so genuinely *good* that it makes me dizzy.

But what would an actual, real relationship with him look like? He's so busy. And I don't question his loyalty, but I know he enjoys the chase. He doesn't get around nearly as much as other guys in our school, but he's no saint, either. He's never been serious about a girl before, and I'm afraid of being naïve and assuming that I can be the one to make him change his ways.

And, most importantly, I'm only at St. Mark's temporarily. I'm only living with the Marshall's temporarily. I've been starting to forget that recently, but I can't. Laying roots is dangerous enough, and I've already done that.

Starting up a romance seems downright lethal.

"It's all so complicated," I groan, following Lainey into a store. "Feelings are so stupid."

"Amen." Lainey stops in her tracks, turning to look at me like something had just occurred to her. "Wait, does Chris know?"

Guilt swirls in my stomach. He doesn't know and I feel *awful* about it. I've been open with him since the day I moved into the Marshall's house. Honest. He's my best friend, and he's done so much for me…

God, I'm a horrible person.

"No," I murmur, shame dripping from my quiet voice. "We haven't told him, because there's nothing to tell."

Lainey cocks a disbelieving brow at me. "Um, regularly hooking up with his best friend isn't nothing, Maize. I'm not saying it's wrong," she adds, probably noticing the flash of panic in my expression. "But… he'd definitely want to know."

I fidget with the strings of my hoodie. "But what if he gets mad at me? I don't know what I'd do if he stopped talking to me, Lainey. I'm scared that he won't forgive me."

And I am. The thought of Chris cutting me off is like a dagger to the chest. It makes me feel unhinged, imagining a world where Chris and I don't play a song before bed, where he doesn't ruffle my hair and call me Maisy Mae. I love our relationship, and I'm scared that the news of Colt and I will ruin it.

"I'd tell him sooner rather than later, though," she suggests. "The longer this goes on, the harder it'll be."

I nod. I'll probably break the news to him after Christmas. I'd hate to ruin his favorite holiday.

We wander aimlessly for hours, but every time I mention going home, Lainey miraculously remembers some distant relative or friend that she forgot to buy for.

I'm sure her great-great aunt Susie is going to love her candle, though.

I'm nervous for Christmas this year. Every other year, the only person I had to let down was CJ. I'd try to scrape together extra cash to afford something little for him, but it was never a guarantee. And Nat was too young to understand the meaning behind any of it, anyway. But this year I have friends and my foster family, people who I'd love to get a gift for, but can't afford to.

Amanda offered me money, but I couldn't take it. Especially because I knew she had plans of going all out for my little siblings. I've gotten better at accepting her help, at allowing her to spend some money on me here and there. But I couldn't bring myself to take what she offered to me.

I made some gifts for people in ceramics class at school, and all I can do is hope that it's enough.

I did something different for Colton, though. He'll probably hate it, but knowing him he'll treat it like the single greatest gift he's ever received.

I've been telling myself that it's the thought that counts. I just pray that the old saying holds some semblance of truth.

<u>Colton</u>

For several grueling hours, Maisy's room looks like a crime scene. Tarps line the carpeted floor, paint cans are scattered around in no particular order. Even though her room is fairly large, having four larger than average hockey players in here at once is less than desirable.

Especially when our creative visions don't exactly align.

I don't dare complain, though, because Davie, Vinny, and Zalinsky didn't have to come over today. They're under no obligation to spend their only free Saturday for several weeks painting a bedroom and placing fake plants and fairy lights. But they do, because that's just the kind of people they are. The kinds of friends they are.

When I called them the other day after our impromptu meeting with Tim and Amanda, none of them even batted an eye. Nope, they were even excited about it.

Davie's dad owns a lumberyard, and he donated some wood, which Vinny and Davie built into a giant bookshelf.

I don't know shit about carpentry, but it's nice. Like really, *really* nice.

We've spent the last few hours painting the walls a soft beige color, touching up the baseboards, and retiling her bathroom. The bathroom didn't take long, seeing that only the inside of the shower is tiled and the rest is painted, but we also redecorated it.

Zalinsky and Chris have alternated between watching the two younger kids while Amanda and Tim helped us in the bedroom. Z has four younger siblings, and Chris is unnaturally attached to those children. So far, there haven't been any hiccups on that front.

Vinny had really wanted to help out with the kids, but the second he reached to pick Nat up she started wailing, a blood-curdling screech that probably could've shattered glass. His eyes had gone as wide as saucers, and he'd resigned his imaginary position right then and there.

Now, the paint job is finished, the tiles are settled, and the floor is cleared. It's like staring at a blank canvas, one that's just calling for us to turn it to something authentically *Maisy*.

She deserves all of this and more. The layout we've drawn up is really nice. Gorgeous, light wood, pale pinks and fluffy rugs and pillows. We even included a reading swing that'll go by the window where her bed used to be.

"C, question," Chris says, walking over to where I'm standing in the doorway. There's an evil glint in his eyes, and I don't like it. Not even a little bit. "Where should I put my cock?"

I whip my head to glare at him, shooting daggers. "I'm sorry, can you repeat that, please?"

He grins maliciously, waving around his *caulk* gun. "My caulk. Where should I put it?"

I let out a sigh, shaking my head. I'd expected nothing less from him. I'm honestly surprised it took him this long to make the joke. "There is something seriously wrong with you, Christopher." I shake my head, trying to bite back a smile. "Go put it in the tool bag."

He wanders off towards the hallway, where we're temporarily storing all of our supplies, still grinning like a fool. Vinny and Davie pass him in the doorway, and I step out of the way as they carry in the new light wooden end table. It matches her new desk and bookshelf perfectly, and I smile to myself as they place it against the wall, right next to where her bed is going.

"Bossman, we did you a solid and threw some Trojans in the top drawer," Vinny says, his tone teasing.

"Ribbed for her pleasure," Davie adds.

For the second time in two minutes, I snap my neck turning to address my friends' obscene comments. "What the hell?"

"C-O-N-D-O-M-S," Davie spells out, smirking. "You can thank us later."

I don't know whether to blush or throttle them. I decide on the latter. "Wanna be a little louder so her brother and foster parents hear?" I grit out, smacking Vinny on the back of the head. "Dumbasses."

They don't know about Maisy and I for sure, but they've speculated, and I haven't denied. I'm sure they've caught on to my staring and general infatuation, though they've had the good graces to not say anything in front of Chris.

Until now, that is.

My point hits home, and they both wince slightly. I tug open the top drawer. Son of a *bitch*, they actually put condoms in there. Assholes. I pocket them before I forget and they traumatize the hell out of Maisy.

We fall into a steady rhythm after their brief period of debauchery, working hard to max out the three hours we have left before Lainey returns to the house with Maisy.

After we have everything hung on the walls—the LED strips, various posters, and, of course, her record wall—and her bed positioned in the corner and made with a fluffy pink comforter and about a dozen throw pillows, there's a soft knock on the open door.

"We just put the baby down for a nap, and little dude wants to know if he can help," Z says, nodding down towards CJ.

He's grinning wider than the Cheshire cat. Come to think of it, I don't think I've ever seen the kid *not* grin. It's a fucking miracle and a show of serious strength, considering what I know about his past.

To have been through what they've been through and still smile, still embrace the world, still *try*… God, these kids are something else.

"Of course he can." I hold out a fist to CJ, which he happily bumps. "How're you doing, CJ?"

"I'm good," he giggles, glancing around the room at my friends. He scrunches his nose up. "Can I leave my shirt on?" His eyes pass between the five of us, all shirtless and sweating slightly from exertion. I nod, but that doesn't stop him. "I was playin' football with the kids down the road, and they said we were playing shirts and skins. They made me be shirts. Said I was so skinny that it was hard to look at me."

He doesn't sound sad about it, just… confused. Like he doesn't quite get what they meant.

Good. I think. *Keep it that way.*

What little assholes. Kids are so cruel sometimes.

Vinny, Z, and Davie glance at each other, identical looks of unease on their faces. I'm more used to CJ's oversharing tendency, though.

"Of course, bud," Chris says, a hint of sadness in his voice. He masks it nicely, though. "We're done painting anyway. You don't have to worry about ruining your shirt."

CJ nods eagerly, and we put him to work organizing the various new books Tim and Amanda bought for Maisy on her new bookshelf. Zalinsky works on organizing her desk, while Davie and Vinny decorate the bathroom with various pictures and fake plants.

Chris and I tackle the reading nook, which includes a canopy-like swing with fairy lights.

By the time it's all done, it looks like something out of a movie. Literally. I couldn't be prouder of the work we've done, or more excited for Maisy to get back and see it. I really hope she likes it.

The more time I spend with her, the more I see how easy she is to please. How… happy, I guess is a good word for it. But it's more than that. Every book she reads is the best one she's ever read. Every song is her favorite song. Every movie she watches is the best one ever made. Every sunset is the most gorgeous thing she's ever seen. She's so agreeable, so in awe with the most mundane aspects of life. She sees the beauty in things that a lot of people skim over.

Including me.

Experiencing real life for the first time through her eyes makes me really stop to think about all of the things I take for granted.

"Guys?" CJ says, snapping me out of my mini trance. He suddenly looks shy, nothing like the outgoing boy I've gotten to know over the last few months. "Thank you for doing this for my sister."

"Of course," the guys all say in unison.

"Your sister is pretty cool," Vinny adds, smiling.

"It's kinda crazy," CJ sighs wistfully, looking around the room. "The people at our old school would never *ever* do something this nice." He scrunches his brow, like he's thinking about something. "They weren't very nice to her. Probably because of our old house, I think." He shakes his head, like it doesn't really matter. "It's good that you guys are gonna make her happy. She deserves to be happy."

The guys and I all exchange sentimental glances.
"We, uh, we like to do nice things for our friends," Davie says awkwardly.

"Yeah," Chris chimes in, clearing the emotion from his throat. "We'd do anything to see her happy."

Chapter 43

Maisy

After several, *several* long hours of shopping with Lainey, she finally pulls Colt's truck up the Marshall's driveway.

I still think it's weird that he let her borrow his truck. She's not a bad driver by any stretch of the imagination, but that truck is his baby. I doubt he even lets Chris drive it.

"Okay, girl. Let's go." Lainey hops out of the truck, waiting impatiently for me at the hood of the car.

I briefly wonder what her rush is, but I've spent the entire day following her around without much of an argument. Why start now?

"Do you mind if I keep a gift bag or two in your bedroom?" Lainey asks, leading me up the staircase and towards my bedroom door. "My parents are major snoops, and if I leave them in my room, they'll totally find them."

She waits for me at the mouth of the staircase. When I catch up to her, she begins following me as I turn the knob on my bedroom door. "Yeah. Of course." I squint, trying to read her expression. "Lainey, why do you look like that?" I ask, noticing the strange, excited glimmer in her eyes. She's smiling, too. Not her usual, sarcastic smile. A *genuine* one.

She shrugs casually. "You'll see."

I don't have a clue what that means, but I also know that my stubborn friend wouldn't tell me, even if I got down on my knees and begged. I push open my bedroom door and freeze in place, jaw slack, eyes blinking in disbelief.

Me being me, I momentarily worried that I'd stepped into the wrong room. That is, until my gaze finds the six boys playing cards on my bedroom floor, smiling up at me like the cats that got the cream.

"Ah, Maisy Mae!" Chris exclaims, his voice oozing delight. "I thought you'd never return."

I'm too stunned to respond to Chris. My gaze darts between the others: from Tommy Zalinsky and Davie, who wave at me amicably, to Vinny, who gives me a wink, and finally over to Colton and CJ, who give me matching ear-to-ear grins.

No matter what direction I look at it from, I can't come to a logical conclusion about what's going on here. "Can someone explain this to me in simple terms, please?"

I hear Amanda's familiar chuckle behind me, and I turn to find her and Tim standing in the doorway. "Well, we weren't sure what you wanted for Christmas. We figured ridding you of the bland décor was a good start," Amanda explains.

But this isn't just décor. It's a whole new room. A new bed frame. A new desk, the most gorgeous bookshelf I've ever seen, records lining the walls…

It's way too much.

"I helped load the bookshelf!" CJ declares proudly, pointing at the shelves filled with brand new paperbacks.

"And before you come at us about the price, we only bought the furnishings," Tim interjects.

How is that even possible? How is any of this possible?

As if he read the questions on my face, Davie pipes up from his spot on the fluffy pink carpet. "My dad owns a lumberyard. He gave us the wood for free."

"But how did it turn into *that*?" I ask, disbelief coating my tone as I stare at the bookcase. "And that, and that?" I add, gesturing towards the end table and desk.

Vinny flexes one arm and kisses his bicep. "Three years of carpentry classes, baby." Colton glares at him dangerously, and he clears his throat, dropping his macho man façade. "Davie and I built them."

"I… I don't…" I push down the emotion in my voice, forcing the words out. "Thank you. All of you."

I don't really know what to do with this. It seems awfully…permanent. What happens when we leave? If Mom wins us back, or if they find a family willing to adopt us? It's an inevitability, sadly.

What happens to all of this work, all of their thoughtfulness, when that day comes?

"I'm sorry we're just… camped out here on your floor," Colt grimaces, flashing me an awkward smile. "We just wanted to see your face."

I assure them all that it's fine—more than that—and deliver at least a dozen more thank yous before Tommy, Vinny, and Davie say they need to go home for dinner.

"So," Chris drawls slowly, his glare probing. It's the look that tells me not to bother lying to him. The look that tells me he'd see right through it. "Now that the parents are out of earshot, do you actually like it?"

I don't hesitate. I nod like a deranged bobblehead. "I love it. Thank you guys," I say turning to my remaining three friends. "Seriously. This is… it's unreal."

I've never had a space to call my own before this bedroom. They took the knowledge that I cherish my space, that my room is like my temple, and amplified it. Made it even more… *mine*.

Truthfully, I'm not sure how much of my past Davie, Vinny, and Tommy know, but somehow that makes it sweeter. That they spent their Saturday helping just to do something nice for me. Totally oblivious to the deeper meaning behind the gift that they were giving.

It hits me hard, the realization of just how strong the friendships I've built are. The fact that I have people in my life who care about me deeply. People who love me, even though they don't have to.

I fall asleep that night, tucked into my new bed, my room illuminated by the dull fairy lights surrounding the perimeter of my room. I fall asleep with an unfamiliar warmth in my veins and a whispering of the word *family* in my ear.

A few days later, real Christmas comes. I'm genuinely not sure who's more excited; Chris or CJ. Both come barreling down the staircase in fuzzy green and red plaid pajama pants. Both hum Christmas carols as they unwrap their presents. Both wear wide, boyish smiles.

The only difference is that one of them is eight, and the other is teetering on the edge of seventeen.

Nat is too young to understand what's happening. She cuddles her new stuffed animals and smiles happily at the various dolls and toys she receives, but that's a gift in and of itself. Her smiling.

Not too long ago, she was this scared little girl who froze at the sound of the wind. Her eyes widened in fear at the sight of a stranger. That version of Nat is nothing like the giggling, babbling baby seated on Tim's lap, clapping happily. Sure, she has her moments. She still hates loud noises. But it's growth. Growth that she never would've had without the love and support from our foster family.

And the mistrusting little boy that walked in the Marshall's front door all of those months ago? He's still in there somewhere. CJ still glances nervously at new people, and he still looks to me for advice. But he's happy. Fully happy, inside and out.

Even I've changed. Grown. That's the biggest gift I could've gotten this Christmas. The knowledge that my siblings and I are so much better off. That we've overcome yet another obstacle, and come out better for it. Together.

Later that night, after Chris passed out on the couch and the kids were tucked into their beds, I'm just about to get into bed when I hear a soft knock on my window.

At first I think it's the wind. A tree branch or something. But then there's another knock, and then another. I walk cautiously towards the window, peeking curiously into the milky black night.

I nearly have a heart attack when my brain registers the face pressed against my window. My heart rate goes down slightly when I realize that the face is only Colton, but it's still pounding heavily in my chest as I slide the window open.

He drops to my floor unceremoniously, brushing his knees off as he stands up to his full height.

"Merry Christmas, Maisy," he says, smiling down at me. His expression is purely lax, drunkenly happy. He leans down and kisses me briefly, sweetly, before pulling our lips apart and murmuring, "not what I came here for."

"I have a lot of questions. First of all, how the hell did you get to my window? I'm on the second floor."

"I climbed," he says in a *duh* tone of voice. Like the answer is obvious. "There's a landing right beneath your window."

He scaled the side of the house, at ten o'clock on Christmas? For *me*?

"I wanted to see you." He shrugs, oblivious to the way my heart turns in my chest at those five words. "And give you your present."

"You didn't have to get me anything." I tuck a piece of hair behind my ear uncomfortably. God, knowing him, he probably did something obscene. I don't have much of anything for him. I know in my heart that he won't care, but still.

"It's okay if you didn't get me anything. I didn't want to make a whole production of it," he says dismissively. "It's more for me than you. I was driving myself crazy over it for weeks." He fumbles in his pocket for a second before pulling out a small box.

"Colton," I say wearily, eyeing the box in his hand like it might explode. "If you get down on one knee right now, I'm running."

He rolls his eyes, a smile tugging at his lips. "Ha-ha. Funny." He pops the box open, revealing a dainty gold necklace with an odd colored stone. "It might not be perfect, but I tried."

He... tried? What does that mean?

I study the stone, the strange light brown color achingly familiar to me for some reason. It's auburn but not really auburn, golden brown but not really golden brown.

And then it dawns on me.

"Colton," I say cautiously, worried that I'm wrong and about to make a total fool of myself. "Did you color match the stone to my eyes?"

The apples of his cheeks flush bright pink. "Yeah." He scratches the back of his neck uncomfortably. "I've never seen anything like them before. It was important to me to get the color perfect. I don't know why, but it was."

Forget fluttering. My heart full on *gallops*. "This is… I don't…"

I try to recall a time when anyone had ever done anything remotely this intimate for me.

Nothing comes to mind.

"God, now my gift feels really stupid," I groan.

Colt sets the necklace on my end table before plopping onto my bed. "I doubt that you're capable of producing anything *stupid*. But humor me."

I pull out my phone, keying in my password and bringing up the link. I share the video with him before shutting off my phone and sliding it in my sweatpants pockets.

I pray for my death by humiliation to be quick and painless.

He eyes me with veiled confusion as he opens up the attachment I just sent him.

We sit in silence for the four minutes it takes for him to watch the highlight reel I had made of his entire hockey career. All of the videos I found online, from various Facebook pages and news outlets that had done specials on the local boy wonder or covered some of his U18 games. It took me forever, but I wanted to do something special for him. He's given me so much, and I wanted to do something for him in return.

He blinks rapidly for a moment, looking simultaneously awed and confused. "Was that the song…"

"That you listened to in the car the day you drove me from school?" I shrug. "Yeah, um, you said you loved it."

He stares blankly at his phone, like he might miss something if he looks away, even though the video has long since ended. "I do."

"I'm sorry it wasn't much. I just… I remembered the song, and I know hockey is important to you, and…"

I can't keep rambling, because he tugs me towards him and presses his lips to mine. "It's perfect. Thank you, Maisy."

I nod. It's all my flustered brain can manage at the moment.

Chapter 44

<u>Colton</u>

Speechless.

I'm absolutely, alarmingly, utterly speechless.

All I can do is stare up at my ceiling, unblinking, letting the thoughts and emotions hit me in confusing, paralyzing waves.

I've been lying like this since I left Maisy's bedroom four hours ago. Just… thinking.

The corners of my lips tug up when I think about the video. Movies are our thing, and she'd made me one of my own. With the song I mentioned once, but that I thought perfectly represented me. And her, for that matter.

The clips she'd used… they went back several years. Some of them I hadn't even known existed, and yet she'd dug hard enough to find them.

Nobody has ever, *ever* done something so thoughtful for me. It's true what they say. It really is the thought that counts.

Whenever I think she can't possibly surprise me anymore, she goes ahead and does it. Watching that video, hearing that song, connecting the dots… In the moment my feelings for Maisy had crystallized, sharpening with blinding clarity.

It isn't a helpless little crush anymore.

No, it's more terrifying than that. More all-consuming. My heart beats faster when she's around. My throat goes dry. I'm instantly aroused, just looking at her. And that's just my physical responses.

My mental responses? That's a whole other story.

I can't focus when she's around. Ironic, considering I'd wooed her by luring her into being my freaking tutor. The thought of making her happy, of seeing her smile, drives so many of my actions, I can't decide if it's pathetic or admirable.

There are whisperings of a four-letter word, but I'm not ready for that. Not yet. But the one thing I do know is that I can't keep going over there for physical relief. I can't keep going into her bedroom hidden behind a textbook, kissing her stupid, and then leaving.

My heart wants so much more than that. It wants all of her. I just don't know how to go about getting that. I have no idea how to go about solidifying things, but the feelings tonight evoked in me proves that our time as something solely physical has run its course. I don't know how things are going to play out.

But I know I have to try.

It's New Year's Eve, and I'm spending it at the Marshall's house. Both of my parents got caught at the garage tonight, which is fine by me. I'd prefer to be here, anyway.

I already have my New Year's resolution figured out.

Being more honest. It should be easy enough, seeing as I'm not a huge liar. Normally. But right now, I owe explanations to two of the people closest to me.

"I lied," I whisper, pausing our movie to deliver my confession. Might as well start with the honesty now. "I never actually needed tutoring."

Maisy chuckles, shaking her head softly. "I had a feeling."

"Lies. You're just saying that so you don't seem naïve," I goad, propping my head up on an arm so I can look at her better.

"Yeah, that's definitely it." She rolls her eyes. "You're the smartest kid in our grade, Colt. I thought it was strange that you needed help from anyone, but from me especially. But I didn't want to say anything. Didn't want to bruise your precious ego."

I can't fight my smile. I never can when she's around, especially not when she's teasing me like this.

"Of course not."

Her features sober suddenly, her expression turning serious. "Can I ask you a question?"

"Always."

"Why?"

"Why did I want you to tutor me?" She nods. *Honesty.* Even if it makes me look like a total loser. "Because I wanted to get to know you, and I wasn't sure how to spend time with you without scaring you away."

She nods again, and we fall into a comfortable silence. We watch the movie she put on for a while, her curled into my side, and my hand drawing lazy pictures on her arm. It's entirely subconscious. I just like touching her, being connected to her whenever possible.

A while later, I pause the movie again. "Maisy, I think we should tell Chris." I feel her stiffen beside me. I feel like shit for ruining her comfortable moment, but it's getting harder and harder to skate around him. I've been drowning in my own guilt for weeks now. "I know it's weird, but it's not going to get any easier."

She sighs. "What are we going to tell him?"

"That we're seeing each other," I answer easily.

"But are we?" Maisy asks, turning her head up to look at me, her voice dripping with insecurity. "Are we seeing each other?"

I choose my next words carefully. "Do you *want* to be seeing each other?"

I know damn well what I want. But this is about her. Her comfort zone. The lines she does and doesn't want to draw between us.

"I don't… I mean, I've never…" She shakes her head, letting out a long sigh. "I don't really know what it would entail. What it would be like. I've never done this before."

I can sense that she's starting to retreat. Her eyes flit away from mine, her hands start fidgeting in her lap. It's like I can see her brain spinning a mile a minute in that pretty little head of hers.

I reach my own hand out, stilling her movements. She still won't look at me, so I use my free hand to tip her chin up, forcing her to meet my eyes. "You think I have any idea what I'm doing?" I ask, scanning her face for a reaction. "I don't. I've never been in a serious relationship before, either. But I've also never felt like *this* before." I exhale a shaky breath, feeling lighter. "I want you, Maisy. I have since the first day I saw you. I want *all* of you."

Her eyes flash with emotion, vulnerability swarming her expression. "Even the broken parts?"

"Especially the broken parts." I tuck a stray piece of hair behind her ear, studying her intently. "I want all of you, and I want to give you all of me. But only if that's what you want, too."

Her whiskey eyes dart between mine. I didn't realize I've been holding my breath waiting for her to answer. I let it out in a quiet exhale, and she nods. "I think I'd like that," she says, smiling softly up at me. I swear to God, it's the sweetest five words I've ever heard in my life.

I fight to bite back the grin threatening to curl my lips. "Yeah?"

"Yeah." She nods again, her smile breaking.

I lean down, closing the small space between us, kissing her softly. It isn't rushed or frantic or hungry. It's not even exploratory. It's more about the connection—of acknowledging that there's nobody else I'd rather be with, nobody else I want.

It's her. Only her. Sometimes I think it's only ever been her.

I tangle my hands in her hair as she tips her head back, deepening the kiss.

It's just her and I. On our own little planet, in our own little universe. Nothing else matters right now.

Just her. Only her.

"What the fuck?"

It takes a pathetic amount of time for the deep timber of the voice to register in my lust-clouded brain. And when it does…

I groan, resting my forehead against Maisy's. "Busted," I mouth, dread and a fair amount of humiliation coursing through me. Maisy smiles.

At least we don't have to find the right words to tell him now.

"Um," Maisy says awkwardly, pulling away from me. I can feel the loss of her heat deep in my bones. "Hi, Chris."

"Hi, Maisy Mae," he chirps, smiling at his sister. Then he turns his gaze to me, and I see the knowing glint in his eyes. I register the smirk, and my heart thunders against my chest.

"You knew," I exhale, still slightly breathless from that damn kiss. "This whole fucking time, you knew, didn't you?"

Chris nods, grinning evilly. "Well, not the whole time. But I had a feeling. You're my two best friends. I know when I'm getting snowed. Not to mention these insanely thin walls." He punctuates the last part with a soft knock on the wall. His expression shifts then, his smile falling as hurt and anger swarm his features. "I was kind of hoping I was wrong. I figured you'd come to me. I figured… I knew you were both in denial of your feelings. I figured I'd let you come to terms with them. But I'm kind of pissed you just…" He shrugs, his smile self-deprecating. "Neither one of you told me anything."

Maisy's expression falls, and I feel horrible. I know how much she worships their friendship, and I know that hearing this from him is killing her. It's killing me, too. I'm just better at masking the hurt hammering my heart than she is.

"Don't be pissed at Maisy," I murmur, forcing my eyes to meet his. "It's my fault. I was afraid you'd be furious with me, so I put off telling you. I'm sorry, Chris." I bow my head, shame filling me at the raw hurt in my best friend's eyes. "Really, really sorry."

He shakes his head, acting like he's fine. But he always does this—pretends not to care, when deep down, it's eating him alive. I get what he's saying, though. He's not pissed that we went *there* with each other, he's pissed that we kept it from him. He's right; we're his two best friends, and instead of being honest with him, we snuck around behind his back for weeks. We took the coward's way out, and it only ended up hurting him worse in the end.

I feel terrible. There's a deep pit of shame in my gut, settling heavily like a stone.

Honestly, though, props to him. If the roles were reversed, I don't know that I'd be able to stay this calm.

"Maisy, I just came to tell you that we're having dinner at five. I'll, uh… I'll see myself out." And just like that, he's gone.

"I should go after him," Maisy says uncertainly, staring at the spot Chris had been standing moments before.

As she stands to leave the bed, I stop her with a hand on her shoulder. "Give him a minute. He won't be ready to talk yet." We've had our fair share of disagreements down through the years. I know him. He'll sulk for a while, go through a brief fit of rage, and then he'll be ready to talk. He needs time to process. "I'll talk to him tonight. Smooth things over. He isn't furious, which is good." It's a relief, actually. "We can work with hurt. Anger… Chris can be pretty petty. It's a good thing we don't have to mend things in that respect." Maisy nods, still looking lost.

It hurts to see the two people I care the most about hurting. Especially because I'm almost wholly to blame for their pain. But I'm going to fix it.

I *have* to fix it.

Several hours later, after we've finished cleaning up from dinner, I've finally worked up the courage to confront Chris.

Dinner was awkward as hell. Chris, Maisy, and I couldn't meet each other's eyes, and we ate our steak and potatoes in awkward silence.

Luckily, CJ talked enough for the three of us, so at least there's that. But both Tim and Amanda picked up on the tension between the three of us, and they spent the entire meal staring between us, visibly puzzled.

I need to work it out with him. The guilt is threatening to swallow me whole, and there's no way in hell I can relax or even remotely enjoy myself when I know he's mad at me.

I rap my knuckles against his bedroom door, my heart in my throat. "Chris? It's Colt."

"Come in."

I can't read his tone. Is he pissed? Still hurt?

God, I'm not cut out for this.

But I got myself into this mess, and goddamnit, I'm going to get myself out of it.

I step into his room, shutting the door behind me and letting out a sigh. "Can we talk?"

Chris is laying on his bed, staring up at the ceiling. It brings me back to the day Maisy moved in, when I found him compromised in the same position.

"Sure." He's monosyllabic. Always a good sign.

"Look, man. I'm really sorry I didn't tell you about Maisy and I. It's still kind of fresh, and I didn't…."

"Are you serious about her?" Chris cuts in, sitting up to stare at me intently, doubt flickering in his blue eyes. "You're not just gonna love her then leave her?"

I glare at him, appalled. "No way in hell. I'm offended that you'd even *ask* that question."

Jesus, does he really think that low of me? I'd never fuck around with her feelings that way. Even if my heart wasn't tethered to the girl, I'd never even dream of hurting her like that.

Chris just shrugs. "Well, you know your reputation with commitment…"

Yeah, namely that I don't have a history of it. I'll admit, I don't have a very good reputation when it comes to girls and relationships. But this is different.

"Not with her," I interject. "She's different. She's… she's everything."

He cocks a brow at me, unease still swimming in his eyes. "This isn't some sort of conquest?"

"Absolutely not," I say instantly. "Chris, I never meant for this to happen, I swear. Actually, I tried my hardest to prevent it." I think of all of the months I spent convincing myself I didn't want her, telling myself that it was too sticky of a situation, that I was too busy… God, I'd tried to ignore her. But you can't ignore someone who's tattooed themselves across your brain. "But every time I tried to ignore my feelings for her, every time I pushed them down, they just came back stronger."

I tuck my hands in my pockets, rocking slightly, suddenly uncomfortable. "I've wanted her for a while. And I am sorry that I went behind your back, but I'm not sorry that I'm with her." *Honesty.* "She's just… she's so damn special, man. She really is.

I've never met someone who cares so deeply about *everything*. She's so thoughtful and strong and so goddamn brave, I can't…" I shake my head, trying to make sense of my thoughts. "And when she laughs? It's just like *woah*."

Chris smiles, awe filling his expression as he regards me. "*Woah*, huh?" He laughs softly. "Damn, Colton Lorenzo, you've fallen hard. Who even are you?"

"I don't even know anymore, Chris," I groan. "Nothing about what I feel for Maisy makes sense. But it's there, and it's not going away."

He nods, and I can see the sincerity in his expression. He believes me. He's forgiven me.

I cock my head at him, taking in his now lax expression. "Why aren't you more pissed at me?"

"Because I'm happy for you. Both of you. You deserve to be happy." He pauses for a moment. "That being said, hurt her and I'll fucking bury you." There's a murderous glint in his eyes that tells me he's not kidding.

"You won't have to. If I break her heart, I'll do it myself."

And I'm not kidding, either.

Chapter 45

<u>Maisy</u>

Two weeks after Colton and I make things official, things are still going strong.

I reconciled with Chris, which was a huge weight off of my shoulders. I still feel awful that I went behind his back for so long, but he assured me that everyone makes mistakes, and that he really is okay with Colton and I being a couple.

A couple… It still sounds weird. I still don't quite understand how someone like Colton fell for someone like me. Not that I doubt his intentions; I can see the way he looks at me, I can tell he cares about me by the little things he does. But it's still strange to me, the notion that my feelings for him are reciprocated.

I've spent the last few weeks on cloud nine. Not even the strange glances or snide comments at school could shake me from my high.

Even the upcoming visit with my mother seems manageable. I feel invincible, ready to take on the world. Ready to survive the visit with my mother because I know that once I leave, I'll be coming back to my *better* life.

But the thing nobody tells you about floating on cloud nine?

Gravity won't let you stay up forever. Eventually, inevitably, you'll fall back down to reality. And you'll hit the ground.

Hard.

I know something's up the second I see my mother's awful, conniving smile. I can tell by the sadness in Wanda's eyes and the defeated expression she tries—and fails—to cover up.

"Why are you…" I narrow my eyes at her, not trusting any part of this situation. "What did you do?"

My mother scoffs. "What a wonderful way to greet your mother that you see once a month," she pouts.

Now it's my turn to scoff. I can't believe I ever fell for her woe-is-me act. It's pathetic, honestly. "So you're telling me that you have nothing up your sleeve? I mean, besides the track marks we all know are there."

I snap my mouth shut, shocked at the words that had escaped. Snide comments and hurtful jabs aren't like me. I'm supposed to be the doormat child. The one that says the appropriate things at the appropriate times, never daring to step out of line.

But I've seen what it's like on the other side. I've seen what love actually looks like. And this isn't it.

"I spoke with my lawyers earlier. We're working on setting up a court date."

Terror bubbles up in my stomach. I know the answer before I even ask the question. I know in my heart what she's getting at, but I really, *really* hope I'm wrong. "For what?" I ask, my voice barely more than a dreadful whisper.

"I finally have a chance at winning you back." Her green eyes well with tears, her face shining with pride. "It's going to be different this time." *Where have I heard that before?* "We're going to be a family again."

I anticipated this news, but the words still hit me square in the chest, sending a wave of shock through me. "Are you insane? Actually, don't waste your breath. We all know the answer." I let out a laugh, which is conveniently void of humor. "We don't want that, Mom. And let's be honest, you don't want us back, either."

Beside me, CJ starts to cry. "I don't want to leave the Marshalls," he sobs, his lower lip quivering.

"It doesn't matter what you want!" she snaps. "I'm the adult here. I'm the one making the decision! Not you!"

I think it's amazing, in an incredibly sad way, how one sentence can make a person dead to you forever.

It doesn't matter what you want.

It never did.

For her, it was never really about us.

I rest my hand on CJ's shoulder, squeezing gently. "Don't worry, bud." I turn back to my mother, feeling my blood boil in a way that it never has before. "We're not your children. No, we're just a status symbol to you. A prize. You want to *win* us back, but not because you love us. No, because you need to have a heart to love, and you're lacking one of those."

Mom blinks back at me, stunned to silence. I think I like her best this way.

"All of my life you've dragged me along. I've tried so hard to love you, but do you realize how hard it is? To love someone who couldn't give two shits less about you? You kept me in hopes that Dad would come back for me. Not out of love. Out of pure selfishness. You kept these two," I spit out, pointing towards my siblings. "For a one-up on two decent men who saw through your special brand of manipulation. You don't want us back because you love us. You want us back because you can't play your stupid little game of chess without your pawns. But you know what? I'm *done*.

"Do you know how nice it is? To have a safe, stable place to live? To be surrounded by people who love us— unconditionally—for who we are, rather than what we can bring them? Do you know how nice it is, to eat three meals a day? To know with absolute certainty that you have food? Do you even *care*?"

There are a billion other things I'd like to say—about the almost-rape that led us to foster care, about her drug use, about everything she's ever said to hurt me. But my baby siblings are right here, and I refuse to make them relive the ugliness. They deserve better than that.

Plus, I can tell by her shattered expression that she knows I'm right.

"You ruined us, Mom. And this nice family has spent months of patience, diligence, and genuine love doing their very best to fix something they had no part in breaking. And now you're going to undo it all, and for what? To say you won?"

I'm out of words to say to her. I'm out of motivation and energy and emotion. I have nothing left to give her, so I simply watch her absorb every word that just spilled out of me.

I look at my mother, and I recall her outlandish words. I think of all of the times she used me as a scapegoat for her hatred of her life. I think of every time she put us in immediate danger to further her romantic pursuits. All of the times she chose drugs over feeding us. Over making rent payments.

But then my mind wanders to the family I mentioned. To the Marshalls. Particularly, I think of Amanda. I think of her kind eyes and soft laughter. I think of our shopping trips, of the light in her eyes helping me pick out cute clothes. I think of her cooking, of the way she tried to console me when I broke down in the kitchen after that horrible day at school.

Amanda isn't obligated to care about my siblings and I, but she does. She's done nothing but prove her love for us since the moment we met her, even though she doesn't have to.

But my mom? The one who's supposed to love us unconditionally? She was the cause of the tears that Amanda dried. She was the one who cut us deeper than anyone else ever had.

"I don't have anything else to say to her," I tell Wanda, purposefully avoiding looking at Mom. "Can you take us back now, please?"

Wanda nods, and I don't think I've ever been more grateful for her.

The moment I walk into the Marshall's kitchen, I fling myself at Amanda. She doesn't ask questions. She doesn't mention that I've never hugged her—not once—she just hugs me back, blindly.

"I'm sorry." I give out apologies like candy on Halloween. I always have. It's the easiest way to stay safe, a self-preservation tactic. But this one I really mean.

"For what? You've done nothing wrong, Maisy."

"I'm sorry I've pushed you away. I'm sorry I made it so hard to care about me. You and Tim opened your home up and I…" I choke out a sob. "I wouldn't let myself get close to you."

I don't think I understood just how important this realization was until I said it out loud.

She pets my hair, like I'm a small child that needs consoling. And in a way, I am. Deep down I'm just a small, broken little girl who had to grow up way too fast. "Sweet girl, the amount you've had to go through in sixteen short years explains it all." She doesn't break the hug, and I thank God for that. I really need the contact right now. "And, for the record, you've never made it hard to care about you. You couldn't even if you wanted to."

I let her words sink in, feeling a massive weight lift off of my shoulders.

This, I think, *is what being loved* should *feel like*.

This is the feeling of stability I've been chasing my whole life.

And even if my mother somehow miraculously wins us back, the lessons I've learned here will make it so that I'll never be her doormat again.

Chapter 46

<u>Maisy</u>

After sleeping on the news I got yesterday, I decide not to tell Chris and Colton about potentially being sent back to live with my mother. I know it's kind of their right to know, but there's too much at stake for them. Colton's taking the SATs today, and he's studied way too hard for me to drop this bombshell on him and distract him.

And Colt and Chris have a game tomorrow for the school team, and I know that the news will mess with Chris's focus.

When the water is clearer, I'll tell them.

Colton came over for a brief hangout before he has to go to the school to take the test. I asked if it was a good idea, if Chris and I would distract him, and he swore it would actually be beneficial. Something about tranquility that he doesn't have at home.

"It's still weird as fuck that you guys are together," Chris muses, reaching in his bag of Doritos for another handful. "Like, I love you both, but *ew*."

Colton rolls his eyes, leaning forward to move his game piece. We got trapped playing Monopoly, per Chris's request. Which we later found out was because he's an absolute real estate tycoon.

I'm already bankrupt, and we haven't even been playing for twenty minutes.

"Thank you so much for that ringing endorsement," Colt deadpans. "Seriously, you should write Hallmark cards."

Chris's response is interrupted by a knock on my bedroom door. I yell for them to come in, although I do find the interruption kind of strange. CJ is at a playdate, and Amanda and Tim rarely come up to my room.

But, sure enough, the door opens to reveal my foster parents, both of whom look deeply troubled. Amanda looks like she's been crying, her usually smooth skin looking blotchy, her eyes red-rimmed. Tim's hair is disheveled, like he ran his hands through it a few hundred times, the lines of his face etched with worry.

"Is everything okay?" I ask, my gut twisting in a way that tells me everything is, in fact, *not* okay.

"Colt, Chris, can you give us a minute?" Tim asks congenially, shooting the boys a glance layered with intensity and hidden meaning.

Colton and Chris look at each other, communicating in that silent way of theirs. Probably deciding whether or not they want to be obedient.

"No, no, it's okay. They can stay." I tuck a piece of hair behind my ears anxiously.

Tim swallows, and I see the unshed tears beginning to well up in Amanda's eyes. "Maisy, there's been an… um… an accident," Tim says, his voice grim.

Panic roars to life inside of me. "Is it CJ? Did something happen at his playdate?"

Tim shakes his head, his expression growing more somber. "It's your mother. She's in the hospital."

Am I a bad person for feeling relieved right now? Probably. But the thought of something bad happening to my siblings is a thousand times more terrifying than something happening to my mother.

"Maisy, honey, your mother overdosed last night," Amanda says, her brown eyes shining with moisture. I know she isn't crying for my mother. She's crying for my siblings and I, for the pain we'll feel from this news. Suddenly, I want to cry, too.

My voice is barely more than a hoarse, dreadful whisper. "She's dead?"

"No, they were able to pump her stomach," Tim explains matter-of-factly. "But she's… she's in rough shape.
The doctors think she might have some, um, permanent damage."

It shocks me, how little this news surprises me. I guess I always knew it would come to this. Every time she took drugs, it was a gamble. There are only so many times you can get lucky. She'd never quit, not permanently, anyway. I've always known, deep down, that she'd keep using until the day she died.

I think back to the things I said to her yesterday. How cruel I had been, whether it was justified or not.

Oh my God. What if that had been the last conversation I ever had with her?

"How did you… how did you find out?" I ask, struggling to keep up with the influx of new information. Trying to sort through the complex emotions passing through me.

Amanda clears her throat uncomfortably. "Wanda called to tell us. With her… unstable condition, we can't bring the younger two to visit her in good faith. But you're almost seventeen. If you'd like to go visit her, we'd be more than willing to take you over. It's your choice, sweetie."

Do I really want to go see her? *Voluntarily*? Or am I just worked up and feeling guilty? "Can I think about it?"

Both of my foster parents nod. "Of course. We'll be right downstairs when you're ready."

They exit my room, shutting my door behind them. It's so quiet that the sound of the lock clicking into place echoes through the room.

I'm not sure what comes first; Colt's strong arms tugging me into his chest, or Chris throwing himself at us, turning it into a group hug.

"I'm so sorry, Maisy Mae," Chris murmurs, his voice muffled against my back.

"Isn't your fault." I squeeze my eyes shut, willing the tears to recede. They don't. Warm streaks burn down my cheeks as I let out muffled sobs into the front of Colt's hoodie.

Chris pulls back, settling himself at the foot of my bed as Colton leans himself back, ridding me of my cocoon of warmth.

"Maisy," Colton whispers, heartbreak lining his voice. He uses his thumb to gently brush away my tears, his soulful brown eyes staring into mine. "Maisy, baby, please don't cry."

“I'm sorry,” I choke out, swiping at my leaky eyes. “I just… I said some really awful stuff to her yesterday. What if…”

“*No*,” Colt says, a bit too harshly. He softens his voice and tries again. “Maisy, no. This is *not* your fault. She's a grown woman. She chose to use those drugs. She chose to risk it. Nothing you did put her in that hospital bed, okay?”

He sounds so certain. I really want to believe him. But I just *can't*. “You d-don't underst-tand. I was a-awful to her.”

“Yeah, and she's been awful to you your whole life,” Chris points out. “You hit your breaking point. It happens to everybody, but it doesn't mean that you're the reason your mother turned to drugs.”

“But she was doing so g-good for so long,” I groan, frustrated. “She was sober for *months*.”

Both Chris and Colton look surprised. “She was?” they say in unison.

I nod, my expression tortured. I'm well past distracting them from their important commitments. Go big or go home, right? “She was trying to win back custody of the kids and I,” I admit. “She's been clean since the day we left. That's why I fought with her yesterday. She actually had a fighting chance of winning us back.”

“Well, not anymore,” Colt mumbles, his voice dark. His expression turns thoughtful as he stares down at me. “Maisy, if you want to go to the hospital, I'll come with you.”

“You c-can't. You have your test in two hours.”

His eyes blaze with something hot. Something like irritation. “You really think I'd choose a test over you?” he asks incredulously. “I'll reschedule it. I'll take it next month instead. You say the words, and I'll be right there with you.”

My heart warms slightly at the gesture, but my brain stamps it down. I can't ask him to do that. I can't allow him to throw this away for me.

I'm about to tell him as much when Chris chimes in. “You can't do that, C. You already paid for it. You go ace that test, Einstein.” He turns his attention to me, giving me a soft, shy smile. “I'll go with you, Maisy. If you want me too.”

As much as I hate the idea of seeing my mother at all, let alone seeing her barely functioning in a hospital bed, I know I'll never forgive myself if something happens to her and I missed the chance to say goodbye. The idea of having Chris there with me makes it a bit more appealing.

I bite my lower lip and nod my head, albeit reluctantly. "Yeah. Okay. Let's go."

The hallways reek of antiseptics. The lights are blinding. There are a thousand different noises, beeping machines and chatting doctors. Every one of my senses is on overdrive, and I feel like I might collapse.

Chris slides his hand into mine, squeezing gently, drawing me back to the moment.

Tim and Amanda offered to come in with me, but I politely declined. I have a feeling stuffing them in a small room with my mother is a horrible idea. She sees them as trying to steal her children, and they see her as a neglectful monster.
Talk about unnecessary awkward confrontation.

The hospital staff allowed Chris to come with me for moral support, but he's not allowed to be in the room. He'll have to wait in the hallway.

"This is her," Chris says quietly, giving my hand another gentle squeeze. "I'll be right here if you need me, okay?" I nod, only half hearing his words over the sound of the blood pumping in my ears and the feeling of my heart slamming against my ribcage. "Remember, Maisy Mae, this is not your fault."

With that, he releases my hand and turns me towards the doorway. I reach up to turn the handle, and my arm feels like lead. All of me feels like lead, actually. Weighed down by guilt and dread and a thousand other metaphorically heavy things.

I step into the hospital room, and the guilt triples. *Quadruples.* The breath leaves my chest in one fellow swoop.

My mother has always been a frail woman, but she has never looked smaller than she does propped in her hospital bed.

Her usually tan skin is ghostly white. IV's and other wires connect her to several different machines, all of which tell me that she's alive.

Barely.

She flashes me a weak smile. "Hi, Maisy."

I swallow past the lump in my throat, forcing my voice to cooperate. "Hi, Mom."

Her happy façade caves, her expression falling. "I'm so sorry you have to see me like this. I didn't—"

"Why did you do it?" I interrupt. "You were doing so well, Mom. Why did you do it?"

I don't have to specify what "it" is. She knows exactly what I mean.

"What's the point of staying sober if you guys don't want to come home? If you testify against me, if everyone thinks you're better off without me, I won't win you back, anyway. What's the point of staying sober when the only reason I tried doesn't want any part of me?"

Her words would be sad. Honorable, maybe. But that's if you miss the hint of bitterness in her tone. The trace of blame and the malice in her eyes.

I stamp the rising guilt down. The boys were right. This isn't my fault. Once upon a time her spiel of manipulation would have worked on me, but I see everything a bit clearer now.

She's been using her whole life; it just so happened that this one time was the one to knock her on her ass. Nothing I did caused this. This was on *her*.

"I thought about what you said yesterday," Mom continues, oblivious to my moment of awakening. "About how I ruined you kids. About how your foster family fixed you. About all of the things they've given you that I never could." She shakes her head sadly. "I finally caved."

Confusion courses through me, replacing my earlier slew of emotions. "You finally caved? What does that mean?"

"I finally gave you kids up. As soon as I'm out of here, I'm surrendering my rights to you and your siblings."

I'm still lost. "When you say finally…"

Annoyance flickers in my mother's green eyes. Apparently, not even a dance with death can cleanse this woman. "That damn *family* of yours is persistent. They've been trying to adopt you kids for months now. Pretty much since the day you stepped foot in their house."

Wait *what*?

"Of course, they couldn't adopt you, not until I fully lost my rights to custody, or signed you over to them. Which was never going to happen. But now…" her voice trails off as she glances around the hospital room. "I stand no chance now. Not after I almost killed myself. Might as well let you stay where you're happy, right?"

I know it's an extremely improper time to be happy. My mother almost *died*, and she's admitting to me that she's forfeiting her rights to the kids and I. I should feel sad.
Devastated.

Instead, all I feel is relief. Relief that I can stay at the Marshall's house. Relief because they really have wanted us from the very start. Because they've been fighting for us for months. Relief because I finally—*finally*—have a family of people who genuinely care about me.

I finally have a permanent place where I know that I belong.

Chapter 47

<u>Colton</u>

As used in the passage above, the term "ethereal" most nearly means… Maisy.

As described in the excerpt above, Aphrodite is best compared to…

Maisy.

Maisy, Maisy, Maisy.

Fuck.

I set my pencil down on the desk, inhaling deeply and running a hand through my hair.

I can't get the image of her horrified expression out of my mind. Every time I try to focus, I picture the way her face fell when she heard the news about her mother. I don't want to be here, in this stuffy classroom, staring at this stupid test. I want to have her in my arms. I want to comfort her.

God, I really want to be with her right now.

Focus. The sooner I finish this test, the sooner I get out of here. The sooner I get out of here, the sooner I get to her.

I take the test question by question, blocking everything else around me out. I focus on the words directly in front of me, and nothing else.

It goes okay. I know the material like the back of my hand. I've been studying for the last six months. I've taken every practice test that I could get my hands on. I just have to trust my own knowledge.

And worst-case scenario, I bomb this test and I retake it in the spring or summer.

When the proctor hands out the final section of the test, I exhale a sigh of relief.

Thirty-five minutes until I'm out of here. Thirty-five minutes until I can make my way back to her.

I burst through the Marshall's front door, the epitome of a man on a mission. Not pausing to say hello to Tim or Amanda, I fly up the staircase, my eyes homed in on Maisy's bedroom door.

I know she's here. All three cars are in the driveway, and there's no way in hell they would have left her at the hospital alone.

I rap my knuckles against her door, barely waiting a full second before I fling it open and step inside.

The sight before me cracks my heart in two. Splinters it right in my chest.

Chris has his arms wrapped tight around Maisy, and she has hers around him. They're both sobbing, and judging by their blotchy cheeks and puffy red eyes, they have been for a while.

"Oh God," I choke out. "Is it really that bad?"

They pull apart, each wiping their tears on their sleeves and giving me watery smiles.

How the fuck are they *smiling* right now? Maisy's mom is in the hospital. She might be getting taken away from us.

It's always been a possibility, but one that I kept at the back of my mind. It hurt too much to think about, so I just… didn't. Out of sight out of mind.

But when she told us earlier that her mother was actively trying to take them back?

I damn near exploded with rage. Her mother had done enough as it is, but now this? Taking her kids who were finally happy and stable back to that hellhole? Taking them from *us*?

Hell fucking no.

Panic flutters in my gut. Is that why they're crying? Are the kids being taken back sooner than we thought?

No. Please, God, no.

"No. Happy tears," Chris chokes out, his grin widening by the second. "Really, *really* happy tears."

Maybe the SAT fried my brain to a crisp, because I'm really confused. "How the hell can you possibly be happy right now?"

"They're taking us," Maisy says hurriedly, smiling ear to-ear. "The Marshalls. It isn't official yet, but after what happened, my mom won't get custody back. Not for a really long time at least. She's signing over her parental rights to Tim and Amanda."

Realization hits me so strong it damn near knocks me over. "They're adopting you?"

Maisy bites down on her lower lip, nodding eagerly. "Yeah. My mom told me they've been trying for months, and they confirmed it. They're going to adopt us."

God, now I want to cry, too.

I can't help the smile that takes over my face when I look at her. God, the difference a few months can make. I still remember the tortured look in her now bright eyes. I remember how skittish she was, how untrusting and weary. That girl is somehow nothing like the girl sitting in front of me now, but also exactly the same.

There isn't a doubt in my mind that Maisy has always had this happy, bubbly girl inside of her. She just needed help coaxing it out of the shell she was forced to wear to shield her from the terrors of her old life.

All she needed was a few good people to take care of her the way she always took care of everyone around her.

All she needed was a few people who would do anything for her.

Chapter 48

Maisy

"Can you tell me now?" I ask for the billionth time in the past week.

Chris has stopped bothering to pretend like I'm not annoying him. He makes no attempt at muffling the groan leaving his lips. "No, Maisy Mae. I couldn't tell you an hour ago, and I can't tell you now."

I have to say, I'm a bit disappointed in him. Chris is horrible with secrets, and I figured he'd crack and spill all of the details Colton begged him to keep quiet.

We're going on our first "real" date tomorrow, when he gets back from the U18 team's away tournament. I say "real" date, because every time we've gone out together in the month and a half we've been dating, he says it doesn't count. The movies? Nope. Ice skating? Also, nope.

I have no idea what he has up his sleeve, but I'm getting tired of waiting. Chris knows what Colt has planned, but unfortunately for me, his lips are sealed.

"He needs to hurry up and get home," I huff, flopping onto Chris's bed and staring up at the ceiling.

I've spent the entire February break with either Chris or Lainey, desperately trying to pass the time so that I didn't think about how badly I miss my boyfriend. The fact that I can barely survive a few days apart from him is pathetic, really.

"Why?" Chris asks, a teasing smirk curling his lips. "Do you miss your man?"

"Shut up," I grumble, throwing a pillow at the side of his head. "He's your man, too, and you miss him just as much."

That part is the truth. The more time that goes by, the more I start to think that Chris and I actually share a boyfriend. The boys are as connected at the hip as ever, and while I tease them for it, it secretly makes me happy that Colton and my relationship doesn't get in the way of their bromance.

"Of course I miss him," Chris admits. "He's my best friend, and the asshole left me for seven whole days. He didn't leave *me* love letters. No, I had to cut my Colton fix cold turkey."

My heart flutters at that word. *Letters*. Colt had left Chris with exactly seven letters, one for each day he'd be gone, with the explanation that I couldn't be trusted not to open all of the letters at once. I couldn't even argue that fact, because it's exactly what I would do.

"Speaking of which," Chris muses, reaching into his desk drawer and withdrawing the final letter. "Go crazy, Maisy Mae. You know you want to."

I take the envelope from him, studying the neat swoops of Colton's letters. He's got the nicest handwriting of any guy I know.

Maisy,

I come home tomorrow. I know I've apologized about a hundred times, but I'm going to apologize about a million more. I'm sorry I had to go, but if it makes you feel any better, you stole my heart a while ago, so at least there's still a piece of me with you in Elksborrough. I'm going to buy you all of the Swedish Fish at the airport store tomorrow, and hopefully I can win my way back into your good graces.

About tomorrow, I'm sure you've been tormenting Chris for information, and believe me when I tell you that that's part of the reason he knows our plans. Somebody had to drive him crazy enough for the both of us while I'm away.

I know I'm pre-writing these letters, but I also know that by the time you read this, I'll be aching to come home to you. A week doesn't seem like a whole lot, until you think about the fact that that's 7,200 minutes that I can't hold you, or kiss you, or do any of the other things that I'm not going to list here because I know

Chris will probably read this letter before you get ahold of it, and I don't want to put him in therapy for the rest of his life.

Anyway, there's nowhere I'd rather be than right next to you. So, get ready for tomorrow, baby, because I'm not letting you out of my sight once I have you in my arms again.

All of my heart,

Colton

"What a fucking dork," Chris snorts. "If thirteen-year-old Colt knew he'd be writing love letters in a few short years, he'd have an aneurysm."

"Did you actually read these?" I chuckle, still stuck on that one paragraph. Chris nods. "And what if he hadn't been vague?" I ask. "What if he'd spelled out the 'other things'?" Chris shrugs, a slow grin creeping across his face. "Nothing would surprise me. You're forgetting one very important thing." I furrow my brow at him, confused. "Our walls are paper thin, Maisy Mae. Paper. Thin."

"Is that him?" Chris asks, his voice eager.

I pull back the curtains and peek at the street. "Nope."

Several seconds go by before the sound of another passing engine reaches us in the sitting room. "Is that him?"

"Still no."

We've gone back and forth like this for almost an hour. I'm perched on the couch by the window, reading my book and trying to make the minutes pass by quicker. Every time we hear a car go by, Chris perks up from across the room and asks me if it's Colton.

There's another car, and before I can even fully process the sound of the engine, Chris pipes up again. "Is that him?"

"Oh my God, Chris," I groan, setting my book down. "It's not going to be—" I do a double take at the white truck parked in the driveway. "Oh wait. It is him."

We barrel towards the front door, and when it swings open, I hang back and let Chris attack Colt first. As much as I want to hug him, and as much as I want to just be in the same space as him, I'm a little bit afraid of getting mauled in Chris's frantic attempt to reunite with his best friend.

"Hey, buddy," Colt chuckles, patting Chris's back awkwardly. "I missed you, too."

"You're never allowed to leave me again, asshole." Chris pulls back, narrowing his eyes at Colt and pointing at me accusingly. "Your girlfriend pestered me about your stupid date the whole time. Like, ten times a day."

"Ah, so my plan worked, then." Colton comes farther into the foyer, stopping right in front of me. "How're you doing down there, Shorty?"

"Not too bad." I shrug, trying to hide my excitement. "How's the weather up there, BFG?"

His face breaks out in my favorite kind of grin. "A lot sunnier now that you're here."

Behind him, Chris gags dramatically. "God, I just ate breakfast. Please don't make me puke."

<u>Colton</u>

I'm really nervous right now. I know I shouldn't be nervous, I know it doesn't make sense for me to be nervous, but does that stop me from being nervous?

No. *No*, it does not.

It's so stupid. I've been on dates before. But it's because this one is with *her*. I'm so desperate for it to be perfect that I'm making myself physically sick over the idea that I could potentially fuck it up.

That's why I've pushed off our official first date for so long. I want it to be perfect and romantic and everything Maisy deserves.

I tug at the collar of my dress shirt, which must have shrunk a size or two in the last few minutes. It's still February, and it's freezing outside, but I'm sweating. Holy hell, I think I've blown a fuse.

Maisy comes down the giant staircase in the Marshall's foyer, walking at a snail's pace in her giant heels that I *know* were Amanda's doing.

She has on a tight black long sleeve dress that hugs her so tightly it makes me want to cancel our dinner reservation and hightail it back upstairs to her bedroom.

It sounds cheesy as hell, but she still takes my breath away. It's the middle of winter, but her tan skin is still glowing, her freckles still dotting her nose. She's got a light to her that makes people just stop and stare. I'm not even joking: I've been there when it happened.

She's just so fucking *pretty*.

I take the time it takes her to reach me to just admire her. To thank cupid, or God, or Aphrodite, or whoever it was that sent her my way for the billionth time.

I clear my throat, pushing past the gravel suddenly lining my voice. "Hi, Maisy."

She smiles up at me sweetly. "Hi, Colton."

"You kids have fun tonight," Tim says, looking between us with a soft smile.

I still find it funny how unsurprised Tim and Amanda were when we told them that we were together. Seriously, I don't think either one of them even batted an eye.

I guess that's a consequence of growing up with people. They know you better than you know yourself at times.

"But not too much fun," Amanda adds, winking at me. I bring my hand to the small of Maisy's back, leading her out of the front door before we get caught up in *that* conversation with Amanda.

"We'll be good," I promise, smiling back at them from the doorway.

I help Maisy into the cab of my truck and start driving towards the restaurant the second I buckle myself in. I have to resist the urge to lean over and kiss her, because I know I won't be able to stop.

She leans her hand over the center console, linking our fingers together. "Can you finally tell me where we're going now?" she asks hopefully.

"Well, first we're going to dinner. I got us a back table at DeAndres." It's the nicest restaurant in Elksborrough by far. And, well, I don't want to bring it up now and kill the mood, but I know how she feels about eating in public. Namely that it freaks her out. The back table is fairly secluded, so I figured it'd be our best bet. "And after that we're going to go to the fields by the school and stargaze."

I threw an air mattress with an automatic pump in the backseat, so we can set it up in the truck bed. I also brought a shit ton of blankets, because you don't plan an outdoor date during a New York winter without coming prepared.

Her eyes twinkle with excitement, and I absolutely love the fact that I put that look there. "You know," Maisy muses, a smiley dancing across her lips. "You should just take me for fast food. I'm not picky, and it'd be a lot cheaper."

I fight the urge to scoff, because I know she's voicing a legitimate idea right now. "Maisy, please don't worry about the money." I bring her hand up to my lips, kissing the back of it.

She knows better than to argue with me, because she knows I'm never going to let her win. Not about this, anyway.

She lets out a defeated sigh. "Thank you, Colt. For the letters, and dinner, just… everything."

"Of course, Maisy." I grin over at her as we roll up to a stoplight. "You know I'd do anything for you."

Epilogue

One month later...
Colton

"I've said this before, and I'll say it again; Colton Lorenzo, you're crazy. No, scratch that. You're *clinically insane.*"

His shocked expression only makes me grin wider. I know that my plan is a bit...extravagant. That's the whole point.

"Can't you just hold up a sign like a normal lovesick fucker?" Chris groans. "Also... aren't you already dating? Isn't going to prom together kind of a given?"

"Well, yeah," I concede, taking the left turn onto Broadway. I purposefully waited to tell him where we're going until we were almost there. I knew he'd try to bail on me. "But she deserves more than that."

There's officially one month until prom, and I've been brainstorming how to ask Maisy for weeks. It wasn't easy to pick from my long list of ideas, but I've finally narrowed it down.

I just want it to be perfect. I just want her to be *happy*. I know she is happy—at least happier. She smiles a lot more lately, what with the stability of having a forever home with the Marshalls, paired with the awesome state of our relationship, plus her friendship with Lainey and her strange bestie/brotherhood with Chris.

But she still deserves more. She deserves everything.

After the last few months of chaos balancing captaining two teams, plus a shitload of coursework, I want to prove to her that she's a priority in my life. She always has been, at least in my mind. The problem is, it's hard to show her that when our time together was limited to lunchtimes and brief meetings on my rare days off.

Plus, I couldn't have been easy to deal with, waiting for the SAT scores to drop. I was an anxious mess.

But we made it through, together. I ended up acing the SAT's, earning myself a near-perfect score. The school team won the division championships, and the state team won nationals. I had my grades, two championships under my belt, *and* I got the girl, which only proved my earlier argument wrong. I really can have it all.

Now that it is all behind us and we have a smooth rest of the year ahead of us, I can finally stop and slow down.

And slowing down consists of some much-needed boyfriendly activities. Like grand gestures and asking my girlfriend to go to the prom with me.

I pull up outside of the small florist shop downtown, parallel parking against the curb and throwing my door open.

"Colton, I'm going to freeze my ass off out there. It's, like, twenty degrees," Chris wines, hesitantly opening his door and stepping onto the sidewalk outside of Rosie's Roses.

I know, it's such a clever name for a florist.

I struck a deal with Rosie, the owner, a few weeks back. I got her and her husband the best tickets to the U18 playoff game at TD Garden, and she's giving me a generous discount on the insane number of flowers I had custom-ordered.

I'm grateful for her, because there's no way my mechanic apprentice pay would've covered this.

"There's no way we're fitting all of these in here," Chris grumbles, continuing to be Debby fucking Downer. Or maybe he's just being realistic. I'd prefer to stick with option number one, though.

"Come on, ye of little faith. It'll work." I take two of the buckets of flowers and carry them outside, setting them in the bed of my truck. There are twelve in total, and after some strategic maneuvering, Chris and I are able to jam all twelve buckets into the bed without even a sliver of space left.

"Well, fuck a duck," Chris muses, admiring our handiwork. "You're not as pathetically clueless as I thought you were."

"Gee, thanks," I say dryly, heading towards the front of the truck to drive before our cargo freezes in the late March chill.

Chris is quiet for the majority of the ride back to the Marshall's house, which is abnormal for him. He taps his fingers against the glass, clearly lost in thought.

When we park in his driveway, Chris turns to look at me, his blue eyes shining with sincerity and a rare sort of seriousness. "As much as I'd like to tease you for being a lovesick idiot, and trust me, I do, I'm really glad Maisy has you."

"I'm really lucky to have her." And I mean it. She's my everything, and I know that might not be healthy, but it's the truth. For the first time in my life, I'm existing outside of school and hockey. My friendships are deeper, my days are happier… Everything is a little bit brighter.

"Welp, good luck, soldier," Chris says, unbuckling his seatbelt and saluting me. "I'll go grab Maisy for you. Don't fuck this up."

I try to push down some of the nerves as I fumble getting out of the car. I spend the next two-ish minutes alternating my weight between my feet, partially to stay warm and partially to combat the anxiety eating away at my insides.

She'll say yes. She has to, right?

"I didn't know you were coming today!" Maisy exclaims, barreling out of the front door and down the driveway to meet me. She's in one of the Raven's hoodies she stole from me, her hair tied up in a loose bun. She's so damn pretty, even in her pajamas.

She flings herself at me and I catch her easily, spinning her around a few times before setting her down on the ground. I glance down, frowning. "Maisy, it's forty degrees," I say, nodding at her bare feet. "Where are your shoes? And socks?"

She shrugs, her smile unfaltering. "Couldn't waste the twenty seconds it takes to put them on. I wanted to see you."

I smile down at her before grabbing her hand and leading her towards the bed of my truck. I had a whole blurb prepared, which I'm completely forgetting at the moment.

Her expression turns quizzical as she takes in the absurd number of flowers. "Did you… rob a plant nursery or something?"

Inhale. Exhale. "No, I um, I wanted to do something special. For you."

I know the books she reads. I know how high her expectations are, so going above and beyond is kind of difficult. But it's okay, because I love a challenge almost as much as I love the girl standing in front of me. Because I do.
Love her, I mean.

I just haven't told her that yet.

"I wanted to ask you to go to prom with me," I continue, scratching the back of my neck nervously. "And I figured signs were overused." I gesture towards the truck bed full of flowers, smiling at the awed look in her whiskey-colored eyes. "So. Prom?"

"Is that even a question?!"

I cock my head at her, taking in her smiling frame. "So that's a yes?"

She nods, biting her lower lip to contain her smile. It doesn't work, and she grins wider than I've ever seen her grin before. "Yeah. It's a yes."

<u>Maisy</u>

"I don't understand how people wear these for fun," I groan, pointing at my heels with a look of intense loathing. "They should be classified as torture devices."

Amanda chuckles, setting the curling iron on the bathroom sink and stepping back to let me admire her handiwork.

She had offered to get my hair and makeup professionally done, but I told her I wanted to do it at the house instead. This time, it wasn't even money related. I've gotten better at accepting gestures and coming to terms with spending money, but I really just wanted to do something mother/daughterly with Amanda.

It's been a few months since I found out Tim and Amanda's plans to adopt my siblings and I, and I've let myself get closer to them. It helps, knowing their intentions. Knowing that they're not going to abandon us, knowing that they love us like we're their biological children.

I went prom dress shopping with Amanda, too, which was the most intimate mother and daughter type of activity I've done in a very long time. Maybe forever. But it felt right, being there with her. Maybe it's because she's more of a traditional mother figure than I've ever had.

We finish my hair and makeup, just the two of us, and when we're completely done, we let Chris and CJ come in to admire our work.

"You kind of look like a princess. But, like, a really short one," CJ says, scrunching his brow thoughtfully.

I chuckle. "Thanks, bud."

"I can't wait to see Colt's face," Chris says with a malicious glint in his eyes. He adjusts Nat on his hip, not caring that he's probably going to wrinkle his expensive-looking tux. "He's going to lose his ever-loving S-H-I-T, you know that, right?"

"I'm prepared for that."

As it turns out, I was definitely *not* prepared for it. Not even a little bit. Aside from Tim and Amanda, I've never seen someone look at another person the way Colton looks at me. I don't know what it is, or how to classify the expression. But he just looks… complete, I guess. Like he knows that he's looking at the other piece of himself.

He's staring at me, slack-jawed, which gives me a moment to drink in the sight of him in his tux. That's one of the perks of dating a hockey player—you get to see their suits *constantly*.

But nobody pulls it off quite like Colton does.

"Quick, somebody take a picture! I could *so* photoshop this," Lainey quips, shooting her cousin an odd look. I know it's weird for her, seeing this side of him. It's weird for Chris, too.

For me, though? I'm used to it. I could've come down here in a sweatsuit and probably gotten the same reaction from him.

When Colton pulls himself together, we take a bunch of photos as a group and individually. I swear we've got enough photos to fill a whole album by the time Tim and Amanda usher us out the front door with the instructions to make good choices.

Prom itself is pretty much like every high school movie I've ever watched. There's a fair amount of PDA, and the usual cliques are all hovering together around their respective tables. Our table consists of Colton and I, Chris, Lainey, Davie, Vinny, and Tommy. We spend most of the night laughing so hard that we cry, and then laughing at the fact that we're crying. I genuinely don't think I've ever had more fun in my whole life.

Nobody in our group really wants to dance, which is fine by me, because it's been so long since I last attempted to dance that I'd probably be horribly uncoordinated, anyway. But when the DJ announces it's time for a slow song, Colt sticks his hand out towards me.

"Dance with me?" he asks, though it doesn't really sound like a question. It's more like an invitation.

I nod, and he drags me towards the center of the room before I have time to change my mind.

Mazzy Star's *Fade Into You* plays softly through the speakers as our bodies tangle together. I'm all too aware of the various people around us, but Colton doesn't seem to notice. It's either that, or he flat-out doesn't care.

He spins me once before pulling me back to him, not stopping until I'm flush against his chest. The smell of his cologne assaults my senses, and I can honestly say that there's nowhere else I'd rather be than right here with him.

"I think I'm falling in love with you," he blurts out, resting his chin on the top of my head casually. Like this is a perfectly normal conversation, not one that sends goosebumps fluttering across my skin.

I never understood love, not fully, at least. I understood obligation. I understood commitment and loyalty, but outside of my siblings, I never knew what love was. It's part of the reason I was so hesitant to say it first, despite what my heart told me. How did I know if I loved him? And what if he didn't feel the same way?

I've been biting the words back for months now, and I feel the weight leave my shoulders at his confession.

I press myself farther into him, hiding the blush creeping across my cheeks. "I think I've already fallen," I admit, meaning every single word.

This should feel more monumental, but I think I've loved him for so long that saying it out loud feels inevitable. We both know what we mean to the other. We didn't need to say the words, because our day-to-day actions prove how much we care about each other.

After the song ends and we reluctantly break apart, we head back to the table, towards our friends that we both know watched every single second of our dance.

"You're not bad, considering you broke my toe square dancing in the fourth grade. I guess you've improved," Chris muses, earning him a dangerous scowl from Colt.

"Moving on from that," Lainey interjects with a soft chuckle. She turns towards me, directing her next question at just me. "Some of the girls and I are going to get ice cream. You want to come with?"

The dance is starting to die down, with most people fleeing to attend one after party or another. I look up at Colt.
"Do you mind?"

He shakes his head. "Of course not. You go have fun. I'll be back at the house when you get back, okay?"

I nod, and both Chris and Colton start heading towards the exit with the other boys right in front of them.

"Bye Maisy Mae." Chris waves back at me, slinging an arm over Colt's shoulders. "I'll see you at home, yeah?"

I nod, my heart and my head stuck on that one word.
Home.
Because for the first time in my life, I have one of those.

Chris and Colton Bromance
Brother- Kodaline

Maisy and Chris in Chapter 24
Train Wreck- James Arthur

Stay With Me- Sam Smith

Maisy about her mom
DNA- Lia Marie Johnson

Colton to Maisy
Fall into Me- Forrest Blakk

Colton, Chris, and Maisy
This Side Of Paradise- Coyoute Theory

Maisy and her mom in the park
i love you-Billie Eilish

Maisy to Chris
Thank You for Being You- Jake Banfield

Comfort Crowd- Conan Gray

Maisy in the last scene
Coming Home- Part II- Skylar Grey

Acknowledgments

First and foremost, thank you, reader, for seeing this book among the millions of others and choosing to immerse yourself in Colton and Maisy's world. I hope you enjoyed your trip to Elksborough!

Thank you to my family, for always supporting me in all of my insane ideas, including self-publishing a novel at eighteen.

To Mimi, Aunt Kim, and Mom, thank you for always beta reading whatever I put in your hands, and for being excited enough about my work to keep me writing.

Dad, thank you for getting me into hockey, and sorry this book disobeyed your first rule of romance: "never date a hockey player."

Mrs. Gallagher, thank you for teaching my junior year creative writing class. Your class inspired me to get back into writing and to start writing novels. This book wouldn't exist without you.

And to Rachael. Thank you for reading the original draft of Anything for You, and thank you for pushing me to take this step. I couldn't have done any of this without your support and friendship.

Readers

If you enjoyed *Anything for You,* please consider leaving a review! Any review, no matter how short, helps spread my book to other readers and gives me feedback for the future!

To follow along with my writing and to stay up to date on future releases, follow me at:

www.mackenziehamelinwrites.com
Instagram: @authormackenziehamelin
TikTok: @author.mackenzie

Keep reading for an exclusive sneak peek at the next book in the Hearts of St. Mark's series, featuring the story of Chris and Isla...

Chris

I'm fairly certain that my best friend is trying to murder me.

I don't know what I did to him, but it must've been bad. He's been upping our gym sessions and literally killing me with the workouts he designs for our pre-season training.

"I've figured it out," I say, stepping out of the locker room shower and tying my towel around my waist. "You're trying to kill me so you get Maisy all to yourself. Greedy bastard."

Colton chuckles from his shower stall behind me. If it were Colton B.M.—Before Maisy—he'd grumble and call me an idiot. But my once grumpy best friend is a big softy now that his hard exterior was melted by his girl.

It was weird at first, my best friend dating my sister, but they're so good together it was hard to stay mad at them for long. The only down side of my sister and my best friend being a match made in heaven is that I have to watch them be all sappy and in love while being chronically single.

They're the kind of sickeningly sweet couple that makes you look at your own life and just sigh.

I've never been much of a relationship guy. I don't have the attention span to make it a realistic option for me. As bad as it sounds, I get bored too easily. But watching them all happy and in love kind of makes me want to try.

"You've figured me out," Colt says, stepping out of his stall and following me back to the benches where we left our clothes. "No, you asshole. We've gotta buckle down before the season starts. You're getting fat." He punctuates this with a few disapproving pats to my core.

I'm not getting fat. My best friend is just a dick. Granted, I don't have his washboard abs and I don't take hockey as seriously as him, so I probably *do* seem like a slacker in his eyes.

I was a rambunctious kid. I still am. I had two wildly successful parents with demanding careers, and they didn't know what to do with a kid like me. Hockey was a way to burn off some of the energy vibrating within me all of the time. It kept me occupied and gave me an outlet.

I keep playing it because I find it fun, and I know that I'm talented. I do love the game, but unlike Colton, I'm not *in* love with it. I'm not going pro.

Hell, I'm probably not even going to play when I go to college next year.

My life exists without hockey.

Colton's... not so much.

I come to the gym with him because I think that having a workout buddy is a good motivation, and honestly, what the hell else would I do in the off season?

I mean, I work shifts at Colt's family's garage, but not because I need the money. I'm good with my hands. Not like that—well, *yes* like that—but I've always had better motor skills than brainpower. Ask me to reassemble and engine, and I've got your back.

Ask me to solve a simple math problem, and I'll get back to you in three to five business days.

I work at the garage to keep myself occupied. Stimulated. But I'm finding it harder and harder to keep myself engaged the older I get. It takes a lot to keep me entertained—thank you, chronically low dopamine—and I'm still searching for ways to make things feel vibrant again.

By the time Colton and I make it out of the locker room and into the parking lot, I'm sore from exertion and my stomach is growling angrily.

I decide that my early morning murder-sesh with Colt warrants a treat, so I decide to make a pitstop at Smoothie Shack for a protein shake before I head home.

I park my car in the lot, making my way into the small shop on the end of the local strip mall. It's kind of a hole-in-the-wall place, but I love it all the same. They make the best shakes here, and it's right on my way home from the gym.

When the overhead bell chimes, the worker turns to greet me with an undoubtably rehearsed and overly cheerful "Welcome to Smoothie Shack!"

The salesgirl doesn't look so peppy when she registers who I am, though.

"Oh. It's you." The blonde frowns at me, looking like she's just smelled the inside of an equipment bag after a tournament weekend.

It's that girl from film theory class. Isla. I remember her name because I thought it was really pretty.

God, *she* is really pretty. There's a lot of pretty girls at school, don't get me wrong. But there's something... unpolished about her. Jagged. She looks like she just wakes up and looks spectacular, while a lot of the other girls I've come across use a visible amount of makeup and products galore.

Her long blonde hair falls over her shoulder in a loose braid, her high cheekbones highlighted by the way she's annoyedly sucking in her cheeks.

This girl really doesn't like me, and that makes me irrationally giddy.

I lean my elbows against the white marbled counter top, smiling at the scowling girl in front of me. "Hello there, Elsa."

"It's Isla," she says, narrowing her eyes at me in a way that I assume is supposed to be menacing but is actually just adorable. She's kind of like a chihuahua. Thinks she's a lot fiercer than she actually is.

Now, I'm not a total jerk. I wouldn't sit here and talk to her if it'd mean I was holding up a line or other customers. But there's nobody behind me at the moment, and I get a strange thrill from annoying her.

She's feisty. I like that.

"You seem more like an ice queen than an Isla." I smile up at her, stifling a chuckle at the way her bright green eyes flare with annoyance.

"Wow, you're such a wordsmith. You should work for Hallmark," Isla deadpans, tapping on the computer screen in front of her like she's bored.

As someone who spends a lot of time bored, she doesn't look it. She looks pissed, and I think she's trying to hide her obvious annoyance by feigning boredom.

She slips her professional mask back on. "What can I get for you?"

"Well, gee, I don't know." I stand up to my full height, pretending to read the overhead menu. "What would you recommend?"

I'm not positive, but I'm pretty sure she mutters "rat poison" under her breath.

"What was that?" I ask, my voice forcibly chipper.

"Oh, um, I said the blueberry kale protein shake," Isla replies, grinning up at me devilishly.

She's got a really nice smile. It's a shame she spends so much time scowling. She's even prettier when she doesn't look like she wants to murder me in cold blood.

"Great. I'll take a large, please." I flash her my best aw-shucks little boy grin, the one that always gets me what I want.

She must be immune to it, though, because she doesn't even bat an eyelash. "Do you have a rewards number with us?"

My face breaks out in a wide grin. "Is that your way of asking for my number, sweetheart?" She growls at me, and my grin widens. "You know, *I* don't have an account, but I'm sure you do." I wink at her, and I notice the way she blushes slightly. Or maybe her face is just flushing red with anger. "Why don't you give me your number?" Her scowl deepens, so I add, "that way you can get the points, obviously."

"Obviously," she repeats, deadpan. "Nice try, Chris. I'm not giving you my number."

"It's for emergencies only," I say, struggling to keep a straight face. Fuck, this is fun. More fun than I've had in a long time. "What if I run into Ana, and she needs to get in touch with you, ASAP? What if Olaf is panicking and needs you?"

She inhales a long, calming breath. I know it's probably childish of me to enjoy annoying her this much, but I'm having too much fun to care.

"I'm not giving you my number," she repeats, her voice colder than ice.

She turns back to the screen in front of her. "That'll be nine dollars."

I hand her a twenty, lips twitching at the shock that widens her eyes when I insist that she keeps the change. "And a non-monetary tip?" I offer, taking the drink from her outstretched hand. "Smile more often. It suits you."

I wink and walk away, not turning around to catch a final glimpse. I can see her slack-jawed reflection in the door in front of me.

www.ingramcontent.com/pod-product-compliance
Lightning Source LLC
Chambersburg PA
CBHW070849160726
48004CB00003B/989